for Susan Krinard's
SHIELD OF THE SKY

WITHDRAWN

"Krinard has written more than a half dozen fantasy or supernatural romance novels, and she is one of the few who take the time to develop the story's background and the psychology of her characters beyond the rudimentry... undeniably well written and should find an attentive audience among manistream fantasy fans as well as romance readers."
—*Chronicle*

"Intriguing characters and nonstop action in a complex and fascinating world..."
—Carol Berg, author of *Guardians of the Keep*

"A unique combination of love, horror, adventure and revelation.... I look forward to subsequent volumes."
—Susan Shwartz, author of *Hostile Takeover*

"There's something for everyone in this novel: a strong fantasy in a world vaguely reminiscent of ancient Greece, a world-spanning adventure and two nicely done romances.... Character-driven [and] enhanced by plenty of adventure."
—*Romantic Times BOOKclub*

Praise for

SUSAN KRINARD

"A master of atmosphere and description."
—*Library Journal*

"The standard for today's fantasy romance."
—*Affaire de Coeur*

SUSAN KRINARD
HAMMER OF THE EARTH

LUNA™

www.LUNA-Books.com

LUNA™

First edition February 2006

HAMMER OF THE EARTH

ISBN 0-373-80224-2

Copyright © 2006 by Susan Krinard

This edition published by arrangement with Harlequin Books S.A.

® and TM are trademarks of Harlequin Books S.A., used under license.
Trademarks indicated with ® are registered in the United States Patent
and Trademark Office, the Canadian Trade Marks Office and in other
countries.

www.LUNA-Books.com

Printed in U.S.A.

As always, for Serge.

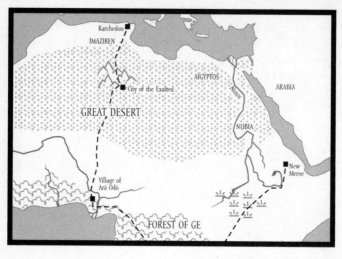

	DESERT		FOREST
	SWAMP		CITIES / VILLAGES
	MOUNTAINS		SEEKERS' JOURNEY

Cast of Characters

Enemies of the Stone God

Rhenna, a warrior of the Free People

Cian, an Ailu shapeshifter

Tahvo, a shaman of the Samah

Nyx, a rebel of Karchedon

Quintus Horatius Corvinus, citizen of Tiberia, son of Arrhidaeos

Philokrates, also known as Talos, philosopher and inventor

Slahtti, a spirit-beast

Servants of the Stone God

Baalshillek, High Priest of the Stone God

Farkas, a simulacrum

Orkos, commander of the Temple Guard

Urho, a simulacrum

Yseul, a simulacrum

The Court of Karchedon

Nikodemos, ruler of the Empire

Danae, mistress of Nikodemos

Gulbanu, a princess of Persis

Hylas, a courtier

Arion, a courtier

Chares, a courtier

Doris, a courtier

Galatea, a courtier

Iphikles, adviser to Nikodemos

Kleobis, chamberlain to Nikodemos

The Court of Karchedon (continued)

Mnestros, a courtier

Kaj, a palace guard

Philemon, a palace guard

Vanko, commander of mercenaries

Annis, a kitchen servant

Ashtaph, a servant of Hylas

Briga, a kitchen servant

Kanmi, a servant of Hylas

Leuke, a servant of Danae

Thais, a kitchen servant

Warriors and Elders of the Imaziren

Berkan, a warrior

Cabh'a, a warrior

Immeghar, a warrior

Madele, a warrior

Mezwar, a warrior

Tamallat, a warrior

Zamra, an elder

Villagers of the Ará Odò

Abeni, a villager

Abidemi, a hunter

Adisa, a Mother of Clan Amòtékùn

Bolanle, a Mother of Clan Amòtékùn

Dayo, a Mother of Clan Amòtékùn

Enitan, a hunter

Monifa, a villager

Olayinka, a villager

The Court of New Meroe

Akinidad, a former king of New Meroe

Aryesbokhe, king of New Meroe

Dakka, chief priest of the Archives

Irike, a former prince of New Meroe

Neitiquert, a princess

Khaleme, a warrior

Shorkaror, a warrior

Talakhamani, priest and prophet of the Sacred Scrolls

Other Characters

Aetes, a Tiberian slave

Arshan, a griffin-rider

Buteo, a leader of rebels in Tiberia

Danel, former lover of Hylas

Geleon, a leader of rebels in Karchedon

Keela, chief of the Alu

Melissa, wife of Philokrates

Deities of the Stone God (the Exalted)

Ag

Erichthonios

Gong-Gong

Huracan

Idiptu

Ninhursag

Ran

Surt

Free Gods and Deities

Aigyptos:

Amun

Apep (Aphophis)

Asar (Osiris)

Aset (Isis)

Geb

Hat-T-Her/Het-Hert (Hathor)

Heru-sa-Aset (Horus, son of Isis)

Inpu (Anubis)

Nut

Re

Sutekh

Tefnut

Hellas:

Apollon (Apollo)

Artemis

Dionysos

Poseidon

Zeus

Ará Odò:

Eshu

Olorun

Other Gods:

Ge, one of the Free Exalted

Tabiti, a goddess of the Skudat

Part I
Seeds

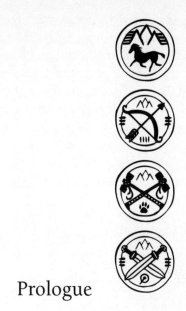

Prologue

Year Three of the Reign of King Amanibakhi of Meroe

As I write, the last of the scrolls have been packed and the people are prepared for their journey. The time has come to leave our home, the one we have known for over a hundred years. Meroe is no longer safe for those who guard the ancient Prophecies. The one whose birth was foretold, the one who will free the Stone, has been born across the sea.

The land to which we travel is unknown to us, a province of barbarians and wild beasts. But already the city is being built anew. The scrolls will remain inviolate, just as when they were entrusted to our ancestors at the time of the second Godwar.

I have but one fear as I gaze upon the years ahead. I foresee that the very beliefs that have sustained our people will become a source of discord, and that which I have learned may be deemed heresy by certain men of power who fear any interpretation of doctrine that differs from their own.

Every child of Khemet and Kush has been taught that before the coming of men, there were more gods in the heavens than there are grains of sand in the desert. These most ancient of gods fought their first great war over the creation of life upon the earth. Gods of fire, earth, air and water quarreled over the shape that life should take, attacking each other in fury and greed. A thousand thousand deities whose names we have forgotten were destroyed, their bones scattered to the far corners of the world.

In time, those who survived agreed that no one god should seek dominion over the others. With one breath, the gods gave life to man and beast, and caused the Great River Iteru to flow in all its abundance.

The first people of those ancient days lived simply, at one with the black soil, the air and water and the sun's holy fire. There were no priests, for any man could speak with gods who trod the earth. Aset, Asar, even Lord Amun, walked among men and blessed us with their eternal wisdom.

But not all were content with peace. Men there were who found the bones of the defeated gods and discovered that these sacred remains contained mighty magic. Desiring to rule over their fellow creatures, these men approached certain of the living gods and offered this magic in exchange for knowledge the deities had long ago agreed to withhold from mankind.

Though most of the gods remembered their agreement, some hungered for greater power. Twelve gods met in secret to teach the greedy men the arts of sowing and reaping grain from the fields, shaping stone for walls to divide each man from his brother, raising fire to forge weapons created for the sole purpose of severing human flesh. In return, the men erected temples to the twelve gods and built a vast city, contending among themselves for the right to rule all other men.

Thus were the first kings born, and priests to exalt the Twelve far above the gods who had not broken their promise. The faithful gods were driven into the wild places, where mankind forgot their existence. Only when the treacherous gods sent their minions to burn the wilderness and lay waste to the earth did the righteous gods take up arms to fight.

Geb and Nut, Amun and Inpu, Aset and Asar, Het-Hert and even Sutekh, made alliance with the gods of other lands. But the Twelve had taught men the way of war, and with every death of man killed by man, they grew stronger. Weakened by the neglect of those who had loved them, the righteous gods mated with mortals to create half-divine heroes and shaped four mighty weapons only these heroes could wield: the Hammer of Sutekh, the Arrows of the Wind, the Sword of the Ice and the cauldron of Fire.

Thus began the second Godwar. So great was its fury that the city of the Twelve was razed to the ground, its fertile plains reduced to desert. The Twelve were captured and imprisoned, but four of their number escaped, carrying with them the Weapons that had brought about their fall.

The righteous gods withdrew to the heavens and the underworld, abandoning their mortal bodies. To the most loyal of their followers—we, the people of the Scrolls—they bequeathed the chronicles of what had gone before and prophecies of what was yet to come, that which even the gods could not alter.

The Prophecies warn of the time when the Eight will escape their prison in the desert and heroes born of the gods must rise again to do battle. For more than a thousand years our people have believed that Sutekh's Hammer must be carried by a son of our royal line—some future prince who will prove worthy of bearing one of the most powerful weapons ever shaped by the gods. Surely such a right belongs to those who have been so faithful in our guardianship.

But in this we have been wrong. In my studies of the scrolls I have discovered that which many will call blasphemy: the

Hammer-bearer will not come from within our city but out of the North, far beyond the borders of Khemet. He will wear the shape of the Watchers, a descendent of beings who failed in the vital purpose for which they were fashioned by the mating of gods and men.

As I write these words, the Bearer's father walks in ignorance among distant mountains. He will come to us as surely as Heru-sa-Aset himself will be reborn to carry the sacred fire.

Now my servant summons me to join the other priests who walk with the wagons and chests that guard our sacred heritage. I do not know what will become of me. It is of no consequence. You who read and believe, make ready for the coming of the Watcher. Make ready for the trials that await you, for you will stand against kings and gods. May the righteous gods stand between you and harm in all the empty places where you must walk.

—from the last scroll of Talakhamani, priest of the House of Life

Chapter One

Karchedon

It was a prison. A luxurious prison, to be sure, furnished in royal style and adorned with every comfort a king's son might wish. Quintus had not seen its like since he was a young boy, not even in Danae's opulent quarters.

He thought it must be a jest, a condemned man's last view of a life he would never have. A life he had never wanted.

Quintus sat in an ivory-inlaid chair, exhausted from a long night's pacing. No one had come to see him since his transfer to Nikodemos's custody. He had expected far less pleasant accommodations, where he could remind himself with every clank of chains and breath of stale air that he was Tiberian.

But he'd been spared a painful and inevitable death at the

High Priest Baalshillek's hands only to face a prospect as bitter as it was unthinkable.

He was the half-brother of Nikodemos, ruler of the Arrhidaean Empire, nephew of Alexandros the Mad. How the absent gods must be laughing.

I am Tiberian.

He slammed his twisted left hand on the chair, relishing the pain. Why had his father not told him? Why had he been allowed to grow to manhood believing that he was a true-born son of Tiberia, of the Horatii, ancient in loyalty and honor? Why had the family of Horatius Corvinus taken the terrible risk of raising the emperor's condemned bastard son?

Quintus stared at his crippled hand. Philokrates had known. Had he been the emperor's agent from the moment he had come to the Corvinus household until he had revealed himself as Talos and fled to the palace? Had he bribed Quintus's adoptive father, or threatened him with a fate worse than mere conquest?

No. No bribe, for Quintus's family had not been saved. And Nikodemos hadn't known his half-brother lived. The only man who could answer Quintus's questions was the one he had loved most and never dared trust again—Philokrates himself.

Quintus jumped up from the chair and resumed his fruitless pacing. It didn't matter how he had come to be here. His future was dubious, at best. He was caught in a war between emperor and High Priest, between his two deadliest enemies. Nikodemos might exploit or discard him, depending on his usefulness—welcome him as long-lost kin or throw him into the sacrificial flames.

But that would be the high priest's Baalshillek's desire. No, if Quintus was to die, it would be by more common and secretive means. And if he were permitted to live…

I will never be a tool. Not his nor the rebels', not even for my own people.

No common tool could turn in the hand of its master. But

Quintus bore in his own flesh a weapon that Baalshillek greatly feared. Boldness and courage would count with Nikodemos, but Quintus must be cunning, as well, if he were to survive Baalshillek's machinations. He couldn't afford a moment of weakness.

His thoughts flew to Danae and the last time he'd seen her, playing the part of his hostage. She must have convinced Nikodemos of her innocence; if Quintus saw her again, it must be as if they were truly enemies.

But she might know what had become of his friends, the companions who had earned his respect and loyalty in the fight against the Stone. Rhenna of the Free People; Tahvo, shaman and healer of the far North; Cian, the shapeshifter who was neither wholly man nor beast but something of both.

Were they still in the city? Had they, too, been captured? Or were they dead by sword or evil Stonefire?

No. I will not believe it....

The door to his chambers swung open. A pair of grim young palace guards snapped to attention, spear-butts hammering the tiled floor. Two more soldiers stood behind them.

"You are to come with us," one of the guards said.

"Where?"

"To the emperor."

The time of judgment was here. Quintus straightened the simple chiton they had given him, adjusted the himation to cover his left arm and joined the guards. They were well disciplined, Nikodemos's men, but they had none of the too-perfect bearing that marked the Temple Guard. They were human, unbound by the Stone. But they would kill him just as swiftly if the emperor so commanded.

The guards marched their prisoner down stone corridors decorated with frescoes of victorious battle, through several doorways and into a wide, columned anteroom. A bust of Arrhidaeos, Nikodemos's father—and Quintus's—stood watch at the golden double doors at the end of the antechamber.

"The emperor holds court," the guard captain said. "You will bow and hold your tongue until he addresses you."

Quintus stared straight ahead as the doors swung open. A vast space lay ahead, echoing with whispers and the shuffling of sandaled feet. War banners hung on the walls, and gold glittered on slender necks and bare arms. Braziers lit the windowless room, carrying the fragrance of rare incense. The voices of flute and lyre mingled in sensual flirtation.

Nikodemos sat on his golden throne like the king he was, thickly muscled arms draped on the lion-faced armrests. Tumbled hair almost covered the plain circlet on his brow. He needed no elaborate headdress to proclaim his position.

His most trusted advisers, a dozen older men and officers near his own age—commanders who had led Nikodemos's troops to victory again and again—stood at the foot of the dais. Danae sat on a stool at his knee. She wore a sheer chiton that left her right shoulder bare, and a fall of delicate golden bells spilled from her neck into the shadow between her breasts. Her hair was arranged in delicate flaxen ringlets. Her gaze was cool, sweeping over Quintus as if he didn't exist.

The other courtiers—the remainder of Nikodemos's favored Hetairoi, or Companions—followed her example. They laughed and posed as if they expected to be judged on the grace of an offhand gesture or the curve of a well-plucked brow. A few armored men stood among them, stolid warriors who bore the look of seasoned veterans. Quintus had no love of their breed, but at least they would weigh a man's worth by the strength of his sword arm and not the cut of his tunic.

With the lift of one finger, Nikodemos silenced the musicians, and all eyes turned from his face to the door.

The escort started forward. Quintus matched his steps to theirs, maintaining a soldier's bearing. He would show these effete courtiers that a Tiberian faced his fate with impeccable honor and courage. If these were to be his last moments on earth, he would not disgrace himself in the eyes of the empire's champions.

He stopped of his own accord before the guards could bar his way closer to the throne. He bowed his head the merest fraction, acknowledgment and no more. The courtiers murmured. Danae hid a yawn with slender fingers.

"Quintus Horatius Corvinus," Nikodemos said, drawling each syllable. A cupbearer obeyed his negligent summons and offered a bejewelled chalice on a chased silver platter. The emperor drank, wiped his fingers on a cloth of white linen and waved the servant aside.

"Son of Arrhidaeos," Quintus said.

Murmurs grew to soft cries of outrage. Quintus stood unmoved, legs braced apart, hands at his sides. This was not his emperor, nor his lord. He would not call Nikodemos "brother."

"Son of Arrhidaeos," Nikodemos repeated. "As *you* are."

The hall fell silent. The courtiers looked from their emperor to Quintus. An older man, standing near the foot of the dais, muffled a cough behind his hand.

Suddenly Nikodemos laughed. He slapped the fanged lion's head under his palm, shaking his head.

"It is polite of my Hetairoi to pretend they know nothing," Nikodemos said, "but I doubt a single one of them is unaware of yesterday's events. Is that not so, Danae?"

She smiled at him, turning Quintus's blood hot and cold by turns. "It is, my lord."

"No one knows quite what to make of it," the emperor said. "Do you, Iphikles?"

The old man of the muffled cough bowed and met his master's eyes. "Such things do not happen without purpose, Lord Emperor," he said. "But I cannot tell what that purpose may be."

"A wise answer." Nikodemos leaned back, stretching his legs. "Who could have predicted the appearance of a royal son believed long dead? Certainly not Baalshillek."

Courtiers tittered. Quintus noted which men kept straight

faces, finding it less than prudent to mock the High Priest even in the emperor's stronghold.

"My brother," Nikodemos said. "Such a strange twist the Fates have brought me. And now I must judge what is to be done with him—a boy raised among my enemies. Raised to defy his own father's empire."

Quintus felt heat rise under his skin. Nikodemos was baiting him, hoping for some betrayal of untoward emotion. Waiting for a vehement denial...or capitulation.

He would get neither. Quintus held his brother's gaze and said nothing. "Alexandros," someone whispered. "Is it truly possible...?"

"Do some of you still doubt?" Nikodemos said in the same tone of lazy amusement. "Uncover your arm, brother. Let my people see how the Stone God left his mark upon you."

Quintus didn't move. One of his guards reached for the himation. Quintus raised a clenched right fist, slowly unfolded his fingers and drew the cloth away from his left arm.

Gasps sighed through the room like a rushing wave. Quintus let them look their fill and then readjusted the fabric.

"You see why my father sent young Alexandros away as a babe, to be raised in safety," Nikodemos said. "Or so he believed." He nodded to his right. A guard brought another man forward—Philokrates, blinking in the dim light, his hair a wild, white halo about his head. "I owe this reunion to Talos, who served Arrhidaeos so ably."

Talos, builder of war machines. Quintus hadn't met his former teacher since he'd learned the ugly fact of Philokrates's true identity, but he detected no change in the old Hellene. If anything, the inventor seemed more confused and uncertain than Quintus had ever seen him.

"Tell me again, old man," Nikodemos said. "Is this my brother?"

Philokrates turned his head slowly and gazed at Quintus. His brown eyes held no expression. "It is, my lord."

"And my father gave him into your care, to instruct while he lived with his adoptive Tiberian family?"

"Yes."

"You told me of his presence in Karchedon so that he could be of service to me, did you not?"

"Yes, my lord Emperor."

"And because you hoped to save his life from the High Priest, believing that I would show mercy."

Philokrates bowed his head. Nikodemos stroked his freshly shaven chin and half smiled at Quintus. "What would you do in my place, brother?" he asked. "If I were the rebel who had killed your men, threatened your chattel, defied your authority—would you show mercy, or risk my continued treason?"

Quintus returned the emperor's smile. "I would never be in your position."

"Such humility," Nikodemos said. "Such foolish courage. But you expect to die, do you not?"

"I expect the same fate as any of my countrymen."

"You refer, of course, to the rebel Tiberians." Nikodemos addressed his Hetairoi. "Should we admire his loyalty? Iphikles? Hylas?"

A beautiful young man stepped from the ranks of Hetairoi and flashed kohl-lined eyes at Quintus. "Perhaps he may be given a chance to prove himself, my lord."

"Indeed. But can the loyalty of such a man be altered?"

"Only if that man is wise enough to recognize his error."

"That may take some time, Hylas. Would my brother prefer imprisonment or death?"

Quintus opened his mouth to answer, but Hylas spoke over him. "He need not be lonely in his captivity," he said slyly.

Nikodemos laughed. "Not if you have your will." He looked sideways at Danae. "Perhaps he prefers other company, my dear."

"I prefer no company in this hall, Nikodemos," Quintus said.

The emperor sat up and frowned. "I think my noble brother

would choose death," he said. "Do you have a last request of me, Corvinus?"

The Tiberian name was like the whisper of a cold blade against Quintus's neck. The decision had been made, and there was nothing left to be lost.

"Withdraw from Tiberia," Quintus said. "Set my people free."

"I am much too fond of your country for such a sacrifice," Nikodemos said. "What do you wish for yourself?"

"An honorable death."

"Honorable. If by that you mean on a sword and not in the Stone God's fire…" He gestured to one of the officers. The man saluted smartly and bowed to his emperor. His face was seamed with old scars, and he clutched a battered plumed helmet to his cuirass. "I can think of no better man than the commander of my Persian mercenaries to perform such a task. Vanko?"

The soldier moved to stand beside Quintus and drew his curved sword. Quintus looked at Danae without turning his head. Her lips were parted, her eyes glazed with sudden fear. She believed Quintus was about to die.

Quintus had sworn to her that his life wouldn't end in Karchedon. He'd been so certain. He had achieved nothing…nothing to make this death worthwhile.

"My lord," Danae said, her voice slightly hoarse. "I beg leave to retire."

Nikodemos glanced at her in mild surprise. "Squeamish, my lady? You do not wish to witness the punishment of the man who so crudely assaulted your person?"

"Forgive me, my lord, but I do not care for the sight of blood."

"Gentle Danae." Nikodemos held out his hand to her. "Would you spare him, then?"

"I would, my lord," Hylas said boldly. "At least until it's clear that he is of no use to your majesty."

"Would you stake your life on his good behavior?"

The slender young man blinked long-lashed doe's eyes. "My life is my emperor's, always."

Nikodemos laughed again. "How can I resist such appeals?"

"Lord Emperor," one of his officers said, "I advise caution."

"And cautious I shall be." He bent his stare on Quintus. "It seems you have allies, Tiberian. And I have more important work at hand. Vanko, your men are quartered in Karchedon."

"They are, my lord."

"Select the best to guard my wayward brother. He is to be confined to his chambers. No visitors without my express permission."

Vanko thumped his cuirass. "As my emperor commands."

Quintus carefully released his breath. It had all been some courtier's game to Nikodemos, a test of sorts, and somehow he had passed. Danae had played into the game, and so had the pretty boy Hylas. Now it remained to be seen what Nikodemos expected of him. And how much Quintus was willing to concede to stay alive.

The guards fell in about Quintus. He turned smartly on his heel and preceded his escort back to his quarters. The door was closed and barred. A little while later a maid brought food and wine, which he barely touched. When the angle of light from the small window indicated day's end, a second visitor tapped on the door.

Quintus recognized the girl who entered, and at once he shot up from his chair and faced the door. Leuke, Danae's servant, bowed to him and took up a stance of prim watchfulness at one end of the room. Danae followed her. The guards wedged the door half open with the shafts of their spears.

Danae settled in Quintus's former seat, smoothing her evening robes over her thighs.

"Come here," she commanded, looking at Quintus down the length of her lovely nose. "I would study the face of the man who dared lay hands on the emperor's woman."

She spoke loudly for the benefit of the guards, and Quintus obeyed. He stood close, positioned so that he could be observed by the men beyond the door.

"I regret my discourtesy, my lady," he said, meeting her gaze.

"No doubt. I confess I was surprised that such a ruffian could be of the royal house. Of course, you were raised by barbarians and know no better. I am inclined, like my emperor, to be merciful."

"You are gracious, my lady."

"And you are extremely fortunate." She glanced at Leuke, and the maid gave an almost imperceptible nod. "If you are very careful," she said in a low voice, "you may even survive. But you will never touch me again."

He heard her words and understood their relentless truth, yet his muscles tightened in rebellion. Tiberian discipline kept him in place even as he breathed in the intoxicating perfume of her hair and the arousing scent of her womanhood.

Danae bent in her chair as if to adjust the lacing of her finely-woven sandal. "I have been blessed," she whispered. "Isis came to me in a dream. She showed me what has become of your friends."

Quintus leaned closer. "Tell me."

"They have been given a great task, and the gods will protect them. But they will not return until this task is complete."

"Where do they go?"

"Into the unknown. That is all I know." Leuke hissed a warning through her teeth, and Danae nodded in acknowledgment. "I care nothing of what happens to traitors," she said distinctly, "but you are my emperor's brother and he will decide your fate."

She rose, beckoned to Leuke and floated toward the door.

"Do you know the emperor's game, Danae?" Quintus asked softly.

"He plays no games," she answered. "He wishes to spare your life. Find reason to let him do so." She paused, resting her cheek against the door's polished wood. Her eyes expressed all the things her lips had not, the confusion and fear and conflicting loyalties trapped in her brave and generous heart.

Do not betray him, her eyes said. *Live.*

Then she walked out the door. The guards closed and barred it. Quintus laid his cheek where Danae's had been.

"You will never touch me again."

He slid to the ground and cupped his crippled arm to his chest. In his mind he glimpsed an image of Rhenna and Tahvo and Cian, standing together outside the walls of the city, looking back as if to bid him farewell.

They were free. But they fought for something bigger than mere freedom: the Watcher, the seer and the warrior, bound to each other and to Quintus by some magic as potent as the Stone itself.

I was not meant to go with them. Mine is a different path.

As quickly as the vision came, it was gone. Quintus stood and walked to the high, tiny window overlooking the citadel square. The sun was setting, but summer heat still blistered the pavement. No one who had not seen it would believe that snow had fallen in Karchedon.

No one would believe that a woman could wield a sword like a hero born, that a man could become a beast, or that a Tiberian could be the son of an emperor.

Quintus had begun to believe.

The old man known as Talos came to Baalshillek in all proper humility, head lowered and body hunched. It seemed the inventor was well aware that he had made a deadly enemy in the High Priest, though the two had never met before this day. Because of Talos, Baalshillek's most valuable prisoner had fallen into the emperor's hands.

Baalshillek expected no little inconvenience from that fact. As long as Nikodemos believed that Quintus's power over the red stones outweighed the risk of his rebellious past, the Tiberian remained beyond Baalshillek's reach.

For the time being.

The Temple Guard left Talos at Baalshillek's door and withdrew. Baalshillek did not invite the old man to sit. He poured himself a measure of wine—in moderation, of course—and regarded the inventor over the rim of the cup.

"Do you know what you have done?" he asked.

Talos raised his shoulders in a half shrug. "Does the emperor know I am here?"

"I doubt he will object to a friendly visit." Baalshillek set down his cup. "He may come to doubt the wisdom of listening to your advice."

The old man peered at Baalshillek from rheumy eyes and looked away. "You would have killed Quintus."

"Perhaps. Perhaps I would have found a better use for him."

"Twisting his gifts to suit your purpose?"

"To the service of the Stone God. But your interference has made that prospect more difficult."

Talos offered no reply. He was either frightened into immobility or a Thespian of considerable talent.

"I could make your life in court extremely unpleasant," Baalshillek said. "I could turn the emperor against you."

"He values me. I served his father well—"

"—until you fled and made a bargain for your freedom."

"To protect Arrhidaeos's youngest son," the old man said.

"A son the emperor never bothered to reclaim. One might even say you failed in your bargain, since you allowed young Alexandros to believe himself a Tiberian, traitor to his own father's blood."

"An unfortunate turn of events."

"Most unfortunate—if your pupil chooses to maintain his current loyalties."

Talos ran his hand over his flyaway hair. "He understands what he faces."

"That I doubt." Baalshillek poured himself another digit of wine. "And what of you, Talos? When will you begin building new machines of war for our ambitious princeling?"

If Talos was startled by Baalshillek's open contempt for the emperor, he didn't reveal it. "Such machines will benefit you, as well," the old man said.

"What benefits the empire benefits my god."

"But the reverse is not always true."

Baalshillek smiled. "You're right, old man. That is why you had best consider carefully whom you choose to serve." He moved to an iron stand that held a wide-mouthed black bowl filled with equally dark liquid. Talos regarded the bowl with wary disgust.

"Do you feel it?" Baalshillek asked, cupping the sides of the bowl. The vessel's heat passed into his hands, and he hissed between his teeth. "My god's power is unconstrained by the petty ethics in which you take such pride." He passed his hands over the surface of the liquid, and it stirred sluggishly.

Talos shuddered. "How many children did you drain of blood to create that monstrosity?"

"How many did you kill with your machines of war?" The mixture in the bowl bubbled and seethed. "You would believe you have changed, old man, since those days of heedless destruction. I know that you had dealings with the rebels who traveled with your former student—the females Tahvo and Rhenna, and the Ailu, Cian. Do you not wonder what has become of them?"

"They are no longer of concern to me."

"That would be a wise attitude, if true. Let me set your mind at rest." Baalshillek lowered his face to the bowl and touched his tongue to the liquid. The metallic taste of blood mingled with the unmistakable tincture of the Stone.

The images began to form at once, figures and faces rising to the skin of the fluid, only to drown again. Rhenna of the Free People, tall and lean, with light brown hair, honey-moss eyes and a four-striped scar on her right cheek; Tahvo, shaman of the North, short and compact, with silver hair and blind silver eyes; sleekly-muscled Cian, black-haired and golden-eyed like his lost brother Ailuri; and the rebel known as Nyx, a woman of the South, with skin the color of ebony and eyes like the night.

"They live," Baalshillek said, letting none of his rage enter his voice. "They escaped the city, and many rebels died to make it so. A few were captured, but they are insignificant." He dipped his finger into the bowl, then licked it dry. "Your friends, however, must and will be stopped."

Talos sighed. "I see no mobilization of troops in the city. The emperor seems indifferent to their escape."

"Because he is wise enough to leave such matters to one who understands them." Baalshillek caught Talos's sleeve, forcing him closer to the bowl. "Your friends believe they serve a prophecy that binds them to seek certain great Weapons...a prophecy that foretells the downfall of my god."

"I know nothing—"

"You know, but it does not matter. Those called the Bearers, the godborn...they have weaknesses to match their supposed powers. And I have sent each of them a gift." He called up new images, new faces. First Yseul, the female Ailu he had created from the blood and essence of his captive shapeshifters. Then Farkas, formed from Rhenna's dread of violation and helplessness. And Urho, Tahvo's twin, dead at his birth but now reborn to haunt her dreams and visions.

"There is no greater weapon than fear," he said. "My creations were made to serve only one master and achieve only one goal: to stop the so-called Bearers and, if possible, bring the Weapons to me."

Talos examined the faces, like and yet unlike those of his friends, and shook his head. "You demand much of mere simulacra," he said. "And perhaps you underestimate simple human courage."

"You know the worth of your constructions, and I have faith in mine," Baalshillek said. He cleared the images with a sweep of his hand. "Your companions are beyond your aid, and you will not be permitted to interfere with young Corvinus again."

Talos stepped away from the stand. "If you are so sure of such things, why did you summon me here?"

"Because you and I are not so different, Talos. They called you 'the Destroyer' in the lands your machines ravaged. Yet you saved many lives by ending wars quickly. You made the rebels see the futility of their resistance."

"Your priests have no need of my devices to achieve the same results."

A rancid smell rose from the bowl, and Baalshillek summoned an omega priest to dispose of its contents. "You are too modest," he said when the servant had gone. "You could make yourself very useful to me."

"You do me far too much honor, lord priest. I fear I must decline the privilege of serving you and your god."

Baalshillek sat and adjusted his robes around his legs. "You may choose to believe so, for now. But you will keep no secrets from me, old man. All that you have done or been, everything you have ever thought will be as an open scroll to me when my agents have completed their work."

"I thank you for the warning." Talos bowed. "If I have your leave to depart—"

"By all means. Return to the court. Draw up your plans and convince Nikodemos that you can put all the world under his heel. I will not tell him that your loyalty is as false as your foolish prophecies."

"True or false, I am unlikely to see their fulfillment," Talos said. "You, however, will be alive to witness your god's downfall."

Baalshillek touched his stone pendant and pointed at Talos. The old man crumpled, and his face whitened in agony.

"You live on the emperor's sufferance," Baalshillek said softly. "*How* you live is within my hands."

Talos hobbled to the door and pulled it open with obvious effort. The victory left a foul taste on Baalshillek's tongue.

No matter. Pain was obviously not sufficient in itself, but the old man had some weakness other than his dubious allegiance to Nikodemos and his fondness for the Stone-killer. Once Baalshillek learned it, no magic would be necessary to convince

Talos where his true interests lay. Quintus Horatius Corvinus, so-called Alexandros, would lose his few allies one by one until he was entirely—and fatally—alone.

Chapter Two

Your powers will come.

Rhenna sat on an outcropping of rock on a barren hill, gazing across the valley at the glittering speck that was Karchedon. Early morning sun beat down on her head. No breeze stirred this scorched place where even the city's fat and glossy livestock did not venture. Yet the fertile croplands nestled between the hills seemed untouched by the scouring storm of dust that had driven the Stone God's servants back behind their walls.

Rhenna could never again draw breath without being aware of the life in the air all around her…the pneumata and the lesser devas of sky and wind who had come at her desperate call. She had no idea how she had done it or if she could repeat the magic. But it had saved them, and she was changed.

Cian tended Tahvo in a sheltered hollow. The little healer was recovering from the effects of sharing her body with a host of divinities and would soon be up on her own two feet. The windstorm had won the fugitives time and a goodly distance from Karchedon, but Rhenna didn't believe for a moment that the priests would abandon their hunt.

"We should move on," Nyx said.

Rhenna looked up at the Southern woman through narrowed eyes. "When was it decided that you should come with us?"

Nyx leaned on her spear. "You need a guide. My home is south of these lands, and I have traveled this country before."

This country. Nyx didn't mean the hinterlands of Karchedon, leagues of rugged hills where the Stone God and the empire held sway. Something even worse than imperial soldiers lay between the seekers and the magical object they sought—an ocean of rock and sand, roasting under a merciless sun by day and bitter cold by night.

"You have crossed the Great Desert?" Rhenna asked.

"Yes. It is a wasteland few can survive in ignorance."

"Yet you did not make the journey alone." Cian joined them, brushing at the dust that clung to his sweat-streaked arms and chest. He had fought in Karchedon as a panther and run naked from the city; the windstorm had bought him time to twist a scrap of cloth around his hips. He was lean and lithe and beautiful, bronzed rather than burned by the sun, an ideal representation of all that was fine in a male physique.

Rhenna had held that body in her arms, felt it move with her own in the most ancient and carnal of dances. She tried to remember what she had vowed to herself when she had agreed to this mad venture. She could not be both lover and leader. She *must* be—

"I had aid," Nyx said, oblivious to Rhenna's turmoil. "There are tribes that live in the desert, men and women who share our hatred of the Stone, and I know where they are wont to dwell."

"Did Geleon command you to help us?" Rhenna asked.

"I do not even know if Geleon survived the battle. I do this of my own will, and because I believe in the prophecies—as did the others who died for the sake of the Bearers."

Rhenna rubbed her sunburned arms. "Many were willing to give their lives based on the words of one woman—"

"*Your* friend, who spoke with the voice of the gods."

"—and because of these scribblings, which are much talked about but never seen."

"Philokrates believed in them," Cian said.

Rhenna snorted. "Philokrates lied about his past with the empire. How can we be sure of anything he told us?"

"The prophecies are real," Nyx said. "I knew of them long before I came to Karchedon."

"How?"

Nyx's expression flattened. "I do not know how Talos obtained his information, but the Stone priests are not the original owners of the sacred texts. Others outside Karchedon have knowledge of the prophecies, and they will be our allies."

"Your people," Cian said. At Nyx's nod, he added, "Then your country hasn't yet been taken by the empire."

"No." Nyx stretched the hamstrings of her long runner's legs. "The desert lies between Karchedon and my mother's homeland. Even the Stone God's minions are not yet prepared to conquer so great a barrier."

"Then what brought you to the city at such great risk?" Rhenna asked. "Did the prophecies send you, or do you have visions, like Tahvo?"

"I need no visions to see the truth. No one on this earth can escape the Stone God forever."

They looked as one toward Karchedon. Cian cleared his throat.

"What did you mean when you said I was to carry the Hammer?" he asked.

Rhenna started. She had heard nothing of this, but there had been little time for conversation since the escape. "You have information about the Weapons?" she asked Nyx.

"They are clearly mentioned in the prophecies."

"Do you know where this Hammer lies?"

Nyx hesitated. "It is somewhere in the South, as Cian guessed. Beyond that, I do not know, but there are those in my village and among the folk of the deep forest who may help us discover its location—now that its true Bearer has been found."

"These prophecies also mention Cian's name?"

Nyx cut the air with her hand. "Any woman with half an eye could see that he is the one."

"Indeed?" Rhenna arched a brow. "One would think you have a personal claim on our Cian. Why is that, woman of the South?"

"He is Ailu. He has power over the Earth, and the Hammer is of the Earth. He—" She broke off, and suddenly rooted the butt of her spear into the gritty soil, chanting in her own language. Tiny buds burst from the polished wood and flared into whorls of green leaves. Living tendrils snaked up and down the length of the spear.

"I also am of the Earth," Nyx said. "The Watcher is more powerful, but I have my gifts. You may find them useful."

Rhenna concealed her astonishment and met Nyx's eyes over the waving leaves. "I put more faith in the other end of your spear, if you're prepared to fight."

"She risked her life for us," Cian said. "I trust you both. Now you'll have to trust each other." He pointed his chin toward the arid scrublands to the south, where only a few miserable goats could hope to find sustenance. "You can find these desert tribes, Nyx?"

"I can."

"And they will be willing to help us?"

"We must be cautious, of course. We will be entering a land where they have fought for survival for thousands of years, but they know the Stone God threatens their very existence."

"And once we're beyond the desert?" Rhenna asked.

"Forests," Tahvo said. She crept up the low hill, feeling her way with outstretched hands. The unbroken silver of that blind gaze was still a shock to Rhenna, filling her with dreadful rage and bitterness.

"I see it in my mind," Tahvo said, smiling sadly at Rhenna as if she had heard her thoughts. "A vast sweep of trees like the pelt of a great green beast. Not like the North."

"Nor like the woodlands in the hills west of Karchedon," Nyx agreed. "You will see many changes between here and my mother's country."

"Will there be villages where we can purchase clothing and supplies?" Rhenna asked.

"There is one we may reach by nightfall." Nyx inclined her head to Cian. "We should continue on our journey before the soldiers find our trail. If you are ready, Watcher…"

Cian looked to Rhenna, waiting for her signal. A small concession, but it warmed her heart. Dangerously so.

I am leader, she thought. *Rhenna-of-the-Scar is no more.*

She hitched up her small pack and started down the hill. Nyx caught up and passed her, using her spear as a staff. Cian followed with Tahvo.

They made reasonably good time on foot, using their limited supply of water sparingly. Nyx's pace never flagged. Tahvo asked Cian's help when she needed assistance over the roughest places, but the healer fared remarkably well with touch, hearing and smell, in addition to the mystical shaman's senses she possessed.

The land gradually gave up its scant moisture, growing more rocky and bare with every passing league. Dry stream beds carved deep gorges out of overgrazed pasture, stripped of grass and all but the hardiest shrubs. An occasional goat paused in its browsing to stare at the interlopers, and jackals poked their heads from behind jutting rocks, laughing at human foolishness. The air grew so stifling that Nyx called a halt in the shadow of a cliff until the noonday heat had passed.

"The village I spoke of is not far ahead," she said. "The people who reside there are kin to the wandering desert tribes. They will have horses, which can carry us to Imaziren territory."

"Imaziren," Cian echoed, helping Tahvo drink from her waterskin. "This is a name I have heard before."

"Philokrates called my people 'Amazons,'" Rhenna said. "A strange similarity."

"*Imaziren* is the word for more than one tribesman," Nyx said. "The singular is Amazi." She glanced at Rhenna. "Among the desert tribes, women fight at the sides of their men. Your women fight alone, do they not?"

"My people have no kin outside the Shield's Shadow, except male offspring who return to their fathers among the steppes tribes," Rhenna said.

"Yet your legends don't tell where Asteria was born," Cian said.

Asteria, First Mother, founder of the Free People. It was true that not even the Earthspeakers, Healers or Seekers of Rhenna's race could be sure of Asteria's origins.

"It doesn't matter," she said, watching waves of hot air rise from the baked earth beyond the border of the cliff's shadow. "As long as these Imaziren help us."

After the four of them had rested and the sun had begun its downward journey to the West, Nyx led them out again. At sunset they reached the borders of a small, mud-brick village beside a small patch of green Nyx called an *amda*. Tall, branchless trees with broad, fringed leaves at their tops shaded the houses and the livestock grazing in a surprisingly verdant pasture.

Nyx, who spoke a little of the local dialect, took the coin the Karchedonian rebels had provided and ventured into the town alone. The people Rhenna glimpsed were brown from the sun, men and women both, but their hair and eyes ran from dark to fair, and they wore light garments befitting the hot weather. They came out of their plain, pale houses to talk and sip beverages from clay cups as the cool of evening brought relief from the day's fierce temperatures.

Rhenna spent most of the next two hours pacing and debating how soon she should go after Nyx. Cian watched her without comment, his chin resting on his knees.

"They are here," Tahvo said.

Rhenna spun to face the healer. "Who?"

"The spirits. It is difficult to sense them in this land. The water runs deep under the ground, and many of those who once inhabited even the dry places have fled."

"From the Stone God, as they did in the North," Rhenna said.

She nodded. "But water rises to the surface in this place, and the spirits linger. Nyx said that the desert tribes rely on the green islands. Perhaps I will be able to talk with the spirits once we are in the sea of sand."

"If Nyx keeps her promises, you won't have to burden yourself. You've had enough dealings with devas to last you half a lifetime."

"But it is not over," Tahvo whispered. "It is only beginning. For all of us."

Rhenna shuddered. "You're still mortal, Tahvo. Remember that, when the devas are so anxious to use you."

But we're all being used, Rhenna thought. *Even the devas.*

Cian sat up, nostrils flaring. "Nyx returns. With horses. And food."

Rhenna hardly thought of nourishment when she caught the unmistakable smell of horseflesh. Nyx led a string of four mounts, one hardly larger than a pony, the others smaller than the steppes breed and far from beautiful, but sturdy enough in appearance.

"It took nearly all our coin to buy them," Nyx said, offering the lead of a bay gelding to Rhenna. "They're desert-bred, able to travel on less water than most."

Rhenna examined the gelding's legs and patted his shoulder as the animal snuffled her dusty hair. "They'll do," she said. She assessed the other horses and chose the tallest gray gelding for Cian, while Nyx took the chestnut mare. The pony might have been made for Tahvo's short stature and uncertain horsemanship. The tack was not of the best, worn and rubbed thin, but it would serve.

Nyx laid out her other purchases, including larger waterskins for the horses to carry and a change of clothing for each of the riders. There were shirts, trousers and headcloths for Rhenna, Tahvo and Cian, dyed the same ocher hue as the landscape. Nyx had chosen a tunic that left her legs bare. She had bought low leather boots for herself and taller ones for the Northerners. Tahvo's were decidedly too large.

The meal consisted of flat bread, a thick stew of beans, vegetables and mutton, and a brown drink Rhenna guessed was beer. When the last of the perishable food had been devoured and the rest packed away, Nyx passed out rough woolen blankets and the group made a fireless camp beneath the scraggly branches of a scrub tree. With the horses bunched nearby, Rhenna could almost imagine she was home in the Shield's Shadow with the herd, back in the days before the devas had spoken to her in voices of wind and blood.

A breeze puffed against her cheek, and she swatted it away. Cian stirred and rolled over to face her, eyes half-lidded and glinting by moonlight. Tahvo snored under her blanket, and Nyx stood watch near the horses, her lean body erect in a warrior's stance.

"You can't sleep?" Cian asked.

Save for brief conversations, the two of them had barely spoken since formulating the plan to leave Karchedon. So many deaths, so many sacrifices stood between that day and this. So many vows that Rhenna wasn't sure she could keep.

"I could ask the same of you," Rhenna retorted. He was almost within reach. If she stretched her arm and fingers...

Cian shivered. "They must be pursuing us," he said.

"Do you know this, or only fear it?"

"I'm always afraid." He raised himself up on his elbow. "I'm afraid for Tahvo, that she'll be driven mad by the powers that consume her. I fear for Nyx and her disillusionment when she sees how unworthy I am of her expectations. And I fear for you." He spread his right hand on the ground between them, the hand that lacked its smallest finger. "Rhenna—"

She willed him not to speak of things that could only create more discomfort for them both. But his eloquent golden eyes said all the words his tongue did not, bringing a slow, heavy throbbing to the core of her body.

"Would you change what happened?" Cian asked.

He had no need to explain himself further. She remembered a garden lush with flowers and trees, untouched by the impossible snow that fell throughout Karchedon. Lying with a man she had wanted without daring to admit it, giving and taking in equal measure. Knowing there could never be a moment's peace or certainty between them.

"I would not change it," she said. "But that was a place out of time, Cian. We can't go back."

He closed his eyes. "If your people could remain free of the Stone God, would you return to them?"

She rolled over, turning her back. "We wouldn't remain free. And the Ailuri are gone. The Free People can never be the same again."

His fingers stroked over her shoulder, so lightly that she felt their heat more than their touch. "None of us can. But we must stay true to what we are, Rhenna. To each other."

Mother-of-All. She tugged the blanket up to her neck. "I swore I wouldn't leave you while our quest continues."

He retreated, and for an instant she thought he had left the camp. She strained her ears for the sound of his breathing.

"I promise the same," he said at last. "I won't leave you, Rhenna, until the Stone God has fallen."

And after? If there was any future to be had, it was far beyond Rhenna's ability to imagine. Survival was by no means assured, not for any of them. The devas knew she would willingly give her life for Cian or Tahvo.

"Go to sleep, Cian," she said wearily. "Surely Tahvo will sense if we're in immediate danger."

But Cian didn't answer. He had gone, perhaps to prowl the night in a panther's skin black as the night sky. Rhenna looked for Tahvo's sleeping form, got up and spread her blanket closer to the healer. She laid her sword within easy reach of her hand.

Tahvo muttered something in a language Rhenna didn't understand. "Heru-sa-Aset," she whispered. She smiled tenderly and began to sing an unmistakable lullaby.

"She speaks of the gods," Nyx said. She crouched beside Rhenna, lean hands dangling between her knees. "Heru. Horus, the Hellenes call him, child of Aset and Asar, Isis and Osiris."

Rhenna sat up, tossing the blanket aside. "I've never pretended to know much of devas. Are these important?"

"They are revered in Khemet, and by some in lands beyond." She peered at Tahvo. "That one knows much she cannot yet say."

"She knows more than any of us can understand."

"Then perhaps she would tell you what I am about to say, though you will not wish to hear it."

Rhenna's heart began to thump in her chest. "And just what is that?"

"You care greatly for the Watcher, do you not?"

"Of course I care for him." Rhenna got to her feet. "We've been companions for many months. We've saved each other's lives. I care for Tahvo—"

Nyx shook her head. "Do not pretend to misunderstand me, warrior. I may not be well acquainted with your past or your customs, but I recognize the gaze of lovers when I see it."

Rhenna flushed. "Perhaps your sight is not as keen as you believe."

"Then you deny that such a relationship exists?"

Relationship. Rhenna hated the sound of Cian's name on

Nyx's lips, but this was a subject she had no wish to discuss with a virtual stranger. "What may exist between Cian and me is our business," she said sharply.

"But it is not." Nyx stood, her dark eyes clouding with anger. "It is the business of the world, of all who fight the Stone God. You have no comprehension of what lies ahead. Through Tahvo, the gods revealed only the smallest part of the battle to come. They revealed that you are one of the godborn Bearers. And Cian is to carry the Hammer."

"You already made that clear enough," Rhenna said. "If you think I'll stand in his way…"

"Perhaps not deliberately. But the Watcher will have no time for ties such as those he believes bind you to him. He must be free."

"He *is* free." Rhenna turned away, fighting to still her trembling. "The Ailuri and the Free People have been allies for all our known histories. I would protect Cian even if I had met him yesterday, just as any of my Sisters would defend any of his kind. But I am a warrior, not one of the Chosen."

"The Chosen," Nyx repeated softly. "Chosen by the Watchers?"

"Chosen by our Earthspeakers to mate with the Ailuri." Rhenna's voice cracked, and she swallowed to bring it back under control. "I owe you no explanations, Nyx of the Unknown Lands, yet I will tell you this. Cian's choices are his own, but he is not all-powerful. I would have come even if Tahvo's spirits had declared me one of the deva-cursed godborn, because he is alone and needs guarding as much from himself as from those who would destroy him."

"And you trust no one else to watch the Watcher."

"I trust very little."

"And yourself? Do you trust yourself, Rhenna of the Free People, who has mated with one who should have been forbidden to you?"

Rhenna reached for the knife at her waist but diverted the

motion, clenching her fist on empty air. "You assume a great deal, Nyx," she said. "You think me weak, like women of the Hellenes. Do not make that mistake."

"Then you will give him up for the sake of our quest?"

Rhenna laughed. "Give him up? Is he a dog to wear a collar? Do I hold his leash?"

"It is not enough to deny your feelings. You must be prepared to push him away if he comes too near. If you refuse, you may bring about his death and the downfall of everything we hold dear." She kicked a pebble with the toe of her boot. "One distraction, one misstep could prevent him from doing what he must to win and hold the Hammer. You could be that distraction, Rhenna."

"Your opinion of Cian is as low as it is of me."

"You are wrong. I have great respect for you, as a warrior and as one of the Bearers. I believe in the Watcher with all my heart. But what men and women call love can be a terrible force. It has no place among the godborn. Cian's attention must be focused on victory. When your time comes to claim your Weapon, you, too, will be alone."

Alone. As if she hadn't been alone all her life. As if that one time with Cian hadn't been born as much of accident as intention.

No accident. The devas themselves arranged it. We were meant to be together....

"No," Rhenna said. "I will not be this 'distraction' you fear. Cian and I are not lovers. But I won't abandon him."

"That is not required." Nyx's shoulders sagged as if she had unexpectedly emerged alive from the heat of battle. "He will need your protection, and one day you will stand together as Bearers. But only as Bearers."

"I thank you for making my position so clear." Rhenna backed away before she could consider striking at this woman with her overweening arrogance. She grabbed her sword and climbed to the hill overlooking the village. Gusts of wind blew first from the North and then the South, sighing the warning that had become so familiar.

Danger.

Rhenna laughed.

Chapter Three

"I say we are wasting time," Farkas said, his lips curling in a sneer. "They can't be very far ahead now. We should attack while we're close to the city."

"When we still know so little about their powers?" Urho said, staring at his fellow male with undisguised contempt. "Can you make a great wind like the warrior female, Skudat? Or are you merely ruled by hatred of the one who helped give you birth?"

Farkas snapped the brittle stick he held between his hands and tossed the two pieces aside. "As you hate the healer? You wouldn't exist without her. At least I—"

"Be silent," Yseul hissed. The males looked up at her as if they were surprised she dared speak. Even after days of traveling together, they quarreled among themselves like infants…and infants these creatures were, only weeks old in the ways of the world.

Yseul was wiser. Baalshillek had brought her to life nearly a year ago, when he had taken flesh and blood from captured Ailuri and created a shapeshifter of his own. Female of a race where females were unknown. Driven by hungers she hardly understood, given new form on the day she met and seduced the Ailu named Cian.

Cian, her enemy. She grew hot and wet at the thought of having him at her mercy once more.

She rose from her seat on the rock above the others and stretched, bending and twisting until the stupid males gaped in mute lust. She had not bothered to clothe herself since her last change from panther to woman, but she wasn't afraid of her companions' frank desire. She wasn't for them, and they knew it.

As for the Children of the Stone, the soldier escort Baalshillek had so generously provided for his creations, Yseul doubted they felt real emotion at all. They seemed no more than three dozen armored puppets. Yet among those warriors was at least one who had been sent to spy on her and her fellow simulacra, one who had been given the independence to judge the progress of their mission and report any failure to Baalshillek.

Sharp pain stabbed Yseul's forehead, and she rubbed at the shard of red stone imbedded in her flesh. Even a mildly treasonous thought was enough to loose the crystal's punishment.

"Farkas," Yseul purred. "Urho." She climbed down from the rock, finding her way easily by moonlight, and stopped before them. "You both know why we were sent to this gods-forsaken land. Our lord Baalshillek has given us but one purpose, and that is to stop the godborn—"

"And take the Weapons," Farkas interrupted.

"If possible," Yseul agreed. She stroked the barbarian's chin with the tip of a long fingernail. "Urho is right. If we attack now, we do so in ignorance. Already Rhenna has proven herself stronger than we anticipated, and her powers may grow. She is to be one of the Bearers."

"How can any female wield a weapon forged for heroes?" Farkas demanded.

Yseul smiled and ran her tongue along the edges of her sharp teeth. "You tell me how Rhenna's people continue to hold the Skudat and other tribes at bay, mere women though they are?"

"I remember taking the bitch," Farkas said, jerking away from Yseul. "She was helpless. I could have killed her any time."

"You seem to forget, my impetuous friend, that it was not you who enjoyed her scarred body. You are but a shadow of that other Farkas…and he did not kill her."

"I *am* Farkas," he said, beating his chest with his fist. "I am more than he ever was or can be. I hold the power of Air."

"Prove it." She folded her arms beneath her full breasts, lifting them high. "Show me your skill, Skudat prince."

He licked his lips as if he dreamed of suckling on her like the babe he was. "I have many skills, woman."

"Then make a windstorm, like the female you conquered."

Farkas snarled defiance and lifted his hands. His dark eyes squeezed shut. Drops of sweat stood out on his forehead. A fitful gust of air played around his feet and scattered dust over his boots.

Yseul laughed. Urho snickered. Farkas swung toward the shaman's double, but Yseul stepped between them.

"You are not ready," she said to Farkas. "And you, Urho…if you had been born to a human woman, you would have had Tahvo's abilities. That birthright was denied you, but our master has given you power over the element of Water. How well can you use it?"

Urho scowled, his pale eyes reflecting light like twin silver pools. "I will learn."

"And learning takes time." She ran her hands over her flat belly and flung back her head. "Time we have, my fellow travelers. Our enemies have far to go. There will be many chances to hurt them and to make them realize the futility of their hopes."

"You speak like a feeble *enaree,* woman," Farkas said. "What will you do when it's time to fight?"

She changed instantly, confronting him with a panther's bared fangs and lashing tail. He flinched, in spite of all his bravado. She could kill him…and earn Baalshillek's undying wrath. Proving her superiority would be far more satisfying, if she were patient. Patient as a cat waiting for a small rodent to emerge from its hole.

With a single thought, she was human again. "I have a power neither of you possesses," she said, almost sweetly. "And I am Ailu. The Earth is mine as much as it is Cian's." She crouched and passed her hand over the dry dirt. A small crack opened at Farkas's feet. He cursed and jumped back.

"Until one of you has a plan worth following, I will lead this party," she said. "I suggest you practice to refine the skills your creator gave you. I would not like to see him disappointed."

Farkas spun on his bootheel and strode away, shoving the Stone's Children right and left out of his path. They closed ranks immediately and looked to Yseul for orders.

Which of you is Baalshillek's spy? she asked them silently, ignoring the pain in her head. *I will find you. I must.*

"At dawn we continue our pursuit," she said, addressing the commander of the phalanx. "You will send scouts ahead to question any villagers in the vicinity…discreetly. We want no dead in our wake. Not yet."

The commander—nameless, just as he was faceless behind his slitted helmet—saluted. His men dispersed to their beds on the hard ground, long spears hugged to their bodies like lovers.

"You have won…this time," Urho said. "Farkas will not be content to follow a female forever."

"Farkas is a fool, and he had better gain wisdom quickly. There can be no failure if we wish to continue our existence."

Urho eyed the Children. "They have been sent to watch, as well as serve us."

Indeed. But perhaps a time will come when we no longer…require their services.

She noted Urho's narrowed glance and smiled. "Do you also have ambition to lead, Urho?"

"Unlike Farkas, I do not hate all females," he said. "But beware, Yseul. If you fail in your vigilance, it will be observed."

"I take your warning," she said. "We must be allies, but we are not burdened by love for one another, as are our enemies. Do you understand love, Urho?"

"I know it is a human weakness."

Like fear, and greed. But not ambition. Not the desire for the power one had been created to wield. "We are not human, Urho." *But Baalshillek is. And if he sees us now, it will not be so forever. Eventually we must venture even beyond the limits of the Stone God's influence.*

And when that time comes…

"Do not worry, Urho. You are a most obedient servant. You will receive your reward."

And so will I. Beware, Cian of the Ailuri. So will I.

Among many of the peoples Cian had known during his youthful wanderings in the North, it would have been unthinkable that two women should lead while the man obediently followed.

Cian did not find it strange. He had been born to a mother of the Free People, those the Hellenes called "Amazons," and lived beside them in the Shield of the Sky until his sixth year sent him back to his sire's race. He knew women could fight and ride with the best of men, and he never doubted their courage.

He had seldom been the only male among females. But he had felt alone many times, both more and less than human, and he had known what it was to be helpless. Now, as he and the band of seekers began the trek across the Great Desert, his only use was to trail behind Nyx and Rhenna, caring for Tahvo as best he could.

Tahvo herself was no weakling, but her blindness was still new. Her other senses were growing stronger, and Cian taught her how to listen and smell in the way of the Ailuri—how to catch the slightest shift in the wind or detect the faint rattle of a bird in a thorn tree. She could already find water in the least likely of places. Yet it was clear that something troubled her.

"What worries you, Tahvo?" he asked when their little group had left the last of the rocky hills and coastal valleys behind. "Do you sense our enemies?"

She shook her head. "It is the spirits. I had hoped to find them once we were far enough from Karchedon, but…" She paused, as if seeking the right words. "If they still exist, they hide deep under the ground or high in the air, where I cannot reach them."

That was troubling news indeed. Tahvo was the travelers' go-between with the devas. Through her, in Karchedon, the devas had explained that the coming war would require all the resources of free men and benevolent gods in every corner of the world. Even the most barren places had their lesser devas…unless they had been destroyed or driven away.

Cian looked out on the flat pan of black rock and sand stretching before them as far as the eye could see. He followed the erratic flight of a small, shiny black beetle as it winged past his horse's ear. The desert was hardly as lifeless as it seemed. Beyond the realm of plowed fields and livestock, where the gravel plain began, wild creatures filled every available living space, no matter how inhospitable to men. Lizards, scorpions, serpents, dust-colored birds, even the occasional big-eared fox, scuttled between larger rocks in search of shade by day and prey at night.

Nyx took her cue from the beasts. When they reached the open desert, she urged travel during the hours of darkness as long as the moon provided adequate light. She usually called a halt by mid-morning, when a haze of heat softened the harsh horizon with the illusion of moisture, and the travelers sought scraps of shade beneath nearly leafless thorn trees or clusters of boulders. Everyone slept, the horses dozing on their feet. As night approached, Nyx built small fires of whatever material was available and made flat cakes out of a paste of grain and water baked in the embers.

Every day was much the same. That first week, and the second and third and fourth passed with monotonous discomfort. The ground remained featureless save for colored swaths of pebbles and the isolated hillock. Only the light itself changed, brilliant ocher as the sun rose in the East and fading to a white-hot glare at noon. There was no rain, no rivers or streams; sometimes the pattern of rocks revealed where flash floods from some rare and ancient storm had scoured channels out of the desert floor.

Rhenna rationed the water carefully, saving the greater part of it for the game little horses. Nyx led them to wells painstakingly dug into the rocky earth where water rose nearest the surface; she, Cian and Rhenna took turns hauling up leather buckets of gritty liquid to refill skins and quench unrelenting thirst. Tahvo always listened for the spirits who should inhabit the realms of Water but found the wells as deserted as the arid plain.

Nyx watched constantly for signs of the desert tribesmen, but the Imaziren remained elusive. Rhenna grew more grim as the leagues passed.

"The animals can't abide these conditions much longer," she told Nyx as the women shared the morning's meager supply of water. "We're almost out of grain, and there isn't enough grazing even beside the wells. Where are these desert folk of yours?"

Nyx gazed toward the Southern horizon. "Have patience," she said. "They will come."

"Patience will not carry us when the horses are dead."

Cian watched the two women in wary silence. Before this journey began, he would have sworn that no woman in the world could be as stubborn as Rhenna of the Free People. But Nyx shared that quality in full measure. In Karchedon she had been one of many rebels, subordinate to the leader Geleon;

she'd been a prisoner of the Stone priests and barely escaped with her life. But there was something in her carriage that suggested a very different past. She was as proud as an Ailu in the days before the Children of the Stone came to steal Cian's people from the Shield, and her courage was admirable.

Admirable. Cian shifted uneasily on his mount's back and tried to wet his cracked lips. He couldn't deny that he was drawn to Nyx in a way he couldn't define. Her powers were of Earth, like his; she was graceful and beautiful. Rhenna had ignored Cian since that night outside the village, and it was Nyx who asked how he fared, who treated him as an honored companion.

Once or twice at the afternoon camp Cian caught Rhenna looking at him by the wan firelight, but she always turned her head before their eyes could meet. He knew that she didn't dare show any sign of weakness now that she'd placed herself at the head of their expedition. Affection was an encumbrance for a warrior, even one who had given her body and some small piece of her heart to the man who rode beside her.

Cian wouldn't beg for her attention. He'd lost nearly all right to pride, but that remnant lingered. When Rhenna kicked her mount into a trot and Nyx fell back to join Cian, he had his emotions under control.

"You are well, Watcher?" Nyx asked.

"Well enough. Where is Rhenna going?"

Nyx adjusted the cord that bound her headcloth over her braided hair. "Ahead, to scout. She won't go far."

Cian scanned the horizon, where Rhenna's vanishing shape was a distorted blur in the rising heat. "What does Rhenna hope to find?" he asked.

"I think she has begun to doubt that we will meet the Imaziren," Nyx said. "Do you share her distrust in me, Watcher?"

Cian sighed. "You've told us very little about your part in this journey. Perhaps if you explained, Rhenna would be less suspicious."

"Of my motives?" Nyx tossed her head. "I intended to do so, but she can make such conversations difficult."

"She prefers action to discussion," Cian said wryly.

Nyx curled her fingers about the shaft of her spear, which rested in a makeshift harness of rope tied across her horse's withers. "Action is not always possible or advisable," she said. "I would have *you* understand, even if she does not."

Cian reined his gelding to a stop. "You had better make clear what you expect of me, Nyx, or I may sadly disappoint you."

"That is not possible." Her dark eyes glinted with passion. "You are the one. The one my father sought, the one written of in the prophecies." She glanced back at Tahvo, who rode her stolid pony with eyes half closed. "I will tell you some of what you wish to know…but I ask you to say nothing of it to the others until I am ready."

"If it puts them at a disadvantage…"

"It will not." Nyx shifted her slender weight and urged her horse into motion again, her spine strong and flexible as a willow branch. "I must begin with my father. You see, he was not born in my mother's land. He came from the East, from a city unknown to all but a privileged few. His people call it New Meroe."

"I've never heard of it."

"If you had, my father's people—*my* people—would be in grave danger." She met his eyes. "New Meroe is the true home of the prophecies, the ancient writings that predict the rise and fall of the Exalted and the Stone God. It was from there that my father left in search of the Hammer of the Earth, and it was his quest that sent me across the desert to find what he could not."

Nyx continued her remarkable tale as they rode through the morning, while Cian listened with astonishment and growing apprehension.

"So at last I arrived in Karchedon," she said, her voice grown hoarse with the story's telling. "I heard rumors of panther men taken captive by the Stone priests. I joined the rebels in the hope that Geleon would work to free the Watchers, but his people hadn't the strength for so desperate an act. Then you came."

"Ignorant of everything but what Philokrates had told us," Cian said.

"As I was ignorant of your presence when Quintus and Talos asked for our help. But after Danae set me free and I met you, I knew you were the one."

"How? Other Ailuri escaped from Baalshillek—"

"They were not chosen."

"I would rather have died with them."

"*No.*" She jerked on the reins, and her horse tossed up its head. "Do you think that Rhenna and Tahvo would long have survived your fall?"

"I didn't save them. I didn't save anyone. Many lost their lives because of me—"

"What you will save is a thousand times more important than any one life."

Cian laughed. "The world?"

For a long time Nyx didn't answer. "Not only the world's body, but its soul."

Cian had learned from experience that there was no arguing with the faithful. "What of the Weapons? We were told that each of them is guarded by an Exalted who escaped the Stone prison. Do your prophecies say which deva took the Hammer?"

"They tell that the god of chaos, Sutekh, created the Hammer to fight the Exalted, but they do not reveal who stole it."

"And the other three Weapons?"

She bit her lip. "My father was able to share with me only what he knew. The priests of New Meroe understand far more than a simple warrior. When we take the Hammer—when *you* take it—we must continue on to the holy city."

Cian heard the conviction in her words and wondered what Rhenna would make of them. She would certainly object to Nyx deciding the seekers' destination, but she knew they had all too little information to go on. If New Meroe held the key…

"Was it your father or your mother who gave you your gift with growing things?" he asked.

"My mother. Clan Amòtékùn is blessed with such abilities, passed from mother to daughter." She hesitated. "What became of the females of your people, Cian?"

The question startled him. "We have no females," he said slowly. *Liar. There is one…unnatural, forbidden….*

He shook himself. "We…take mates from among the Free People, whose country borders our mountains. Male children of such matings return…returned to us in their sixth year."

"No female has ever been born with the shapeshifting gift?"

"None. Female children of Ailuri sires usually became leaders among the Free People, but they did not change their shape. Why do you ask?"

"Did you not find it lonely without mates of your own kind?"

Cian looked away. "Our elders said we were meant to be alone, close to the devas and apart from man. We had no need of such companionship."

"Yet you left your people."

"I was not content with the life to which I was born, so I left the mountains. When I finally returned my people had all been taken."

"And you blame yourself. This is an indulgence you cannot afford, Watcher."

He almost smiled, thinking again how much she sounded like Rhenna in one of her more reproachful moods. "I doubt there will be many indulgences for any of us," he said.

"Sacrifice is necessary if great deeds are to be achieved."

"What else do you demand of me besides saving the world?"

She looked into his eyes. "Your courage and strength, when the time comes to leave behind all that you love."

He knew what she meant, and the beast within him howled in protest. The blood raced hot in his veins. His mount plunged, feeling the wildness simmering under his skin.

Nyx reached across the space between them and took his

hand. "I have faith in you, Cian of the Watchers. You will defeat the god of evil and take your rightful place."

"Where? On a temple pedestal, with priests of his own to worship him?"

Rhenna's voice was tight with feigned amusement, and her eyes were slits in a dust-coated face. She drew her horse alongside Cian's and pushed straggling hair from her forehead. "It seems I've missed a fascinating discussion," she said. "Perhaps you can share it with me."

"I doubt you'd find it of interest, warrior," Nyx said. She and Rhenna glared at each other. A sharp burst of wind blew up from beneath the horses' feet, carrying grit into Cian's eyes.

"The wind is rising," Tahvo said, trotting up to join them. "We must find shelter."

Cian sneezed. The air was already laced with tiny particles of dust and sand, blotting out the horizon and turning the very ground into a whirlpool of earth and pebbles.

"This should not be," Nyx said. "It is the wrong season for windstorms, or I would have been prepared—"

"Prepared or not, it comes," Rhenna said. "Where do we ride, Nyx?"

The Southern woman sat still on her trembling mare. "Cover your faces and follow me."

She turned her mount into the wind. It seemed insanity, and as the gusts grew more violent the sting of spinning gravel became lashing whips, tearing at skin and cloth with equal viciousness. The air was too thick to breathe. Cian lost sight of both Nyx and Rhenna. Guiding his horse with his knees, he reached for Tahvo's reins and tugged her pony as close as he dared.

Soon every step was a struggle for the terrified, half-blinded horses. The exposed portion of Cian's face was a mass of tiny welts and abrasions. Blood trickled into his eyes. If shelter lay ahead, he couldn't sense it. He and Tahvo might have been alone in a world of unbeing.

"It is Rhenna!" Tahvo shouted, muffled by the cloth wrapped over her mouth. "This wind is of her summoning."

"I can't see her," Cian replied. "I can barely smell her. Can she control it?"

"Only if recognizes her own magic. She must understand…."

But Rhenna obviously didn't understand. If she'd created this storm as Tahvo claimed, it had come not from her will but from her anger. And if she didn't find a way to bring it under control, she would surely kill them all.

Chapter Four

Rhenna reined her gelding away from the wind and rode back to find Cian and Tahvo. Their horses walked with lowered heads, barrels heaving, eyes shut against the flaying wall of sand. Rhenna pulled the last of her spare clothing from her pack and cut the linen into strips, dismounting to fasten makeshift blinkers over the other horses' heads, as she'd done with her own mount.

Nyx reappeared, harsh coughs wracking her long body. "We can't stop!" she cried.

Rhenna fixed blinkers on Nyx's mount. "We'll have to lead the horses," she said. "Do we have far to go?"

"Not far." Nyx slid to the ground, and Cian helped Tahvo to dismount. They turned back into the wind. The storm grew more savage by the moment. Rhenna murmured to her weary horse and waited until Cian and Tahvo caught up.

Step by step Nyx led them through the rain of grit and gravel.

A journey that seemed to last many hours might have taken only a few thousand heartbeats; the sun was invisible, the heat unabated. Boulders rose monstrous and strange out of the haze. They stood like old men with hard gray skins, seamed and scarred by the elements.

Mountains. They were nothing like those Rhenna had known, as alien to her as the desert and just as forbidding. But as the travelers gained altitude, the force of the wind gradually died from a raging blizzard of sand to a mere tempest. The horses' hooves skidded and echoed over the slick surface of a massive sheet of granite. Sand and dust blew across the rock in swirls and eddies, movement without life or purpose.

"There are caves among these mountains," Nyx called. "We will take refuge there until the storm abates."

"Is there water?" Rhenna asked, as much to Tahvo as Nyx.

No one replied, and that was answer enough. Nyx continued to lead them higher, where ancient wind and water had carved sandstone cliffs into bizarre shapes, pinnacles and pillars like the ramparts of a city. A few ragged brown tufts of grass pushed between cracks in the stone. The horses were trembling with fatigue by the time Nyx found the shelter she sought.

The mouth of the cave was wide and unobstructed, easily large enough to accommodate the horses. Rhenna remembered another cave in very different mountains, the first time she'd held a real conversation with Cian after his escape from his Neuri captors. There had been a new, strange intimacy between them then, even with Tahvo standing between them. Rhenna hadn't acknowledged it at the time. Now she had to pretend it no longer existed.

She forced the useless anger away and followed Nyx under the overhanging arch of dark-polished rock. The horses came readily enough, nostrils flaring as they sucked in breaths of cool, clean air. Rhenna led the animals to a place where the wind couldn't reach but there was still enough light to see. She stripped the blinkers from the horses' eyes and spat out a mouthful of grit.

"Where are we?" she asked Nyx.

"In the mountains the tribes call Speaking Stones. This is Amazi territory." She peered out at the gray afternoon light. "It's too late to continue today, but if the storm breaks, I'll scout for sign of the Imaziren."

"The horses must drink soon."

"Give them my water." Nyx turned her back on Rhenna and began to remove her mare's pack. Rhenna went to her own mount and untied waterskins and the collapsible leather dish Nyx had bought to serve the horses. She poured as generous a helping as she dared, and the animals crowded close.

Cian had already unpacked his gelding and Tahvo's pony. He accepted a waterskin from Rhenna without touching her hand.

"Where is Tahvo?" Rhenna asked.

Cian looked around in surprise. "She was with me a moment ago. Perhaps she's looking for the spirits."

"I hope she finds them. They aren't speaking to me."

"But you still speak to them."

"What do you mean?"

He shrugged. "I'll find Tahvo." He set off into the darkness at the back of the cave, his panther's vision keener than any human's.

Nyx had started a small fire with twigs and branches she had collected from the rare trees and shrubs that grew beside the desert wells. "It grows cold at night in these mountains," she said, "but we have little left to eat."

"If there were game here, I could hunt," Rhenna said. "At least there's some grain left for the horses. When that is gone..."

"I know." Nyx rubbed her high forehead with the palm of her hand, revealing the brown skin beneath the dust. "We will reach the Imaziren soon. They do not permit strangers to pass unchallenged. When we—"

"Rhenna."

Cian's voice was a hollow whisper, as if it came from a great distance. Rhenna snatched up a burning stick and strode the way Cian had gone. She found him much sooner than she'd expected, standing beside Tahvo in an alcove off the main chamber.

"What are you two doing?" she demanded. "Tahvo—"

"She found them," Cian said. "The Speaking Stones."

He pointed to the nearest curved wall. At first all Rhenna saw were pale scratchings and lines on the darker rock, and then she picked out the images by firelight: men and beasts, graceful drawings and engravings of hunters and horsemen, animals of impossible features and proportions. Indeed, the stones did speak. They told stories of people who had lived in this harsh country in another age, an age when the desert had nurtured abundance that had long since vanished.

"I felt them," Tahvo said. She sat cross-legged on the floor, an arm's length from the painted wall, eyes closed, hands resting on her thighs in an attitude of prayer or contemplation. "The spirits are no longer here, but some part of them remains in the stone. Can you tell me what you see?"

"They are the ones who came before," Nyx said. She settled to her haunches, gazing up at the pictures with reverence on her face. "The ones who hunted here when the desert was grass, when the *àgùnfón* and *àjànànkú* walked beside the rivers. They who gave birth to the Imaziren and saw the Exalted's City fall."

Rhenna held the torch closer to the walls. "Here men hunt beasts on foot with spears," she said to Tahvo. "But I've never seen such animals. One is spotted and has a neck as long as its legs. Another creature has a head that is all mouth, with broad feet and tiny ears—"

"The *akáko*," Nyx said. "They still live in Southern rivers."

Rhenna moved a few steps deeper into the cave. "People— women—are dancing. Herds of deer with strange horns. Men with bows and arrows."

Tahvo ran her fingers across one of the lowest engravings. "There is more," she said. Slowly she got to her feet. "Yes, I hear." She spread her arms wide and crept along the wall. "It is the story of the coming of the Exalted."

There were no voices. The spirits had gone long ago, just as Tahvo had told the others, but their bones were here, infusing the paints with which vanished artists had made these pictures.

Rhenna had described images of men hunting and women dancing in a time when fantastic creatures roamed a vast plain. And Tahvo could see it: rolling steppes dotted with trees, rivers filled with the great-mouthed water horses and horned beasts of enormous size.

"When the desert was grass," Tahvo repeated. "When men lived in harmony with the spirits, before the Exalted came."

"She's having a vision," Cian said. "Tahvo, are you all right?"

"I am well." The pictures flooded her mind—not motionless drawings like those she had painted on her own drum in the lands of the Samah, emblems shaped to call the spirits, but moving representations of the distant past.

"The great City was here," Tahvo murmured.

"Here?" Rhenna echoed.

"Not in this cave," Tahvo said impatiently. "On the plain that is now wasteland. A world of plenty destroyed by evil. What else do you see?"

"Symbols," Rhenna said. "Spirals, waves, discs with wings."

"The Elements. The spirits, as men once saw them," Tahvo said. "Can you find the place where the drawings change?"

Tahvo heard Rhenna step around her and walk beside the wall. "The light isn't bright enough, but not all the pictures are made in the same way."

"I can see the difference," Cian said. "They start with the scenes of hunting and dancing, and then the symbols. These drawings are cut into the rock."

"They are the oldest, from the time before the City," Tahvo said. "And the next?"

Cian moved farther away and sucked in his breath. "The next group are painted in red."

Red. The color of the Stone God's fire. "What do they reveal?"

"Men and women bowing to other beings...like men but taller, more powerful."

"Devas," Rhenna said.

"Some have the heads of animals," Cian said. "Some are male and some female. Some are painted dark, some light." He counted under his breath. "Twelve. Twelve gods, and many men to worship them."

Tahvo shivered. "The people gave the Exalted more than their worship."

"Men hold the symbols of the elements in their hands. They place them before the Exalted, and the gods...devour them."

"The bones of the spirits destroyed in the first great war," Tahvo said. "Men gathered them from the wild places and made offerings to the Exalted in exchange for greater power over other men."

Cian's fingers whispered over the rock. "New animals appear. Cattle and goats. Horses. The strange beasts from before are gone."

"Hunted to destruction for the sport of killing," Tahvo said, her eyes wet with tears at the sounds of the animals' dying screams. "The Exalted taught men the way of binding the gentlest beasts to their service."

"And growing grain," Rhenna said. "Men with scythes and women gathering the harvest with backs bent under their burdens."

"Fire," Cian said. "Forges and new weapons. Men facing each other with swords in their hands."

Tahvo scrubbed her face. "War."

"Naked men carry stones to the Exalted," Cian said. "Some lie crushed under the weight of the blocks. Others strike at the bearers with whips. A city rises from the plain."

"The spirits of nature grow weaker as men turn their backs on the old ways, the old reverence," Tahvo said.

Cian's voice floated from deeper inside the cave. "The city dwarfs everything around it. The people are as insects."

"No more than insects to the Exalted," Tahvo said. "But men are too blind to see. They flock to the City, to learn the new ways, to fight and to kill. And the Exalted become fat on the blood of their willing servants."

"But the pictures change again," Cian said. "The paint here is ocher, not red."

"The nature spirits awaken to their peril," Tahvo said. She heard the murmur of fear and despair rustling among the leaves of the trees in the Southern forests and the icy woodlands of her own ancestors, rushing in streams and rivers as yet unpolluted by the taint of the City. "They know they must fight or perish."

In her mind's eye Tahvo saw what the ancients had drawn, trying to depict what human hands could never capture. Symbols of the elements swirled together, and from their union rays of power reached out to touch mortal life. Out of the rays emerged the shapes of men bearing shields that carried the emblems of their divine parents.

"Godborn," she said. "Heroes to stand against the Exalted. The Weapons are forged."

"A hammer," Cian said. "A bow and arrows. A sword...and a circle of fire."

Tahvo envisioned the first three Weapons clearly, but the fourth remained a mystery except in its element. "A hundred thousand clash in battle," she whispered. "The good spirits sacrifice much. Many die. Yet they are victorious. The Exalted are defeated."

"The City lies in ruins," Cian said. "The fields are razed. The desert claims everything."

"Ailuri gather to create the Stone that will bind the Exalted for all eternity," Tahvo said. "But Four escape—"

"A withered leaf, a black spiral, a dagger of ice, a red flame. Each with one of the Weapons beside it," Rhenna said.

"Eight Exalted are trapped in a great circle of many-colored rings. Ailuri dance around it." Cian paused for a long moment. "There is no more."

No more, because the ancient artists had believed the story ended with the enemies' defeat. They had not foreseen that the Ailuri would abandon their duty, or that the Exalted would be released from their prison.

"There's nothing here we didn't already know," Rhenna said. "Come, Tahvo. You must rest."

She took Tahvo's arm. The images began to fade from Tahvo's mind. She touched the wall one last time, hoping to feel living spirits as well as those long dead. But those who had survived the Godwar had fled the region of the City when it was destroyed. They were still beyond her reach.

As the Stone's sickness spreads, Slahtti had told her, *many gods who survive have chosen to hoard their strength rather than aid mankind. They will retreat until no place remains for them to hide.*

Perhaps once Nyx located the Imaziren, Tahvo would find the spirits again. Surely no humans could thrive in their complete absence. Yet she had seen men in the North who existed with only the Stone God and its evil priests to guide them. Water flowed and grain sprang from the earth without the blessings of the spirits. But that life was as false as the Stone God's promises of peace and perfect order.

If the Exalted devoured all the spirits, the world would wither before the Stone fulfilled its desire to remake the earth in its corrupt image.

Tahvo swayed, and Rhenna caught and carried her back to the front of the cave. Darkness had fallen outside, but the wind continued to howl in the lowlands and whistle among the mountain peaks.

When everyone had eaten the last of the food and settled down for the night, Tahvo crept to Rhenna's blankets. She sat beside Rhenna until the warrior sighed and rose up on one elbow.

"Bad dreams?" Rhenna asked in the way of one who knew the flavor of nightmares all too well.

Tahvo shook her head. "You are angry with Cian," she said.

"Angry with Cian?" Rhenna lowered her voice, and Tahvo imagined her glancing toward the Ailu where he slept beside the smoldering ashes. "Why should I be?"

"Nyx honors Cian as the fulfilment of her prophecy, and she wishes you to stay away from him. Is this not so?"

Rhenna snorted. "Nyx has many strange ideas, some of which I am not prepared to accept. But her fears about me and Cian are without merit. I won't interfere with his sacred destiny."

"You are part of his destiny."

"Oh, Nyx admits that I must protect him. I am, after all, one of the Bearers." Her loose braids thumped against her shoulders. "I am not jealous, Tahvo. You need not be concerned with my feelings."

"But *you* must. Your anger has consequences—"

"I'm not likely to challenge Nyx over any male, even Cian," Rhenna said. "What he and I…shared in Karchedon will not be repeated. And I am not angry."

"The winds say otherwise."

"What do you mean?"

"The storm that came upon us yesterday…it was not made by the spirits."

Rhenna shifted as if to rise and stopped with a sharp breath. "Are you suggesting I caused it?"

"I know you did." Tahvo ducked her head to take the sting from her words. "Your powers are new, as yet untried and untested. They respond to the dictates of your heart as much as to your will."

"You think I would put us all in danger?"

Tahvo grasped Rhenna's clenched fist. "The winds know

what you feel. They answer to your godborn blood, even if you do not yet accept it."

"I thought the spirits had abandoned this land."

"Not all that lives is moved by spirits alone. And even the bones of the gods—what Philokrates called pneumata—can be summoned and controlled by one with skill."

No longer able to contain herself, Rhenna got up and paced away. After a hundred heartbeats she returned.

"I didn't ask for these abilities," she said. "I have tried not to feel—"

"Your denial works against you. Your power is as much a part of you as your skill in battle. You can learn to shape it, as Cian shapes his body."

"Tell me how."

"Knowledge is the first step." Tahvo hesitated, searching out words Rhenna would understand. "As a child, you practiced with your weapons to become a warrior at womanhood. You did not learn these things in a single day. You studied how to move, how to breathe, how to calm your mind. Now you are like that child again, with a weapon you have never held and a new skill to master."

"Can you teach me to master it?"

"Only you can understand the nature of your power. You will need it when you find your own Weapon, the Arrows of the Wind."

"The bow and arrow were matched with the black spiral in the paintings."

"A symbol of Air," Tahvo said. "The emblem of the Exalted who stole the Arrows, as one of Earth took Cian's Hammer."

"So Cian and I will meet these Exalted and fight them with powers we hardly understand?"

"Not with power alone, but with courage and loyalty. With love."

Rhenna laughed under her breath. "You don't make any of this easier to bear, my friend."

"I know. I am sorry."

"No. Your burdens have always been greater than mine." She swallowed. "How do you endure…not seeing?"

Tahvo closed her eyes, though it made no difference to her vision. "The spirits give me sight when I need it," she said. But she knew she deceived both her friend and herself. Every day she longed for the sense she had taken for granted since she was old enough to find joy in the fresh green of spring leaves or the purity of a gentle snowfall. Now all the world was darkness, and even the dear faces of her companions were lost to her. She had never let them see her tears.

"I am all right," she insisted, though Rhenna had not spoken. "There is always a price to pay for magic, and for the spirits' favor."

Rhenna touched her shoulder, seeking to give comfort. Tahvo crawled back to her own blanket and tried to sleep.

She woke to the smell of morning and the sound of quiet voices.

"I'll go," Rhenna said. "The storm was my doing, so I should be the one—"

"Your doing?" Nyx interrupted. Her feet tapped out an angry rhythm across the cave floor. "You forced us to take shelter here, and yet you complain—"

"I didn't know."

"How could you not know, when you called the winds outside Karchedon?"

"She's telling the truth," Cian said. "Six months ago, neither of us knew anything about godborn powers or prophecies, let alone our part in them. Rhenna didn't ask for this fate."

"But I must learn how to deal with it," Rhenna said.

"Storm or no storm, you'll soon find yourself lost in these gorges," Nyx said, resignation in her voice. "I will accompany you."

"We'll go together," Cian said. "Tahvo can stay with the horses."

"Tahvo comes, as well," Rhenna said.

"Do you rely on the Healer to help if you fail to contain what you started?" Nyx asked.

"She can't stop it for me. But I will accept her advice in matters pertaining to devas…or their bones."

Tahvo slung her half-empty waterskin over her shoulder and went to join Nyx. Rhenna had already left the cave, Cian at her heels.

"Is it true that Rhenna can't control her powers?" Nyx asked, offering the support of her arm.

"Your dislike does not help her," Tahvo said. "You must not fight over Cian."

"*I* do not fight over the Watcher. And I do not dislike…" She trailed off and fell silent. Tahvo took Nyx's arm. Together they hurried out of the cave. Tahvo heard the skittering of an insect on the rapidly warming rocks. Sunlight struck her face, and she knew that the storm had passed, along with Rhenna's anger.

But danger hummed in the morning air.

"What is it?" she asked Nyx.

"We are being watched," Nyx whispered.

"Horsemen," Cian said, his footsteps so soft that even Tahvo didn't hear them. "Archers, hidden among the rocks."

"Imaziren," Nyx said. "I will hail them. They'll do us no harm once I give my name."

Rhenna and Cian escorted Tahvo back to the cave. "Nyx's friends look none too hospitable," Rhenna said.

"How do they appear?" Tahvo asked.

"Lightly dressed, for warriors, without armor of any kind, though all carry bows and javelins. Skin of a tone between mine and Nyx's. Hair worn close to the head." She clicked her tongue. "From what I could see at a distance, they must be excellent riders. Their horses wear no bridle or saddlecloth. There are women among their fighters."

"On equal footing with the men," Cian said. "That should please you, Rhenna."

"That their women aren't treated as slaves? I—"

A shout echoed in the distance, followed by another. Rhenna hurried away and returned with Nyx.

The Southern woman was breathing hard as she sat beside Cian. "The Imaziren have been following us for almost two days," she said. "They remember me."

"But there is a problem," Rhenna said.

"The storm. They claim it is not natural, that such wind does not rise in this season of the year. It can only have been brought forth by evil sorcery."

"Did you explain the truth?" Cian asked.

"The tribes stay well away from Karchedon. They will have heard little of what has occurred since you arrived there. They know only that we have come from the North, and that we bear potent magic. We could easily be servants of the Stone God, who is their most bitter enemy. Even the suspicion that we are its allies could earn us our deaths."

"What will they accept as assurance of our benevolence?" Rhenna asked.

"They demand that the sorcerer who raised the storm come to them unarmed and surrender himself for judgment."

"Impossible," Cian snapped.

Rhenna's boots crunched on gravel. "This talk of judgment is not promising. Will they hear me out if I go to them alone?"

Nyx sighed. "I don't know."

"I have no intention of allowing superstitious barbarians to kill me without a fight."

"The alternative is equally unpleasant," Nyx said. "They will not allow us to leave the mountains. They'll hold us here, away from food and water, until we die of thirst and starvation."

"There must be another way to make them understand."

Nyx rose and joined Rhenna in her restless pacing. Cian growled under his breath. Tahvo felt the full measure of her helplessness without the spirits to guide her, to be her eyes and reveal all that was unseen.

"The spirits have given me the gift of tongues," she said. "I will speak to these people. A blind woman can do them no harm."

"No," Rhenna said. "We know nothing of the Imaziren save what Nyx has told us, and even she isn't sure of them."

"It was not I who…" Nyx paused, sucking air between her teeth. "I spent several weeks among the Imaziren, enough to learn something of their customs. Once I witnessed a bitter quarrel between two families, one that could not be resolved by the elders of their tribe. It was decided that the matter of right and wrong would be settled by force of arms, the champion of one family against the chosen warrior of the other."

"And how did the battle end?" Cian asked.

"One champion was victorious, and his family was declared to be in the right. The defeated family gave a gift to the winners, but their own warrior survived."

"You suggest that Rhenna offer to fight one of their warriors to prove her innocence."

"I see no better prospect."

"But these battles are sometimes to the death?"

"It is possible."

"Then Rhenna will not do it."

"That is my choice to make, Cian," Rhenna said. "It's a small enough risk when weighed against our inevitable deaths in this cave. And I *am* responsible." Her pacing stopped. "Nyx, will the Imaziren extend their customs to an outsider?"

"They are an honorable people, not murderers."

"Then I'll go with you now. Offer the challenge. Tell them I invoke their ritual of trial by combat. If I defeat their champion, they must accept our word that we are enemies of the Stone God. Furthermore, they must agree to guide us safely to the borders of your land."

"It may work," Nyx said grudgingly.

"Good." Rhenna untied the knife from her belt. "Cian, you and Tahvo wait here," she said, handing the sheath to him. "If this goes wrong, take Tahvo out of the mountains and find water."

"If you believe I—" Cian began.

"Am I leader? Will you obey me?"

He walked away without answering. Tahvo felt for Rhenna and grasped the warrior's wrist.

"We have faith in you," she said. "You will succeed."

"I'll pretend that is a true vision, my Sister, and not a hope." She kissed Tahvo's cheek—a brusque peck of more violence than tenderness—and strode off. Nyx went with her.

"I won't let her be killed," Cian said roughly.

"These Imaziren are a warrior people, like her own," Tahvo said. "Perhaps she understands them better than we do."

"*Perhaps* is not good enough."

"This is only the first of many such battles we will face," Tahvo said. "When the next one comes, Rhenna may be forced to let you meet the enemy alone."

"Now you speak like Nyx."

"Each of us sees only a part of the whole."

"I intend to see much more." He took her arm. "Can you climb, Tahvo?"

Chapter Five

Rhenna sat on the smooth granite bank in the posture of warrior's meditation, making her mind and body ready as Nyx issued her challenge to the Imaziren. In her quiet state she was aware of the eyes watching her, the whisper of many breaths, tension in the air as taut as a bowstring.

She was grateful. For weeks she had felt the helplessness of being a leader in name only, dependent upon Nyx while her own skills shriveled in the desert's relentless heat. Now she would be a warrior once again, and her purpose was clear.

Nyx spoke the Amazi tongue in a strong, carrying voice. When she was finished, the tribesmen were silent for some time, consulting among themselves while the sun rose higher in a leached-blue sky.

"One comes," Nyx said.

Rhenna opened her eyes. The vast face of rock upon which

she sat sloped down from the cave mouth, ending in a water-less river of gravel. Sheer cliffs rose from the river, and from behind the cliffs came a lone rider mounted on a small but handsome horse. The warrior wore a single plain garment, a tunic belted about the waist, and his dark brown hair was cut close to his head. His horse bore neither saddle nor bridle. He guided the animal with a braid of rope around its neck, as much at one with his mount as the finest riders of the Free People.

It was only as the rider dismounted, carrying both round ox-hide shield and throwing spear, that Rhenna recognized the slender legs and narrow waist of a woman. The warrior planted her spear in the ground and called out in her lan-guage.

Rhenna got to her feet. Nyx exchanged a few brief sentences with the Amazi female, then returned to translate.

"Her name is Madele," Nyx said. "She has been sent to speak for her tribe and to answer the challenge. She wishes to know if you are the sorcerer who brought the wind."

Rhenna nodded slowly. "You explained the terms of my offer?"

"I did."

"Then I'll speak to her, and you translate what I say." Rhenna glanced toward the cave. "Whatever happens, do your best to get the others to safety as soon as the agreement is struck."

"The tribes will not let us go unless you have won the battle."

"Cian won't surrender without a fight, bargain or no bargain. If you believe in your vaunted prophecies, you'd better find a way to make them come true."

Rhenna walked down the rock slope, Nyx behind her. She stopped within easy reach of the tribeswoman's javelin and held out her hands to show them empty of weapons.

"I am Rhenna, warrior of the Free People," she said. "I am the one who brought the wind, but I mean you and your peo-ple no harm. We seek only to cross the Great Desert."

The young woman met Rhenna's stare with gray eyes in a

lean, sun-bronzed face. Her bare arms and legs rippled with long, sleek muscle, scarred from many battles. Rhenna had no doubt that she was an able and even deadly fighter.

"Are you a servant of the Stone God?" Nyx translated.

"I am its enemy."

"And you would prove this with your life?"

Rhenna glanced at Nyx to be sure she understood. "She wants a fight to the death?"

"So it seems." Nyx spoke again to the warrior, who answered in a harsh, low voice. "It is as I told you. The Imaziren will take no risks with sorcery."

"Is she willing to risk that I will not turn sorcery against her in our fight?"

Madele made a short, eloquent gesture with one hand. "You will not," Nyx translated, "because if one breath of wind rises as we do battle, you will be pierced with a thousand javelins, and your companions will die."

Rhenna shook her head. "I will use no deliberate magic. But whatever she and her people may believe, I do not control every movement of the air. These terms are not acceptable." She turned to go.

"Wait," Nyx said. She consulted with the desert warrior. "Madele says that their own elders can judge sorcery from natural causes."

"And can her elders be impartial in their judgements?"

"Yes." Madele spoke again. "She asks why you call your kind the Free People."

Rhenna faced Madele again. "Because we are women who fight to live free of the yoke of men."

"Yet there is a man among you."

"Under my protection, as are all my companions."

"They will give themselves up to us before the challenge."

"They are not warriors," Rhenna said flatly. "You can take them easily enough if I fall."

The warrior's hard face closed as she weighed her thoughts

on some inner scale. "Can you fight astride?" she asked through Nyx.

"My people are born on horseback."

Madele raised a brow. "The horses with you are from your country?"

"We bought them in a village to the north."

Madele's expression made clear what she thought of such poor, scrawny beasts. "You will have your choice of horses from our herd. We will fight mounted, each with three javelins. If neither is killed in the first round, we will dismount and continue with knives until one is dead."

"And if I survive," Rhenna said, "I and my friends claim the aid of the Imaziren to travel across the Great Desert. You will swear this on whatever gods you honor most."

Nyx conveyed Rhenna's words and waited for an answer. Madele reached for her javelin, lifted it high and hurled it into the loose rock at Rhenna's feet.

"The Imaziren accept."

The chosen battleground was a level plain of sand and pebbles some thousand paces from the cave. As Rhenna accompanied Madele through a narrow notch in the cliffs, Imaziren emerged from their places of concealment until nearly a hundred men and women, all bearing knives and javelins, escorted their champion and her challenger.

A handful of stretched-hide tents marked the Amazi camp. Rhenna noted a swell of movement beyond the outermost tents and caught her first sight of the tribe's horses, a herd of small and fine-boned animals bred for speed and endurance.

Instinctively Rhenna turned for the horses. Madele fell in beside her, pride in her brown face. There was no need for words between them. Rhenna thought that under other circumstances she and the warrior might have been friends; Madele reminded her of Alkaia and dozens like her, back home in the Shield's Shadow.

She quickly smothered such thoughts. Any weakness now could be fatal, for she had no doubt that Madele would fight with every intention to kill. She must do the same. At least the Imaziren recognized the fighting ability of their females; if Rhenna died today, she would do so at the hands of a true equal.

If she died today, all would be lost.

Several small children of both sexes ran ahead of the horses as Rhenna approached, waving thorny sticks like swords. Madele spoke to the herders and gestured for Rhenna to move freely among the animals. She breathed in the rich smell of horseflesh, touching withers and rumps, manes and muzzles. Big heads bumped her chest and shoulders. She stood still and held out her arms.

Soft lips stroked her cheek. She opened her eyes. A bay mare with a white star on her forehead gazed at Rhenna, sucking in her scent with a flare of wide nostrils.

"Tislit-n-unzar," Madele said, gesturing toward the mare.

"Tislit-n-unzar," Rhenna repeated, stroking the silky coat. "You shall carry me well today."

The mare bobbed her head and snorted. Rhenna kissed the horse's muzzle and led her from the herd. A child brought a braided rope, which Madele slipped around the mare's neck. Without waiting for permission, Rhenna jumped onto Tislit's back and felt the quiver of the animal's flesh between her knees. Like any good war mount, Tislit knew this was to be no ordinary day.

Madele left her own horse with one of the young herders and strode for the camp. Imaziren—warriors in their short tunics and tribeswomen with children in hand—began to gather in a ragged line at the edge of the plain. Men and women in longer robes emerged from the largest tent. Madele knelt at their feet. They spoke words of ritual over her, perhaps offering a blessing, and then sent her to meet her fate.

A young male warrior brought three light javelins to Rhenna and offered them with a slight bow. A young woman presented her with a knife, hilted with silver and bone. Rhenna tucked the knife in her belt and tested the javelins' balance. They were made entirely of iron and yet surprisingly light, tipped at both ends with needle-sharp points. She chose one of them and returned the other two to her attendants.

They gestured for her to follow them five hundred paces across the plain. The young male warrior instructed Rhenna with sweeping motions of his arms, acting out a charge on horseback and flinging the javelin, then turning his imaginary mount back to retrieve another weapon. Rhenna nodded her understanding.

The crowd fell silent. Rhenna felt their eyes on her, not hostile but only expectant. If they feared sorcery, they showed no sign of it. Even Madele, taking her own javelin in hand, revealed neither fear nor hatred.

Rhenna prepared herself with a warrior's chant, spoken only in her heart lest she convince the Imaziren that she was working some sorcery. Across the open space that lay between them, Madele made peace with her own gods.

One of the long-robed elders lifted a twisted ram's horn to his lips. Its wailing drifted above the camp like shimmering waves of heat. Rhenna secured a cloth about her forehead to keep the sweat from her eyes, shifted her grip on the javelin and waited for the signal to charge.

Madele gave a high-pitched cry and kicked her horse into motion. Rhenna bent low over Tislit's back. At her lightest touch the mare sprang forward. Pebbles crunched under the mare's hooves. Rhenna lifted the javelin and aimed at the rider hurtling toward her.

She threw. The javelin whistled a song of death. Madele's weapon slashed by Rhenna's temple, narrowly missing flesh, and suddenly Madele's horse was galloping past.

Rhenna let Tislit fall into a trot and wheeled the mare about. She thought she had heard a shout from the crowd, but her pulse pounded so loudly behind her ears that she couldn't be certain. Madele sat her mount unharmed.

The warriors passed each other again as they returned to their original positions. Rhenna took the second javelin from her attendant and ran her hands along its smooth length. This time it was she who broke first, urging Tislit from standstill to gallop in a matter of moments.

Tislit didn't fail her. The mare threw her heart into her run, never wavering. Madele's horse was equally fearless. The two beasts seemed bent on collision when Rhenna threw her javelin and saw it strike a glancing blow from Madele's shoulder. Madele's spear sliced through the sleeve of Rhenna's shirt, drawing blood.

Pain came swiftly, but it was a small thing and easily dismissed. Madele had suffered the worst of the second encounter. She clutched briefly at her shoulder, and her hand came away stained with red. She exchanged a few harsh words with her own attendants, took up the last javelin and turned toward Rhenna.

The last charge flew by as if in a dream. Tislit became insubstantial between Rhenna's legs, a creature of mist floating above the ground. The javelin was weightless in Rhenna's hand. Madele and her horse were a blur of motion, a streak of light. The desert warrior's javelin arced toward Rhenna's chest.

Rhenna twisted her body to the side, and the javelin hissed past. Madele's horse was almost upon her. Rhenna stiffened her arms and wielded her weapon like a club. Madele knocked it from her hands as she swept by.

The sun beat down on Rhenna's head, and her mouth was dry as bone. She drew Tislit up and leaned over the mare's sweating withers. The young female warrior offered Rhenna a waterskin. Rhenna drank, watching Madele accept a drink from her aides. Then Madele tossed the skin to the ground, dismounted and drew the knife at her waist.

This, then, was the final round, from which only one warrior would emerge alive. Rhenna slid from Tislit's back and gave the faithful mare a firm pat.

"Thank you, my friend," she said. She smiled at her attend-ants. "Take good care of her. She has a great spirit."

The boy and girl bowed to Rhenna, respect in their eyes. The boy led the mare toward the tents, but the girl lingered, search-ing Rhenna's face. Rhenna thought of Derinoe and all the young initiates of the Shield's Shadow who waited so eagerly for their first test at arms. She touched the girl's hand and walked away.

Madele waited, the left shoulder of her tunic soaked with blood. She grinned at Rhenna and flexed her arm to show that she was far from disabled. Rhenna stopped, bowed and drew her knife.

The Amazi woman lost no time in attacking. She lunged with a backhand slash at Rhenna's arm, and Rhenna felt the blade slice her flesh before she dodged and struck in turn. Her knife's edge nicked the back of Madele's hand, releasing a spray of blood.

Barely pausing, Madele stabbed toward Rhenna's neck and angled her body at the last moment, cutting for Rhenna's leg. This time Rhenna was better prepared. She spun on her toes as she feinted, narrowly missing Madele's cheek. Madele lashed out with her foot and caught Rhenna in the knee. She dove as Rhenna fell, so swift that Rhenna saw with cold clarity that she would not be able to block the thrust.

It will end here, she thought in the strangely quiet space be-tween life and death. *Devas have mercy on my friends....*

A gust of air swirled up from Rhenna's feet, spattering dust and tiny pebbles into Madele's face. She fell back, pawing at her eyes, and a cry of rage roared from the watching Imaziren.

...if one breath of wind rises as we do battle, you will be pierced with a thousand javelins, and your companions will die. Those had been Madele's words. The very air had betrayed Rhenna, com-ing to her defense against her will.

Running feet pounded the earth. Rhenna rolled to her knees, knowing there was no protection against five score warriors bent on her destruction. She clutched the knife and waited for iron to pierce her flesh.

There was no blow, no pain. The shouts of the tribesmen faded to a murmur. The gentlest of breezes licked at Rhenna's sweat-soaked hair.

She opened her eyes. A black streak sliced between her and the Imaziren, tail lashing and yellow eyes ablaze. Stones rattled and bounced beneath Cian's paws. The ground under Rhenna's knees bucked and shuddered.

Madele cried out, her voice hoarse with warning. The surging crowd stumbled to a halt as if with a single will. Rhenna reached for Cian's shoulder, burying her fingers in his fur.

"You shouldn't have come," she said. "Now they'll kill you."

Air shimmered before Rhenna's eyes, and supple beast became naked man. Cian turned to catch her hands in his.

"If we die, we die together," he said. "Tahvo and Nyx are safe. They—"

A collective moan rose from the Imaziren, silencing Cian. One of the long-robed elders pushed from the throng, wielding a staff of polished wood inlaid with metal and stone. He stared from Cian to Rhenna with mingled awe and disbelief.

"It seems we have made an impression," Cian said.

"You showed them that you're not human," Rhenna said. "If these people revile all magic…"

The elder struck the ground with his staff. Every face turned toward him. Madele took a step forward and spoke a word in a tone of reverence. Others repeated it, over and over again until it became a wave rushing from one edge of the crowd to the other. Then a new ripple of motion started far back in the gathering, an invisible wedge scattering tribesmen like a dull sword thrust into sand.

Nyx broke through the Imaziren, leading Tahvo by the hand. The Southern woman showed no expression, but Tahvo faced Rhenna and Cian with a smile.

"Tahvo," Rhenna whispered. "Why?"

"They will not harm us," the healer said. She turned her head back and forth, following the swell of chanting. "Do you know what they say?"

"Guardian," Nyx said slowly. "The Guardian has returned."

The tent had been hastily abandoned by its former occupants, set aside for the unexpected guests while Amazi elders and warriors talked and argued among themselves in the day's growing heat. A party of half-grown boys brought the village horses from the cave to join the Amazi herd; a silent woman came with bandages, a jug of water and some sweet fruit drink, quickly departing before Nyx could ask a single question.

Cian was not eager to hear the answers. He had intervened in the fight as he'd planned from the beginning, prepared to join Rhenna in death. He should have known that Tahvo and Nyx were no more likely to obey his orders than he had Rhenna's.

He hadn't reckoned on surviving long enough to suffer Rhenna's anger.

"You did not know of this?" Rhenna asked Nyx as Tahvo cleaned and bound her wounds. "You haven't heard the Imaziren speak of Cian's kind before?"

"Nothing," Nyx said. "I would have approached them very differently if I had suspected such a reaction."

"*I* did not expect him to provoke it," Rhenna said with a hard glance at Cian. "But what's done is done. Tahvo seems certain they'll do us no harm."

"They will not," Tahvo said serenely, tying off the bandage on Rhenna's arm. "The Imaziren will reveal their purpose in time."

"Time." Rhenna snorted. "Time for any who follow us to catch up. Perhaps you'd better explain to these people once again, Nyx. Surely we're still being pursued—"

The tent flap opened, and Madele stepped inside. Her shoulder was bound in cloth bandages, but she continued to move with an easy grace that Rhenna observed with wary calculation. The tribeswoman nodded to her former adversary and bowed in Cian's direction before addressing Nyx.

"She apologizes for keeping us here without proper explanation," Nyx translated, "but it seems there is an argument among the elders about what Cian's arrival portends."

Cian got to his feet. "What is the nature of this argument?"

Madele met his eyes and quickly looked away. "I do not wish to offend," Nyx translated.

"Do they debate whether or not to kill us?" Rhenna asked bluntly.

Nyx conveyed the question. Madele blanched beneath the bronze of her skin and sat down on the woven carpet just inside the tent. *"Oho,"* she said. *"Oho."*

"No," Nyx said. She waited as Madele continued to speak, then passed on her words. "You fought bravely and well, warrior. Had the Imaziren known the Guardian was among you, the challenge would never have been accepted."

"In spite of my sorcery?" Rhenna asked.

"Even so. You are one who protects the Guardian." Madele looked almost shyly at Cian while Nyx continued to translate. "Many of us have waited for their return."

"Return?" Cian said.

"To the land where the Guardians were born. To the land of your mothers."

Cian crossed the tent and sat opposite Madele. "The Speaking Stones showed Ailuri," he said. "My brothers said our ancestors imprisoned the Exalted in some forbidden wilderness, and Alexandros discovered the Stone in the South, but we have no tales of living in this country."

Madele listened gravely and frowned. "Do you not know how the Guardians first arose from the desert?"

"We believed that our homeland lay in mountains far to the north," Cian said.

"It is from there you have come?"

"Yes. My companions and I travel south to seek the means of defeating the Stone God."

"You did not seek the Imaziren?"

"Only as guides in our journey. Before I came to Karchedon, my people knew nothing of yours."

Madele's muscles tensed, as if she would leap up and commence some furious motion to match her thoughts. "It would be best not to speak of this to others of my tribe," she said through Nyx. "There are those who do not regard your arrival as a sign."

"A sign of what?" Cian asked.

"That the Imaziren must rise up and fight the Stone."

Rhenna crouched beside Cian. "It seems Nyx is not the only one with prophecies of Ailuri," she said. "What do they want of Cian?"

Nyx repeated the question to Madele. The desert warrior grabbed the jug of water and poured herself a cup. Her hands shook.

"Our oldest stories," she said, "speak of the war of the gods, and how the gods made warriors to fight the evil ones."

"Like the drawings in the caves," Rhenna said.

"The Speaking Stones," Madele said. "They tell much, but not everything. They do not say how the gods walked among the Imaziren and chose our women above all others to bear the first Guardians."

"Mothers of the Ailuri," Tahvo murmured.

Cian shivered. "You believe we were created here in the desert?" he asked Madele.

"In ancient days there were many rivers and herds of great beasts in this land. The Imaziren were a simple people who lived in peace, hunting and gathering the earth's bounty. But the good gods knew they were strong and worthy to raise those who would one day shape and guard the Stone."

"Worthy," Cian repeated bitterly. "Do your stories also speak of how my people abandoned their duty?"

"*Wajá.*" Madele met Cian's gaze. "My tribe fought bravely in the war of the gods, and we were rewarded with great honor. All the lands that once surrounded the City were given into our keeping, including the place chosen for the binding of the evil gods. Other tribes fled to Khemet or the shores of the sea, where life was easier, but we would not abandon our kin, the Guardians who held the Stone in their keeping."

"Where was the Stone?" Rhenna asked.

"My people traveled from *amda* to *amda* with our horses and cattle, but we did not venture into the Guardians' domain. We did not know for many years that they had left, until the curse of the Stone was let loose upon the earth. That was when our elders declared that we would stay far from the evil ones' empire…until the sign came again that we should fight."

"When the Guardians returned," Cian said.

"And now you are here. But it is not simple, after so many years. Some agree that our time of waiting is at an end. But others…"

"Others wish us gone," Rhenna said.

And I will gladly oblige them, Cian thought. "It is not safe for us to remain here when our enemies may still be on our trail."

"You have seen these enemies?" Madele asked.

"Not yet," Rhenna said. "But I don't believe they'll give up so easily. Will your people guide us across the desert?"

Madele averted her gaze. "I do not know."

"What must we do to convince them?" Cian asked.

"The elders will wish to speak with you, Guardian. They believe that your coming has purpose."

Cian got up. "I already have a purpose." He glanced at Rhenna, quenching the fury of his emotions. *They would have killed you. They would have killed us all.*

But he saw no malice in Madele's eyes, only a distant hope. Hope that he had come to fulfill some unknown destiny. Nyx had already laid that claim upon him, but he was only one man, human or not, godborn or otherwise.

"These people have no claim on you," Nyx said, cutting Madele out of the conversation. "We must continue south without delay."

Cian dragged his hand across his face. "If they are the Stone God's enemies, we should be allies."

"Unless they wish to keep you," Rhenna said.

A cold knot of memory settled in Cian's stomach. He had always feared confinement, even when he had more freedom than any of his Shield-bound people. But then he had learned what it was to be a slave, prisoner of the barbarian Neuri, caged like a wild beast. He had been driven to near madness by the red stones, and for a brief time he had shared imprisonment with the last of the Ailuri in Karchedon.

"They won't," he said with a growl.

"They will be our friends," Tahvo said. "Even with the Weapons we cannot fight alone. Many must join us."

"The Imaziren are few," Nyx said. "You will find stronger allies in the South."

"Who will demand nothing in return?" Rhenna asked.

Madele got to her feet. She addressed Cian and Rhenna, bowed, and left the tent.

"She said she will help if she can," Nyx said reluctantly. "Many of their warriors are weary of hiding from the Stone God's soldiers. But if they believe you answer their prophecies, they may expect more than you are willing to give." She held Cian's gaze. "You must not let these people divert you from your purpose."

"Enough," Rhenna snapped. "He didn't ask for this."

"We seldom ask for the burdens to which we are born."

And I have always tried to flee from mine, Cian thought. "Tahvo is right. We may need their friendship one day, and I intend to keep it if I can."

"As long as you don't take any foolish chances," Rhenna said.

"No more than you."

"Cian—"

"They search for their gods," Tahvo said, her voice soft and detached. "They had almost stopped believing. Faith is what you bring to them, Cian. They will accept the gift."

Tahvo had the last word. Cian, Nyx and Rhenna resumed their seats, silenced by the stifling heat and the pall of uncertainty. As the day drew to an end, women brought lamps, bread and a stew of meat and beans. Madele came for Cian at dusk. Nyx rose to follow, but the warrior blocked her way.

"She says you are to have a tent of your own, befitting your place among the Imaziren," Nyx said, disapproval stark on her face.

Madele spoke again. "The elders have not yet reached a decision about the meaning of the Guardian's appearance," Nyx translated. "We will break camp at midnight and travel to the City."

"The City of the Exalted?" Tahvo asked.

Nyx ignored her. "We must continue south. Make them understand that this is necessary, Cian."

"Even if it is necessary to speak of your prophecies? And the Hammer?"

Madele hurried Cian out the tent before Nyx could answer. He blinked, his eyes adjusting to the darkness. Flickering light from a handful of fires scattered about the camp turned staring faces into golden masks of awe and doubt. Madele passed them without stopping and led Cian to a small tent set apart from the others.

The tent was furnished with skins, bright woven carpets and a plate heaped with small, dark fruits. Madele gestured for Cian to sit, then knelt and poured him a cup of sweet-smelling wine. Cian set the cup aside untouched. Madele gazed at him for a long, uncomfortable moment. Cian knew she wanted something of him and searching for a way to make him understand. She asked him a question. He shrugged helplessly.

With a firm, smooth motion, Madele untied her belt and pulled her tunic over her head.

Cian bolted to his feet. Madele sat blocking the tent's exit, her sleek and youthful body a more potent barrier than a dozen swords. He could no longer doubt what she asked, or why she had wanted him alone.

Cian sank back to his heels. She was beautiful and, yes, desirable. No male could fail to respond to such a blatant offering. Madele was too much like Rhenna in her strength and bearing, in the tautness of waist and curve of hip. Cian's body stirred.

"You do me honor," he said hoarsely, "but I cannot accept."

She hesitated, reached for his hand and set his palm on her flat belly. He snatched his hand away, but not before he fully grasped her meaning.

"You want a child of the Guardians," he said, looking everywhere but into her honest, fearless eyes. "I am not the one, Madele." He struggled for words. "Rhenna…"

"Rhenna," she repeated. She asked another question containing Rhenna's name, but Cian could only shake his head.

"Rhenna," she said again, sighing. She took up her tunic and pulled it over her head. Then she left Cian alone with his racing thoughts, aching with need for the woman he could not have.

Chapter Six

Karchedon

Five weeks into Quintus's seemingly endless confinement, his guards announced the arrival of the emperor himself.

Quintus nearly upset his cup of wine and the small table on which it stood. Two palace soldiers drew their swords and stood to either side of him, ready to gut him at the slightest provocation. Four other men formed a square at the door, and Nikodemos strode in.

He was smiling, clean-shaven and handsome as a young god. He glanced at Quintus's wary face, laughed, and sprawled in the chair across the table.

"Are you so astonished at the honor of my presence, brother," he asked, "that your tongue cannot find a suitable greeting?"

Quintus gripped the stem of his goblet as if it were the hilt of a sword. One of the guards stepped toward him. Nikodemos waved his hand, and another attendant brought him a cup, filling it to the brim.

Nikodemos drank and wiped his lips with the back of his hand. "Not my best," he said, "but good enough for a rebel bastard half-brother, is it not?"

Quintus recovered and matched the emperor's smile. "Good enough for a Tiberian," he said.

Nikodemos laughed louder than before, and Quintus wondered if he was already drunk. But an instant after the thought had passed through his mind, the emperor lunged across the table and Quintus felt the keen edge of a dagger at his throat.

"Are you a Tiberian now, I wonder?" Nikodemos asked.

"To my last breath."

The dagger was gone as quickly as it had found his flesh. "Foolish child," Nikodemos said, sheathing the blade. "Have you learned nothing in all these weeks of contemplation?"

Quintus bit back his immediate reply. He had expected any number of fates since his strange reception in the emperor's court. He hadn't foreseen becoming the recipient of such wry and casual affection.

Affection he had certainly not earned and wanted no part of. "Why are you here, Nikodemos?"

Swords twitched. Nikodemos sighed. "Put your swords away, all of you. I didn't come for a battle." He cocked his head at Quintus. "If you think to insult me by using the name my father gave me, you must work a little hard, brother. I demand loyalty, not worship."

"Then I regret to inform you that these weeks of contemplation have not altered my loyalties, son of Arrhidaeos."

Nikodemos stared at him, leaning heavily on the table, and abruptly rose. "Out," he addressed the guards. "Philemon, Kaj—remain outside the door until I call."

"My lord," Philemon protested.

"I am in no danger." He grinned at Quintus, shifting between one emotion and the next as casually as a man blinks his eyes. He handed his sheathed dagger to Kaj. "Our Tiberian is too honorable to attack an unarmed man."

His soldiers were too well trained to argue, but they moved to the door with reluctance. Philemon closed the door very slowly.

"There," Nikodemos said. "Now you have no reason to mistrust me."

Quintus was in no mood for humor. "No reason?"

"We haven't talked as brothers, you and I."

Quintus got up from his chair and walked to the opposite end of the room. "We had the only necessary conversation in the hall among your courtiers, Nikodemos."

"Under formal circumstances, soon after you had just learned the truth of your parentage."

"Nothing has changed."

Nikodemos made an impatient gesture. "You know this cannot go on forever, young Alexandros. You have no allies here…save perhaps Hylas, who seems to find you desirable."

And Danae, Quintus thought, but it was more hope than certainty. He hadn't seen her in weeks, and he missed her far too much.

"Hylas amuses me," Nikodemos said, "and you have amused me, as well. But if you continue to defy me like a petulant child while I hold Baalshillek at bay—"

"I did not seek your protection. You keep me alive for reasons of your own."

"True enough." Nikodemos resumed his seat and refilled his wine cup. "You are my brother."

"If I am your kin, it's only by an accident of birth. Why risk your master's anger on my behalf?"

Nikodemos slammed his cup on the table. The door burst open.

"Get outside and stay there!" Nikodemos bellowed. His men retreated. He turned hot, furious eyes on Quintus. "You dare to call that creature my…" He bristled like a boar about to charge. "Do you truly believe the gods will protect you?"

Quintus felt his legs bump the low couch that served as his bed. He could retreat no farther, nor risk his pride by showing any reaction to the emperor's impressive rage. Pride was all he had left.

"I believe in no gods," he said steadily.

Nikodemos sent cups and wine jar flying with a sweep of his hand. He sat down, staring into the pool of spilled wine as the flush left his face.

"We are not so different, you and I," he said. "We believe in ourselves above all else. Like our illustrious uncle." He met Quintus's eyes again. "You taunt me even though you know I could have you killed in an instant, just as you know I am no tool of the High Priest."

"How do I know that?"

"Because you're still here. Baalshillek would prefer to take you back alive. But he'll accept you dead, if that is the only way to remove the threat you present."

Quintus turned to gaze out the tiny window that looked down on the harbor and its swarming Stonebound occupants. "You want my loyalty, Nikodemos, yet I am as much a threat to you as to Baalshillek."

"I know you can destroy the stones, but that does me no harm—as long as you stand at my side."

Quintus heard the grudging words with amazement. Nikodemos spoke as if they shared a common past, common interests. As if they could be anything but enemies. Unless…

"Stand at your side…against Baalshillek?" he asked.

"Yes."

"Why?"

Nikodemos scraped his chair across the tiled floor. "What I tell you now I say only because I know you hate the Stone God as much as any man on earth. Because you are my kin, and we share that hatred." He walked to stand behind Quintus. "You have seen the evil committed by the priests in the name of their one god. I have no intention of allowing the High Priest to conquer the world and then destroy what I have built. He will try, once all lands are under the empire's rule. You and I, my brother, can stop him."

Quintus remembered Danae's words: *"…he is the man who will defeat the priests and the Stone God."* Now Nikodemos spoke with that same righteous sincerity, a beloved general exhorting his troops to seemingly impossible victory.

Any man would have believed the emperor in that moment, as Danae believed.

Quintus turned slowly to face his half brother. "You claim I am no threat to you," he said. "If I am your brother, then I, too, am Arrhidaeos's heir. Could I not take your throne as you took our father's?"

Nikodemos froze, shocked beyond rage or laughter. "And they accused our uncle Alexandros of hubris."

"You killed Arrhidaeos, or had him killed," Quintus said. "You destroyed thousands of my people, allowed the Stone God to devour innocent children. And you want me to help you."

The emperor's smile was long in coming, and it was icy cold. "You asked me in the great hall if I would permit you to die with honor. I would grant your request if I loved my people less."

Their gazes locked. Quintus felt the full potency of the man who had won or compelled the allegiance of so many and struck terror into the hearts of those who defied him. This was no ordinary tyrant, no sneering villain out of some Hellenic melodrama.

Nikodemos looked into Quintus's soul and saw him for what he was—a mockery of rebellion, defiant because he had only words with which to fight. Words, and the courage he had struggled to maintain every day of his nearly unbearable isolation.

Nikodemos *knew* him. He knew Quintus feared death as much as any other man. He knew his half brother's loneliness.

He saw through the years of childhood rejection, hard faces turned away from the imperfect child in a land where there was little sympathy for weakness. He recognized needs that Quintus refused to acknowledge, even to himself.

"You do not wish to die," Nikodemos said, almost gently. "You feel the value of life too keenly. But there are things you fear far more than death."

Quintus looked away. "You speak in riddles, Nikodemos."

"I think you are the riddle, young Alexandros," Nikodemos said, using the name of his birth. "The Tiberians never accepted you, did they...even when they knew nothing of your true heritage? You fought to prove yourself their equal when you were always superior."

"I was...I *am* one of them."

"I wonder what they would give to have you back now? What price would they pay for the one who can kill the Stones?"

It was a reasonable assumption from an intelligent man, but it struck Quintus like a fist in the belly. As a child, he had been ignored and sometimes reviled for his deformity, even by his own brothers. But once his hidden powers had been discovered by his adoptive people, the Tiberian rebels had held him captive, treating him as an invaluable weapon that could be used but once in a single deadly strike against the empire.

Had Philokrates told Nikodemos of that captivity—how Quintus had escaped in defiance of his own elders' commands? Was that why Nikodemos was so sure he could turn his half brother against his former allies?

"They care nothing for you as a man, Alexandros," Nikodemos said. "I would not have you waste all you could become by throwing your life away on a hopeless rebellion. Not when I can help you gain what we both desire."

"Mastery of the world?" Quintus asked bitterly.

"The strength to counter Baalshillek in his ambitions—to keep him from seizing secular as well as spiritual control once all resistance has been crushed. For it *will* be crushed, brother." Nikodemos took a step forward, hands open before him. "Don't you see? The Stone God's power was established in our father's time because he was too weak to recognize his own folly in permitting the cult's rise from obscurity. Now my men—my administrators, Hetairoi and generals, my loyal soldiers—hold key positions in the empire. The priests and Stonebound will destroy the old gods, and only the edifice of iron and human lives I have forged will hold steady when all else falls and the greatest battle begins."

The greatest battle. Nikodemos saw it as the final conflict between the empire and the Stone God, not a struggle that would topple the empire itself.

"There is yet another thing to consider," Nikodemos said. "Baalshillek uses his sorcery to find your barbarian friends who escaped the city. You may yet save them when they are brought back to Karchedon in chains."

"My friends may be more resourceful than Baalshillek believes."

"Perhaps. But do not underestimate the High Priest."

Quintus wondered if Nikodemos himself underestimated Baalshillek. He risked a great deal by confiding his plans to an enemy. He assumed that Quintus hated the High Priest and the Stone more than he despised the emperor and his troops.

He presumed too much. He expected Quintus to accept everything he had said, without proof. Yet Nikodemos had been honest about his desire to use Quintus's powers against Baalshillek. He preferred direct speech to subterfuge, like Quintus.

Danae trusted this man. She claimed to love him.

"Let me be sure I understand you," Quintus said. "You will not return me to Baalshillek, whatever my decision. I serve you, or I die."

"That is your choice." Nikodemos smiled wryly. "It is not so terrible a fate, brother. I demand your loyalty, but you won't be my servant. Your life will have true purpose again."

If I turn my back on everything I believed. If I am prepared to fight this battle in a way I never imagined and become the tool of an emperor instead of the rebellion.

But if Quintus could hold his own in Nikodemos's court and learn the workings of the emperor's mind, he might find the opportunity to bring down both empire and Stone God with a single blow.

"You have no further need to prove your courage, Alexandros," Nikodemos said. "Think on what I have told you." He turned to go, leaving his back exposed to the chance of attack. Quintus didn't move until the emperor had passed through the door and the guards had bolted it from the other side.

That night he didn't sleep. His luxurious couch might have been a bed of swords for all the comfort he took upon it, and his mind hummed like a hive of angry bees. He spent the next day pacing his room, ignoring the ample meals palace servants provided.

At dusk Danae's servant, Leuke, slipped in the door, followed by her mistress.

Quintus backed away, more concerned for Danae's position of trust with Nikodemos than for the ready swords of the guards. But the soldiers did as they had before, leaving the door slightly ajar while Danae seated herself for an interview with the prisoner. Leuke took up her position to watch and warn her mistress of any attempt at eavesdropping.

"My lady," Quintus said, bowing. "To what do I owe this honor?"

"My lord the emperor has sent me to discuss a certain matter with you," Danae said loudly. "It has come to his attention that you lack the companionship befitting the son of a king."

For one startled, heart-stopping instant Quintus dared to believe that Nikodemos was giving Danae to him. She quickly robbed him of such childish hopes. "The emperor wishes to provide you with a woman," she said, avoiding his eyes. "I am here to ascertain the kind of female you prefer."

Quintus stifled a laugh and pulled a chair safely away from the table. "The emperor is most considerate," he said. "But was it truly his idea?"

Danae looked up. "It was mine," she said. "But we have little time to talk. I suggested to Nikodemos that you might be more inclined to cooperate if you had all the necessities of a pleasant life to enjoy during your confinement."

"I thank you, but I want no such—"

"Hear me out," she whispered with a glance at Leuke. "I convinced Nikodemos that I could best learn what servant would suit you, and he granted me permission to visit your quarters for this purpose only. But I did not arrange it for your comfort."

"I am grieved, my lady."

Her green eyes sparkled with mingled pleading and annoyance. "I need your help, Quintus."

"My help?"

"Yes." She noted Leuke's nod and continued in a low voice. "There is a girl…a young kitchen maid who must be hidden from the priests until we can get her out of the citadel. She is marked with a defect that would have sent her to the Stone God's fire at birth, except that she was concealed by other servants in the kitchens. Now her secret has been exposed."

Quintus remembered the children Danae had saved from sacrifice in spite of the danger to herself. He had admired her courage, but he questioned her sanity now. "You wish me to hide a girl in my prison?"

"It will not be necessary to hide her if she comes cloaked as a woman brought for your pleasure."

"How old is this girl?"

"Old enough, if anyone should discover her with you. But that should not happen if we take the proper precautions. You would risk little—"

"My position is unlikely to become more delicate than it already is," Quintus said.

Danae met his gaze, and her eyes warmed with concern. "I know. I have prayed daily to Isis, asking her to show you the truth. Have you decided, my friend?"

My friend. It was a simple phrase, and yet from Danae it meant more than a casual address.

"It is not a decision to be made lightly. If I had more proof—"

"Perhaps I can arrange to present it," Danae said. "Nikodemos honors your courage and loyalty, Quintus. That alone should tell you that he is not an evil man. You are more alike than you think."

Quintus laughed shortly. "What do you wish me to do about the girl?"

"Tonight I will bring her to you, disguised under a cowl and cloak. All you need do is accept her, keep her with you and cover her face if the guards enter your chamber. With Isis's blessing, I should be able to come for her within a few days' time."

"And if Nikodemos chooses to visit me again?"

"I will make sure he does not."

Quintus declined to dwell on how she would accomplish that mission. "I'll do what I can," he said, "but I trust you have considered every other way of saving this child."

"I trust I have proven that I am no fool." She rose, nodding to Leuke. "The emperor will be pleased that you accept his gift," she said for the benefit of the guards. "Good night, Lord Alexandros."

She left, and the guards bolted the door. Two hours later, by the water clock in Quintus's chamber, the door opened again and Leuke brought in a cloaked figure whose face was concealed in a deep hood. Leuke retreated before Quintus could question her.

Quintus cursed under his breath and studied the still, silent girl before him. She was small and fragile-seeming within the enveloping cloak, and made no move to uncover herself.

"It's all right, girl," Quintus said gruffly. "Danae explained why you're here. I won't hurt you."

She didn't answer. Quintus poured a cup of wine and set it on the table. "Sit down," he said. "Drink."

The girl sat, one fine-boned hand emerging to arrange the folds of her cloak to conceal any hint of the garments beneath. She ignored the cup.

Quintus sat opposite her. "Danae must have prepared you for this," he said, "but there was a great deal she didn't tell me…only that you must be taken out of the palace. I'm to keep you here until she finds a way to do so. You needn't be afraid."

"I'm not afraid."

The girl's voice was lower than he expected, trembling a little but otherwise clear enough. Quintus nodded. "Good," he said. "That's a beginning. My name is Quintus Horatius Corvinus, of Tiberia. What are you called?"

"Briga." She hesitated. "You are the emperor's brother."

"So I am told."

Her head lifted at the wry humor in his words. "You are a prisoner in the palace?"

She was bold and well-spoken for a servant, but Quintus had learned that courage and intelligence could be found in unexpected places. "They would prefer to call me a guest," he said, "but Danae thought you would be safest in a place the priests would be least likely to look for you."

Briga reached for the cup but made no move to drink from it. "I'm not afraid of the priests," she said.

Quintus liked the girl already, and his initial annoyance vanished. "You know they're your enemies, as they are mine."

"Yes."

"Then you and I must be allies."

"Do you mean…like friends?"

"Yes."

"I have not had many friends," the girl said, without self-pity or regret.

"Did not the kitchen servants protect you from the priests?"

"Yes. But they couldn't do it anymore."

"Why not, Briga?"

Her other hand emerged to join the first on the table, slender fingers clutching each other until the bones showed white under pale, almost transparent skin. "Danae said the priests would have killed you when you were a babe."

This conversation was not going at all as Quintus intended, but he had to set the girl at ease. "I was found to be…defective," he said, remembering what Danae had said about Briga's "secret." "Someone sent me away before the priests took me."

"What was wrong with you?"

Quintus touched his left arm without meaning to, instantly defensive. He had no need to be. Everyone at court knew of his deformity—indeed, it was proof of his identity as the younger son of the former emperor Arrhidaeos.

Slowly he uncovered his arm, revealing the twisted muscle and flesh that reached from elbow to wrist and made a near-claw of his hand.

"It was damaged when I touched one of the red stones," he said.

The girl shifted in her seat, and Quintus knew she was staring. He let her look her fill and then covered his arm again. "Is there more you need to know before you will trust me?" he asked.

She flinched from his tone, and her hands disappeared within the folds of her wide sleeves. Then, with a reluctance Quintus recognized all too well, she pulled back her hood.

Briga's face was as pale and delicate as her hands…young, so painfully young, blue eyes huge under the faint tracery of straight brows and vivid red hair pulled tightly back from her forehead. She didn't look like a servant. She might even have been pretty, save for the glaring blemish that covered her right cheek: a wine-colored stain in the shape of a three-forked flame licking the side of her nose and each corner of her eye.

Briga stared at Quintus, daring him to comment, to show a single sign of revulsion at her terrible flaw. Her eyes were full of anger so like his own at that age...fifteen or sixteen, proud and defiant, eager for acceptance yet expecting the inevitable rejection.

"I know it is ugly," Briga said. "The priests would have killed me because of it."

Quintus pushed the wine cup toward her. "Drink," he said.

This time she did as he asked. She drained the cup, beads of wine the same color as her scar clinging to her lower lip. Quintus poured himself a cup and drank, as well.

"You were born with this?" he asked.

"Yes." The girl moved as if to cover her face again but stopped, refusing to submit to her fear. "My mother and others in the kitchen covered it up with flour paste. Not everyone knew. Something happened...."

"You were exposed," he said, gentling his voice.

"There was an accident. I didn't mean..." She broke off again, clutching her empty cup. "It was a mistake. I didn't know I could do it."

"Didn't know you could do what, Briga?"

The girl bit her lip and looked down at Quintus's cup and the small measure of wine that remained in it. Quintus followed her stare, and as he watched, the liquid began to bubble. Steam curled from the cup. He snatched his hand away as the cup grew too hot to hold, and the wine boiled to nothing but a dark residue.

"I was angry," Briga whispered. "Thais said something about my face...I don't remember what. And suddenly the fire came up from the ashes in the hearth, and I could feel its heat in my hands, but it didn't burn me." She spread her fingers in the air before her as if they were foreign objects.

"You controlled the fire?"

She shook her head. "It...*talked* to me. I could hear it, but I couldn't make it stop."

Sickness gnawed at Quintus's belly. "Did you have one of the red stones, Briga?"

She jerked, eyes filled with reproach and pain. "The red stones are evil, like the priests."

Quintus closed his eyes. Not the Stone God's fire, then. He'd seen Stonefire burn a boy to cinders, but it was no natural flame. The girl spoke of something entirely different.

He flexed his own right hand, remembering what it had been like to destroy a priest and his red stone with one over-whelming blast of power. He was not alone in possessing abilities beyond those of ordinary men. Philokrates had once told him that all matter was composed of the four elements—Earth, Air, Fire, Water—and Quintus had seen for himself how the Ailu Cian could manipulate the element of Earth.

Briga spoke of a similar power over natural fire. Such a girl would be of more than passing interest to the Stone priests, even if she weren't already marked for sacrifice. Danae had for-gotten to mention that slight complication.

"Nothing like this ever happened to you before?" he asked Briga.

"Never."

"Did any of the kitchen servants go to the soldiers or the priests to report what happened?"

"The other servants were afraid of what I did. Mother said they wouldn't tell anyone, but I had to escape from the palace."

"How did Danae find out about you?"

"My mother heard that she had helped children who were supposed to be sacrificed." Briga flushed, turning her blemish a deeper red. "She begged the lady to take me out of the citadel."

And of course Danae would not have refused, no matter what the risk. "You aren't grateful for the lady Danae's assis-tance?" he asked.

Briga bolted from her chair, fists clenched. "I could have found a way out myself. I could—"

Someone thumped on the door. Quintus snatched at Briga,

pulled her close and pressed her head into his shoulder. He buried his face in her hair just as the guard entered, bearing a tray with the evening meal.

Quintus looked up and fixed his coldest gaze on the guard. "I was told we were not to be disturbed."

The soldier blinked, taken aback by the prisoner's royally arrogant tone. "I am...forgive me, Lord Alexandros," he stammered.

"See that this does not happen again."

"Yes, my lord." The guard bowed his way out, and Quintus released his breath.

Briga pushed free of him, patting at her hair where he had touched it. She had the startled look of a girl who had never felt a man's embrace, which was almost certainly true, given her young age and her lifelong need to hide her mark. But she had lived that life among slaves and could not be entirely ignorant about the relationships between men and women.

"I didn't intend to surprise you," Quintus said, "but Danae must have explained the pretense under which you were brought to my chamber."

Briga pulled her hood halfway over her head. "Lady Danae told me—" She met Quintus's gaze, swallowed and started again. "I am to pretend to be a woman sent to you for your pleasure."

"Then you do understand."

She took a step away from him, and he laughed. "I won't touch you, Briga, unless it's necessary to keep the guards from seeing your face."

"Am I very horrible?"

The laugh stuck in his throat. "No," he said, confounded again by the unfathomable ways of females. "Only very young."

She lifted her chin. "I am fifteen. Other girls…" She stared at the floor between them. "Why are you helping me?"

"Because Lady Danae asked." He pushed the hood back from her head and unfastened the pin that closed the cloak at her throat. "You should appear comfortable, or the next guard may think you haven't pleased me."

Briga stood absolutely still while Quintus eased the cloak from her shoulders and draped it over one of the chairs. Beneath it she wore a simple floor-length chiton caught around the waist with a braided cord. Her body had the underfed, coltish look of a girl at the threshold of womanhood, but no one could doubt that she was about to step through that fateful portal.

"Sit on the couch," he told her. "I'll remain near the door unless someone comes."

Hesitantly Briga went to the couch and sat, plucking at the folds of her chiton as if she had never worn such a garment before. A kitchen slave might own a single scrap of cloth to serve as clothing for all occasions. Quintus noticed that her hands, slender as any aristocrat's, were roughened and chapped from constant work. Hands that had summoned fire to her unwitting call.

"Do you love Lady Danae?"

The girl's question startled Quintus from his thoughts. He sat down at the table and refilled his cup. "What makes you ask such a thing, Briga? Do you know who she is?"

"She is the emperor's hetaira. His mistress."

"Then how could a mere prisoner love her?"

"Everyone must love her. She is so beautiful."

Quintus sighed and glanced over the delicacies that had been provided for their dinner. "Are you hungry, child?"

She began to bristle at the word, blue eyes bright enough to spark her hair into living flame. Her stomach rumbled loudly. She pressed her hands over her ribs. "Have you any bread?" she asked.

"Better than that." He picked out the best slices of meat, selected a piece of fruit, tore off a chunk of bread and arranged the food on a smaller platter. "You had better eat all you can now, since we don't know when Danae will come for you." He took the smaller platter to Briga and set it on the couch. "Do you know where she intends to take you?"

"Only out of the citadel," Briga said. She stared at the food, licked her lips and chose a morsel of meat with the uncertainty of one unused to such rich fare. "I have never been outside the palace."

Quintus had little difficulty imagining a life of such confinement. He had grown up in a noble Tiberian house, fiercely protected by his adoptive mother and seldom allowed beyond the confines of the estate. Even when the empire took the city and his family fled to the hills, Quintus's period of freedom had been brief.

Since the day he had escaped the Tiberian rebels' custody, he had seen much of the world and the cruel empire that ruled it. Soon this child would face more challenges than she could begin to imagine.

"You will have a great deal to learn," he told her. "Many things will be strange to you. Watch and listen. Speak seldom. Keep your anger under control. Let Lady Danae guide you."

Briga took a large piece of fruit. "Were you truly a rebel?"

"What do you know of rebels?"

"They fight the Stone God. In the kitchens they talked of how the emperor stole you from the High Priest," she said, swallowing the fruit a little too quickly. She hiccuped and belatedly covered her mouth with her hand. "The priests are afraid of you."

"What makes you say that?"

She grinned, subtracting several years from her age. "They said Baalshillek was very angry. People get angry when they're afraid."

"Perhaps the High Priest would fear you if he learned of your ability with fire."

Briga pushed the plate aside. "I couldn't hurt him," she said. "But I wish I could."

"Because of what they would do to you?"

"Because of what they did to my mother." Her voice dropped

to a whisper. "She isn't really my mother. The priests took her son when he was only a baby and gave him to the Stone God. They took her man, as well. She would have been taken, too, except she came to work in the palace. The emperor doesn't let the priests take his servants. But Lady Danae said even the emperor can't protect everyone."

Quintus wanted to tell the girl that Nikodemos was not the noble champion she seemed to believe, but it was more important that Briga trust Danae than that she comprehend the complexities of a world beyond her ken.

"Did you ever know your real mother?" he asked.

"No. I was too little when I came to the kitchens. But Annis always loved me." She speared Quintus with a look of fierce defiance. "You think no one could love me."

"I see no reason why you should not be worthy of love, Briga."

She met his gaze. Her lips parted, and her eyes widened in her pale, freckled face. Abruptly she snatched at the chunk of bread on the rejected plate and tore it into two pieces. "Are you going to escape, too?" she demanded.

"If I can."

"Then I want to stay with you."

Quintus flinched from the unreasonable worship in her eyes. "That is not possible."

"I could find a way to hide. I'm good at hiding. I won't make another mistake with the fire."

"You must do as Danae tells you."

"I could serve you as well as anyone else," she insisted with artless innocence.

"It's far too dangerous," he said. "You don't even know me, Briga."

"Danae said you were a good man."

"I may die here, today or tomorrow."

"But you are the emperor's brother."

"I am also his enemy."

"Then I would die with you."

Her naive passion tore at his own foolishly weak heart. "I can account only for my own life, Briga. You do not belong to me. I own nothing, control nothing. Whatever you may think, I—"

Without warning the door opened again. The intruders entered boldly and came for Quintus before he could get to Briga. Two guards forced Quintus's arms behind his back while two other men snatched Briga from the couch.

"No!" Quintus said. "Why are you taking her?"

"By the emperor's command," one of the guards said, twisting Quintus's deformed arm until the bones seemed ready to snap. The moment his fellow soldiers had Briga wrapped in her cloak and out the door, he and his partner released Quintus.

Quintus hurled himself at the closing door and struck it with his fist. Briga was gone. All her innocent, bold plans had been ground into the dust beneath Nikodemos's sandals, and there was nothing Quintus could do but curse. And mourn.

"If you hurt her," he swore softly, "if you touch one hair on that child's head, Nikodemos…"

He slumped against the door and thought of Danae. Somehow her plot had been exposed. There was no telling how the emperor might punish her for scheming behind his back, or what he intended for Briga. Even if Quintus pleaded for the emperor's mercy, he might only make matters worse for both of them.

Unless this was all a part of Nikodemos's game, and he knew his brother better than Quintus knew himself.

If that were so, gods help the world. Quintus could no longer lift a finger to save it.

Chapter Seven

Baalshillek paced in the reception room off the emperor's private suite, counting each slow drop of liquid from the water clock in the wall niche. The emperor was making him wait, as always—a petty display of his majesty, that he alone could keep the High Priest of the Stone God idle.

The High Priest was not unduly perturbed. He gathered his patience, with which he was plentifully supplied, and imagined Nikodemos's screams as Stonefire devoured his flesh.

"I trust you have not been waiting long, Baalshillek." Nikodemos entered the room and sprawled in his fur-draped chair, regarding his guest over tented fingers. "I was detained by matters of great importance."

"So I have heard," Baalshillek said. "Perhaps these matters had something to do with the recent fire in the palace kitchens."

Nikodemos raised a brow in disbelief. "When did you

begin to take an interest in the domestic arrangements of my household?"

"Only when your servants evince certain powers that fall under the purview of my god."

The emperor snorted and poured himself a cup of wine. It was his habit to dismiss even his most trusted slaves when he met with Baalshillek…a wise precaution, given the nature of their conversations.

"Why don't you tell me what you think you know, Baalshillek?" Nikodemos said. "I might find it amusing."

"No doubt. Servants will gossip, and you are a most lenient master."

"Because I don't feed my people to your altars?" Nikodemos shrugged. "There was a fire in the kitchens a day or two ago. It did little damage."

"A fire started by a young female servant."

"Indeed. That sort of carelessness will, of course, be punished."

"Perhaps you have already located this careless slave."

"As you said, servants will gossip."

"Especially when the subject of their talk is one who can summon fire from ashes without touching them."

"Is that what you've heard?" Nikodemos sipped his wine, eyes hooded in apparent boredom.

"I also hear that the girl in question is marked in such a way that she should long since have been given to the Stone God…if the palace servants had been properly tested."

Nikodemos yawned. "My physician said she was burned in the fire…disfigured. Perhaps that is punishment enough, eh?"

Baalshillek wearied of the game. "If this child has power over fire, she must be examined."

"As you 'examined' my brother?"

"You should have no objection to my priests questioning a slave."

"Except that your priests can be imprudent in their interrogations. Death by torture seems an extreme penalty for a foolish accident."

And Nikodemos prided himself on keeping his household, staff and soldiers free of the Stone God's influence. That was provoking enough, but Baalshillek had received new reports of an even greater insult to the god's power: the emperor was seeking out children and youths who showed any signs of godborn heritage, those very children who should have become priests or breeding females for the Temple.

This slave who had manipulated fire might be one such discovery, and Baalshillek could not allow the emperor's scheme to go unchallenged. Nikodemos might only be testing the Temple's sources and means of intelligence or be playing yet another infantile game. But he could also be attempting to build or breed his own private army of godborn, unlikely though his chances of success might be.

"You try my patience, Nikodemos," Baalshillek said gently.

"Alas." Nikodemos began to pare one of his fingernails with the blade of his dagger. "I will have Kleobis inquire as to the present whereabouts of this dangerous child. Is there something else you wished to discuss?"

Baalshillek smiled. "I wish to propose a wager, my lord Emperor."

Nikodemos paused in his trimming and eyed Baalshillek with surprise. "I didn't know you were a wagering man, priest."

"Only when the odds are sufficiently intriguing." He stroked the great stone pendant on his chest. "Now that you have had the young rebel Alexandros in your care for many weeks, have you come to a decision regarding his fate?"

"You mean whether or not I've decided to give him a place at court?"

"Then you intend to let him live."

Nikodemos swept nail shavings from the table with the side of his hand. "I do not like being hurried, priest. What I do with my kin is my own concern."

"Not when it affects the entire empire. Then it also becomes mine."

The two men stared at each other, blue eyes meeting icy gray. "You said you had a proposal," Nikodemos said. "What is it?"

"You may talk of kinship and blood, Lord Emperor, but even you dare not risk the chance that young Alexandros will turn on you the moment he is given his freedom."

"Your concern touches me deeply, Baalshillek, but—"

Baalshillek raised his hand. "Surely you intend to test him before granting him power he might use to destroy you."

"It's your own destruction you fear, priest."

"If I thought you were so naive as to believe that the Stone God's fall would not result in your own, then I would be forced to call you a fool. And I do not think you have become a fool…yet."

The emperor rubbed his chin with his hand and scowled like a thwarted child. "Of course I'll test him. I have only to choose the method."

"Then let me suggest a means that will satisfy us both."

Nikodemos listened, unmoving save for the steady tapping of his thumb against his jaw. His eyes narrowed as Baalshillek finished, and then he smiled with grudging admiration.

"It was only a matter of time before my own agents discovered this Buteo's plans," he said, "but I could not have devised a more effective trial myself."

Baalshillek inclined his head. "I thank you, Lord Emperor. You see that there could be no better opportunity than this."

"And what stakes do you propose for the wager?"

"Only what you would expect. If Alexandros ignores the bait and thereby proves his ultimate loyalty to you over the rebels, I will no longer object to his place at your side."

Nikodemos leaned far back in his chair. "That is a great concession, lord priest. You would surrender all claim to my brother?"

"All."

"Even though his particular power threatens only your god and its priests?"

Baalshillek swallowed rage and feigned only the mildest reproach. "You jest, my lord. Palace and Temple are allies. One cannot exist without the other. If Alexandros is your sworn vassal, then what cause have I to fear that his power would ever be turned against us?"

Nikodemos grunted. "And if he falls into your trap?"

"Then the emperor will give the rebel up to the altar for sacrifice…and surrender the servant with power over fire and any similar individuals of whom he has knowledge."

Nikodemos stretched out his long legs and closed his eyes. He almost appeared to be sleeping, but the tension in his body and the rapidity of his breathing gave him away.

"If I knew of such…individuals," the emperor said at last, "I would agree. As it is—" He shrugged. "I accept your terms as to Alexandros's fate."

Baalshillek let the tension drain from his muscles. "Your judgment is, as always, impeccable," he said.

Nikodemos opened his eyes and stared balefully at his guest. "I agree to the wager on the condition that I and my chosen men have equal part in laying the trap and are privy to all its details."

"Naturally, Lord Emperor."

"Then I'll summon Kleobis and Iphikles to witness our bargain."

Baalshillek shook his head. "Even the highest of servants gossip. The more who know in advance, the better chance that the boy will learn of the trap before it is sprung. What need of witnesses when our vows are heard by the God and your own honored ancestors?"

Nikodemos lunged up from his seat. "Curse you, Baalshillek. If you play me false…"

Baalshillek also rose. "I have weighed the odds and the consequences, my lord, and I find them suitable. I have no reason to cheat you."

"Then prepare to be disappointed, priest." Nikodemos went to the door and opened it. "You will lose this wager, and I shall drink to victory with Alexandros at my side."

The first Quintus learned of his new freedom came in the form of an invitation.

The request for Quintus's presence at a feast to be held in the emperor's hall was delivered by the young courtier Hylas, who arrived at Quintus's door with a faint, provocative smile and a sly offer to help the emperor's brother select attire appropriate for the celebration.

"You have only today to prepare, my lord Alexandros," Hylas said, looking Quintus over with the boldness of an experienced whore. "I am accounted to be very good at arranging matters of dress...at least among my friends."

Quintus glanced past Hylas's shoulder through the open doorway. Not a single guard stood watch there. Hylas's servants, a pair of boys almost as pretty as he, bore draperies of fine fabric and trays of wine, fruit and pots that smelled of paint and perfume.

Hylas cleared his throat. "May I come in, my lord?"

Quintus backed away, leaving room for courtier and slaves to enter. Hylas sat and arranged his long embroidered chiton with the fastidiousness of a beautiful woman. He looked around the room and clucked under his breath.

"This is where they have kept you for so many weeks?" he said. "I was right when I feared you would be lonely. What an ordeal for such a strong and vigorous young man as yourself, my lord."

Quintus found himself unable to laugh. Last night the guards had taken Briga away; he'd heard nothing since, and now— many weeks after he'd been presented as a prisoner before the emperor and his court—he was told to prepare for a second public appearance for reasons he could not begin to guess.

"My name," he said stiffly, "is not Alexandros. Why are you here?"

Hylas raised kohl-darkened brows in wounded surprise.

"But I thought I had made that plain, my lord Alex…Quintus. The lady Danae desires your presence at a celebration to be held for our lord Nikodemos this very night, and she will be devastated if I do not return to her with a guarantee of your attendance."

Danae. Quintus leaned against the wall and collected his disorderly thoughts. She must be well enough if she was to play hostess at the emperor's feast. Either her part in Briga's attempted escape hadn't been discovered, or Nikodemos knew and approved of her work.

"Are you here to answer my questions, or merely to make me presentable for your friends?" he asked Hylas.

The courtier grinned. "That depends, my lord. If you will allow me the privilege of selecting your garments and your mask, thus permitting me to uphold my reputation, I will of course do all I can to provide any information you seek."

Quintus met the young dandy's eyes and tried to read what lay behind them. Certainly there was shrewdness, intelligence hidden by facetiousness, and a very real measure of stubbornness. But he was no rebel. Hylas was offering a bargain already approved by his master the emperor.

"Where is the girl who was brought to me last night?" Quintus demanded.

Hylas's brows rose even higher. "Girl? Were you given a girl, my lord?" He shook his braided locks. "What a pity."

Suppressing the urge to take the ingenuous catamite by his delicate neck and give him a good shake, Quintus folded his arms and stood over Hylas's chair. "Her name was Briga. Was she given to the priests?"

Hylas lifted his hand to his throat. "My lord, do not glower so. I swear I do not know. The emperor would never surrender one of his own to the priests, of that I am certain. But if you will be patient…" He gestured to one of his servants, who bent close to hear his whisper, set down his tray and quickly left the room. "Kanmi will inquire about the female. Now…"

He beckoned to the other servant. "I have bought some of the finest chitons for your perusal…no, Ashtaph, not the green. The blue…ah, yes, the blue." Hylas took a sweep of finely pleated blue linen from Ashtaph and held it up toward Quintus. "It brings out the brilliance in your eyes, lord Alexa… Quintus."

Quintus sprawled in the nearest chair and rubbed a week's growth of beard. "What is the purpose of this feast?" he asked. "Why is the emperor permitting me to leave my room?"

"It is not for me to speak for the emperor," Hylas said, sorting through a bundle of braided cords and sashes. "You have only to rejoice in your good fortune." He carefully drew an elaborate, many-stranded belt from among the rest. "Ah, yes. This will do very well indeed." He smiled at Quintus disarmingly. "If I may be so bold…does the name 'Corvinus' not mean 'crow' in the Tiberian tongue?"

Surprised at the man's knowledge, Quintus nodded. Hylas clapped his hands. "Excellent. I have the perfect mask for you, and the black himation will be the crow's wings."

"Hylas—"

The courtier returned the fabric to Ashtaph. "Leave us," he said to the servant. The boy gathered up the bundles and slipped from the room.

"Now," Hylas said. "I will tell you what little I know. For reasons the emperor has not vouchsafed to me, he has decided to permit you the freedom of the citadel." He leaned forward, reaching across the table as if he would touch Quintus's hand. "I advise you to use this gift wisely. Earn the emperor's trust, and he will repay you a thousandfold."

"Did the emperor send you to make this speech?"

Hylas withdrew his hand. "I speak only for myself," he said with pained dignity. "I was in the hall when you were brought before Nikodemos. I heard your words of defiance, and they were most courageous and admirable. But by now you must realize they will not win you what you most desire."

"A man like you could not imagine what I most desire."

"No?" Hylas smiled, but his dark eyes were as soft and wounded as a child's. "Whether or not you choose to believe it, Quintus Horatius Corvinus, I wish to be your friend. I know you will not be deceived or convinced of anything you do not see with your own eyes. That is why you must allow my servants to prepare you for the feast. Attend as the man of nobility you were born to be. Listen and observe. You can lose nothing by setting aside your pride for a single night."

He seemed about to say more but thought better of it, glancing toward the door. A moment later Kanmi entered and knelt to whisper in his master's ear. Hylas nodded and addressed Quintus.

"The servant Briga has been taken into the emperor's direct protection," he said. "More I cannot tell you now, but if I obtain any additional information, I will bring it to you."

"My thanks," Quintus said gruffly.

Hylas rose and bowed with his hand over his heart. "I will leave you now, but Kanmi will remain to shave you and prepare a bath. Ashtaph will return with your clothing and give you any further assistance you may require." He turned to go.

"Wait," Quintus said. *Did Danae send you?* But he dared not speak the question aloud when he knew that Hylas might be the emperor's agent. "Your assistance is...appreciated."

Hylas's eyes sparkled. "You are most welcome to any service I can render. We will speak again soon, my lord." He flashed a grin of pure mischief and swept out of the room, leaving servant and tray behind.

Quintus shook his head, off-balance and bemused. Hylas was the sort of soft, pleasure-loving man true Tiberians most despised, and doubtless he was a polished court schemer. Whether he'd been sent by the emperor or Danae, or come for reasons of his own, he couldn't be trusted. Yet his advice was sound: Listen and observe. Almost the very words Quintus had spoken to Briga.

Now the girl was supposedly under the emperor's protection, Danae was apparently safe and Quintus would have an unforeseen opportunity to walk among the emperor's Companions. If there was a weak link in the chain of loyalty surrounding Nikodemos, Quintus intended to find it.

"My lord?" Kanmi said. "If you permit, I will have a basin brought for your bath."

"I can bathe myself," Quintus muttered.

"Would you prefer that I send maids to assist you?"

"That will not be necessary."

"Then if I may shave you and paint your eyes—"

Quintus shuddered. "No paint."

Kanmi bowed. "No paint, my lord," he said with a sigh.

Doubtless his master would share his disappointment, but there was a limit to the concessions Quintus was willing to make, even for the privilege of attending the emperor's feast.

He endured the next several hours with all the Tiberian stoicism he could muster. Two muscular servants arrived with a heavy earthenware basin, and a succession of slaves brought hot water to fill it. The basin was not large enough to lie in, so Quintus was compelled to abandon modesty while Kanmi poured water over him, scrubbed his back and dressed his hair. The shave, at least, was welcome. Some time later Ashtaph appeared with the garments chosen by Hylas—blue chiton belted to mid-thigh, flowing black himation deftly arranged over Quintus's chest and shoulders, copper-studded sandals and intricately worked gold armbands.

At the end of the almost interminable day, Ashtaph brought the mask. Quintus hadn't known what to expect when Hylas had mentioned it, and later he had forgotten. But when Ashtaph placed it on the table with a flourish, a crow's head of beaten bronze complete with wickedly curved beak and serrated feathers, Quintus understood that this was no mere decoration.

The servants would only tell him that everyone at the feast, men and women both, would wear unique masks of symbolic import. And when they fitted Quintus with his, binding it to his head with leather cords, he felt strangely powerful, anonymous and yet marked for all to see: Corvinus, the Crow, a bird both plain and bold. Quintus Horatius Corvinus, Tiberian.

Soon after nightfall, guards came to take Quintus to the hall. He carried the mask under his right arm, striding ahead of his escort as if he owned the tiles upon which he trod. As they approached the hall, courtiers on their way to the feast paused to stare and whisper. A portly functionary in rich garb met Quintus at the great double doors.

"Lord Alexandros," he said, bowing. He dismissed the guards with a flick of his plump hand. "I am Kleobis, chamberlain of the House of Arrhidaeos. Be so kind as to put on your mask, and follow me."

Servants rushed ahead to open the doors, which creaked on their heavy hinges. Sound burst from the hall—laughter, the wail of pipes, the clatter of wine cups. The chamberlain led Quintus at a measured pace down the center of the hall, where he could observe the long tables heaped with food and the couches occupying every available space between the marble columns on either side.

It was a glittering company indeed. Men had been seated to the left, women to the right; all wore masks, just as Ashtaph had promised. Every garment was embroidered or painted in complex designs and fixed with fibulae and pins of silver, bronze and gold. Only the servants, one for every couch, wore unadorned white linen.

The throne on its dais at the head of the hall was unoccupied. Quintus could not locate Danae in the crowd. Kleobis took Quintus to a couch very near the foot of the dais, where the most gorgeous creatures claimed their rightful place. Faces of birds, beasts and gods turned to stare.

"Welcome, my lord."

Quintus knew the voice, though the features were obscured

behind a golden mask. Hylas rose from his adjoining couch and placed his hand over his heart. "I am pleased that you took my advice. You are as magnificent as I had hoped."

Glancing down at his fancy dress, Quintus shrugged. "A crow is plain indeed among so many birds of brilliant plumage."

"And all the more striking in its simplicity." Hylas twitched a finger, and the servant standing behind Quintus's couch knelt to offer a cup of wine. Hylas took a cup from his own servant's hand. "I drink to you, Lord Quintus Alexandros."

Quintus hesitated, thinking of clear heads and sharp senses. Then he tilted the cup under the beak of his mask and drank. The servant offered a plate of exotic fruits, tiny birds swimming in highly spiced sauce and other delicacies for which Quintus had no name. Quintus waved the food aside and addressed Hylas.

"Where is the emperor?"

"He is to arrive later. I am told there will be a special entertainment."

Quintus's spine prickled at the thought of what such jaded folk as these must consider entertaining. Musicians played pipes, drums and lyres, lending a constant and sensual backdrop to the hum of conversation. A pair of perfectly matched, nearly naked girls danced to the muted rhythm. Yet the vast room was almost hushed, as if its occupants waited for the true diversion to begin.

He focused his attention on the nearest masks, while their owners surreptitiously studied him in turn. At first the visages seemed to represent several sorts of animals and many varieties of human faces, some noble and some hideous. But as Quintus examined the details, he noticed the subtle emblems and symbols worked into hair and headdresses.

These were not the representations of men and women, but gods and goddesses—deities of Hellas, Aigyptos and Persis, and perhaps even of lands beyond. One man wore the hawk-mask of the Aigyptian sun god, Re; another impersonated Poseidon, mighty sea-god of the Hellenes, with conch shells and tiny golden tridents wound in his beard. Among the women Quintus recognized Artemis the Huntress, a serpent deity of Persis, and the Aigyptian cow-goddess Hathor.

Hylas looked at Quintus with the fixed, lazy grin of a perpetual drunkard: Dionysos, Hellenic god of the grape. He was depicted in his youthful mode of sublime beauty, grape leaves twined in curling locks.

"Do you see?" Hylas asked, leaning close. "The priests seek to ban all deities but the Stone God, and yet our emperor allows this celebration, so that our ancient customs will not be forgotten."

Or because it was yet another way of defying Baalshillek and his minions. No priests were present at the feast, yet they must be aware of everything that happened in the palace.

If the emperor had lied about desiring the Stone God's ultimate downfall, he had a very odd way of declaring his devotion.

Quintus examined the women's masks again, trying to guess which goddess Danae would choose. Often she had mentioned Aigyptian Isis, but Quintus saw no face that matched his limited knowledge of the deity. Perhaps she, like Nikodemos, had yet to arrive. He felt along the sharp beak of his own mask and searched his memory for a god represented by the black bird.

"You wonder at your divine identity," Hylas said. "Some say crows are the messengers of death, but among the Keltoi he is sacred to many gods, and he is a servant and prophet of Apollon. I prefer to think of you as Apollon himself."

Quintus shifted on his elbow, uncomfortably aware of the courtier's intimate tone. "As I recall my childhood stories, Apollon punished the crow for bringing bad news by turning him from white to black."

"But crows are said to have guided your glorious uncle to the Oracle of Amun at Siwa, in the Great Desert," Hylas said, "where he was declared a god."

"I am no god."

"Do not play at modesty," Hylas purred. "You are far more than you seem, Quintus Alexandros, and your destiny will be mighty."

Quintus was about to reply when the music suddenly ceased and every face turned toward the dais. A figure stepped up to stand beside the throne—a man in golden armor molded to represent the muscular torso of an ideal athlete. His mask was that of the king of gods, Zeus, bearer of thunderbolts, crowned with lightning.

Nikodemos had arrived at last.

Chapter Eight

The emperor raised his hands. "Welcome," he said. His mask swung toward Quintus, and Quintus sensed the smile under the stern lips of the god. Nikodemos turned toward the musicians and nodded. At once they struck up a tune almost chaotic in its line, wild and primitive, as if to summon up the most ancient of spirits.

A man dressed in red-dyed leather, wearing a bull's mask with high, curving horns, leaped through a doorway at the head of the hall. He ran about the room, tossing his head at the guests, snorting and pawing at the floor. His dance was unbridled, powerful, that of a savage beast eager to mate or kill. Men laughed and ladies shrieked, but all sound ceased when the girl appeared.

She wore a tight-fitting bodice that cupped her bared breasts and a short apron reaching only to her upper thighs. Her mask was that of a flawlessly beautiful woman. In one hand she grasped a staff shaped like a twisting serpent. She approached the bull with mincing steps, teasing, flirting.

One of the musicians began a slow, steady rhythm on his drum, a thump like the beat of a heart. The girl danced toward the bull, waving the serpent staff. The bull-man wagged his horns from side to side and stamped his feet. They circled each other in time to the drum, eyes locked, opponents and rivals playing out the eternal language of desire.

Suddenly the bull-man charged, horns lowered to gore. The girl jumped straight up, twisted in midair and landed on the bull's shoulders. She balanced there for an instant and floated to the ground as lightly as a grain of wheat.

Courtiers cried out their approval, but the bull was far from defeated. He charged again, turning his body to strike from the side. Once more the girl was ready. She flung herself up and out, arms spread, and vaulted over the bull's head. Then she prodded at the bull with her staff until he bellowed with rage and grasped her in his powerful arms.

Ladies gasped. Men rose to their feet. Quintus leaned forward, knowing this dance was but an act and yet feeling its danger. The girl struggled in the bull-man's embrace. He pushed her legs apart, intent upon taking his prize.

Nikodemos stepped down from the dais, carrying a sword shaped to resemble a jagged bolt of lightning. He strode up to the bull and thrust the sword against the dancer's side. The bull-man jerked; he roared, flung his head in a mimicry of death-throes and released the girl, who fell into the emperor's arms.

The audience broke into applause as Nikodemos carried the girl up to his throne. She stretched her length against him, slid down his body and bowed at his feet. He raised her and removed her mask.

Danae's golden hair spilled down her back. Nikodemos kissed her, and the courtiers clapped and pounded the tables. Quintus half rose and settled back again, fist clenched beneath his himation.

"Is she not brilliant?" Hylas said behind him. "Who can help but admire such grace, even in a woman?"

Danae turned to accept the adulation of her peers, skin flushed and eyes bright. Once she glanced toward Quintus, but her expression told him nothing. He averted his eyes from her near-nudity until Nikodemos himself covered her with his cloak and led her to the seat below his.

Gradually the musicians took up their instruments and conversation resumed throughout the hall. Quintus conceded the need to keep up his strength and accepted meat and bread from the servant, though they tasted like ashes in his mouth. Curious courtiers, singly and in small groups, drifted by his couch to gawk and whisper about the emperor's rebellious Tiberian brother. Otherwise, Quintus was left alone.

Hours passed that seemed like days. Nikodemos fed choice morsels to his mistress and listened to her sparkling laughter. The emperor's Hetairoi grew more noisy as they drank, singing and dancing in defiance of the music, and some left on the arms of friends and lovers.

Quintus felt only disgust and shame. He did not belong among these people, accepting a false rank meant only to mock all he believed. He debated returning to his room but knew such a move would be a concession of defeat. He had to speak to Danae, to ask her about Briga's fate.

Hylas appeared at Quintus's couch. "Lord Alexandros," he said, his silken voice only slightly slurred by drink. "You are weary of the feast. Come with me. I know of a quiet place."

Quintus sat up and met the courtier's eyes. "I prefer to be alone."

Hylas flushed, though Quintus doubted that anything could shame or embarrass such a man. "I will not deny that I would treasure your regard, my lord, but that was not my intention. There are others who wish to speak with you."

"What others?"

"Friends of Danae. Those who share her distaste for sacrifice."

Quintus searched the room for any who might be watching him with more than casual interest. While Hylas had claimed his attention, the emperor and his mistress had vanished.

"You propose a secret meeting," he said. "Will Danae come?"

"If she can. It is safe, my lord, I assure you. Still, it would be wise to feign a degree less sobriety."

"Surely guards will follow me."

"You have been granted the freedom of the palace, my lord. The emperor keeps his word." He held out his hand.

Quintus hesitated, ignored the courtier's offer of support and jumped from the couch. At the last moment he feigned a bout of unsteadiness, took a few weaving steps and chuckled at his own clumsiness. Hylas threw his arm around Quintus's shoulder, and the two men made their way toward the end of the hall.

No one followed, not even the servants. Once they had reached an empty corridor, Quintus pulled Hylas behind a column and waited, watching and listening. The corridor remained silent.

"Come," Hylas said. He walked with surprising swiftness down the corridor, turned into a narrow passage and emerged into the residential wing of the palace. After several more turns, he stopped at a door and knocked once.

The door was opened by a young woman with dark hair and eyes decorated in the Aigyptian style. She stepped back and allowed the men to enter.

The room was comfortably large and well-furnished, with embroidered pillows and furs scattered across the floor and against the walls. Three other young men and a woman sprawled or sat among the cushions, their masks beside them.

One of the young men got up and bowed to Quintus. "Welcome, my lord," he said. "I am pleased that you could come. I am Chares."

Hylas greeted the others and found a seat beside one of the men, but Quintus stayed close to the door. "Who are you?" he asked Chares.

"A humble servant of the emperor," the young man said, smiling. "As are we all."

"Why am I here?"

"Did not Hylas tell you? Please, sit, my lord. You have nothing to fear in this room." He gestured to his companions. "You met Doris at the door. These are Arion, Mnestros and Galatea."

Quintus studied the bland, pleasant faces and found no threat in them. To the contrary, he would have judged each one of the room's occupants as harmless sycophants, pleasure-loving youths who enjoyed every privilege they received as members of the emperor's court. Their clothing was fine, their manners easy and expansive as only those of the very rich—and protected—could be.

Doris approached and offered him a cup of wine, smiling with painted lips. Quintus shook his head. She glanced at Hylas.

"You must understand Lord Alexandros's position," Hylas said. "Until this day he was confined to his rooms, and he has no reason to trust us."

"But that is why you are here," Chares said to Quintus. "You have friends in the court, Lord Alexandros—those who admire your fight against the Stone God."

"And against the empire?"

The courtiers glanced at each other, more amused than nonplussed by his bluntness. "We understand why you feel as you do," Chares said. "But we had hoped to help you see that your brother is not your enemy."

"I have heard this before," Quintus said. He reached for the door latch.

"I told you he was stubborn," Hylas said, gazing at Quintus through hooded eyes. "He is not easily persuaded."

"So Danae mentioned also," Chares said.

"You are friends of Lady Danae?" Quintus asked sharply.

"We have that honor. We hope that she will join us later." He gestured toward a cluster of thick cushions. "Will you not be seated, my lord?"

Quintus located a chair near the wall and sat straight-backed on its edge. Chares resumed his place next to the woman Galatea, a slender beauty who had worn the mask of the cat-goddess Bast during the feast. She stared at Quintus through tilted hazel eyes.

"What did you think of Lady Danae's performance, my lord?" she asked.

"Very skillful."

"Indeed. Many men envied the emperor tonight."

"The lady seems devoted to him."

"Yes," Chares said, "because she knows our emperor is the only one who can end the Stone God's reign."

Quintus swept the group with his gaze. "Did Nikodemos arrange this meeting?"

"The emperor knows nothing of it. But we have heard tales of your defiance of Baalshillek, and any inconvenience given to the High Priest brings great pleasure to us."

"Because Nikodemos protects you."

"It is true," Hylas said, "that some of us would not be alive if the emperor did not hold the priests at bay."

"He saves you while he forsakes the common people and destroys any who defy him."

Chares sighed. "You were right, Hylas. But we mustn't abandon the attempt."

"To convince me that your emperor will save the world by smashing it under his heel?" Quintus asked.

"It will take more than words to convince him," a feminine voice said from the doorway. Danae closed the door and stood with her back to it, meeting each of her friends' eyes in turn. Finally she looked at Quintus. "Is that not so, Lord Alexandros?"

He stared at her, dry-mouthed and foolish with anger and desire. She was fully dressed in a simple chiton, her hair arranged close to her head and her face clean of paint—far more lovely than when she had flaunted her legs and breasts before the court.

"I've heard many arguments," he said slowly, "but I have seen no proof."

"Tiberian stubbornness and royal will," Danae said to the others. "A dangerous combination."

Quintus stepped in front of her. "I must speak to you."

"There is no safer place than this," she said. "Chares—"

"Alone," Quintus said, gripping her arm.

She nodded toward the doorway of an adjoining room. He pulled her through the door, out of sight and hearing of her friends. For a moment he held her pinned to the wall, feeling the softness of her breasts against his chest, and then he stepped away.

"Briga was taken last night," he said.

"I know." She searched his eyes. "I had no way to reach you until now. She is well."

"So Hylas claimed. What happened, Danae?"

"Nikodemos…learned of what I had done."

"He caught you?"

She shook her head. "He was not angry…not as you would expect. He had the girl taken to a safe place where Baalshillek cannot take her."

Quintus cursed and struck his fist on the wall. "What does he intend to do with her?"

"No harm, Quintus. He told me that I must bring others like her directly to him from now on, and that he will protect them."

"For purposes you do not know."

"Whatever his purpose might be, it will not help the High Priest," she said. "I did not tell Nikodemos about Briga because I didn't want to place him in a dangerous position."

"You feared his punishment if he were to learn that you were acting without his knowledge."

She frowned at him, eyes flashing. "I have long suspected that Nikodemos knows of my work with the children. He cannot acknowledge it, but he hasn't tried to stop me."

"He merely allows other infants to feed the Stone God's fire."

Danae raised her open hand and let it fall again. "You will continue to believe what you wish, no matter what I say."

"Nothing has changed, Danae, even if the emperor has given me the freedom of the palace."

She turned from him, disgust plain on her face. "And I was the one who suggested that Hylas and Chares speak with you."

"To what end? They'll only repeat what you've already told me…what Nikodemos himself said when he honored me with his presence."

"I see in your eyes what you think of my friends," she said. "You judge them weak, inconsequential creatures who would do anything to keep their pleasures. But Nikodemos is wise enough to recognize the value of their alliance. Arion is of a leading family in Makedon, the country of your uncle Alexandros's birth. Mnestros is a general's son and Chares is a wealthy merchant in his own right. Galatea is of the house of the Ptolemies, rulers of Aigyptos under the empire. Each one of them possesses wealth and power, free of the Stone, that will be at the emperor's command when it is time for him to act."

"Against Baalshillek?" Quintus said mockingly.

"They would be your allies as well. They trust the emperor and are trusted by him. Do not discard their goodwill so lightly."

"And what of your goodwill, Danae?"

"That has not altered."

He cupped her face in his hand. She stiffened and then slowly relaxed, meeting his gaze. Her lips parted, soft as ripe berries.

"You've stayed away," he said.

"It would do neither of us good if the emperor knew we have spoken as friends."

He dropped his hand, afraid of losing his own self-control. "It was truly a magnificent performance tonight, Danae. I didn't realize the extent of your talents. Was the dance your idea, or the emperor's?" He clenched his fist. "Was it for my benefit, Danae?"

She laughed. "Should every entertainment be designed for you, my arrogant Tiberian?"

"Nikodemos openly defied the High Priest with his display of the gods," he said. "I was meant to be impressed."

"Were you?"

"I don't know."

"Then there is hope for you yet." She brushed her fingertips across his cheek.

He caught her hand against his face. "Show me why I should believe you. Make me understand."

"Quintus," she murmured, eyes closing. "You—"

He kissed her. Her lips softened under his, and then she pushed him away.

"Don't," she said. "It isn't possible."

"Of course not," he said harshly. "Only *my* loyalties must change." He stalked away. Her footsteps hurried after him.

"Do not hate me, Quintus. Turn your hatred toward the destruction of your enemies, not your friends."

"You've given me no reason to love your emperor."

"Then tell me how to change your heart."

By giving me yours, he thought, but kept his teeth locked over such puerile sentiments. "Let me see Briga," he said.

She turned aside, tugging gently on the lobe of one delicate ear. "Perhaps it can be done," she said. "Give me a few days to make arrangements."

"Without the emperor's knowledge."

She nodded. "There is one thing I would ask of you in return."

"Only one?"

"Be gentle with Hylas."

"Why does he require my gentleness? He seems capable enough to me."

"Don't you see? He is enamored of you."

Quintus snorted. "Because I am the king's brother?"

"Because he recognizes your nobility, your belief in your cause. Your courage."

He flushed, remembering Hylas's words at the feast: *"I will not deny that I would treasure your regard, my lord."* Quintus had heard of Tiberians who inexplicably preferred the love of their own sex to that of women, and he knew the Hellenes were more open about such matters than his countrymen.

"I have no interest in his kind," Quintus stammered.

"His kind," Danae taunted. "A man of vast loyalty who wears a mask to hide his tender heart."

"I will not hurt him unless he compels me to do so."

"That is all I ask."

"And you will help me see Briga?"

"Trust me."

Quintus was well aware that he had little choice. He let Danae go, briefly taking his leave of the others before returning to his own rooms. No guards intercepted him. Several times in the night he checked his door and found it unwatched—at least by anyone detectable by his senses.

Two days later Leuke came with a message from Danae. Quintus was to attend one of Hylas's frequent nightly gatherings in his rooms, where he would spend several hours while Hylas's servants watched the corridors to make sure Quintus's movements remained unobserved. From there he would go to meet Danae in one of the many courtyards that adorned the residential section of the palace, a tiny garden generally unused, save by servants.

Quintus received a warm welcome from Hylas, who flirted shamelessly but stayed just within the boundaries of propriety. The servant Ashtaph escorted Quintus to the small garden well after most of the palace folk had taken to their beds.

Danae was beautiful by moonlight, but she gave Quintus little chance to admire her. She swept him off through a maze of corridors, a circuitous route of twists and turns that must have covered the better part of the palace. When she stopped it was before the door to an unoccupied room in a wing that had the look and smell of age and abandonment.

"This is the oldest section of the palace," Danae whispered, allowing Quintus to push open the heavy door. "Nikodemos intends to have it torn down and rebuilt, but this room holds a secret of great value to us now."

Quintus stifled a cough at the whirlwind of dust that rose with each step. "What is this secret?"

In answer, Danae approached one of the bare walls, felt along a seam in the stone and pushed with all her weight. The wall groaned. Taking his cue from her, Quintus added his efforts. The larger portion of the wall swung inward, a door hung on seemingly invisible hinges. A rush of dank air spilled from the opening.

"Tunnels," Danae said with a grin of triumph.

"Under the palace?" Quintus asked.

"Yes. I discovered them some time before we helped Nyx escape. Most of the entrances are in rooms inaccessible to us, but this one has been forgotten."

Quintus leaned into the musty darkness and drew in a sharp breath. "Who else knows of this?"

"The emperor, of course. Undoubtedly some of his closest advisers. And Baalshillek."

Quintus jerked back. "They are not aware of your knowledge?"

Danae wrinkled her nose. "Am I a fool, Quintus? Nyx used these tunnels to escape the palace. I thought they might become useful again one day, and so I took some time to explore them. One of the branches runs close to the soldiers' barracks, and that is where they keep Briga."

"Then the guards don't use these tunnels."

"I have never seen one in them. Nikodemos employs them but rarely."

Quintus couldn't quite control his excitement. "This is a great thing, Danae. If you'd told me earlier—"

"I told you now only because you insisted upon seeing Briga. We must not visit these tunnels too often. Come inside and help me close the door."

He did so, and Danae withdrew an unlit lantern from within her cloak. "There are torches set at intervals along the walls," she said. "We must get to the first one by feel, and then light the lantern."

With confident steps that proved her familiarity with her course, Danae started down the lefthand corridor and descended a narrow, steep flight of stairs. The dank smell grew stronger, but cool air flowed constantly through the tunnels. Soon enough the first torch came into view. Danae lit the lantern and set off at a faster pace. Sometimes Quintus heard strange echoes, voices that came from everywhere and nowhere; once he nearly jumped out of his skin at a violent quarrel that seemed to emanate from the walls themselves.

"The sound plays tricks here," Danae said. "We pass near many rooms that do not connect and a few that do. Let us hurry."

They continued past several more torches and a number of portals before Danae called a halt. "The barracks," she said. "Most of the soldiers are sleeping." She pressed her ear to the wall and listened. "I hear nothing." She put out the lantern. "Let us open the door slowly."

She showed Quintus the clever mechanism that released the portal and helped him swing the slab inward. Quintus pushed ahead, moving cautiously in the darkness of a narrow hall.

Someone coughed. Danae caught Quintus's arm.

"It is only the children," she said.

"Children?"

"Come." She tugged at his himation and guided him down the center of the hall. A sliver of moonlight from a high window provided just enough light to distinguish one step from the next. Squat, motionless shapes projected from the walls— benches or pallets, each with a sleeping occupant. Danae crept from bed to bed, peering into each face. Finally she stopped beside the last pallet and knelt to touch the sleeper's cheek.

The girl sat up with a start, and Danae covered her

mouth. "It is Danae, Briga," she whispered. "Danae and Quintus."

"Quin—" Briga swallowed her cry and flashed white teeth in a grin. Quintus crouched by the other side of the pallet and found himself enveloped by thin, strong arms.

He patted the girl awkwardly and set her back. "Are you all right, Briga?" he asked, careful to keep his voice low.

"Yes. When the guards came for me I was frightened, but they didn't hurt me. They brought me here, to the others."

Quintus exchanged glances with Danae, knowing this was not the place for explanations. "The emperor didn't threaten you in any way?"

"No. I did not see him."

"No…no man has touched you?"

"They leave us alone, except to bring our food or take us into the courtyard." She searched his eyes. "You are all right, too?"

"Yes." He turned to Danae. "Will she be safe?"

"Safer than anywhere else in the city. I'll explain later."

The child on the next pallet stirred, mumbling something about her mama. "We should go," Danae said. "You see that Briga is well and will remain so." Her mouth twisted in a half smile. "You can trust me again."

"I can't go with you?" Briga asked, the words thick with disappointment.

"Not this time," Quintus said. He hesitated and stroked her hair, letting its fiery strands sift through his fingers. "I won't let anything happen to you, Briga. That I promise."

"I know." She gave him another fierce hug and lay back down. "I'm not afraid. Good night, Quintus."

He kissed her forehead and retreated, watching the girl until she disappeared into the gloom. Danae already had the portal open. Quintus stepped through and closed it behind them.

"Who are these others Briga spoke of?" he asked Danae as they set off again.

"All children and youths like her. Each of them is gifted in some way…what I have heard called 'godborn.'"

"What gifts? The control of fire?"

"And of other elements." She paused at the first torch to relight her lantern. "Most such would ordinarily have gone to Baalshillek, but these were rescued by Nikodemos and his men and brought here."

"What purpose do they serve for Nikodemos?"

"He has not told me. But I would not lie to you, Quintus. They are safe." She continued the next hundred paces in silence. "You are very fond of Briga after such a short time together."

"She is a child, an innocent. You put her in my safekeeping."

"It was a mistake. Now I know I can go to the emperor."

"But not with everything, Danae."

She stopped abruptly. "No. Not with everything. I—"

Her words were muffled by the loud creak of a hinge and a trio of rough voices. Quintus pulled her hard against the wall and held his breath. The sounds came not from the tunnels but just outside, and they rang clear as cymbals.

"…the prisoner?" one of the voices said.

"The emperor's agents took him yesterday as he attempted to enter the city," another answered. "He comes within the hour."

"One of their great leaders, so I hear. Their rebellion will suffer without him."

"They call him Buteo…the hawk."

"Tiberian scum," another said. "His wings have been clipped. At least Baalshillek won't have the chance to destroy him before our interrogators can do their work."

The voices faded, and Quintus released his breath. *Buteo.* He knew the name as well as his own…the hard soldier's face, the close-cropped hair and piercing eyes. Nausea curdled in his throat.

"We must go," Danae said.

"Where are we?"

"Near the dungeons, I think."

"Where you rescued Nyx."

"Yes."

"Where is the portal?"

"A hundred paces ahead. Quintus—"

"How did you get Nyx out of the palace?"

"There is a tunnel leading to a door in the outer palace wall."

"You must show me this door."

He could hear the growing alarm in her voice. "Whatever you are thinking—"

"Those men spoke of a new prisoner, a Tiberian. What have you heard of this?"

"Nothing."

"I knew him," Quintus said. "Buteo. Why would he come to Karchedon?"

"Perhaps we can learn more," Danae said, "but not here."

He relented and let Danae lead him back through the tunnels, but he committed every turning to memory, counting doors and torches until he was sure he could find his way back unaided. He worked the mechanism to open the door into the abandoned suite and preceded her, listening for intruders. He carefully observed Danae's path from the uninhabited section of the palace back to the servants' courtyard.

Ashtaph was waiting to meet them, clearly uneasy at their long absence. The moon had set.

"Ashtaph will take you back to your room," Danae said. "Good night."

Quintus caught a handful of her cloak. "I must know more about this Tiberian prisoner. Will you learn what you can?"

"I no longer have any connection to the Resistance, if any of the rebels still survive."

"You know all that goes on in the palace."

She met his eyes, and her own gleamed with concern. "There is nothing you can do, my friend. If this Buteo has fallen into the emperor's hands, Nikodemos must act."

"To expose the rebels in Tiberia? I know Buteo. He would never speak."

"You cannot save him." She touched his good arm. "Please, Quintus. You have come too far to turn back now."

"Will you listen, and tell me what you hear?"

She withdrew her hand. "I can promise nothing. Be cautious, Quintus. Be safe." She hurried into the shadows.

"My lord?" Ashtaph said.

Quintus nodded, and the servant set off ahead. Quintus turned half his attention to memorizing Ashtaph's route, but the rest of his mind was in turmoil.

Buteo was a prisoner of the empire. He, most honored of all the Tiberian rebel leaders, had taken the grave risk of coming to Karchedon, where somehow he had been exposed. Quintus could think of only one reason why he would have attempted such a dangerous journey.

He had come to look for Quintus. And now Quintus, alone of all the inhabitants of the palace, had both motive and means to help his countryman escape his inevitable fate.

If Quintus was prepared to give his own life for Buteo's freedom. If he chose to throw away his unique opportunity to change the empire from within.

The time for choices was almost over.

Chapter Nine

The fallen City of the Exalted had lain buried for thousands of years, and yet Cian knew they had arrived long before he saw the first broken stump of some ancient monument jutting out of the sand.

The journey from mountains to City had taken three days of steady travel to the southeast, passing through many leagues of flat gravel plain and entering at last into a country of high sand hills. Tiny golden grains infiltrated mouths, hair and every fold of clothing; sand sank and shifted under the horses' hooves, yet the beasts seemed well adapted to the endless climbs and descents, as well as to the careful rationing of food and water that made such journeys possible.

Hunger and thirst were the least of Cian's concerns. He tried several times to join Rhenna and the others, but he was kept in a kind of respectful but implacable isolation. Madele sent young warriors to bring him refreshment, and he was surrounded by the constant coming and going of curious tribesfolk who wished to catch a glimpse of the legendary Guardian.

Once the party of Imaziren and their guests stopped at an island of fruit-bearing trees and grasses surrounding a large spring, one of many such sources the tribe claimed in its vast and hostile territory. Horses and men drank their fill, the waterskins were replenished, and Cian let himself imagine what it might be like to lie beside the cool water with Rhenna in his arms.

Such dreams were futile. Cian saw nothing of Rhenna, nor did he learn anything more of the elders' decision regarding the significance of his coming. Just as he had decided to approach the elders directly, he felt the change that vibrated through his horse's legs and lodged in his own belly like the rumble of a distant avalanche.

He crested a tall hill with his escort and looked down upon a level ocean of sand, a full league in diameter, dotted with hundreds of tents and countless lumps of dark stone. Far across the plain was a patch of green, the remnants of an ancient lake or river; a few herds of lean cattle and horses straggled to or from the waterhole.

"The City," Nyx said, riding up beside him. "I never believed I would see it."

Cian turned in surprise to find the Southern woman with Madele. "How are Rhenna and Tahvo?" he asked quickly.

"Well enough. They asked the same of you."

"Why do the Imaziren keep us separated?"

Nyx sighed. "I have listened carefully to the Imaziren during the past several days. They are still in disagreement about the meaning of your arrival." She patted her horse's sweating neck. "You see, the Imaziren believe their gods abandoned them in ancient days, after the Godwar. Though the tribes earned great honor in the battle with the Exalted and were given all this land as their own, still the gods for whom they fought chose to leave them."

"Then this is why Tahvo complained that she couldn't find her spirits," Cian said. "Why did the gods disappear?"

"The Imaziren do not know, but they consider it a grave betrayal. For millennia they have had no priests. They work no magic and regard most such powers as evil sorcery. Yet their legends predict the coming of the Guardians...and it is also said that when the Guardians return, so will the gods."

"And some do not wish the gods to return."

Nyx nodded. "They have lived so long without them. Some believe the Imaziren would lose the freedom they cherish and resent the thought that any god should demand their reverence. They would deny the great changes your coming portends."

"And the others?"

"Like Madele, they believe the Imaziren have lost their purpose and now have the chance to find it again. They have struggled to survive in a difficult land, and this has made them strong as a people. But if the gods return and the evil one is defeated once and for all, the desert will become a paradise as it was before the Godwar."

Cian laughed. "So I am to determine the future of an entire race."

"You see why your presence is the source of much confusion."

"Then it might be best for all concerned if I remove the source of conflict. Can we escape?"

"It is unlikely the Imaziren would harm you or our companions even if you attempted to leave." She paused, shading her eyes against the sun's glare. "But I cannot be sure of finding the safest route through the Southern desert."

Madele spoke, interrupting their conversation. Nyx cast her an impatient glance. "I have been asked to interpret for you now that we have reached our destination," she said. "Madele says that this is their tribe's true home, their most sacred dwelling. Their herders and warriors may wander far in search of forage for their beasts, but to the City they always return. None but the Imaziren dare intrude—on pain of death."

Cian shuddered. He could not imagine why anyone would challenge the Imaziren for such a place. Old evil persisted here, deeply buried but not forgotten; when he slid from his horse's back Cian felt it in stone far beneath the sand. Ruins of the Exalted's creation.

"Madele says that you need not be afraid," Nyx said. "The evil ones have no power here now."

Cian knelt and sifted a handful of sand through his fingers. "Her people are not troubled by what lies under their feet?"

Nyx consulted Madele. "We were given this City by the gods," she translated. "It cannot hurt us."

Cian closed his eyes, slipping his hand under the hot golden surface. He felt as far as he could reach, seeking the poison he had sensed in Hellas and Karchedon. There was none; it had been leached from the earth long ago, driven out as thoroughly as the flowing waters and fertile fields destroyed in the Godwar.

Yet evidence of the City remained. As he, Nyx and Madele rode down the long slope toward the encampment, Cian saw the first of the stone blocks and wind-scoured obelisks that had defied the centuries. Most were shapeless, all hard edges and sculpted details smoothed away by the desert's unforgiving caress. But some—like the great head buried to the chin, dwarfing the tents beside it—still preserved a faint likeness to what they had been: the faces of the gods.

Cian stared up at the immense visage and almost felt the helpless rage locked behind blind eyes and pitted lips. To which of the Exalted had such a massive monument been erected? Did the Imaziren know the names of the gods who had brought ruin on the world and might bring it again?

He had no chance to ask the question. Madele's warriors—and several hundred new ones from the dead City—closed in around Cian, herding him and Nyx toward the innermost encampment. Some tribesfolk reached out as if to touch him, but most simply repeated the word he had come to recognize as "Guardian."

At the center of the tent city was a group of a dozen dwellings larger than the rest, staked so firmly in place that Cian doubted they were often moved. Goats wandered among them, and children peered out from behind the flaps of ocher-dyed goatskin that served as doorways. The sand closest to the tents was smooth and white, as if it had been recently swept clean.

Cian was asked to dismount before one of the biggest tents, and Madele dispersed the crowd with a few sharp words. While Nyx and Cian waited outside, Madele and several senior warriors entered the tent. They emerged with a trio of elders in long robes the deep blue of a clear evening sky. The elders addressed Madele and examined Cian with dark, unreadable eyes. One of them spoke to Cian.

"He asks you to change," Nyx said, disapproval clear in her voice.

Cian held very still, banking his anger. Nyx began to speak, but Madele interrupted. Her hands drew elegant shapes in the air, illustrating the story of how Cian had appeared at the end of her duel with Rhenna.

"She tells them that she witnessed your changing," Nyx whispered. "She gives her most solemn word that you are of the Guardian race."

The elders consulted among themselves and, after some disagreement, went back into the tent. Madele's shoulders dropped.

"A full council must be held to discuss these events," she said through Nyx. "Come. You may rest and take refreshment."

"I wish to see my friends," Cian said.

"Please be patient. They will be well cared for."

Cian stared at Madele and finally relented with a shake of his head. Nyx spoke to Madele. "I am to stay with Rhenna and Tahvo," she said. "Go with Madele, and I will come when I can."

Ill at ease, yet not prepared to challenge the Imaziren outright, Cian went with the warrior to the tent they had made ready for him. He was left alone with a generous supply of flat bread, roasted meat, small fruits and a tart beer that he ignored in favor of plain water. The stifling heat gradually gave way to the coolness of dusk.

Voices rose outside the tent. Cian opened the flap and found Nyx and Madele arguing softly. Nyx saw him and broke off.

"Madele asks if the Guardian will honor the Imaziren with his presence," Nyx said. She glanced at Madele and moved closer to the tent. "Something is about to happen, Cian. Perhaps they plan to resolve their arguments with a test."

"As they tested Rhenna?"

Nyx addressed Madele, who answered Cian directly. "She asks you to trust her," Nyx said.

Cian met the desert warrior's gaze. "She swore to her elders that I was of the Guardians. Does she also swear that my companions will come to no harm no matter what her people decide about me?"

Nyx conveyed his words. Madele extended her hand and then drew it back to touch her chest.

"She swears," Nyx said.

"Then I will come." He and Nyx followed Madele to an open space between the tents, where there waited a delegation of elders in their long robes, and warriors in short tunics, cloaks and headbands set with the gray and black plumes of enormous feathers. The warriors and elders bowed to Cian. Something in their manner demanded both formality and absolute silence, and Cian knew that Nyx was right. This was indeed to be some ritual test meant for him to pass or fail.

The tribesfolk turned and set off from the encampment, striking across the plain toward the dark blotch of the distant waterhole. Broken black stone pillars thrust from the sand like decayed teeth, radiating malignancy. The Imaziren ignored them. They climbed a gentle rise to the bank of the *amda*, where trees with broad, fringed leaves hung over a carpet of lush grasses.

The elders and warriors knelt and lay on their bellies in the sand. Madele signaled for Cian and Nyx to do the same. A hush of expectation settled over the group. Cian's heartbeat drummed in his throat.

Something moved on the hill beyond the waterhole. A wedge-shaped head on a long neck lifted to smell the air. The creature climbed over the rise and descended toward the water, bizarre and nimble, hump-backed and knobby-legged, its wooly hide gleaming in the moonlight.

Madele grabbed Cian's arm and squeezed it hard enough to bruise. The strange beast snorted and flicked its small ears toward the watchers. A second animal joined the first. The two creatures stood as still as the ancient pillars, waiting in the breathless quiet.

And Cian understood. He got slowly to his feet. No one moved to stop him. He crested the hill and walked along the bank of the *amda,* footsteps whispering in the grass. The beasts watched him come, nostrils flared to capture his scent. He passed the trees and the far edge of the water, and still they did not flee.

Cian held out his hand. Flexible lips drew back from strong, yellow teeth. The larger beast extended its neck. Long-lashed brown eyes gazed into Cian's. Immense, two-toed feet shuffled in the sand. Then the creature gave a deep groan and bent its legs before and behind, settling into a surprisingly graceful crouch.

The short, pale fur was both soft and harsh under Cian's fingers. He stroked the ugly head, scratching between the beast's intelligent eyes. The second animal pressed forward and pushed its muzzle against his free hand. Cian laughed.

Tahvo woke with a start. Nothing had broken the quiet of the Amazi camp; she felt no change in the thrum of awareness that had seized her mind since their arrival in the City of the Exalted. Her dreams here were filled with vague premonitions that always evaporated in the light of morning, but it was still night.

She listened to the sigh of Rhenna's breathing. The warrior slept as she hadn't done for days, exhausted by her constant vigilance and worry over Cian. She desperately needed the rest, and Tahvo had no intention of waking her for so small a reason as a peculiar feeling inside her head.

Tahvo crept to the tent flap and eased it up. She could hear no guards outside, nor any stirring among the other tents. Yet the very quality of the silence itself was more telling than the roar of a crowd.

Wrapping her cloak about her shoulders, Tahvo slipped out of the tent. The sharp, welcome cold of the desert night stung her cheeks. She crossed the open space between the tents and traced the deepest silence, avoiding the piles of stone that murmured with the voices of an ancient evil. At last she found a depression in the sand made by many feet. She heard a ringing in her ears, as if someone spoke just beyond the range of her hearing. Then came distant shouts, cries of shock and agitation that pierced the stillness like the crack of falling branches.

Tahvo turned away from the noise and began to retrace her steps back to the tent. Her thoughts raced so far ahead of her feet that she didn't sense the beast until it was almost on top of her. It half reared, casting a spray of sand.

"Tahvo," Cian said from a place above her head.

"Cian?"

"Do you hear them?" he asked.

She reached toward the warmer air in front of her, and her hand came in contact with the matted fur of the beast's shoulder. It was no horse nor any animal she knew. It nibbled at her hair with soft, mobile lips.

Come.

"I hear them," she said in wonder. "What are they?"

Cian didn't answer. His hand grasped at her cloak, urging her closer. She felt a long, arched neck and humped back sliding under her fingers, and then a second questing muzzle. Two beasts, one already bearing a rider.

Come.

Obeying instincts she hardly understood, Tahvo felt her way

back to the tent. Rhenna slept on undisturbed. Tahvo found a loaf of bread and a handful of fruit left from the evening meal, wrapped them in a bit of cloth, and returned to Cian and the beasts.

"We must go," Cian said. "Can you mount?"

Stretching her hands out before her, Tahvo clambered across the crouching animal's bony rump and grasped at the sloping back, pulling herself up until her legs dangled at the animal's round sides. It heaved to its feet, hindquarters first, so delicately that Tahvo never lost her precarious hold.

"Where are we going?" she asked Cian in a whisper.

Once again he gave no answer, and she knew he was as ignorant as she, caught up in some spell of his own. His beast turned toward the South. Her mount followed. They began to run with a swaying, rocking rhythm that lulled Tahvo into a sense of perfect safety.

"Rhenna."

Rhenna opened her eyes at the sound of Nyx's voice and rolled to her knees in a single fluid motion, feeling for the knife at her belt. Nyx caught her arm just as Rhenna saw that Tahvo no longer lay beside her.

"Where is Tahvo?" Rhenna demanded, shaking free of Nyx's hold.

"Gone." The Southern woman retreated to kneel at the opposite side of the tent, hands fisted on her thighs. "Gone with Cian. No one knows where."

Rhenna sheathed her knife and fought sudden panic. "They escaped?"

"We were never prisoners here," Nyx said. "But last night…" She hesitated and met Rhenna's gaze. "Last night the Imaziren took Cian to see the creatures they call sand horses. These animals are sacred to the Imaziren and have not been ridden since the Godwars, but Cian—"

Rhenna got up and flung back the tent flap. Harsh morning

sunlight lanced through her eyelids. Warriors, talking and gesticulating in a fury of sound and motion, turned to stare as Rhenna and Nyx emerged from the tent.

"It was a test," Nyx said, her voice subdued. "I had no chance to tell you. They have said that Cian is safe and will return."

"Return from where?" Rhenna strode away from the tents, her feet sinking in the sand with every step. "Where was he last seen?"

Nyx caught up as the Amazi warriors fell in behind her. "I told you the Amazi legends of those they call the Guardians. Last night I learned the one tale I did not know—that only a true Guardian can tame and mount the sand horses."

Rhenna came to a halt in the shadow of a black pillar, scanning the rolling horizon for any sign of movement. "Sand horses? What are they?"

"Ugly creatures that bear no resemblance to true horses." She knelt in the sand and drew a shape with her finger, marking four legs, a crooked neck and humped back. "They reside only here, near the City. It is said that they can go for leagues without food or water, walk where the strongest horse could not, and survive even the most ferocious of storms."

Rhenna stared at the drawing as if she could will it to come alive and lead her to Cian. "You said these beasts are sacred to the Imaziren?"

"Their tales say that the sand horses were created at the same time as the Guardians, to bear the ancestors of the Imaziren into battle against the Exalted. But the sand horses grew wild when the old gods left this land. Some have believed that the Guardians will return to tame the beasts and make the Imaziren invincible warriors again."

"So Cian obliged them by mounting one of these creatures and simply rode away?"

"Into the desert, with Tahvo," Nyx said.

"Tahvo." Rhenna kicked at Nyx's sketch with the toe of her

boot. "Whatever madness was in Cian's head, *she* wouldn't have gone without good reason."

"Such is the magic of the sand horses—so the Imaziren believe—that no rider can come to harm in their care. Madele says this must be part of the test."

Rhenna snorted. "Tests and more tests. Will these people be satisfied only when we are dead?"

"Cian has proven himself," Nyx said. "I believe they will agree to help us now."

"I would hear this from their own elders," Rhenna said. "Tell Madele I wish to speak with them."

Nyx grinned, suddenly of one mind with Rhenna. "Come with me."

She led Rhenna to the cluster of expansive tents at the center of the Amazi encampment. Warriors standing watch came to attention, snapping up their javelins. Nyx addressed them, mentioning Madele's name, and one of the warriors slipped inside the largest tent. He emerged a few moments later and beckoned the women inside.

Like Rhenna's quarters, the elder's dwelling was simply furnished with woven rugs, skins and intricately decorated storage bags that hung from the tent poles. Madele sat with three elders and several other warriors near the back of the tent, where a portion of one wall had been opened to let in a light morning breeze.

Madele beckoned Rhenna and Nyx to join them, inclining her head. Rhenna brusquely returned the bow.

"These are leaders and elders among the Imaziren," Nyx said. "They give you greeting—"

"Will they send warriors to look for Cian and Tahvo?" Rhenna interrupted.

Nyx turned to the elders, two men and a woman whose faces were scored by age, sun and weather. The old female smiled tolerantly and addressed Nyx.

"Zamra says there is no need," Nyx translated. "The Guardian will return when the sand horses are ready."

"I prefer not to leave the fate of my friends in the hands of animals, no matter how intelligent they may be."

"They are not mere animals," Nyx said, relaxing Madele's irritation. "You would know this if you had seen them. They are a gift from the gods."

The gods who abandoned you, Rhenna thought. "And where have they taken Cian and Tahvo?"

"Only the sand horses know."

Rhenna kept a fragile hold on her patience. "They'll keep their riders from dying of heat and thirst?"

"As they did our people in ancient times."

She glared at Madele. "We have enemies other than the desert."

The elders murmured to one another. Madele answered for them. "No man or beast can catch the sand horses, or enter the City undetected."

Rhenna glanced at Nyx. "You told them that our enemies may still be pursuing us?"

"I did."

"Clearly it wasn't enough. We must tell them everything… about the prophecy, Baalshillek and the Weapons."

Nyx nodded slowly. She faced the elders again and spoke at length, occasionally punctuating her tale with graceful gestures. The Imaziren listened intently. Women brought fruit and cool water to wet Nyx's dry mouth, but she never faltered.

When she was finished, Madele looked at Rhenna with new interest and touched her hand to her chest.

"Now she understands why you are such a formidable warrior," Nyx said, "and how it is that you command the winds without the use of foul sorcery."

"They believe our story?" Rhenna asked, hiding her relief.

"The Guardian has proved that all you say must be true." Nyx paused for one of the elders to speak. "The sand horses would not permit one tainted by evil to touch them. Most of our people now accept that the time has come for the Imaziren to take up arms and fight the Stone God."

"Most?"

The female elder, Zamra, smiled as Nyx translated. "Some still resist, but they will come to understand." She studied Rhenna through clouded gray eyes. "Your people live in the North, near the home of the Guardian?"

"Our country lies in the shadow of mountains we call the Shield of the Sky."

"Where all is green, and water flows freely, as once it did in our homeland. You have protected the Guardian in his journey to us."

"In our journey to find the Hammer."

"We understand this. The Guardian cannot remain in the City."

"Then you will help us cross the Southern desert?"

"We will provide all the assistance you require. But there is a thing that you, warrior, may give us to strengthen the faith of those who doubt."

Rhenna straightened uneasily. "What is that?"

The elder spoke to Madele, whose face took on a tinge of red beneath sun-browned skin. Nyx was silent for a long while afterward.

"What did she say?" Rhenna asked, the back of her neck prickling.

Nyx drew in a deep breath. "She knows that you and Cian have been mates. She asks if you are prepared to give the Guardian up for a single night, so that he may father a child who will become a great leader of their people."

Rhenna's cheeks flamed to match Madele's. With an effort she kept her seat. "I am not…the Guardian's keeper."

"He—" Nyx began, and coughed. "He refuses all other women because of you."

A curse bubbled up and died in Rhenna's throat. She stared hard at Madele, who refused to meet her gaze. Her chest tightened with an ache that stabbed through heart and belly like a lethally cast javelin.

"I am not the Guardian's mate," she said. "He is free to…lie with whomever he chooses."

A heavy silence fell over the Imaziren and their guests. After a while Zamra spoke, face and voice solemn.

"We will make preparations for the Guardian's return," she said. "And for your journey to the South."

Rhenna rose and bowed stiffly. She turned to go.

"Rhenna," Nyx said. "Zamra has one more question."

"Ask."

"Do you…do you carry the Guardian's child?"

For a moment Rhenna was blind and deaf to everything around her, hurled back to that exultant, terrifying day when she and Cian had lain together in the magic-bound courtyard of Danae's house. Her belly was as flat and hard now as it had been then, untouched by an Ailu's potent seed. Shameful tears came to her eyes.

"Tell them I do not," she said, and left the tent without another word.

Chapter Ten

For two days the hump-backed beasts carried Tahvo and Cian across the desert, over endless hills of sand and flat expanses of pebble and stone. Several times each day the sand horses found waterholes, where they stopped to allow their riders to dismount, drink and rest. The animals themselves drank little but slept kneeling in any shade they could find.

Tahvo shared her scant ration of bread and fruit with Cian, but he had no appetite. He did not suffer from the oppressive heat, nor did his skin burn like hers. He had felt nothing since leaving the Amazi camp…nothing but a sense of waiting, a strange certainty that some new trial lay ahead.

On the third morning he found the bones.

His mount came to a shuddering stop just below the crest of a sand hill. There was no shelter, no shade nor water, but the beast grunted and sank onto its knees, refusing to move another step. Tahvo's animal did likewise. Cian dismounted, placing his feet carefully on the shifting ground, and struck something other than sand.

The bone was bleached white by sun and scoured by wind, half lodged in the desert's ever-shifting surface. Cian crouched to pick it up. He recognized its origin by its length and shape, yet he felt no sorrow for the man or woman who had died in this barren place.

Tahvo joined him. She didn't speak; they had done without talking during the journey and had no need of it now. But she picked up the bone carefully, fingers curled as if she feared to touch such a symbol of extinction.

Cian let her take it and climbed the hill. Fierce sunlight needled his eyes. His boots found a second bone, and then a third. Two dozen bones lay behind him by the time he reached the top of the hill, but he was not prepared for what lay on the other side.

The land fell away in a vast crater, stretching two stadia from one edge to the other. The hue of the depression was neither the gold of sand nor the brown and gray of stone. It was the white of bones beyond counting, piled a hundred deep as far as the eye could see. The entire crater was a single mass burial ground.

Cian fell to his knees. An empty-eyed human skull grinned at him from amid the twisted skeleton of a horse. The fleshless claws of predators mingled with the spiraled horns of goats and cattle, and the tusks and spines of bizarre and unimaginable creatures. The silver of long discarded weapons glinted like beacons among the bones, shields and spears and swords cast aside as if at the very moment of their wielders' deaths.

But this was not merely a place of slaughter. Cian felt the same power here that he had sensed in the City of the Exalted, a thrumming in his belly both loathsome and triumphant. It sang to him with the voices of his ancestors, summoning him to change and dip his claws in the blood of his enemies, dance out his victory on gut and bone and sinew.

Cian crawled away from the rim of the crater, the taste of decay foul on his tongue. He stumbled to his beast and attempted to mount. It cast him off with a heave of its shoulder. Tahvo sat cross-legged in the sand, clutching the long human bone so tightly that her knuckles stood out sharp and pale through the burned skin of her hands.

"Tahvo," Cian whispered.

She turned toward him, her blind silver eyes as bleak as a grave. "They are here," she said. "All that remains of a hundred thousand gods. Do you see them?"

Cian collapsed to the ground beside her. "No gods," he said. "Only bones."

She shook her head. "I feel them, Cian. They gathered here for the greatest battle, and they died."

Her words stripped away the last of Cian's defenses. He pried the bone from Tahvo's fingers and took her hands in his. They were cold as ice. "Where are we?" he asked.

"Do you not know? This is the place the beasts intended to bring us. It is the prison of the Stone."

The prison of the Stone. Cian hurled the bone over the crest of the hill. A part of him had guessed from the moment they had arrived; part of him must have known the sand horses' destination before they had ever left the Amazi camp. He understood the sickness that claimed him, the dread and exultation that warred to a bloody standstill in his Ailu heart.

This was where his people had wielded their magic of Earth to bind the Stone for all eternity. That magic still lingered, perverted by Ailuri treachery. But a greater power overwhelmed even the memory of the shapechanger's enchantment, for here the Stone had lain for millennia, its concentrated evil sustained by the remnants of all those creatures, mortal and divine, who had died to defeat it.

"This is where Alexandros found it," he said. "Found it and moved it to a place hidden from all but the highest priests of the Stone God."

Tahvo rocked back and forth, her arms clamped over her stomach. "Part of it endures, even now. Enough to destroy. Enough to—" Her body arched violently, and her eyes rolled up beneath her lids.

Cian caught and held her as she convulsed through the fit, wedging his thumb into her mouth so she wouldn't bite through her tongue. The hump-backed beasts drew close, craning their long necks and groaning mournfully. Tahvo gave a final shudder and went limp in Cian's hold.

"Tahvo," he said, stroking matted hair away from her face. "We must leave this place. *Tahvo.*"

She opened her eyes. "I saw him, Cian. I saw my brother."

"Your brother?"

"He died. But he is still alive. He came to me in Karchedon. I promised him everything if he would help me save you…."

"Hush." Cian pulled her close, terrified that she had finally succumbed to madness. "Can you ride, Tahvo?"

She struggled against him. "Do you hear them? They are drawn to the prison of the Stone like crows to a carcass." She clutched his shirt. "They are coming, Cian."

"Who?"

The earth shivered. Bones rattled. Loose grains of sand bounced down the hill like miniature boulders in an avalanche. The hump-backed beasts surged to their feet, baring great flat teeth.

Cian left Tahvo and ran up to the lip of the crater. The sky was black over the field of bones. A plume of fine sand rose beyond the right edge of the pit, dust from the marching of many feet.

Cian plunged back down the hill and swept Tahvo into his arms, carrying her to her sand horse. The animal tossed its ugly head and danced away. The other bellowed, snapped at Cian and raced toward the crater's edge, leaping over it in a single jump.

There was no hope of escaping on foot from whatever was coming. Cian set Tahvo at the base of the hill and ran after the smaller of the beasts. It flung up its feet and followed the first into the crater. Cian swallowed the rising nausea in his throat and pursued, his feet rolling on the upper layer of bones as he skidded into the depression. Smaller bones cracked under his weight, releasing a stench of corruption as if they still bore rotted coverings of flesh.

The sand horses stood some five hundred paces down the slope of the crater, where the ground began to level. They trembled on their long, knobby legs, heads turned toward the approaching plume of dust. Cian held out his hand. The beasts let him near enough to touch them, but they refused to move a finger's breadth from their position.

"Do you think we'll be safe here from whatever comes for us?" Cian asked his mount. "This is a place of evil."

"They know," Tahvo said. She slid down the side of the crater on her rump, no better able than Cian to keep from touching the animal and human remains. Her lips curled in sorrow and horror. "They know what comes. It is the warriors of the Stone."

Cian grabbed Tahvo and pulled her up beside him. "You've seen them?"

She nodded. "I think they have been pursuing us since Karchedon, but I did not sense them until now. I am sorry, Cian."

"No. We all realized Baalshillek wasn't likely to let us go without a fight." A spike of dread sliced through him. "I should have heard the red stones long before they got this close. They haven't called me since I found my people in Karchedon."

"Then at least they cannot draw you to them," Tahvo said.

"That seems small consolation at the moment." He sniffed the air. Over the reek of bones rose the scent of men's living bodies and sun-heated metal. "At least twenty, I think," he said grimly. "Did they believe they could take us without difficulty after we left the others?"

"Perhaps they were already drawn to this place," Tahvo said. "Their masters' power lingers here even though the Stone is gone."

"Then we have little chance unless the beasts will carry us."

Tahvo rested her palm against her mount's quivering side. "They came into the pit for a reason," she said. "They intend us to fight."

"How?"

"You, too, have power here," Tahvo said softly. "The power of your ancestors."

Cian could not deny what he himself had felt, but he had no idea how to tap that latent magic. Every time he shifted his weight, his legs sank knee-deep in bones. He couldn't guess how far down he would have to reach to touch clean earth.

He tried to remember everything he had observed of the Stone's soldiers when they had hunted him in the North and taken him prisoner in Karchedon. They possessed strength and endurance far beyond that of ordinary men, were difficult to kill and knew no fear. Any one of them would keep fighting even after suffering a deadly wound. And these had tracked their prey across two hundred leagues of hostile terrain.

But the children had weaknesses. They were creatures of rigid order and obedience to their priestly masters. They fought ferociously but without individual volition.

Perhaps the sand horses were not so stupid after all. If the soldiers attacked in formation, their phalanx would be broken by the uncertain footing in the crater. They would be forced to separate, and the more they fought alone, the more vulnerable they would become.

"I will do what I can to find the magic of the Guardians," Cian said. "Hold on to the beasts, Tahvo. If they run, go with them."

"I can fight," Tahvo said in a small voice.

Tahvo had performed works of great magic in Karchedon and before, in the North, when she had joined with the spirit-beast Slahtti and spoken with the voices of gods. But there had been no Slahtti and no gods since Karchedon.

"Protect yourself," he ordered. "Carry the warning back to Rhenna."

Tahvo's jaw set in stubborn defiance, but there was no more

time for argument. The plume of dust had reached the edge of the crater. The first rank of soldiers appeared above it, brutal sunlight striking sparks from greaves and speartips. Booted feet stepped into a quagmire of bone.

Cian thrust his arm into the white crust. Blade-sharp edges, horns and teeth scraped his skin. Then came terrible pain…fire that ate flesh and seared muscle to useless filaments. His fingers numbed. He screamed and pushed deeper, all the way to his shoulder, and felt the very marrow of his being sucked dry by the ravenous bones.

A small, blunt hand touched his hair. Tahvo gave him her strength, chanting to her absent spirits, and Cian found the will to reach beyond what his body could endure.

Bones clattered. Cian's vision went dark. Tahvo pulled at his shoulders, and with a howl he yanked his arm from the voracious teeth of the dead. His shirt was in shreds, his skin bloodied and raw.

Cian sat up. Two dozen soldiers were halfway to the sand horses, their formation fracturing as they struggled to find solid ground. They lowered their long spears, ready to pierce and impale.

"I failed," Cian gasped. "There is nothing—"

"Listen." Tahvo held her breath, and Cian heard a rattle and clink like metal striking metal. The bones under his right hand leaped upright and shivered with unholy life. A man's leg bones snapped together, tottering as they joined with feet and pelvis, spine and arms and grinning head.

"They are waking," Tahvo whispered.

Cian ignored his heaving stomach and pushed Tahvo against the terrified sand horses. There was no other shelter from the horror stirring on every side. Skeletal men rose from their open graves, reaching for swords as sharp as the day they had last cut human flesh. Horses arched necks of bleached vertebrae, smashing skulls beneath narrow hooves. And there were other creatures, things made of plates and spines and far too many teeth, fitted together piece by piece like some monstrous puzzle.

Dead men and animals and monsters turned hollow eye sockets to Cian. One creature leaped out in front of the rest, snapping its tail over its pale, pitted flank. A semblance of black fur settled over its oddly graceful bones. It opened its noseless muzzle impossibly wide.

Brother, it said in Cian's mind. *Kill.*

Cian closed his eyes. Then he turned to face the Stone's warriors. They had stopped for an instant when the dead had come to life, but now they pressed forward again, unafraid.

Cian flung off his clothes and changed. Blood beat wildly in his chest and throat and ears. He filled his mind with thoughts of revenge, of bloody retribution for his people who had died, here and in Karchedon. The skeletal Ailu came to crouch at his side. They leaped as one.

Metal scraped under Cian's claws as he dodged the thrusting spear of his chosen prey. The ghostly Ailu batted at a soldier's head as if it were an infant's plaything. Warriors built of naked bone hacked at limbs and helmeted heads in eerie silence. Monsters rattled spines, clamping massive jaws on greaves and armbands, crushing bronze and iron like brittle papyrus.

Cian lost himself as he had done at the last battle in Karchedon. The taste of enemy blood washed away all that was human. The dead were more real than the living. The living must be destroyed. Chaos ruled the world, and Cian laughed.

He laughed while the soldiers were slaughtered, one by one. He laughed as the skin was stripped from their bones to feed the legions of death. He laughed when their stinking corpses collapsed to join the ranks of the long-lost fallen. He could not stop laughing even when nothing of the soldiers remained and the skeleton army turned, unsated, to the only creatures that still drew breath.

Warm air ruffled the fur of Cian's shoulder. Tahvo knelt beside him, her fingers locked in the heavy pelt behind his ears.

"Come back, Cian," she said. "We must leave now."

He growled and snapped toward her hand, but she didn't let go. The dead ones moved closer. The Ailu clacked its teeth, and the man-creatures behind it hungrily stretched fleshless fingers.

"There is too much evil here," Tahvo said. "They hate all that lives, and they will kill us."

They cannot kill a god, Cian thought, but his mouth would not form the words. He changed to human form, and the hundred cuts on his body bled afresh.

Pain did what Tahvo could not. Cian stared at the red-streaked human hands, wondering if they belonged to him. Gods could be wounded. They could die.

"Cian!"

He stared into the woman's silver-blind eyes. The hump-backed beasts sank to their knees and moaned impatiently.

Cian grabbed Tahvo's arm and shoved her toward her mount. He lifted her up over its rump, made sure she had a firm hold on its fur, and ran to catch his own beast. The sand horse lurched up under him almost before he gained his seat. Earth rumbled.

As one the beasts galloped up the slope, scattering bones like pebbles. The skeleton soldiers pursued. Cian and Tahvo mounted the rim of the crater, and their sand horses bellowed as the sand rippled like tossing waves. The silent scream of a thousand dead voices exploded from the crater.

Cian glanced over his shoulder in time to see a funnel of bone and sand shoot up from the pit behind them, ripping the grotesque creatures apart with its fury. Arrows of slivered bone hissed past Cian's ears. Sand stung his eyes, blinding him. An indescribable wail shrilled in his ears, the lament of beings who would never again know life or light. Cian's mount stumbled as the earth gave one final, agonized heave.

Then there was silence. The beasts slowed as if they had exhausted their strength, snorting and panting. Cian reached out, feeling for Tahvo's mount. His fingers clutched at dust-laden cloth.

Tahvo caught his hand and squeezed it. Together they dismounted, legs trembling, and gazed back the way they had come.

Dust and wind settled, leaving behind an unbroken expanse of sand where the crater had lain. The hungry dead were gone, along with their Stonebound enemies, every last bone sucked into the maw of the earth.

"It is over," Tahvo whispered. She felt Cian's arm. "You are hurt."

"It's nothing." He shivered. "There may be others waiting for us."

Tahvo tore a strip of cloth from the hem of her shirt and tied it around Cian's forearm. "The beasts will take us home."

Home. No such place existed for any of them. But he and Tahvo had survived another day.

"Let's ride," he said.

Yseul stared into the slight depression where the bone pit had been, where the Children had gone to do battle with an Ailu, a blind healer and a pair of ugly riding beasts. The bones were gone, and so were the Children. Not one drop of blood remained.

She had underestimated Cian. She had made the decision to leave the vicinity of the Amazi camp to follow him and the female, waiting for the moment when they would be alone and at their most vulnerable. But Farkas had grown impatient. He had ordered all but a dozen of the Children to attack, certain that the vestiges of the Stone's sorcery would be enough to defeat the enemy.

He had been wrong. Cian had drawn upon the power of his ancestors, and it had been enough to rouse the Stone-killed dead to a fury of mindless destruction. The Children had fallen. Now the few that survived stared at the new-made grave of their brethren with a look in their eyes that almost hinted of rebellion.

Yseul dared not hope that those who spied for Baalshillek would be among the dead.

She turned from the crater and stared the way her enemy had

gone. He would return to the Amazi camp and warn his allies of the attack. There was no stopping him when the Children had just suffered such a grievous loss. The survivors must be used carefully, and only when their sacrifice would win a certain victory.

"What now?" Urho asked.

Yseul glanced from the pale-haired shaman to Farkas, who brooded in angry silence. "Indeed," she said. "What now that Farkas has lost us two-thirds of our troops?"

Farkas snarled wordlessly. Yseul smiled. "Perhaps now you will listen to my counsel," she said sweetly.

Urho grunted and drained the last drops from his water skin. "What do you suggest?"

"You are not rash like our brother. You understand that we can make no more mistakes. That is why we will find the nearest spring and you, Farkas and the Children will remain there while I return to the Amazi camp."

"Alone?" Farkas snapped.

"I can travel more quickly than the horses, and with greater discretion than a larger party. We must know what the seekers intend, and then we must hinder them in any way we can."

"Hinder but not destroy," Urho said.

"Precisely." She bent closer. "A time will come when our enemies will be weak, but we must be patient. You will control Farkas while I am gone." Her tongue flicked against the lobe of his ear. "I can trust you, Urho."

He breathed out harshly. "I do not trust *you*, woman."

She laughed. "How far have you progressed with your control over your Element?"

"I can find water."

"Excellent. Continue to hone your powers, my friend. Perhaps we shall need them when I return."

Chapter Eleven

Karchedon

The lower city and harbor were exactly as Quintus remembered them. Below the citadel of palace and temple, all the world was in perfect order. Shopkeepers and bakers, cloth dyers and laborers went about their work with serene and smiling efficiency. Shoppers at the market murmured to each other but never haggled over prices; women congregated at the fountains to fill their amphorae but seldom paused to gossip. Not a single beggar, cripple or petty thief worked the streets or the agora.

There was no obvious reason for such unnatural calm. The soldiers and priests, who watched for deviants or troublemakers, did not worry the Stonebound populace. Nothing could pierce their impenetrable facade of contentment.

Nothing save for Festival, and that Quintus could not forget no matter how many times his aristocratic companions extolled the wonders of Karchedon. He looked into the blank eyes of a fruit vendor and saw the mindless, snarling mask of a killer; he regarded the pretty face of a docile servant and recalled a wild-haired female, blood spattered on her smooth cheek, tearing with nails like claws at the unprotected flesh of a lame child.

He could not forget those things any more than he could forget that tonight was his last chance to set Buteo free before he was given to Baalshillek.

"My lord," Hylas said, lightly touching Quintus's arm. "Will you not look at the ships?"

Quintus came back to himself and focused on the vessels in the harbor. There were hundreds, ranging in size from tiny fishing boats to the evil black ships, casting shadows over their lesser brethren like gods among scurrying ants. But the ships to which Hylas drew Quintus's attention were of ordinary size, driven by wind and oar rather than the depraved magic of the Stone.

"You see how our emperor looks to the welfare of his people," Hylas said, pointing toward the fleet of merchant vessels being loaded with amphorae of grain, oil and wine. "His advisers and satraps send reports on those regions of the empire that have a surplus of crops and other goods. This surplus is sent to the provinces where food is scarce, where there has been starvation and drought. In this way, none are without the necessities of life."

"And does he pay the merchants and farmers from whom he takes these goods?" Quintus asked.

"Some sacrifice is required of the most prosperous citizens of the empire so that all may benefit."

Quintus laughed. "Do you truly believe this, Hylas, or is it simply what Nikodemos commanded you to tell me?"

"My lord," Hylas protested, color rising in his smooth cheeks. He glanced about at the privileged young men and women who made up Quintus's entourage, chattering as they drifted along-side the dark water. "I know that many more would suffer if not for the peace that has come with the empire."

"Peace." Quintus gestured toward the people in the wharf-side marketplace. "What do you see when you look at the common citizens of Karchedon, Hylas?"

"I see men and women unburdened by illness, hunger or fear. People who are content—"

"Because all the sick, defiant and imperfect have been given to the altars," Quintus said, choked with memory. "Because the rest are bound by the Stone."

"This is not the emperor's doing."

"But it happens with his approval…here, and everywhere the empire rules." *Even in Tiberia, once the priests succeed in putting down the rebellion.* "Have you seen Festival, Hylas?"

Hylas would not meet Quintus's eyes. "From a distance."

"Because you know what it is, and what it makes human beings become. Animals, savages, loosed from their chains for a night of madness. And Nikodemos allows this to continue."

"Because he must," Hylas said with a sudden show of temper. "Can you believe that our emperor approves of what the Stone demands?"

"I know he protects those he considers worthy," Quintus said. "You, Danae, Chares, Galatea…we are safe because we live in the citadel, free from the priests' rule, while the plebeians are forgotten."

Hylas sighed. "Not forgotten, my lord. In order to keep his advisers and generals unbound—so that he is not entirely dependent on the Temple for his administrators and armies—the emperor must make terrible choices." He lowered his voice. "It is all compromise, my lord Alexandros, until the time when such concessions are no longer necessary."

Quintus watched a beta priest and his escort of soldiers stroll along the pier. None of the merchants or their customers glanced up from their wares. "And when will that be, Hylas?

When all the world is under the emperor's control, the Stone will be too powerful to overcome."

"Not if Nikodemos has your help," Hylas whispered. "You could be the factor that guarantees victory. I had hoped…" He sucked air through his teeth. "I had hoped that by showing you the good done by the emperor, even in the face of evil, you would come to see that he is the only man capable of defying the Stone God. He alone has the strength of will and purpose to watch and wait until he has gathered every resource necessary to take back what the priests have claimed."

Quintus rubbed the deep groove between his eyes. "I have heard this before, Hylas."

"Then I beg you to listen," Hylas said. "Every one of us, none more than the emperor himself, despises what the High Priest has made of the empire. Believe that the Stonebound will be set free, and there will be true peace."

"It must be easy to have such faith when you have never suffered from the Stone's oppression."

"You think not, my lord?" Cat-eyed Galatea took Quintus's arm and drew him away from Hylas. "We have all lost something to the Stone, in spite of our emperor's favor. Hylas is no different." Her hand slid up and down Quintus's arm in a soothing caress. "You have noticed that Hylas has little of the usual interest in women."

"It has not escaped my attention," Quintus said dryly.

"Hylas had a lover in the lower city, a man who had escaped the priest's testing."

"I have no wish—"

"Do you know what it is to love, Lord Alexandros, and see the one you love torn from your arms?"

"Yes," Quintus said, snatching his arm free. "The empire took my family."

"And do you know what it is to be condemned to death because your love is forbidden?" Her eyes glistened with anger and sorrow. "The priests give to the Stone God any man,

woman or child who does not submit to their order. They
deemed Hylas's lover defective because he failed to conform to
the accepted ways of men and women. When Hylas learned
that the priests had exposed Danel, he begged the emperor to
intervene."

"Did he?"

"At great risk of the High Priest's wrath. Nikodemos sent soldiers to escort Danel to the citadel, but it was the night of Festival, and they could not find him. Hylas endangered his own
life to search for his lover. But they were reunited only when
Hylas found Danel dying in the street, torn apart by the mob."

Quintus stopped, his throat thick and tight. "I understand
why Hylas has no sympathy for the common people."

"Danel was a commoner, Lord Alexandros. Hylas knows
what they suffer. Many of us came to Karchedon to petition the
emperor on behalf of the people in our own homelands, and
we remained with him willingly when we recognized his true
greatness." She met Quintus's gaze. "I lived in Aigyptos. I saw
what the Stone priests did to the ancient gods of Khemet and
any who dared worship them. The emperor will restore what
the priests took away from us. We would die for him."

Quintus shook his head, but he could not deny Galatea's passion. She and Hylas were not merely posturing sycophants
eager to win their lord's favor by bringing the emperor's brother
into the fold. They were believers, as devoted to Nikodemos as
the priests were to their One True God.

Galatea led Quintus back to join the others in their return
to the citadel. Gently angled winter sunlight gave the day a
cheerful cast, sullied only by the beams emitted by the obelisk
atop the great Temple of the Stone. Quintus walked ahead,
desperate for a chance to think.

If he allowed his suspicions to run away with him, he might
have believed that today's excursion to the fruitful Karchedonian countryside, and then to the harbor with its laden ships,
had been undertaken only to turn his thoughts from the Tibe-

rian prisoner in Nikodemos's dungeon. He and Danae hadn't spoken in the two days since their visit to Briga's dormitory, when Quintus had asked for her help in learning more about Buteo's capture and ultimate fate. She must know Quintus would not forget that he'd found a means to set the rebel free.

He had thought of little else, by day or night. Now his time was nearly up.

He reached the citadel gates and strode through, ignoring the salutes of the guards. They treated him like the emperor's brother, a man of power and influence. A man who might turn the tide on the Stone God's rule. And he could risk it all with one toss of the dice, testing Tiberian courage and conviction against the feast of possibilities his newly discovered Alexandrian blood laid out before him.

You have come too far to turn back now....

Soldiers cut across Quintus's path, marching in lockstep with a bound prisoner in their midst. The prisoner turned his head as he passed, cool eyes locking on Quintus's. The eyes widened in shock and recognition. Lips moved to form a single word.

Quintus.

Then the soldiers and the prisoner were gone. Quintus stood frozen, his heart slamming against his ribs. He knew that face.

Buteo. Leader of Tiberian rebels, patrician, soldier. A man who had sacrificed everything to fight the empire. Who had held Quintus captive for four years, waiting for the ideal moment to strike with the most powerful weapon in Tiberian hands.

"My lord," Hylas said. "Are you well?"

Quintus shook himself and continued toward the palace. "Perfectly well," he said.

Hylas stared after the soldiers and ran to catch up with Quintus. "If you are not too weary, my lord, there is something more I would show you."

Quintus almost dismissed Hylas before he remembered what Galatea had said of the courtier's loss. "What is it, Hylas?"

"Patience, my lord." He turned to speak briefly with his

friends, bade them farewell and took possession of Quintus's arm. He led the way into the palace and the emperor's wing, where most of Nikodemos's Hetairoi kept their rooms. They entered a courtyard with which Quintus was not familiar, desolate and bare of greenery or fountain.

In the center of the courtyard stood a pedestal surmounted by the head and shoulders of a man, sculpted in marble and painted in lifelike tones from golden hair to piercing gray eyes. It was a hero's face, handsome and noble, but that was not what made Quintus stare. Save for the color of the hair and a few small, Quintus might have been looking at his own reflection.

"Your eyes do not deceive you," Hylas said. "This is your uncle, Alexandros, founder of the empire."

Alexandros the Mad, Quintus thought. He studied the sculpture with a shiver of unease. "When Nikodemos first came for me in the Temple he said he had never seen Alexandros."

"Not in the flesh, of course," Hylas said. "Yet he knew you for his brother as soon as he saw you."

No one who had seen this likeness could doubt the kinship, but the bust was hidden away where few would view it, and then only those loyal to the emperor.

"Nikodemos often comes here to contemplate his uncle's deeds," Hylas said.

"And you brought me here to remind me who I am."

"More than that, my lord." Hylas touched the perfectly shaped curls of Alexandros's hair with gentle reverence. "They called him 'The Mad' because near the end of his life he turned his back on the vast territories he had conquered and fled to his home in Makedonia. At the peak of his power, he retired to a life of solitude and would see no one, not even his most trusted generals. Only the loyalty of his troops kept his spear-won territories from falling into the hands of rivals and enemies."

"But he was not mad?"

Hylas smiled sadly. "He was the one who discovered the

Stone, recognized its power and moved it from the Great Desert. He founded the priesthood, little knowing what he had begun. And he carried a piece of the Stone, as the priests do now. It was this that drove him to insanity. He recognized that he lacked the strength to hold the Stone's influence at bay and took his own life rather than become a slave to the Stone God."

Quintus stared into the statue's tranquil eyes. "How do you know this?"

"Alexandros left a papyrus to Arrhidaeos, declaring that he had committed a terrible error in releasing the Stone. But Arrhidaeos ignored his brother's warnings. He let the priests take even more power, so that he could maintain control over Alexandros's empire." Hylas moved closer to Quintus, his voice low and urgent. "Nikodemos had no choice but to arrange for Arrhidaeos's death. His father was becoming a puppet king, as Alexandros would have been. Only Nikodemos saw this clearly. But he was forced to invade Tiberia in order to distract the priests and soothe their fears of rebellion."

"My people did not agree to make such a sacrifice."

"Would they have refused if they knew their suffering might check the Stone's power on the earth?"

Quintus turned away, remembering the brave and stoic Tiberians who had given their lives in the fight for freedom. There had been times when he hated them for their harsh judgment of anything they perceived as weakness…hated the rebels for refusing to let him wield a sword in Tiberia's defense, hated Buteo for holding him captive. They had rejected him even without knowing he was not of their blood.

"You could be the new Alexandros," Hylas whispered, his breath warm on Quintus's ear. "Not the Mad, but the Great. Alexandros the Great…"

Quintus bolted from the courtyard. After several wrong turns he found his way back to his own rooms. He paced the tiled floor for the remaining hours of daylight, rejecting the food servants brought to him. Danae did not come, and even Hylas stayed away. Midnight passed before Quintus fell into an exhausted sleep, tossing and turning on his luxurious couch.

And he dreamed.

"Remove his hood."

Hard, brisk hands whisked the cowl from Quintus's head. He blinked, his eyes adjusting to the darkness.

A group of men stood before him, men he knew only by their voices and the bynames they gave each other. Hoods shadowed their faces. Illumination came from a single torch bracketed to the curving wall. The heavy scent of wet stone and earth filled Quintus's nose, along with the sweat of men long in hiding.

"Corvinus."

The voice came from the depths of a hood like all the others, but Quintus could not mistake its authority. This man was the leader called Buteo, the one to whom he must prove himself.

"You have come to the end of your journey," Buteo said, the edges of his cowl fluttering with each breath. "Either you will leave this place as one of us, or leave not at all."

"I agreed to your terms," Quintus said. "It was I who came to you."

"Yes." Buteo signaled with an upraised hand. His sleeve fell back to reveal a battle-scarred wrist and long, capable fingers.

He was a veteran of the Invasion, like most of the rebels—men of all classes who had set aside their differences to defend Tiberia against overwhelming odds. So many of them had fallen. So many were slaves to the Stone God, helpless as children.

Quintus had been too young to fight in the War. He had been hunting high in the mountains the day Corvinium fell. He had seen the smoke, heard screams like the calls of birds across the valley. The Stone God's priests had done their work by the time he scrambled down to the village, legs and arms scored with cuts and bruises in a mockery of battle wounds honorably won.

His father and brothers had died defending Corvinium. He had been left with the ashes.

"You seek revenge," Buteo said. "We seek no less than the destruction of our enemy, no matter what the cost." He took a step forward, radiating the force of banked rage and power. "You will surrender all personal desires to our cause…if you survive the test."

Quintus stood very straight. "I will do what must be done."

"We shall see." Buteo inclined his head. A man came forward, bent with age. A wiry fringe of white beard projected from the jet oval of his hood.

"The auspicia are favorable," he said.

The wall of men about Corvinus broke apart. Just beyond them lay a pedestal and, upon that, a featureless wooden box. Light came from the box—not the hot, clean brilliance of fire, but a pulsing crimson, like blood.

Quintus knew what it was. His stomach knotted and tried to expel its meager contents.

Coward. Would you surrender now, when the sword is all but in your hand?

"The augur will conduct the initiation," Buteo said, unmoved. "You will not speak again until permission is given."

Quintus bit his lower lip and stared at the box. The augur shook his sleeves away from palsied hands and spoke words of ritual, summoning Tiberia's forbidden gods. He trembled so violently that his hood slipped away from his forehead, revealing brows heavy as sheep's wool. He thrust his hand inside the box.

A strange little sound came from his throat. He gripped a small object between his thumb and forefinger as if it were something vile.

A ring. A ring that shed unnatural radiance, bright enough to paint dark cloaks with splashes of red.

The augur lifted the ring. Its faceted stone shone in Quintus's eyes, compelling all his attention.

"This ring was bought with many lives," Buteo said. "It will decide your fate."

Even had he wished to run, Quintus could not have moved.

His legs had become marble pillars sunk into the cave's floor. The augur approached, flanked on either side by the rebel fighters. The ring's luminescence seemed to shine through the flesh of the old man's hand, exposing muscle and bone. Crimson filled Quintus's vision. A sword's edge of pain cleaved his skull. He cried out.

As if driven to expiate his shameful weakness, his legs refused to give way. He bore the agony, and his imagination turned the sinister light into a thousand javelins thrown by a mortal enemy's hand. He raised his shield. The javelins struck and rebounded from good Tiberian oak. The enemy screamed in rage.

Quintus braced for another attack. There was only silence.

"Hold him," Buteo said.

Had he failed? Quintus struggled to clear his vision. The red light had vanished. The hush was so profound that Quintus could hear water dripping deep in the earth.

Buteo held the ring in his cupped palm. Dull gold caught the firelight. He turned it about so that the stone was visible to all.

What had been bright was now cracked and dull, as if it were common glass struck by a blacksmith's hammer.

"It is not possible," the augur whispered.

Buteo dropped the ring into the box and closed the lid. "Consult your auspicia again, pater." He raised his hands to his hood and pushed it back. "Quintus Horatius Corvinus. Do you know what you have done?"

"I have passed your test."

"You have destroyed it."

It was neither accusation nor praise, but the soldier's words filled Quintus with dread. They must not reject him now.

"I offer apology," he said stiffly. "Tell me where to find another and I will bring it to you."

Buteo's face froze in astonishment, and then he began to laugh.

"Silence!" The augur pushed forward, his quavering voice gaining strength. "If the gods have spoken at last—"

"He has ruined our only means of testing," a new voice said. "He could be an agent for the priests."

A rumble of agreement echoed through the chamber. Buteo raised his hand. "The priests would surely not permit such a man to live," he said. "He might become a powerful weapon against the empire."

"You see clearly, Buteo," the auger said. "This one must be protected."

"I have no need of protection," Quintus protested. "Let me fight beside you and I will destroy every stone in Tiberia, in all Italia."

Both men stared at Quintus, and their eyes held an emotion he had almost forgotten.

Hope.

"Do not let him go," the augur said. "The gods will tell us when and how he is to be used. Until then—"

"Until then," Buteo repeated. "I understand."

Quintus also began to understand. "*No.* I came to fight. Only show me what I must do."

Buteo shook his head. The soldier's men closed in around Quintus, a cage of bodies hard as iron.

"'Tiberia has no children,'" Buteo quoted softly. "You are no longer boy nor man, Quintus Horatius Corvinus, but a gift of the gods. Will you swear the sacred oath to serve Tiberia, to obey without question, to give your life for the cause of freedom?"

Corvinus reached for the sword they had taken from him and clenched his fists on empty air. "I will see the Arrhidaean Empire fall," he said, "even if I must tear it down with my own hands."

A muffled stillness fell within the cave, as if someone had shaken out a vast shroud of black linen. The torches flickered and shrank to near embers.

Buteo's eyes narrowed to slits in his sunburned face. "I believe you will," he said. "But not yet."

* * *

Not yet.

Quintus cast off his furs and sat up on the couch, breathing hard. He wiped the perspiration from his upper lip and went to the window.

The world was silent. The red beams of the obelisk pierced the darkness, but no priests stirred in the vast square between Palace and Temple.

Quintus threw on a woolen chiton and listened at the door. He opened it with care, watching, hearing nothing but the splash of the courtyard fountain.

Go, his heart insisted. He shut off the rational protests of his mind and stepped out into the corridor. As with every night since Nikodemos's feast, his room was unguarded. He called into memory the route he had memorized on his venture with Danae, retracing their steps to the abandoned section of the palace and the room with its secret entrance. Not so much as a mouse crossed his path.

He slipped into the room and pressed the wall to open the hidden portal. The dank smell of the tunnel took him back to the cave in the dream, and he paused on the threshold, shaking with mingled fear and pride, like the boy he had been nearly five years ago.

I am Tiberian.

He closed the portal with the weight of his body and felt his way along the tunnel to the first torch. He counted them as he passed, took the side passages Danae had shown him and slowed his pace to a near-crawl. Disembodied sounds echoed from invisible chambers behind the tunnel wall. He stopped a hundred paces short of the last torch before the portal to the dungeon, clinging to the darkness with sweat-damp palms.

This was the moment of decision. He had always known there was a strong possibility that his learning of Buteo's capture and imprisonment was an elaborate ruse, a deliberate attempt to catch him in an act of treason, with Danae as an unwitting pawn laying the trap. When he opened the portal he would commit himself in a way that might destroy any future chance of using his power under the emperor's aegis. If it was a ploy to expose him and he failed, Nikodemos would never trust him again.

The gods knew he had no cause to love Buteo, who had imprisoned a naïve, grieving boy for four lonely years. But Buteo was badly needed in Tiberia, where he had the love and loyalty of his people.

Hylas had said that Nikodemos had been compelled to invade Tiberia to distract the priests and soothe their fears of rebellion. He had asked if Tiberia would have agreed to bear the invasion if her suffering might check the Stone's power. Would not Buteo, too, be willing to give up his own life to save the rebels' greatest hope?

Quintus laughed silently. Such justification made him no better than Nikodemos. If he turned away now—if he agreed with Hylas that the greater good must be served by his concession to his brother's subtle schemes for the Stone God's undoing—then he would lose any right to call himself Tiberian. He would live with the knowledge that he had chosen not to save a man who had made his youth a misery. And he would forever wonder if his decision came of wisdom…or simply of the desire to preserve his own life.

He closed his eyes and laid his hands against the portal. Push or walk away. Become the reckless youth once more, or assume his brother's mantle and sacrifice his soul for a future of patient, brutal intrigue.

I am my brother, he thought with distant horror, and turned away from the wall. With halting steps he left the portal, dragging the chains of self-loathing behind him.

An arm snatched at him from the darkness. He spun on his heel, striking out with all his strength. Quintus grabbed a handful of cloth and threw the cloaked figure against the wall. He tore the hood from his enemy's head.

Hylas shrank from his fist, the courtier's eyes black pools of fear and determination. "My lord," he gasped.

Quintus released him. "What in Hades's name are you doing here?"

"Danae told me of the tunnels and your previous visit. She believes that someone has been watching her, and feared that you might attempt to set the Tiberian rebel free." He felt for Quintus's shoulder. "Come with me now, I beg you."

Quintus choked on his own laughter. "Your intervention was unnecessary, Hylas."

"My lord?"

Quintus took the courtier's elbow and steered him toward the tunnel exit. "Danae believes this to be a trap set by Nikodemos?"

"If there is a trap, surely it is the work of the High Priest himself."

Quintus felt no joy knowing he had been wise in his decision to abandon Buteo. "It seems that Baalshillek will miss his prey this night," he said grimly. "What more did Danae tell you?"

"Only that you should return to your room at once, my lord." He pushed ahead of Quintus through the portal into the empty room, found the way clear and gestured for Quintus to follow.

They made their way unhindered back to Quintus's rooms, where Hylas left him. Quintus slumped to the floor at the foot of his couch. There was no going back. Unless he could find some extraordinarily clever means of convincing Nikodemos to spare Buteo, the rebel leader was as good as dead.

Quintus spent what remained of the night turning a thousand improbable plans over and over in his head. Dawn brought no promise of redemption, nor any word that his clandestine activities had been discovered. Halfway through the next day, after he had declined two meals and refused all other visitors, Philokrates came to his door.

The old man hadn't changed in the weeks since Quintus last saw him. He stood in the doorway, white hair wild and beard untrimmed, waiting for his former pupil to embrace or reject him.

Quintus sighed and got to his feet. "So," he said, "should I call you Philokrates or Talos?"

Philokrates bowed his head. "The man once known as Talos has been dead for many years," he said. "It was never my intention to restore him to life."

"But your past was exposed by the rebels. Didn't you expect—" Quintus broke off and glanced at the door.

"We will not be overheard," Philokrates said. "I have been asking to see you since Nikodemos took you from Baalshillek. They would not permit it until today, but now it seems we may speak freely."

Because the emperor has nothing to fear from either one of us. Quintus sat at the table, his legs suddenly too unsteady to support him. "Did you ever intend to tell me the truth?" he asked.

Philokrates took the chair opposite Quintus, groaning softly at some ache in his aged bones. "I did not betray you, my son."

"Didn't you?"

"I did not expect to be recognized, at least not among the Karchedonian rebels. I considered the small risk worth taking."

Quintus stared at the table between them. "Why did you come to Karchedon?"

"I thought I might be of assistance to you and learn more of the prophecies—"

"You knew who I was from the beginning," Quintus interrupted. "You chose not to warn me. If I had known—"

"You would never have believed me. Just as you would not have believed I was Talos. The very idea that you were not of Tiberian blood, that you could be of the imperial house…" He poured a cup of stale wine, sniffed it and set it down again. His fingers trembled. "I could not keep you from coming to Karchedon. I hoped…I hoped that if you should fall into enemy hands, I could make use of my former identity to gain the emperor's ear."

"And you saved my life." Quintus snatched up the cup. The wine was bitter on his tongue. "You knew that Nikodemos would accept me as his brother."

"No. But I knew that Baalshillek would eventually break or kill you." He raised his hand, forestalling Quintus's protest. "I also knew that Nikodemos would object to leaving such power as yours in the hands of the High Priest."

"And now you have given me more power than I dreamed possible."

"Power to change the fate of the world."

Quintus knocked the empty cup from the table. "But not to save my countrymen," he said. "Not to set a single fighter free."

Philokrates bent stiffly to pick up the cup, turning it around in his wrinkled hands. "I heard something of this Buteo," he said. "He was one of those who held you captive in Tiberia, was he not?"

"Yes."

"And you broke your oath to serve Tiberia without question. You escaped. You chose your own path, as Buteo chose his."

Quintus jumped up from his chair. "What if he came here to find me?"

"Then he knew what he gambled by entering Karchedon. Honor him for his courage, Quintus, but do not blame yourself for being what you are."

"A traitor."

"A man torn by conflicting loyalties," Philokrates said. His voice broke. "Do you think I do not understand? Perhaps you have heard that Talos was a creator of terrible machines of war made to crush the empire's enemies. You have reason to despise such a man. Yet Talos recognized his error and attempted to leave the life he had grown to hate." He rubbed at his eyes. "He did not succeed, yet if his rebirth helped spare young Alexandros for his destiny, then perhaps the guilt is a small price to pay."

"My destiny." Quintus gazed unseeing at the small, bright square of his window. "What more do you know that you haven't told me?"

Philokrates shivered and wrapped his arms around his narrow chest. "What did Baalshillek tell you when you were in the temple?"

Savage memory shook Quintus in its merciless jaws. "He spoke of one called the Annihilator. And the 'Reborn.'"

"It is what he most fears," Philokrates said. "He must believe that you are the prophesied Annihilator…the one who can destroy the Exalted."

Nikodemos believes it, as well, Quintus thought. "If Baalshillek is so certain, why does he let me live?"

"Because he is not yet ready to overthrow the secular government of the empire. But make no mistake…you must be always on your guard. If Baalshillek can turn the emperor against you, he will do so. You must keep that victory from him, my son."

The victory he might have won last night. Quintus pounded his fist against the wall. "Then you would have me submit to Nikodemos."

"I would have you survive. Nikodemos is your best protector until you have found your path."

"And what of those who traveled with us, old man? What of Cian, the Watcher of whom your prophecies spoke so highly? Who protects them, now that they have escaped the city?"

Philokrates slumped in his chair. "She called them 'godborn,'" he murmured.

"Who?"

"Tahvo. Before she and her companions left Karchedon, she came to me here, in the palace, by magical means. She said the daimones had spoken to her. She asked me to give her all the knowledge of the prophecies I had gathered in my years of study." He released a long breath. "All I had recorded in my memory device, my mnemosyne, I gave to her. That was the last I heard of our friends, but I know Tahvo did not waste the gift. I pray they find what they seek."

Quintus dropped onto the couch. "Now that you have determined the roles each of us is to play, what of you? Will you make more machines for Nikodemos?"

Philokrates flinched, twisting the folds of his chiton in gnarled fingers. "I must not alienate the emperor if I am to be of use to you. But I will not create more weapons of death."

"How can you avoid it?"

He closed his eyes. "When I fled Arrhidaeos's court, knowing fully what I had done, I could think of nothing but my shame. But it was not my own heart that made me see the error of my ways. There was a woman, Quintus. A woman of great beauty and courage who showed me how my devotion to my own creations had turned me into a murderer."

Quintus stared at Philokrates. "A woman?"

"Even I once knew love." He chuckled, the sound raw and filled with pain. "She was…exceptional, the only female who could force me to look beyond my inventions. Once she had opened my eyes, there was no returning to what I had been. But when I decided to leave Karchedon and the court, I believed she would be better off remaining behind than risking her life in defiance of the emperor." Tears seeped into his eyes. "I know now that she was given in sacrifice to the Stone God, and I curse myself every moment of my life for failing her. That is why I will not build even a single new device for the emperor."

Quintus walked over to the old man and rested his hand on the frail shoulder. "I am sorry, Philokrates. If I can help you—"

"My fate is ultimately of no importance. But you, my boy…you must find a way to use your position here for the world's benefit. Never allow yourself to forget your true purpose. You will face many temptations in the court, as I did. Many trials await you. But you will not fail. And you will not lose faith."

Quintus laughed. "What *faith,* Philokrates?"

"In yourself." Philokrates covered Quintus's hand with his own. "You face one danger even greater than Baalshillek, my son, and that is your pride. Your power is great, and so must be your self-control."

"I am still—" *Tiberian,* Quintus had been about to say. But that was no longer true. "I won't forget, old man."

Philokrates blinked rapidly. "Lend me your arm."

Quintus helped Philokrates rise and walked him to the door. "We'll talk again," the philosopher said. "For as long as I live, you are not alone, my son." He turned to clasp Quintus's hand. "Remain steadfast at all costs."

"I will. I swear I'll shake the very foundations of this empire."

Philokrates laid his hand on Quintus's cheek. "Patience, my son. Patience, humility and caution." He turned and hobbled through the door, an old soul bent under the burdens of two separate lives.

Patience. Quintus closed the door and drank the last of the wine directly from the jar. Patience was all he had left…that and the memory of what he had sacrificed for survival.

I will avenge you, Buteo. I will see the Arrhidaean Empire fall, even if I must tear it down with my own hands.

"Your agents have returned from Attika, my lord."

Baalshillek looked up from the papyri spread across the table, banking his rage at the interruption. Orkos had the sense to speak plainly, unlike the foolish omega priest whose physical shell and psyche had fed the Stone's fire not an hour past.

The priest had badly misjudged his master's mood, which had been foul ever since Quintus Horatius Corvinus evaded the trap laid for him the night before. That failure had been vexing enough, but it was not quite the disaster it might have been. Not while Buteo remained the Temple's secret captive. Baalshillek had no intention of sacrificing a tool that might still prove of use, even if he must wait many months to set the bait anew.

No, Quintus's narrow escape had not been the worst of the news that had come to Baalshillek that morning. He had just discovered that the simulacra he had created to hinder the god-born—creatures so carefully shaped to match the Bearers' power—had blundered in their attack on the Ailu and the Northern priestess. The fools had not only thrown away the lives of two dozen Children, but they had utterly wasted the residual power that lingered in the Stone's former prison.

At least the Stone's Child who served as Baalshillek's spy among the simulacra still lived and would continue to serve as his master's eyes for as long as he survived. Even so, Baalshillek had begun to doubt how well the simulacra would carry out their mission. They had yet to master their elemental powers. Yseul had held much promise, and clearly she was the cleverest of the three. But she had also proven to be unpredictable.

Perhaps he had given his creations too much free will. But if he had made them like the Children, unquestioningly obedient and single-minded in their duty, they would be neither clever nor adaptable enough to meet the challenges ahead of them.

Baalshillek crumpled the sheet of papyrus under his hand. It seemed increasingly possible that his simulacra might betray him. But even if he must take other measures to acquire the Weapons, the Exalted must never know that their High Priest intended to take them for himself.

Just as they must never realize the threat Quintus presented. Not until he was completely subject to Baalshillek's will.

Or dead.

Baalshillek snapped his reed pen between his fingers and flung the pieces to the floor. "What do you have for me, Orkos?"

The commander of the Temple Guard gestured to the Children in the doorway. Two soldiers half carried an elderly man into Baalshillek's chamber and let him slump to the floor.

"They found this man," Orkos said. "He was a servant in the household of the elder Corvinus before the conquest, and he knew the one who once called himself Philokrates."

Baalshillek rose and walked around the table. The old slave trembled, fixing his blank gaze on Baalshillek's feet. "You have questioned him?" Baalshillek asked.

"Yes, my lord, to determine how much he knew. Talos confided something of his past to this slave. It was understood that you would wish to question him yourself."

"You've done well, Orkos." Baalshillek crouched and caught the old man's chin in his hand. "What is your name?"

"Aetes," the slave whispered.

"Have they told you who I am?"

The old man squeezed his eyes shut and nodded.

"You served in the household of Horatius Corvinus in Tiberia?"

"Yes...my lord."

Baalshillek stroked the slave's bruised and wasted cheek. "Your time of suffering is almost ended, Aetes. Only a little more pain, and then it is finished."

Spittle dripped from the corner of the slave's mouth. "No," he croaked. "I beg you..."

Baalshillek seized the man's head in one hand and his pendant with the other. Heat radiated from the red stone, turning the gold setting into a burning brand that would have damaged the flesh of a lesser being. It barely warmed Baalshillek's fingers.

"Open to me," he said gently. "Give your thoughts to me, Aetes. Accept the peace of the Stone."

The slave keened through clenched teeth. Blue veins pulsed in his temple. His eyes rolled up behind his lids. Baalshillek pierced the common mind as if it were made of the softest curd, sifting through a lifetime of ordinary memories with no regard for the damage his search left behind. The stone lit his way. When he found what he sought, he curled imaginary fingers and scooped it out like pulp from an overripe fruit.

The man's body collapsed, stripped of what had made it human. Not even enough psyche remained to make it of use as a sacrifice. Orkos signaled his men to take the empty husk away.

Baalshillek rose, leaning on the table as he returned to the world. "Hyberborea," he murmured.

"My lord?" Orkos said.

"You may go."

Orkos bowed and left the room. Baalshillek listened to the stirrings of the gods inside his head.

Hyperborea, Ag said. *Who?*

Baalshillek surrendered to the Exalted's bidding and walked the long tunnels under the temple to the sanctum of the Stone. He dismissed the attendant priests and stood before the glowing rock, bathing his icy body in its perpetual fire.

He summoned the Exalted of the Elements and asked them what they knew of the Hyperborea. He listened while they told him of the hidden land far to the North, the country whose veil of magic even they had never penetrated. They spoke of the great machines that kept the ice at bay, of mages who were said to rival the gods in their power, who could manipulate time itself.

Time. Baalshillek smiled, and Ag perceived the direction of his thoughts. The High Priest spent the next hour placating the eight gods who incessantly demanded to be set free from the crystal that bound them.

That time was not yet. But today it had come closer. Today Baalshillek had knowledge shared by only one other living mortal. And that mortal would serve the Stone. He would build his machines, but not for something as trivial as mere victory on the battlefield.

Baalshillek left the sanctum and consciously blocked the Exalted from his mind. He shared much with them, but not all. They believed their High Priest would grant them free reign over the earth when they claimed their newmade, perfect bodies. But they also believed that their human servants would be content to let them divide the world between them, reducing all that lived to the Elements of Earth, Air, Fire and Water. When they had finished the transformation, nothing that remained would bear any resemblance to what had come before.

Baalshillek had no intention of dying for his gods. Their power would be his…his to turn on the men and nations who clung to their foolish dreams of freedom. When the Exalted walked the earth again, they would be under one man's control—the sole mortal who could master the lords of the Stone and wield their magic in the service of perfect order.

And nothing Quintus Horatius Corvinus could do would stop him.

Chapter Twelve

Rhenna was first to see movement on the horizon. She squinted against the glare of afternoon sunlight and urged her mount to the top of the sand hill. A few moments later Nyx rode up to join her.

"They have returned," Nyx said, her voice ragged with relief.

Rhenna disguised her own emotions, but her heart pounded as her Amazi mare raced down the hill and across the flat. Indistinct shapes, shimmering with waves of heat, became two long-legged sand horses with humans perched atop their steeply sloping backs. Rhenna had her waterskin in hand by the time she reached Cian and Tahvo.

Her impatient questions died in her throat when she saw Tahvo's drawn, exhausted face and the makeshift bandage tied around Cian's forearm. She dismounted and thrust the waterskin at Tahvo, ignoring the irritable snap of the sand horse's broad yellow teeth. Tahvo clutched the skin and drank, hands trembling.

Nyx was at Cian's side by the time Tahvo had finished. His mount sank to its knees with a groan, and Nyx helped him to the ground.

"You're injured," she accused.

Cian met Rhenna's eyes over Nyx's head. "Not badly," he said. "But Tahvo is very tired. We must get her back to camp."

Madele arrived, along with several of her warriors. She addressed Nyx.

"Madele asks how you received these injuries," Nyx said. "And *I* ask why you left without a word of explanation."

Cian sighed and rubbed the dirt from his face. "The thing you must know now is that we are not alone in this desert. Our enemies have found us."

"Who?" Rhenna asked.

"The High Priest's soldiers. Two dozen attacked us, but there may be more."

Nyx translated for Madele, who spoke sharply to her followers. Two kicked their mounts into a run back to the City. The rest closed in around the sand horses, faces hard and javelins at the ready.

Rhenna rode between Cian and Tahvo, her nose full of the heavy odors of beasts, dried blood and human sweat. "I am glad to see you survived," she said dryly to Cian, handing him her waterskin. "How did you manage it?"

He laughed. "With great difficulty." He drained the skin. "And with the help of my ancestors."

Rhenna arched a brow but said no more until they had reached the Amazi encampment. Tribesmen, women and children paused in their work to stare and mutter. Warriors gathered in agitated clumps. The sand horses ambled as far as the elders' tents at the center of the City, knelt to deposit their riders and set off at a swinging lope for the waterhole.

The elder Zamra emerged from the central tent and bowed

to Cian. Nyx conveyed her invitation to take refreshment, which Cian gratefully accepted. Madele ushered him inside, while Rhenna and Nyx supported Tahvo between them.

Tahvo disregarded Rhenna's advice that she rest and insisted on looking after Cian's arm, asking the Imaziren for whatever herbs and medicines they used among themselves. A messenger ran off to fetch the tribal healer. Women brought fresh water in deep bronze bowls and built a malodorous fire of cattle dung outside the tent.

Consulting with the healer, Tahvo prepared an acrid paste of dried desert plants and unwrapped Cian's arm. His skin was raw and seeping, torn in a hundred places as if by countless tiny claws and teeth.

Rhenna hissed in sympathy. "The soldiers did this?" she asked.

Tahvo and Cian exchanged glances. "Not the soldiers," he said. "We found the original prison of the Stone."

The tent fell into a strained silence as Cian related how he and Tahvo had let the sand horses carry them into the desert, how they had found the crater of bones and faced the Karchedonian troops in a desperate fight for their lives. Cian's voice cracked when he described reaching into the ground to summon the powers of Earth and his Ailuri ancestors. Rhenna tried to imagine the bones rising to walk, lifting long-abandoned swords to do battle with men as fearless as the dead themselves.

"After the soldiers had fallen," Cian said, "the bone-warriors turned on us. We escaped, and the ground swallowed them all."

"Your doing?" Rhenna asked.

"I don't know. There is still much about this I do not understand."

"You saw no soldiers on your return?"

"None, but the ones who attacked had obviously been following us without being detected."

"If there are others near the City," Nyx said, "Madele's warriors will find them." She cast Cian a stern look. "You never told us why you went alone. It was most foolish, Watcher."

"The sand horses spoke to us," Tahvo said, tying off Cian's bandage. "They had purpose in showing us these things."

"Why should such creatures seek your deaths?"

"They knew we would not die." Tahvo felt for Nyx's arm and patted it reassuringly. "Perhaps they saw that Cian's power would come to him again."

The elder broke in, commanding Nyx's attention. "Zamra says that no man or woman of the tribe has dared approach the place of bones since the Stone was taken," Nyx translated. "The sand horses set the Guardian a test, and he has passed it. Every resource of the tribe will be put at his disposal."

Cian bowed to the elder. "Give her my thanks."

"Anything the Guardian wishes, he may have," Nyx said. "Now the elders desire that the Guardian remain with them while he recovers from his ordeal. Zamra's daughter, Madele, will serve him with her own hands." She hesitated. "The Guardian's companions should return to their tents to rest while food and fresh clothing are prepared."

Cian flushed as if he understood exactly what the Imaziren wanted of him in return for their devotion. Rhenna glanced at Madele. The Amazi warrior gazed at Cian with an intensity that made the hair bristle at the back of Rhenna's neck.

She pushed aside her anger and helped Tahvo up. Cian rose to follow. Madele held him back with a firm touch on his arm.

"Rhenna," Cian said.

She paused at the tent entrance. "You're in good hands," she said roughly. "I'll look after Tahvo." She pushed the flap aside and guided Tahvo into the cool evening air. Nyx stepped out after her.

"Do not let him stay with them," she said.

Rhenna struggled to keep all expression from her face. "If your claim on him is as strong as you believe, you have nothing to fear."

"And you?" Nyx demanded. "You would give him to Madele?"

"Are you not the one who urged me to set Cian free?"

"Not so that you could surrender him to these people."

"Cian will be of no use to anyone if he can't make his own decisions. I trust he will make the right one." Rhenna softened her voice. "We have more urgent matters to consider now, Nyx. The Stone God's soldiers are on our trail, and I doubt a single defeat will stop them."

"What would you have me do?"

"Find out how soon we can continue on our journey and what provisions the Imaziren have made to watch for our enemies."

"They already have patrols sweeping the area of the City," Nyx said. "You can be sure they will send warriors to scout ahead of any escort that accompanies us across the Great Desert."

"I wish to ride with the scouts."

"And I," Tahvo said, reminding Rhenna that she, too, had a will of her own. "I failed to sense the soldiers' approach before, but I will not make the same mistake again."

Nyx kicked at the sand. "Very well," she said. "I'll make arrangements with the senior warriors." She set off at a fast walk. Rhenna and Tahvo returned to their tent, and Rhenna attempted to sleep while the camp hummed with activity through the long night.

Before dawn the Imaziren had nearly completed preparations for a significant journey, breaking down tents and packing goathide sacks of supplies. Several teams of scouts were assembled to precede the main column of fifty warriors, servants and elders who were to escort the Guardian and his companions to Nyx's homeland in the South. The strongest horses were selected from among the impressive herd, and Rhenna chose her previous war mount, Tislit-n-unzar, to carry her again.

By the time the sun rose, she was far out in the desert with Tahvo and five other warriors—the women Cabh'a and Tamallat, and the males Berkan, Immeghar and Mezwar—riding ahead on the route the escort would follow. Though she could have pushed herself to keep up with the experienced desert riders, she was grateful that the Imaziren had set a more modest pace for Tahvo's sake.

Rhenna distracted herself through the long hours of monotonous landscape, dry mouth and burned skin by learning something of the Amazi language and teaching Hellenish to the Imaziren. Tahvo revealed to the Imaziren her spirit-born gift of tongues and joined Nyx in acting as interpreter. They conveyed to Rhenna the tribal names of the hardy plants and beasts that survived in the seemingly barren land, and patiently translated Rhenna's replies.

Pretty, light-haired Cabh'a, and Immeghar, a giant of deceptive grace, proved to be willing teachers and eager pupils. Slender Tamallat and handsome Mezwar spent most of their time riding alone together, a young man and woman who could think of little but each other. Rhenna pretended not to notice.

No sign of enemies appeared by light or darkness. It seemed that the Karchedonian soldiers had vanished. Rhenna didn't allow herself to believe it. Each day, when the outriders found shade in a stand of thorn-trees or an isolated cluster of boulders, Immeghar displayed his prowess with the javelin and taught Rhenna how to hold the light spear to best effect. She practiced the Imaziren knife-fighting techniques with Berkan, carefully observing the maneuvers she had first encountered in her duel with Madele.

She saw little of the warrior leader, Nyx or Cian. That was exactly how she wanted it. Occasionally one of the Imaziren would fall back to the main party to monitor their progress, but the scouts had little to report save that a small herd of sand horses were trailing behind the entourage, lending their blessing to the endeavor.

On the seventh day Tamallat and Mezwar returned from their patrol with grim expressions and haunted eyes. Tahvo listened to their clipped conversation with their fellow Imaziren and dropped back to ride with Rhenna, her own face drawn with worry.

"They say the water is gone," she said.

"What water, Tahvo?"

"The *amda* they expected to find within a few hours' ride. They say—" She broke off as Cabh'a joined them. The young woman spoke, and Tahvo nodded. "She says this should not be possible. It is a spring they have used for generations, always a reliable source of water and grazing for the animals. She asks us to come." Tahvo kicked her pony into a trot, and Rhenna followed.

Three hours later, as the sun began its afternoon descent, they reached the *amda*. There was no evidence that it had once been green, or that the darker depression in its center had been filled with cool water. A few brittle wisps of what might once have been grass blew around the horses' feet, and the shriveled sticks of trees, bare of their fanlike sweeps of leaves, quivered in the hot breeze.

Tahvo dismounted, walked to the edge of the darker sand and sat down, hands resting on crossed legs. The warriors stood in bleak silence with their thirsty horses.

Rhenna crouched beside Tahvo. "What is it?"

Tahvo rocked, muttering under her breath. "This was not meant to be," she said. "It is unnatural. The work of evil."

"The Karchedonians," Rhenna said.

Tahvo took a handful of sand and squeezed it in her fingers. The last particles of moisture seeped into her palm. "Not soldiers," she said. "Not priests. Someone else…"

The vision took her without warning or constraint. She found herself walking in the forests of the North beside a rushing stream, her sight restored, listening to the chatter of birds as she had done a thousand times in her youth. She could see blue sky between the feathery branches of pine and fir, count each stone beneath the stream's clear water. But the beauty of the Samah lands was distorted by a sense of wrongness, a haze of red that stretched from tree to tree like a veil of firelit fog.

A man came out of the wood to walk beside her. He was nearly her height, and his hair, like hers, was silver.

"Sister," he said. "How long has it been?"

Tahvo stopped, but the man caught her arm and forced her to continue. "Why are you here?" she asked.

"Because I long to see my kin," he said. "I must remember what was stolen from me."

"You are dead," Tahvo whispered.

"Am I?" He laughed. "Do the dead have names?"

Tahvo shivered. "Who are you?"

"I am your dear brother, Urho." He swung her toward him and kissed her hard on the lips. The touch seemed to suck all the moisture from Tahvo's mouth, coating her tongue with dust. She gasped as the stream went dry and the leaves and needles on every tree and bush shriveled to brown skeletons. Her own bones rattled inside the desiccated husk of her body.

"I will not let you go," Urho said. "Not until you give me what is mine." He grabbed her arms and shook her, shook and shook until her clothing and then her skin fell away in brittle strips that clattered and crunched under her fleshless feet....

Warm, firm hands snatched Tahvo free of the nightmare. Murmuring senseless words of admonishment and comfort, Rhenna cradled Tahvo's head and helped her sit up.

"A vision?" she demanded.

Tahvo nodded.

"Who is Urho?"

Tahvo reached for the waterskin hung at her belt, fumbled with the plug and lifted it to her mouth with trembling hands. Rhenna steadied the skin until Tahvo had eased her terrible thirst.

"Urho," Tahvo said, tasting the horror of the name. "He is my brother."

"Your brother?"

"He died when we were born. He came before me, but he did not survive his birth."

"You spoke to him as if he were alive."

"He came to me in dreams when I was young. He came again in Karchedon." She rubbed at the grit trapped behind her eyelids. "I think he is real. I think he was here, in this place."

"How is this possible?"

Tahvo tested the strength of her legs. "I do not know."

She heard the rustle of sand as one of the soft-footed Imaziren arrived. "We must report to the elders," Cabh'a said, her voice thick with strain. "Berkan will ride back to warn them that the *amda* has gone dry and there is no water or grazing for the horses." Tahvo felt the warrior's curious stare. "Are you well, Healer?"

"Yes. What would you have us do?"

"There is another *amda* two days' ride south of this one. If we are careful with our rations, we can reach it without endangering the horses. Would you come with us, or return with Berkan?"

Tahvo passed the Amazi warrior's question to Rhenna, who gave an unequivocal answer. Tahvo agreed. If the next *amda* was unaltered, Tahvo would have a means of comparing the dead with the living. But if the next spring had also been touched by magic…

She quelled that unpleasant thought and let Rhenna help her mount again. The Imaziren rode quietly, uneasy and alert, no longer singing or exchanging jests as they had done before. Rhenna was equally tense. Tahvo breathed shallowly and listened for the distant clank of metal or the scrape of bones.

Tahvo knew the second *amda* was dry before she heard Immeghar's shout of anger and despair. The air was leached of moisture. Her pony came to a halt and nosed the sand as if he hoped to find some remnant of fodder.

"We will remain here until the elders and the Guardian reach us," Cabh'a said. "We cannot continue until we know what is to be done."

"This is the work of sorcery," Immeghar said.

Tahvo slid from the pony's back and walked through the

crackling stumps of dead grass to the smooth sand where water had stood. She felt the ground with the palms of her hands, and her fingers brushed a mark formed of several oval hollows, a single large one surrounded by five smaller depressions arranged in a familiar pattern.

"A track," Rhenna said behind her. "It looks like…like Cian's."

The print of a great cat, here in the middle of the desert. "Cian is behind us," Tahvo said. "The Imaziren have not seen another Ailu."

Rhenna knelt, her fingers touching Tahvo's as she traced the print. "Perhaps Cian can tell us more when he comes. Rest, Tahvo. We may need your wisdom later." She led Tahvo to the shade of a sand hill, spread a blanket and pressed a fistful of dried fruit into Tahvo's hands.

Tahvo dozed as the day's heat waned and the shadows grew long. She, Rhenna and the four Imaziren huddled close in the night, enduring the plunge of temperature without the comfort of a fire. Halfway through the next morning, Tahvo heard the whoops of approaching warriors and smelled the scent of many people and horses.

She and Rhenna were left alone as the scouts met with the elders. Cian and Nyx found their way to their friends and shared their half-empty waterskins. The feelings between Cian and Rhenna were almost thick enough for Tahvo to touch.

"Do you know what has caused this drought, Tahvo?" Cian asked. "The Imaziren claim that it must be sorcery."

"I fear they are right."

"Stone priests traveling with the soldiers?"

"Tahvo found something," Rhenna said. "You should see it, Cian."

"I will try to learn what the elders are saying," Nyx offered. The three of them left, and Tahvo listened to the sharp, anxious voices of the Imaziren as they speculated on the evil that had been done in the very heart of their land.

Cian and Rhenna returned first. Cian sat down heavily beside Tahvo, and she could feel his agitation. Neither he nor Rhenna spoke of the cat print. An uncomfortable time later Nyx arrived with Madele.

"The elders are troubled by these signs," Madele said as Nyx translated. "Such a thing has never happened in living memory. Some of the warriors believe that our aid of the Guardian has brought some sorcerer's wrath upon us, and that more wickedness will come if we do not turn back."

"We cannot go back," Rhenna said. "Cian and I will speak to the elders—"

"It is true," Tahvo said. "Our enemies wish to hinder us and make our allies fear to help us." She drew a shuddering breath. "This is the work of the Stone God's servants."

"Then what are we to do?" Madele asked her. "We can kill their warriors, but we have no magic to counter sorcery."

Rhenna cursed. "Tahvo, do you sense anything of these enemies, anything we can use to fight them?"

Tahvo pushed aside her fear and spread her hands on the sand before her. She emptied her mind of all thoughts and images save one: water. Water more rare and precious than the purest gold. Water deep under the sands, hidden from sight and touch and smell.

Her palms began to burn. She pressed them flat, gasping with pain. "Cian!"

"I'm here. What do you need?"

"Help me."

She knew he understood when he grasped her hand and plunged his arm into the sand. He drew her down, down into earth that resisted with every grain, clawing and scraping flesh. Faces sprang into her mind, snarling masks of unrelenting hatred. One of them was her brother's.

She almost withdrew then, almost surrendered. There was no Slahtti to help her, no spirits to lend her their strength. But Cian was there. His courage flowed into her. She lay on her belly, breath mingling with Cian's. Her fingers extended nearly to breaking.

And she found it. Water, leagues away in the South, across the dry wasteland. Water that flowed freely in wide rivers, fell out of the sky to make the earth green and fruitful. Spirits untouched by the Stone, hundreds upon hundreds, voices uncounted.

She chanted and sang to the spirits, begging their favor, drawing upon the water as like calls to like. One presence broke away from the rest. Ancient power gushed through her hand.

Who are you? it demanded.

Tahvo answered with all her being, withholding nothing. Half-familiar coolness lapped at her fingertips. Abundant life sang in her ears.

Hat-T-Her, Tahvo said, hearing a name that had not been spoken for a thousand years. *You have slept long. It is time to awaken.*

The spirit entered her, sifted her mind, examined her soul. *You are not of my people.*

Enemies have taken the water from your people, Tahvo replied. *The long silence is ended.*

The goddess stretched, testing the limits of Tahvo's mortal consciousness. *Let me see,* she said.

Tahvo opened her eyes. Brilliant, blessed light overwhelmed perpetual darkness. She saw Cian's worried face a hand's-breadth from her own, Rhenna and Nyx beyond, Madele with her sun-bronzed features. She remembered what it was to know that her life had meaning and purpose.

Then the goddess swept her away.

She woke cradled in Cian's arms, Rhenna's cool palm resting on her forehead. The darkness had returned. She felt across Cian's arms to the ground beside him, and her fingers found moisture.

"You did it," Rhenna said, stroking her damp hair from her forehead. "You brought the water back. The *amda* is filled."

Tahvo closed her fist around wet sand. "It was not me," she whispered. "The goddess…"

"Hat-T-Her," Cian said. "She spoke through you, Tahvo."

Tahvo tried to sit up and slumped again, exhausted. "She is...one of the lost spirits of the Imaziren."

"So Madele told us," Rhenna said. "'Queen of the West,' she called her."

"Madele..."

"Has gone with Nyx to speak to her elders. You've done more than call the water back, Tahvo. You've restored one of their gods."

Tahvo shook her head. "It was not—"

"I know," Cian said, laughing and sighing at once. "It wasn't your doing."

"You helped me to reach her," Tahvo said. "She was very far away."

"I could never have found her alone." Cian eased Tahvo down onto a blanket. "Did you hear what this Hat-T-Her said?"

"No. I...went away."

There was a long moment of silence, and Tahvo imagined Rhenna and Cian exchanging troubled glances. "She said that all the waterholes from here to the Southland have been sucked dry by the same sorcery," Cian said. "Your goddess was very angry."

Tahvo nodded weakly and listened to the commotion of men and women gathering on the bank of the *amda,* filling waterskins to overflowing. Rhenna bathed her face with cloth soaked in cool water.

"I don't know why their gods abandoned the Imaziren," Rhenna said, "but this one was not eager to relinquish your body. She—" Rhenna paused as footsteps approached. "Nyx and Madele," she said.

Madele crouched before Tahvo. "Wise one," she said, her voice soft with respect, "the elders would speak with you."

Tahvo took Cian's offered arm and got to her feet. Rhenna fell in at her other side, and the five of them made for the bustle of the main camp. Madele led the way into the cool shelter of a spacious tent. Cian and Rhenna sat with Tahvo safely tucked between them. The very air sang with tension.

"The elders thank you for coming," Madele said. "Zamra asks if it is true that you understand our words."

"I do," Tahvo said.

"To comprehend many tongues is a great gift of the gods," Zamra said. "We did not know that one so favored walked among us until Berkan arrived with his message. We hope you will forgive our neglect, wise one."

"There was no neglect."

Bodies shifted uneasily. The elder cleared her throat. "Hat-T-Her has spoken with your voice, wise one. This is of great significance to my people."

"I understand."

"The Queen of the West has said that the servants of the Stone have drained our water supplies from here to the desert's edge."

"But Hat-T-Her has the power of the waters," Tahvo said. "She can restore what has been taken."

"Yes. With the Divine Cow's favor we may continue to aid the Guardian and those who share his burden. You understand what must be done?"

Nyx offered a belated translation, and Rhenna jumped to her feet. "Tahvo knows nothing of this," she said.

All the Imaziren began to talk at once. Cian placed a firm hand on Tahvo's back.

"This is not the first time a god has possessed our friend," he said, waiting for Nyx to relay his words. "What more do you expect of her?"

"Only what the goddess demands," Zamra said. "A mortal shape in which Hat-T-Her may walk the earth again, and advise her people. The wise one must remain with us."

"No!" Rhenna cried.

Tahvo closed her eyes, remembering the warning Slahtti had laid upon her in Karchedon. *If you agree to accept this trial, you will become the voice and the body of the spirits whose primal pow-*

*ers may decide the course of this war. You will not die, and yet you
will surrender your life. You will sleep long and wake in places you
do not know. You will be feared by many and loved for what you
can never be.*

"You will have great honor among the Imaziren, wise one,"
the elder said. "Nothing will be denied you, and your companions will have all they need to complete their journey."

"This is not possible," Cian said.

"Out of the question," Rhenna snapped.

Iron blades hissed in their sheaths. Tahvo reached for
Rhenna's boot and held on with all her strength.

"You wish me to become the living incarnation of the spirit,"
she said to the Imaziren.

"It is what the goddess requires," the elder said. "If we do
not do as she asks, our people will suffer."

"Tahvo is not of your people," Cian protested.

"We will continue alone," Rhenna said. "If you fear the Stone
so much, let us go."

"But the goddess has said—"

"*Stop.*" Madele's voice rang clear over the cries of outrage.
"We fight the Stone because we would not be slaves like the
men of the cities. Is this the answer, my people, to steal the very
freedom from one we honor? Must a stranger be the only acceptable offering?" She knelt before Tahvo, pushing past the
barrier of Rhenna's body. "Wise one, is it true that other gods
have spoken with your mouth?"

"It is true," Tahvo said. "Other gods, of other lands."

"Then your companions will need you in the days ahead. Tell
me what I must do to take your place."

Tahvo touched Madele's face, tracing the long bones and
muscle under weathered skin, finding the wetness of tears.
"Do you know what you say?"

"Your gift is too great to remain with my people alone,"
Madele said. "I have no skill in magic, but if the goddess will
have me..." She bowed her head. "Only show me the way."

Tahvo tucked her head between her shoulders. Madele was prepared to make a great sacrifice…to surrender her very being with no true comprehension of what she might lose. In that respect she was very much like Rhenna. But if the goddess accepted such a substitution, Madele would *see* as none of her people had done in millennia. She would become more than anything a simple warrior could imagine.

And Tahvo would once again be blind. Until the spirits found another use for her.

She clasped Madele's chapped hand. "Take me to the water."

"Tahvo?" Rhenna asked. "What is happening?"

Nyx repeated the conversation to Rhenna and Cian while Madele guided Tahvo from the tent. The elders and other warriors followed. Tahvo cleared her mind and waded into the *amda*, stopping when the water lapped around her waist. She gripped Madele's fingers. "Do not let go," she said, "no matter what you feel." Then she called the goddess.

Hat-T-Her came swiftly, entering Tahvo with no warning. Tahvo fought to keep her mind clear, balanced precariously between the will of the Amazi spirit and her own determination. She saw herself and Madele standing in the water—a plain, short woman with silver hair beside a warrior lean and tall— and offered her hand to the beautiful goddess whose arching horns cupped a disk that shone as brightly as the desert sun. The goddess's power surged through her. She felt it pass into Madele, shared the moment when Hat-T-Her examined the warrior's soul and found it worthy.

Tahvo fell to her knees. Water flooded her mouth. Cian and Rhenna lifted her from the *amda* and carried her to the bank. For a moment longer she could see, clinging to the last remnants of the spirit's power.

Madele was Madele no longer. She shone with an inner luminescence, the very essence of life itself, and above her head rose Hat-T-Her's horns and sun disk. She lifted her arms in a gesture of benediction. The Imaziren bowed to the ground.

Darkness came. The mouth of a waterskin pressed to Tahvo's lips. She drank, pushed the skin away and felt Rhenna's face.

"Madele?" she croaked.

"She changed," Rhenna said. "Your goddess took her, for a time. But she is herself again."

"The Imaziren have no need of you now," Cian said. "You're free, Tahvo."

Free. Free to be weak and blind and uncertain. Free to be alone and apart. But in the South there were other spirits, other voices, other eyes with which to see. And they would demand everything Tahvo had to give.

The sacrifice had only just begun.

Part II
Emergence

Chapter Thirteen

"One journey ends," Nyx said, "and another begins."

She stood with Rhenna, Cabh'a and Immeghar on the river's edge, watching the brown water slide between the muddy banks. To the north, fifty Imaziren and their horses were only a column of dust rising up from the scrublands, tracing a path toward the sand hills a hundred leagues beyond. On every side lay a rolling steppe thick with new shoots of green grass and stands of broad-canopied trees. Rhenna could see herds of deer or antelope to the east and west, fearless of the strange men and beasts in their midst.

Cian broke off his conversation with Immeghar and came to join the women. "How far?" he asked, gazing across the river.

Nyx grinned. She had been smiling constantly since she, the three Northerners and four Imaziren warriors had reached the plain. Rhenna couldn't blame her. After three long months of walking and riding over endless sand hills, gravel plateaus and salt pans, she was profoundly grateful to have seen the last of the desert.

"In a hundred leagues we shall be home," Nyx said. "In fifty we reach the border of my people's country."

Cabh'a crouched on the bank and tossed a stone into the current. "I have never seen a river," she said carefully in her newly-mastered Hellenish. "Is it true there are many where we go?"

"Many," Nyx said in the same tongue. "And before two full moons have passed, you will see water fall out of the sky."

"Rain," Immeghar said dismissively. "*I* have seen it."

"*You* are an old man," Cabh'a said, pitching a smaller pebble in his direction. "But I'll wager my best mare that even you will see things you have never imagined."

"Of course. Why else would I have come?"

A laugh rose from the water. Tamallat and Mezwar splashed each other in the shallows, uninhibited as children. They had proven no more loquacious since they had volunteered to join the outlanders on their travels to the South, but it was clear that the young lovers relished their freedom from the curious eyes of their fellow tribesfolk.

Rhenna would as soon have left them behind. She wanted no reminders of such bonds between male and female, nor any distraction from the dangers ahead.

She cast a covert glance at Cian. He had been increasingly restless, pacing the perimeter of each night's camp, sometimes disappearing for hours at a time when the moon rose high. Perhaps the change had started when Rhenna had shown him the big cat print at the dry *amda;* perhaps it was simply because they drew ever nearer to their destination. But she worried for him, as she never ceased worrying for Tahvo. And she wondered if he had finally given his seed to the Imaziren.

She climbed down the bank, well away from the noisy lovers, and found Tahvo sitting with her bare feet in the warm water. Rhenna sat beside her.

"I feel them," Tahvo said softly. "There are so many."

Rhenna didn't have to ask what Tahvo meant. Deaf though she was to most devas' voices, even Rhenna could almost hear the spirits of this land. They were like the wild devas from the borders of the Northern steppes, bound to no human's bidding, answering to no prayer. The wind spoke to her in some half-understood language; even the sky hummed, as if with the buzzing of countless invisible insects.

"Do they disturb you?" Rhenna asked.

Tahvo shook her head. "I cannot yet sort them out, and their essence is strange to me. They are not like Hat-T-Her or any of the spirits I knew in the North. Some, I think, have never been named by men."

Rhenna squeezed Tahvo's shoulder. "Don't demand too much of yourself, my friend. I wouldn't see you lost to some nameless god."

"You will not lose me. Are we to camp here?"

"It is not wise to stop too close to the river," Nyx said. "The *ònì* live in such waters."

"*Ònì?*" Cian echoed, dangling his legs over the bank above them.

"A creature as long as three or four men, with scaly skin, long tail and great toothed jaws," Nyx said. "A single beast could break the neck of a horse."

Cian snatched his legs away from the water. Nyx laughed. "I see no *ònì* now," she said, "but we must be wary when we cross. There is a low place a little way to the east, and a circle of rocks two leagues to the South. We will spend the night there, and follow the river's course to my people's home." She glanced at Rhenna. "That is, of course, if you agree."

"This is your country." Rhenna got up and stretched her arms over her head. "Is there anything else besides these *ònì* we should watch for?"

"We may see *ìkàrìkò*…like spotted dogs, but low in the hind-quarters…and lions—"

"I have seen a lion in the hills south of Karchedon," Immeghar said. "Sometimes the city folk venture out from behind their walls with spears and chariots to hunt them."

"They would not kill *our* animals so easily," Nyx said, "but even lions of the South are no match for an Ailu."

Cian's nostrils flared, and Rhenna could almost see the hair standing up on the back of his neck. "Let us hope it doesn't come to such a battle," he said dryly.

"They will not attack a large party unless they or their young are threatened," Nyx said. She arched a brow at Immeghar. "Have you seen an *elephas,* warrior?"

"I have heard of them. Large gray creatures with long noses."

"Very large. My people name them *àjànànkú.* We will stay away from them, and from the fat water-beasts we call *akáko.* We will find enough game without disturbing the lords of this land."

"And what of men?" Rhenna asked.

Nyx met her gaze. "The people of the South have had little reason to fear those who walk on two legs," she said. "They have been as innocent as children. We, who bring tidings of the Stone, will be the worst enemies they have ever known."

That evening the travelers camped at the circle of tall rocks. Nyx saw to the horses, and Rhenna and Cabh'a went hunting. They returned with an antelope that had been too slow to escape their spears. Tamallat and Mezwar, still laughing and whispering together, gathered wood from the nearest stand of trees and made a fire, while Immeghar skinned the carcass and dressed the meat for cooking. Dog-sized beasts emerged from the darkness to yelp and giggle as they skirted the fire's light, eyes gleaming red. Cian got up once to chase the animals away. They didn't return.

The next day Rhenna got her first glimpse of the creatures Nyx called *àjànànkú,* monstrous beasts with curving tusks and snakelike proboscises that could snatch leaves from high branches as neatly as any human hand. The animals watched the humans' passage with small, intelligent eyes, and the biggest male trumpeted a warning. Rhenna was more than willing to give him a wide berth. On the second river crossing Cabh'a spotted the *ònì*, which snapped at the horses' hooves but were driven away by Imaziren spears. The broad, brown heads of *akáko* pushed out of the water, flicking tiny ears.

Everywhere was an abundance of game, vast herds of antelope ranging in size from delicate, deerlike creatures to horse-sized beasts with sweeping horns. Raptors and scavenger birds circled the sky, searching for prey or carrion. Dry grasses rustled with the constant movement of snakes and rodents. Save for the peculiar nature of Nyx's beasts, Rhenna almost felt as if she were home on the steppes.

But that was illusion. Even when the travelers reached the first cultivated fields, set apart from the grasslands by low walls of stone, Rhenna could not mistake them for the farmsteads of her people. The men who worked the earth with wooden hoes were dark, like Nyx, and lightly dressed for the warmth of the South. They paused in their work to stare, curious but not hostile, and some lifted their hands in greeting.

Still Nyx urged her companions on, past scattered villages of round huts and herds of cattle and goats tended by wide-eyed youngsters. Patches of wooded land grew more frequent. Well-worn paths became roads of a sort, earth scraped bare and packed firm by generations of hooves and human feet.

It was at the crossing of two such roads that they first saw the dog. The beast sat directly at the junction of the paths, a small, wheat-colored animal with triangular ears and a tightly curled tail. It grinned at the travelers with a lolling pink tongue, looking for all the world as if it had been waiting for them to arrive.

Nyx reined in her horse, signaling for the others to stop. She stared at the little dog with as much suspicion as she might regard a poisonous serpent.

"We must go around," she said.

Immeghar laughed. "After all the mighty beasts we have seen," he said, "you fear this one?"

Nyx cast him a sour look. "Things are not always what they seem, warrior," she said. "You may laugh at your peril."

Immeghar shrugged. Nyx led the way off the road and through the grass and tangled bush, pointedly averting her face from the dog. Tahvo rode up beside Rhenna.

"Nyx is right," she whispered, glancing back over her shoulder. "It is not just a dog."

"A deva-beast, like Slahtti?" Rhenna asked. "It seems an odd choice of shape for a god."

"Its nature is not clear to me. I cannot tell if it wishes us good or ill."

"Then it isn't very different from most devas. Stay close to me, Tahvo, and tell me if you sense any other dangers."

Tahvo agreed, clearly distracted, and they rode on for several more days without encountering the dog. One morning Nyx suddenly kicked her mount into a gallop, racing past stands of fan-leafed trees. Rhenna and the others followed at a more leisurely pace, and soon they began to see plots of land where men dug holes in the earth with pointed sticks, preparing for the planting of some unfamiliar crop. Handsome dark-skinned children left their parents and rushed to the side of the road, shouting to each other in excited voices. The boldest of them darted toward the horses, nearly touched them and dashed away again, laughing.

"Innocents," Cian said with a touch of grimness. "Nyx said they had no enemies."

Immeghar grinned and feinted at one of the boys who came too near. The child squealed in mingled delight and terror.

Nyx returned on foot a few minutes later, calling to the children and the workers in the fields. Men and women put down their diggers and hoes. Nyx was beaming, her face more joyous than any time Rhenna had seen it in all their travels.

"Home," Cian said, his voice rough with emotion. "How long will it be for us, Rhenna?"

He clearly didn't expect her to answer. Rhenna dismounted and helped Tahvo down from her pony. The healer turned her face from side to side, listening intently. Nyx's people pressed closer, many smiling, eyes fixed on the Northerners' pale skin as if such coloring were a fascinating mistake of nature.

"You are welcome to our village," Nyx said, encompassing all the visitors with her wide gesture. "Messengers have gone to alert the Fathers and Mothers, the heads of our clans. Soon we will have *ishu* cakes and *emu òpe,* palm wine."

She led them along the path between the fields, through groves of tall trees and past a group of men at work smelting iron for spear-tips and knife blades. An old man, his face marked with a pattern of scars, sat on a wooden stool carving the surface of a gourd. Women washed bits of cloth on flat rocks beside a stream, and children herded goats and small cattle in search of forage. It seemed impossible to Rhenna that the Stone God or any evil could touch such a haven of peace.

Clusters of huts and larger houses, mud-walled and thatched with serrated leaves, soon replaced the open fields. Nyx stopped often to greet the men and women who welcomed her home. But Rhenna saw that many of the faces were solemn, and the people seemed to avoid engaging Nyx in long conversation. Eventually even Nyx's smile disappeared, and she hurried on to the center of the village.

Three elderly women waited at the doorway of one of the larger houses, a compound of dwellings set apart from the others. Men from the surrounding compounds gathered to watch at a respectful distance. Nyx bowed deeply to the women and spoke at length, introducing the visitors by name.

The oldest woman, her tightly curled hair washed gray with age, sent several young boys to take the horses and beckoned the strangers closer. Rhenna stepped forward, inclining her head to the elders.

"This is the Mother of my House, Adisa, who is also head of Clan Amòtékùn," Nyx said. "And these are her sisters, Bolanle and Dayo. Adisa offers you the shelter of the House and the clan." Adisa spoke, and Nyx's face clouded. "My Mothers wish to speak with me. Will you come inside and take refreshment?"

"Give them our thanks and gratitude," Rhenna said, smiling at Adisa and her sisters. The old women returned her smile and indicated that the guests should enter the house.

Rhenna took Tahvo's arm and bent to walk through. She found herself in a dark, spacious room that smelled of earth, leather and dry vegetation. The two pretty young women inside got to their feet, greeting the strangers with soft voices. Rhenna eased Tahvo down on one of the woven mats, while the healer answered the startled villagers in their own language. One of the girls touched Tahvo's hair and burst into giggles. As soon as everyone was settled, the young women hurried out the back door of the room.

"They will bring food and drink," Tahvo said. "I think they are very curious about us."

"About your hair, at least," Cian teased.

"But they are not afraid." She stared at the ground with sightless eyes. "They are like my people, who never had anything to fear."

"They have been fortunate," Rhenna said, surprised at her own anger, "but even they will not be safe forever."

The Imaziren glanced at each other. No one spoke. Soon the young village women returned with carved wooden platters of dense cakes, fish and dark soup in small bowls of baked clay. Smothering laughter, the girls mimicked lifting the bowls to their lips and urged their guests to eat and drink. The flavors were unfamiliar to Rhenna, but she and the others ate with enthusiasm after so many weeks of game and the occasional cooked root.

Once they were finished eating, the girls brought in a heap of tanned skins and furs, addressed Tahvo and left again. "They ask us to be comfortable and rest," Tahvo said. "When the proper rooms are prepared, the men and women will be given their own quarters in the compound."

Rhenna glanced at Cian and quickly away. "The next time they come, tell them we prefer to remain together. We—"

She broke off as Nyx entered the room. Her eyes were red and swollen, and her full lips were set in a hard line. She sat down between Tahvo and Cian.

"I have spoken to the Mothers," she said. "They understand why we have come and what we seek."

"You have been weeping," Tahvo said softly.

Nyx looked away. "I have just learned that my father is dead."

Tahvo touched her arm. "I am sorry."

Nyx sniffed and raised her head. "It happened many months ago," she said. "I was not here to bury him, but he lies in honor beneath the rooms he shared with my mother. He is with Olorun."

"And all that he would have done now falls upon you," Cian said.

Rhenna stared at him, remembering the times he and Nyx had spoken alone together. "Who was your father?" she asked the Southern woman.

Nyx sighed. "He was the one who brought knowledge of the prophecies and the Hammer to the Ará Odò."

She began to speak in a halting voice, telling Rhenna and the others of a secret city in the East: New Meroe, true home of the prophecies.

"My father was born in New Meroe," she said. "His people— the People of the Scrolls—have guarded the sacred writings for over three thousand years, and the city's holy men spend all their lives studying them to learn the will of the gods. My father taught me to revere the faith of his fathers."

Suddenly a number of things began to make a great deal more sense to Rhenna. "Now I understand why you always insisted that the prophecies were true," she said. "But in Karchedon you said you didn't know how Philokrates had obtained his knowledge of them."

"None from New Meroe would willingly give an outsider access to them. He must have found texts stolen by the Stone priests. But they would be copies, made before my father's people fled from Khemet to Meroe, and then to the new city."

"Khemet, which the Hellenes call Aigyptos," Cian added.

"Yes. After the Godwar, the City of the Exalted was no more, and men wandered in search of new homes. The gods gave mortal heroes of the war all the sacred texts to hold inviolate for the future. These heroes were among those who unified the land of Khemet, building new cities out of the desert. They stood beside the first Pharaohs, and they became priests of an order devoted not to a single god but to the fate of men and gods alike."

"More priests," Rhenna muttered.

"Never mistake them for the evil ones in Karchedon," Nyx said. "For one hundred and fifty generations, these priests served the good, living and working in their own secret citadel...until the Libu kings conquered Khemet. My father's people fled south to the land of Kush and were given shelter by King Kashta, who later became Pharaoh—"

Rhenna held up her hands. "These names mean nothing to me."

"For now it is enough to know that the rulers of Kush welcomed the People of the Scrolls, who then numbered only a few thousand, and the royal family of Kush intermarried with their leaders to create a new dynasty that would stand until the Time of Reckoning. But again the people were forced to flee when the priests foretold the birth of Alexandros the Mad, who would free the Exalted from their prison."

"This part I know," Rhenna said. "Alexandros conquered Hellas, Persis and Aigyptos before he died. He moved the Stone from the desert."

"He let the Exalted escape," Cian said, staring at the packed earth floor. "The Ailuri weren't there to stop him."

Nyx touched Cian's knee. "You will redeem your people, Watcher."

"Continue with your tale," Rhenna said brusquely.

Nyx withdrew her hand with a sharp, knowing look at Rhenna. "Driven from their second home in the city of Meroe," she continued, "the People of the Scroll built New Meroe in a barbarous land in the East, hidden from unconsecrated eyes. There they have lived, safe from the Stone God, for the past sixty-five years. There my father was born.

"He grew up devoted to the prophecies…especially to the cult of the Watchers, who made ready for the one born to bear the Hammer of the Earth. He served as a warrior, training every day for the Time of Reckoning and the final battle with the Stone. But he was impatient. He hoped to be the one to locate the Hammer and bring the Watchers to the holy city."

"The Ailuri were still in the Shield of the Sky, even five years ago," Rhenna said.

"My father's people had only rumor, faith and cryptic writings to guide them. Still, my father took what knowledge he had and journeyed west, over mountains and through endless forests, to the land of my mother's people."

"This village."

Nyx nodded. "Though my father was both courageous and skilled, he reached this land only to be attacked by a wild beast and was severely wounded. My mother, a daughter of Clan Amòtékùn, found him and brought him here. She nursed him back to health. But his injuries were such that he could not continue his quest. He married my mother and was accepted into her clan."

"He became an exile," Cian said.

"He spoke often of the city he had left behind, never forgetting the great quest that had driven him to risk his life. And when I was born, he told me every tale of his people that he could remember. He taught me of the empire and the evil to come. I grew up a disciple of the prophecies, as he was."

"You determined to finish what your father started," Rhenna said.

"I listened to every rumor that drifted across the Great Desert, sought out those few who crossed it and survived. From them I learned of Karchedon, and how well the Stone priests had succeeded in forcing their evil god upon the conquered peoples. I knew I must go north and find the Watchers, even if it meant my death."

"You found what you sought," Tahvo said.

"I completed my father's quest, but I did not return in time to tell him, or to show him…" Tears shone in her eyes. "My mother's people had no knowledge or prophecies of the Stone God before my father's coming, yet most have come to believe his claims. Their own gods, the *òrìshà,* have given signs that the heavens and earth are disturbed by forces they do not understand."

"I feel these spirits," Tahvo murmured. "They are still strange to me."

"The Ará Odò have no priests," Nyx said, "but they make offerings to the *òrìshà,* and the gods sometimes answer."

Rhenna got up and paced from one end of the room to the other. "Why did you not tell us of your father's quest when we left Karchedon?"

"I told Cian because he was most directly involved. Telling you would have changed nothing."

"Perhaps you feared we might trust you less if we realized that your ambition to bring Cian here was more a personal quest than a desire for the salvation of the world."

Nyx held Rhenna's stare. "Do you think I hate the Stone any less than you?"

"I think there is more you may be hiding from us."

Cian pounded his fist on the packed earth floor. "Enough," he growled. "We must find the Hammer, and Nyx's people know far more than we."

His sudden ferocity startled Rhenna. "I'm sure Nyx can also explain exactly what we are to do when we find it," she snapped.

"Finding it will be no easy task," Nyx said. "The forested lands are wide and difficult to penetrate. The Mothers will consult with the People of the House and with the Fathers of the other clans to decide what must be done. They will almost certainly wish to call upon the *òrìshà* for their aid. Until then, rooms in the compound have been prepared for your comfort." She rose. "Abeni and Monifa, the girls who brought your meals, will show you. Ask for anything you require."

She left, deftly evading Rhenna's attempt to detain her, and shortly afterward the girls arrived to lead their guests to new quarters. Immeghar, Cian and Mezwar were given one hut near the center of the compound, while Tahvo, Rhenna, Cabh'a and Tamallat took another near enough that Rhenna saw no good reason to object to the separation. Tahvo retreated to one corner of the room, focused inward on the voices of her spirits, and Tamallat sat near the door and sighed over Mezwar.

Rhenna practiced warriors' exercises with Cabh'a in the open area between the huts, observed by curious children, and waited for Nyx to make her next report. At nightfall, after the second meal had been brought and Nyx had still not appeared, Rhenna went to the men's hut to look for Cian. She suspected he knew more of the Southern woman and her motives than he had admitted.

But Cian wasn't there. Immeghar said that he'd slipped away sometime after the meal. He was not in the village. Rhenna knew better than to chase after him.

She crouched outside her hut and watched the black edge of the forest beyond the cleared fields, listening to the strange hoots and howls from the broad canopy of the treetops. They were seductive, those cries, thick with wild longing and the rejection of all that humans called civilization. The forest's call was far darker and more primal than the stark serenity of the steppes or the mountains. And as she breathed in the heavy, rich scents of the Southern night, Rhenna realized that she was more terrified of losing Cian to this place than she had ever been of his bonds to Nyx, the Imaziren or his own people.

Cian might enter such a place and never return.

Nyx found Cian an hour's walk into the forest, where he had paused to drink at a stream. She stood on the opposite bank and watched him toss twigs and stones into the water, not speaking, until he could no longer pretend he was alone.

"How did you find me?" he asked.

"Why did you leave the village?"

He cocked his head, breathing shallowly to keep his mind clear of the intoxicating scents that swirled around him. "Do you seek your gods in this place, Nyx?"

"Sometimes," she said, "when I come to the forest alone." She curled and straightened her long body in a sensuous stretch. "Is that why you ventured here, Cian? To listen to the gods?"

He swallowed his laughter. "That is Tahvo's gift," he said. "The devas don't speak to me."

"Are you so certain?" She crossed the stream, her own scent mingling in perfect harmony with the fragrance of earth and water and growing things. "I understand you better than you know."

She was close. Too close. "Go back to the village," he said. "I'll come to no harm here."

"Do you think I fear for your safety, Watcher?" She shook her head. "None of my clan fears the forest or its creatures. The first of our Mothers was a part of it." She gazed up at him, her dark eyes catching some distant glimmer of light. "You asked how I found you. I can see in the darkness almost as well as you."

"Because you have the gift of Earth magic. Your ancestors were godborn."

"Yes. And no. The other clans of the village believe that my clan's founder was a panther woman who met a man of the Ará Odò and fell in love with him. She left her skin in the forest and took human shape to bear the man's children."

Cian backed away. "A panther?"

"Does that shock you, after all the things you have learned in your travels?"

He thought of Yseul, and the evening's unfamiliar meal churned in his stomach. "What are you?"

"I, too, have wondered, ever since I was old enough to understand my father's stories about the Watchers. It was a question he could never answer, though he knew my mother's nature when he married her." She leaned against the wide trunk of a tree, stroking its smooth bark. "The legends of my clan say that because of her ties to the forest, my ancestress brought great good fortune to the village. She began a new House of her own, and her husband went to live with her. That is why Clan Amòtékùn has Mothers to lead us instead of Fathers, and why our gifts are passed through the female line."

"But you...cannot change," Cian whispered.

"It is said that the last of my clan who could take panther shape died three generations ago. But all of us are bound to the Earth. Like the Watchers." She knelt at the base of the tree and laid her palm on the ground. A dozen tiny seedlings sprang from the soil, growing before Cian's eyes.

He circled around Nyx, heading for the faint trail that led back to the village. "Why do you tell me this now?" he asked. "Why not before?"

"My answer to you is the same as it was to Rhenna. I told you what I thought was necessary for you to know." She rose and brushed the dirt from her fingers. "My father's prophecies speak only of male Watchers. In the North, I asked you what became of the females of your people. You claimed the Ailuri have none, and no legends of them."

Suddenly he saw what she was implying. "Are you suggesting that your ancestress was a female Ailu?"

"Is it so impossible? The Imaziren claim that their women were chosen to bear the original Ailuri, but even they did not know how their godborn offspring reproduced after the first generation. Your people are not immortal, Cian. They must have required children after the Godwars. What if there were females who also guarded the Stone? What if they were separated from their mates long before your people went to the North, in a time lost even to legend?"

He held his arms out in front of him, warding her off. "Of what use is such speculation, now that my people are dead?"

"Perhaps not all." She came no closer, recognizing that he was on the verge of flight. "My father believed that it was no mere coincidence that he found my mother. He believed there might be others like my clan's distant ancestress still living in the forest, others who might hold some connection to the Hammer itself."

"He never looked for them?"

"His injuries prevented it. But he knew that even if a clan of female shapeshifters did exist, they would not be the ones to bear the Hammer. That may only be done by a male of Watcher blood." She held Cian's gaze with fierce determination. "If females of your kind exist in the deep forest and hold some tie to the Hammer, as my father believed, they may either help or hinder us in our quest. You must be prepared for whatever may come. Above all else, you must never give in to temptation."

Chapter Fourteen

Temptation.

Nyx spoke in ignorance, Cian told himself. She knew nothing of his meeting with Yseul in Karchedon, nothing of his self-contempt and loathing whenever he thought of the panther woman with her pliant body and voracious eyes. She couldn't know that he would never find such a creature tempting again.

Cian strode back for the village, not waiting to see if Nyx followed. Tahvo sat in the darkness at the edge of the forest. She got to her feet as he began to pass by, her face turning toward him.

"Cian?"

He sighed and went to her. "Tahvo."

"Rhenna was concerned when you left the village," she said. "You are well?"

He knew a lie would be pointless, and suddenly he was weary

of secrets. He took Tahvo's arm and led her away from the huts. "You remember the cat print we found at the dry *amda?*"

"I remember."

"How did you think it came to be there?"

She slowed, pulling Cian to a stop. "You know?"

He glanced toward the forest as if a score of lust-crazed Ailu females might appear between one breath and the next. "I was afraid to accept it," he said. "I didn't believe, until Nyx…" He shuddered. "My people never saw a female of our kind. Such creatures did not exist, not even in legend. But I met one in Karchedon, Tahvo. It was because of her that Baalshillek captured me and delivered me to my brothers."

Tahvo patted his arm. "Tell me."

So he did, choking on his own shame as he spoke of Yseul and how he had let her take his body and his mind. "She made herself look like Rhenna," he said, "but even when I knew she was not…even then—" He shook his head wildly. "She was a creature of Baalshillek's making, shaped from the substance of my people. He intended that she and I should…begin a new race of Ailuri to serve the Stone. I didn't see her again after Rhenna and I escaped from the temple. I thought she was the only one of her kind. I was wrong."

"Nyx?"

Cian didn't wonder how she knew. "She told me that her clan is descended from a panther woman who came out of the forest to mate with one of the villagers. Her father believed there must be others, that they may live in the forest even now."

"And these females cannot be Ailuri?"

"I don't know. It seems impossible, but…"

"Surely Baalshillek could not have created them as he did Yseul."

"Even he isn't that powerful. But if they are Ailuri, they were separated from my brothers in a time before memory."

"Then perhaps there was purpose in such a separation," she said. "Your race still survives, beyond Baalshillek's reach."

Cian tried to feel the hope in Tahvo's words, but it eluded him. "The print in the *amda*," he said. "I think it belonged to Yseul."

"She followed us from Karchedon?"

"She is Baalshillek's minion. What if she was at the Stone's prison when the soldiers attacked us? What if she was responsible for drying up the waterholes?"

"Does she have such abilities?"

"I don't know. I never even sensed her presence. If she possesses the ancient Ailuri powers of Earth…"

"She is not alone," Tahvo murmured. "Do you remember when I told you that I had seen a vision of my brother in the crater of bones?"

"The brother you said was dead?"

"He died at birth, only moments before I was born. But I have seen him before, Cian…in Karchedon. Now I know that his spirit walks the earth as a man, and he is somehow bound to the Stone."

"Are you saying that he was created, like Yseul?"

She shivered, and Cian took her into his arms. She pressed her face against his shoulder. "They meant to stop us in the desert, Cian. They will try again. We must tell Rhenna."

"Yes. But not everything. Not about Yseul and me."

She peered into his face. "She would not hate you, Cian."

He winced and quickly changed the subject. "Can you feel anything from the devas in this place? Do they sense the ones who follow us?"

"I have never walked in a land with so many spirits. They call to me in a thousand voices. I am afraid…" She bit hard on her lower lip. "If I open to them, I may not come back."

Her terror dwarfed his own. "Don't risk it, Tahvo. If our enemies were all-powerful, we would already be dead. There will be other ways to fight them." He smelled dawn in the air and stretched his cramped muscles. Beasts who walked and hunted by daylight were stirring in the forest, and soon the village would wake. "Go back to Rhenna. Tell her what you must and try to rest. We—"

A flash of motion commanded his attention. A small, wheat-colored animal trotted around the corner of a hut and sat on its haunches, tongue lolling. It was the dog they had met at the crossroads, the one Nyx had so pointedly warned them to avoid.

Tahvo stiffened, clutching Cian's hand. Her eyes rolled up in their sockets. Cian caught her as she began to convulse, her arms and legs flailing like the limbs of some helpless creature pinned at the end of a spear.

Cian snatched her up and carried her to the village at a run. The dog didn't follow. Just as he reached the women's hut Rhenna came to meet him. She helped Cian ease Tahvo to the ground.

"What happened?" she demanded, stuffing a piece of cloth between Tahvo's chattering teeth.

"Tahvo said there were too many spirits," Cian said, "and then that dog appeared…"

Tamallat ran out of the hut, and the men emerged from theirs. Nyx arrived with several of the villagers.

"The Mothers are invoking the *òrìshà*," she said, her voice strained and breathless. "Healer, do you hear me?"

Tahvo opened her eyes and abruptly sat up, staring across the compound. The yellow dog trotted into the open space, yawned, and rolled onto its back, waving all four feet in the air. Nyx froze.

"Eshu," she whispered.

"What is it, Nyx?" Rhenna asked. "What is this Eshu?"

The dog vanished as if it were no more than a trick of the dawning light. Tahvo spat the cloth from her mouth and laughed. She shook Cian off and stood, turning slowly as she flexed her fingers one by one.

"So long," she said hoarsely. "So long since I have walked in the shape of man." She ran her hands over her body. "Or woman."

Nyx fell to her knees. "Eshu," she said, bowing low. The other villagers did the same.

Tahvo looked down at the Southerners with a smile of indulgent amusement. "I know you, Daughter of Olayinka," she said. "You have been away from the lands of your people."

"Olorun knows that I have been in the North, fighting the evil ones," Nyx said humbly.

"I have heard it said that you are very brave, child, and yet you tremble. Can it be that you hoped I, alone of the great *òrìshà*, would not come to your aid?"

"We honor all the *òrìshà*," Nyx protested.

"Still, you would not look upon me at the crossroads. You warned your guests against me." Tahvo sighed with mock regret. She stared at Cian. "Do you know why she fears me, Child of Shadows?"

Cian searched Tahvo's silver eyes and recognized the capricious, unpredictable power seething behind them. "What have you done with our friend?" he asked.

"The one you call Tahvo is here, but she cannot speak." Tahvo leered at him and glanced from Rhenna to Nyx, licking her lips. "Would you lend me your body instead, Bearer of the Hammer? I would find an excellent use for it."

Rhenna stepped forward. "What do you want of us?"

"What do I want?" Tahvo gestured dismissively toward Nyx. "Did she not explain that her people have called upon the *òrìshà* to aid in your quest? Such ingratitude." She yawned and scratched behind her ear. "Tell them who I am, Daughter of Olayinka."

Nyx straightened, averting her eyes from Tahvo's mocking gaze. "He is Eshu," she said slowly. "Servant of Olorun, Divine Messenger, Bringer of Accident and Chance."

"And all men fear Chance, do they not?" Tahvo said. "Especially those most certain of their destinies. Yet I knew *you* were coming, Hammer-Bearer, and perhaps I will choose to help you."

Nyx opened her mouth as if she would speak, then firmly shut it again. Two of the villagers scrambled to their feet and rushed away, disappearing among the huts. Tahvo ignored them. "You do wish to find what you seek?" she asked Cian.

"That depends upon the price of your aid," Rhenna said. "Let Tahvo go."

Tahvo's eyes grew hooded as if in boredom, and she sat down with the loose-limbed carelessness of a willful child. "*You* have little fear of the gods, Rhenna of the Winds."

"You are not *my* god, and perhaps I'm not so certain of my destiny."

"Rhenna," Cian said in warning. He crouched before Tahvo. "If you know about our quest, you must know of the Stone God."

"Olorun, Lord of the Sky, sees all things."

"You must have Tahvo's knowledge, as well. Her memories. You see that the Exalted and their priests mean to destroy every deva in the world to feed their lust for power and dominion over the earth. Even these lands across the Great Desert are not safe."

"And *you* will save us, little man?"

Cian shifted uncomfortably. "Tahvo has often said that devas and mortals must work together to defeat the Stone. If you know where the Hammer lies…"

Tahvo traced a shape in the dirt with one blunt finger. "It lies deep in the forest, beyond many dangers. What will you give to obtain it?"

"Whatever is necessary."

"No," Rhenna said sharply. "We strike no bargains with devas who demand sacrifice." She faced Tahvo. "You will help us to save yourself."

Tahvo sprang to her feet, her face twisted in fury. "You dare speak so to Eshu, mortal?" She stretched up and up, reaching for the sky until her feet dangled above the ground.

Cian stepped in front of Rhenna and braced himself for a deva's wrath. A deathly hush fell over the compound. A trio of Nyx's clan Mothers rushed from the largest house, coming to a stop when they saw Tahvo. Tahvo began to spin, whirling round and round until her body was a blur. The wheat-colored dog sprang out of the spinning shape, gave a wailing cry and vanished.

Tahvo collapsed to the ground, still shuddering with the remnants of Eshu's power. Rhenna was at her side in an instant. Nyx and the clan Mothers drew near, debating softly among themselves with many uneasy glances toward the forest. Cian helped Rhenna carry Tahvo inside the hut. Rhenna bathed the healer's face while Cian looked on, knowing there was nothing he could do but wait.

"Perhaps it wasn't wise to provoke a foreign deity," he said.

Rhenna's hands trembled as she squeezed excess water from a cloth and laid it across Tahvo's forehead. "I saw no reason to trust a deva of 'chance and accident,'" she said. "Especially not when he had Tahvo in his power. We'll find another way to the Hammer."

"Not if we anger every god the villagers bring to help us."

She rocked back on her knees and glared at him. "Tahvo can't endure much more of this."

Cian offered no argument. Tahvo's skin was pale, almost transparent, and she slept like the dead. Even her generous courage had its limits.

He plucked at a twig caught in the weave of his shirt. "Tahvo and I have reason to believe that not only the Stone's soldiers followed us from Karchedon," he said. "There may be…creatures of Baalshillek's making who have been sent to stop us."

Rhenna frowned at him. "What creatures?"

He couldn't yet bring himself to speak of Yseul. "They have human shape," he said, avoiding her eyes, "and possibly powers we can't predict. Tahvo wasn't able to tell me everything before Eshu came, but she thinks that one of these minions dried up the desert springs."

Rhenna peered into his face. "Why do I feel that you're keeping something from me, Cian?"

The sorrow in her voice, the emotion Rhenna believed she concealed so well, twisted in Cian's heart. If he could not reveal one truth, he might at least relieve her mind of another unacknowledged fear. "I…I was never with Madele, Rhenna."

Astonishment and something far more vulnerable crossed her face just before her expression hardened into a mask of stubborn pride. "Did I ever demand to know?"

"No." He laughed inwardly at his own stupidity. "You never asked." He got to his feet. "I'll speak to the villagers," he said, and left the hut.

Nyx and the Mothers waited outside, their dark faces creased with worry. The Imaziren crowded close.

"How fares the little healer?" Immeghar asked.

"She needs rest, but she should recover in time," Cian said. He turned to Nyx. "Your Eshu has left her very weak. She may be in danger if other devas come to claim her."

Nyx translated for the Mothers, who put their heads together for several moments of intense discussion. "They did not understand Tahvo's power to attract the spirits," Nyx said. "The òrìshà sometimes possess the bodies of those who call upon them, but never with such force." She bowed her head. "It is I who am at fault. I should have realized what might happen after Hat-T-Her's appearance in the desert." She paused to listen to the Mothers' words. "It is always dangerous to anger an òrìshà as mighty as Eshu. He delights in disrupting the intentions of men and turning them against their purpose. But it is also dangerous to trust him, for he has his own desires that no man can understand."

"Could he be an ally of the Exalted?" Cian asked.

Nyx gave him a startled look. "He is not an evil god, only unpredictable."

"Then it's just as well he's gone," Cian said. "Is there another way to find the Hammer?"

The Mothers consulted again. "If anyone knows where such a thing exists," Nyx said, "it is the little people of the deep forest. They live very close to the òrìshà who inhabit the bush."

"Why should these little people help us?"

"They are secretive and have few dealings with outsiders, but they have as much reason as any of us to fear the Stone God.

We will send hunters of the clan to seek their help. Until then, our healers will do all they can to help Tahvo."

The Mothers returned to their house to make their arrangements, and Cian reported the conversation to Rhenna. Tahvo continued to sleep, untroubled by the comings and goings of villagers bringing food, or the solemn healers with their chants and herbal concoctions.

Helpless to intervene, Cian sought the forest. Even by day, its shadows were dark and seductive, hinting at secrets only a wild beast—or an Ailu—could interpret. He lost himself amid the lush scents and mysterious calls, drowsing in soft hollows of fallen leaves and pungent earth, while tiny creatures skittered over his outstretched hands.

Cian.

He stirred reluctantly, unwilling to heed the voice that hummed inside his head.

I am here.

Who? he asked, half awake. No answer came, only an image of fierce beauty and restless hunger. Cian snapped to full alert, the air squeezed from his chest by a fist of terror.

Yseul.

All the forest was her lover, and Yseul could not get enough.

She stripped off her ragged clothes, and coated herself in moist soil and decaying vegetation, preening as if they were the rarest oils and spices from the distant East. She hunted by night, glorying in the deaths of the small, hapless beasts that fell under her claws. And sometimes, when she felt charitable, she brought a carcass back for her sullen companions, who did nothing but complain of the heat and brood over their failures.

Three times since leaving the desert, Urho and Farkas had challenged Yseul's leadership. Each time she had fought them back with her own strength and will, reminding Urho that Tahvo had defeated his efforts to drain the waterholes and Farkas that his one attempt at direct attack had ended in disaster.

But it was not logic or her own superior intelligence that kept the males in line; they submitted because even *their* dim minds understood that she held all the advantages in this place. It was as if she had been born here instead of in the dark rooms beneath Karchedon's great temple. As if the forest had been waiting for her all her short life.

She knew exactly where the enemy hid. She knew of the village and the naive mortals who lived in it, believing they could compel their savage, ignorant deities to aid the godborn. She felt Cian's presence like a constant ache in her belly.

Now, as the light of the day drove the night-hunting creatures to their nests, and the damp, stifling warmth dropped its stillness over the forest, Yseul carried her latest kill to camp and tossed it into Farkas's lap.

He pushed the bloody carcass away with a curse. He had shed most of his clothing, and his muscular chest gleamed with perspiration. Urho glanced up with seeming indifference and resumed sharpening his knife on the rock he had found buried under a mat of leaves. The Children of the Stone sweltered in their armor, unmoving save in direct obedience to their commander's orders. Their long spears were useless in the tangle of undergrowth beneath the canopy of interlaced branches, and even Farkas glared at them as if they were more hindrance than help.

Yseul still watched for the one Child whose eyes were too knowing…for the moment when Baalshillek's spy would reveal himself and seal his fate.

She rubbed at the stone in her aching forehead and nodded at the discarded meat. "Not hungry?" she asked Farkas with false concern.

He scowled and smeared a spot of blood on his arm. "Where have you been?"

"Watching the village."

"No movement?" Urho asked, his blade rasping on stone.

"Only the usual human scurrying." She kicked the carcass toward the Children's commander. "You. Prepare this for cooking."

The man met her gaze for the span of a heartbeat, rose and retrieved the dead animal with the smooth, efficient motions typical of Baalshillek's unnatural soldiers. He drew a knife from his belt and began to skin the carcass while his men looked on without expression.

"How long must we wait here?" Farkas asked, aiming a mouthful of spittle at Yseul's feet. "Can you learn nothing more?"

Yseul stepped daintily over the puddle. "Always you ask the same questions, Farkas, and always my answer is the same. We have tried to stop them, you with force of arms and Urho with his magic. We will not win this battle by confrontation but by cunning…a skill with which you have little acquaintance."

He thrust out his hand and curled his fingers around her ankle. "When I learn to wield my power…"

"But you have not." She jerked her leg from his grasp. "At least Urho has an understanding of his Element and the discipline you lack. *He* almost succeeded." She knelt and gathered a handful of soil. "The forces of Air might have been some use in the desert, but not here. This is the realm of Earth. My realm."

"It will not be so forever."

"Then you had best become more than a sack of wind forever wailing and groaning, unless you want Baalshillek to return you to the filth from which you sprang."

Farkas scrambled to his feet, fists swinging. Yseul dodged him easily. She sprang up into the nearest tree, agile as one of the long-tailed, clever-fingered beasts she had killed at dawn. "Surely you can summon up a little breeze to shake me from these branches," she said, laughing.

Farkas roared. His rage dislodged a few leaves from the end of the smallest branch. The air remained thick and still. He paced across the small clearing, snatched one of the Children's spears and slammed its shaft against the tree trunk.

"Oh, very good," Yseul purred. "Why don't you take your weapon to the village and demand our enemy's surrender?"

"Give me one of the females," Farkas said. "Give me that bitch Rhenna and I will break her."

"Not while an Ailu protects her." Yseul jumped down from the tree, landing well out of Farkas's reach. "Not until they have led us to the Hammer."

"And when we have it?" Farkas tossed the spear, narrowly missing a blank-eyed soldier. "Do you think to keep it for yourself?"

The red stone in Yseul's forehead throbbed again with warning pain. "What would I do with it?" she asked innocently. "I have no part in the prophecies. They—"

"Silence," Urho hissed. He cocked his head toward the edge of the clearing. A moment later a small animal trotted out from among the trees, its fur the color of dried grasses, its nose sharply pointed beneath a wrinkled brow and triangular ears.

Farkas drew his knife and prepared to throw it at the beast. Yseul struck his wrist, spoiling his aim.

"You fool," Urho said softly. "Do you not recognize a spirit when you see it?"

"That?" Farkas scoffed.

Yseul drew near to the dog, searching its bright brown eyes. "Yes," she said. She closed her eyes and drew on the wealth of memories Baalshillek had bestowed upon her on the day of her birth. So little of it made sense to her, even after a year of life, but now she sifted through the names and images of a thousand gods, deities who had fought in the Godwars for and against the Exalted. And a few who had been clever or lucky enough to remain apart from the slaughter....

"Eshu," she said.

"I am Eshu," the dog said, though its mouth didn't move. "You know me."

"I know *of* you," Yseul said, crouching before the beast. "Southern god of tricks and deceptions. You were present at the great battles of the Godwars, but you did not take part in them."

The dog yawned and winked one glittering eye. "It was not

our battle," he said. "Your Northern quarrels were never of concern to the òrìshà of the forest. Olorun sent me to observe, not fight."

"As your Lord of the Sky has sent you now?"

Eshu flicked his ears. "I see all that goes on in the forest," he said. "I saw the first pale-skinned strangers come to seek the help of the òrìshà, and I watched you watching them…servants of the Exalted."

Farkas lunged for his discarded spear and made as if to fling it at Eshu. The shaft snapped in half. The iron point spun about, sliced the flesh of Farkas's hand and buried itself in the trunk of a tree. Farkas cursed and sucked at his injured flesh.

"That was not at all wise," Eshu said mildly. "Yet what more can be expected from soulless beings shaped not by Obatala, like all natural living things, but by the priest of defeated gods?"

Yseul shivered, sickened to hear such words from the mouth of a smug little spirit who had no notion that his people's time was nearing its end. But even this creature still had his power, as he had proven to Farkas.

"The gods you call defeated have escaped their captivity," she said, swallowing her rage. "They grow more powerful every day, and their priests rule many lands. Can it be that even your great Olorun does not see everything?"

Eshu bared his teeth. "Make no mockery of the Lord of the Sky," he barked, "or you will never find what you seek."

"And what is it we seek, great Eshu?"

"That which was stolen by your masters' former allies. That which was made to defeat them."

"The Hammer," Urho said. He crept forward on his knees and bowed to Eshu. "Have you come to help us find it, mighty one?"

Eshu turned to sniff at Urho. "This creature, at least, shows the proper respect." He scraped at the earth with his hind paws, and a shower of leaves and bark fell from the trees. "This is my land," he said, "and here you are intruders. You have come far and have much farther to go. I could stop you. I could cause you to lose your way in the forest until your flesh rots from your bones and the worms burrow into your eyes." He grinned. "But perhaps I have come to help you. Perhaps I have come with a bargain from my brother and sister *òrìshà*."

"A bargain," Farkas said. "A bargain to spare the lives of weaklings and traitors when the Stone sweeps across the Great Desert to devour you and all your kind?"

A branch snapped from the tree above and clattered down on Farkas's head. He toppled over and lay still.

"Now that fool will be silent until our business is concluded," Eshu said. He licked a forepaw. "Will you listen, or shall I go to your enemies?"

"We listen," Urho said.

Eshu groomed his other leg, fastidious as a cat. "It is true that I bring an offer from the *òrìshà*," he said. "We know that your Eight masters stir again in the North. We know they hunger to rule all the earth and consume every god in their path."

"Every god who opposes them," Yseul said.

Eshu gave a strange, wavering cry very much like human laughter. "So you say. We, the *òrìshà* of this land, hold this forest and its people for our own. We have no interest in the world beyond. We wish merely to be left alone."

"And you would lead us to the Hammer," Yseul said, "if the Exalted agree to leave your forest untouched."

Eshu snapped at a hovering insect and crushed it between his teeth. "It is a fair bargain. Your masters are mighty, but they are not without weaknesses. They could not compel us to fight in their wars. The Eight may find that we are not helpless *ekute* to be eaten up in one bite."

Yseul smiled. "Why do you believe that we can negotiate for our masters, unnatural creatures that we are?"

Eshu gave another howling laugh. "There is no certainty," he said. "All is accident and chance. It is my whim to trust you, female of the North. And perhaps we are not without other strategies, should your masters betray us."

"They will reward those who serve them," Urho said. "This is the promise of the Stone God."

"We do not serve," Eshu said with a lift of his lips. "But you will take the Hammer to your masters as proof of our...friendship."

"And we should, of course, trust you," Yseul said softly.

Eshu leaped into the air, spun about and landed exactly where he had left the ground. He trotted over to the Children and sniffed them one by one. None stirred save for a single soldier, who twitched his hand away from Eshu's questing nose.

And Yseul knew. She pretended not to notice the Child's misstep and met Eshu's eyes with the slightest of nods.

"Trust me or not, as you choose," Eshu said. "But I alone know who guards the Hammer. They are females, and they hate all men." He grinned at Urho. "You they might kill swiftly. But that one—" He pointed a paw toward the immobile Farkas. "He is most ill-mannered. He might die very slowly indeed."

"Who are these females?" Yseul asked.

"They are like you. They walk in fur and hunt when the moon is high."

"Like me?" Yseul sprang toward the little god and barely stopped herself from seizing his scrawny neck. "They are Ailuri?"

"They call themselves Alu. They guard the compound of a foreign goddess whose name is only whispered, even among the òrìshà."

But Yseul hardly heard the rest of his words. *Alu.* The name could be no coincidence. Unless Eshu lied for his own purposes, she was not the only female of the Watcher breed. And even the Ailuri had not known it.

Neither had Baalshillek.

"Alu," she said with a show of indifference. "Have these creatures always lived in the forests of the South?"

Eshu saw through her pretense. "They, unlike you, were

given life by Olorun," he said. "But perhaps they will not kill
you if you prove your worth."

"Take me to them, and I will."

"Even if they let you pass, you must face the outlander *òrìshà*. It is she who holds the Hammer and will never let it be
taken, save by her death."

Yseul's heart beat fast with excitement. "It is said that the four
Exalted who betrayed the Eight stole the weapons and carried
them to the farthest corners of the earth. Is this goddess one of
the Four?"

"Who can say? No mortal or *òrìshà* has approached her compound in a thousand years."

"But you can lead us to it."

"If you and your human servants can endure a journey of
many days and nights being attacked by beasts, bitten by insects and soaked by rain, then I will show you the way."

"We will endure whatever trials you set us."

"Then make yourself ready. And remove those accursed
stones, or the Alu will know you for what you are." Eshu flattened his sharp ears behind him, as if he followed some distant
sound. "I go. Be prepared to travel at dawn tomorrow."

He ran off into the forest as quickly as he'd come. Farkas
stirred with a groan.

"Where did it go?" he croaked.

Yseul gave Farkas's head a cursory glance and judged him
unharmed save for the large lump on his thick skull. "Eshu has
agreed to take us to the Hammer."

Farkas sat up. "You trusted him?"

She shrugged. "It is possible that these *òrìshà* truly hope to
spare their own lives by giving us what we seek."

"The Stone will never let them go."

Yseul pressed her finger over Farkas's lips. "Cunning, my
stubborn friend. Let them believe." She glanced at the Children, her gaze sweeping casually over the soldier who had betrayed himself at Eshu's examination. The depleted ranks of

Children would sadly lose another of their number before this day was ended.

The crystal in her forehead began to burn. Yseul took Urho's knife and stared at her reflection in the polished iron. The stone was a baleful third eye, an excrescence, a malignancy that would continue to weaken her as long as it remained a part of her. But she had been born out of the Stone. If she severed herself from it…

Better to die now than live as a slave.

She lifted the knife's blade to her brow and laid it to her flesh.

Urho caught her arm. "What are you doing?"

"Eshu said to remove the stones," she said calmly.

"You're mad."

She wiped at the blood trickling from the first cut and licked her fingers. "Be rid of them," she said, "or let the Alu kill us. Which do you choose?"

He backed away, silver eyes hollow with dread. "The stones sustain us. Without them—"

"Without them we may become more than the 'soulless beings' Eshu named us."

"Baalshillek will send punishment."

"Not if we succeed in our task."

"What of the Children?" Farkas asked.

"They will stay here until we have the Hammer. Perhaps you would care to join them?"

Farkas sneered and unsheathed his own blade, wetting his lips as he contemplated the prospect of self-mutilation. Urho sat down hard, shaking his head. The Children made not a sound.

Yseul smiled and continued her grisly work.

Chapter Fifteen

The portal to the country of the little people was as formidable a gate as one might find in any stone fortress of the North. Even in her blindness Tahvo could feel its power, and as she and her companions rested at the end of many days' travel through the heart of the forest, she remembered what she had learned of the place the Ará Odò called the Cave of Dreams.

"The cave is the entrance to the only passage through the mountain," Nyx had explained as she made final preparations for the journey. She had gathered Tahvo, Cian, Rhenna, the Imaziren and two village hunters at the edge of the village, distributing packs of provisions while she revealed what the little people demanded in exchange for their aid in locating the Hammer.

"The little people have long been our allies," she had said, "but they do not trust what lies beyond their forest. They believe that no evil can pass through the Cave of Dreams."

"Another test," Rhenna had grumbled. "Will there ever be an end to them?"

Cian hadn't spoken, but Tahvo had felt his weariness. She herself had struggled during the long march beneath the giant whispering trees. Rhenna, the Imaziren and the villagers set a modest pace, but often she had been compelled to accept Cian's help when the path grew rough. Sometimes her knees trembled, or she heard voices that were not there. And always she felt the multitudes of forest spirits dancing around her, drawn to her soul as the swarms of biting insects sought the sweet taste of human blood.

Now it was just past dawn, and the insects were at their worst. She pulled her head between her shoulders and tried to pretend that her skin was as tough and impenetrable as a turtle's shell.

"Are you all right?" Cian asked, settling beside her.

She tried to smile. "I did not sleep well last night."

"Who could, in this cursed heat?" he said, killing a dozen winged biters with one slap of his hand. "How you must be longing for your snowfields now."

She thought that Cian must be speaking as much for himself as for her. "Do you miss the mountains?" she asked.

He went very still, barely breathing. "It's strange," he said slowly, "but at times I think I belong here more than I ever did in the Shield."

"The Imaziren say your people were created in the South."

"Thousands of years ago," he said. "But there is something in these forests, Tahvo, like a fever in the blood. It frightens me."

She touched his arm. "It is not like the call of the red stones?"

"No." He gave an uneasy laugh. "That's the one thing I don't hear." He pressed a piece of dried root into her hand. "Eat while you can. Nyx said we're soon to enter the cave."

The dread in his voice confirmed Tahvo's own fears, but she took a bite of the root and forced herself to chew. If she concentrated on each mouthful of the bitter plant, she could almost forget the anger that flowed from the mouth of the mountain—anger and hunger—as if half-mad spirits were held unwilling prisoner in perpetual darkness. As she was.

She remembered nothing of her possession by the god called Eshu—knew nothing of him save for what Rhenna and Cian had told her—but she would have welcomed his return. Such a powerful spirit would not be afraid. He would not tremble when Nyx announced that each man or woman must enter the cave alone.

Rhenna and Cian refused to leave her behind. They allowed Nyx, the village hunters and the Imaziren to go ahead, and guarded the cave mouth while Tahvo blundered her way past the drape of vines overhanging it. They shouted encouragement when a damp and heavy wall of air struck her face and flowed over her body like a second skin. She pushed forward, arms stretched before her, but not a single obstacle appeared in her path.

"Rhenna?" she called. "Cian?"

Her voice echoed, bouncing from wall to wall. She heard no footsteps, no breathing other than her own. She continued to feel her way, trying to ignore the increasingly crushing weight that bore down on her head and chest.

She knew the pressure was not physical, yet it was very real. Her legs moved as if through deep snow or the thick mud left after a flood at snowmelt, each step requiring all her strength and concentration.

Thirty paces beyond the cave entrance she could no longer sense the world outside. After another ten paces the spirits began to gather. At first they hovered, pacing her like starving wolves. And then they descended, alighting on her clothing and skin, brushing her face like cobwebs, skittering over puckered flesh, pricking like invisible gnats. Faint itching turned to stabs of pain as hundreds of spirits became thousands.

Had they been ordinary spirits like the benign dwellers of the forest, their assault would have been terrifying enough.

Tahvo had long since acknowledged the danger of losing herself to the spirits who borrowed her body, as Eshu had done. But these beings threatened more than a simple loss of control or memory.

These were not true spirits at all. They did not have minds, not like even the tiniest creatures that dwelled in drops of water or particles of earth. They did not wish to speak to Tahvo or assume her shape. They had no message to impart.

Pneumata. The "bones" of gods destroyed in the Godwars, fragments that still contained enough power to be wielded in magic by those who understood how to command them. Most were neither good nor evil, lying neutral and dormant until they were made to serve some mortal or godborn purpose. But the pneumata of the cave were driven as surely as if they had desires of their own…driven by hatred and appetite that had only one purpose: to devour utterly.

Tahvo cried out. Darting, stinging motes burrowed into the roof of her mouth and coated her tongue. They tore her clothing from her body, leaving her naked to their foul assault. Soon they would consume every bit of flesh, face and belly and limbs, and then gnaw away at her bones until there was nothing left but dust.

And they laughed. Not the witless pneumata themselves, but the ghosts to whom they had once belonged: gods of evil, allies of the Exalted who had been defeated in the last and most brutal of the Godwars. She tasted their undead lust for power, their desperate search for a way back to life. The roar of their voiceless whispers pounded against the drums of her ears: *She was made to carry the gods. Take her apart and create anew.*

They would do worse than destroy her. They would turn her into a thing of pure evil, fit only to do their will.

Fight them. She thought the words were her own, though she had no tongue left to give them substance. But as she struggled with what remained of her body, writhing in agony on the cave floor, a new vision came to sightless eyes: the dog Eshu, crouched beside her, his warm tongue stroking the scalded flesh that still clung to her skull.

Fight. She clutched at Eshu's short coat with fingers stripped to the bone. His divine strength flowed into her, mingling with her determination to survive. Or die free.

I will not become a thing of evil. If it ends here, then let my soul rejoin the waters and flow back to my people....

Eshu gave a wailing cry that silenced the evil spirits' yammering. He leaped into Tahvo's body, dancing in the cage of bones where her heart had been, and lifted her from the cave floor. Through his eyes she saw the whirling specks that sought to undo her very being. Hatred overwhelmed her fear. She shared Eshu's laughter and delight as she crunched the evil pneumata between powerful jaws. She felt obscene joy in their obliteration.

Crush your enemies, little sister, Eshu whispered. *Take what is yours by right.*

Tahvo opened her hands and snatched pneumata from the air, consuming them with savage hunger. They became a part of her, feeding her strength, introducing her mind to a new world of possibility, a world she had never dared to see for what it was.

To destroy evil was glorious in itself, but to transform it, to force it to serve the good...was this not the purpose of true power?

Yes, Eshu said. *Now you understand....*

The empty sockets of Tahvo's skull overflowed with light. She looked, and saw—not through Eshu's eyes, but with her own—saw the cave walls glazed with an eldritch luminescence, saw each drop of water that slicked the stone, saw Eshu leaping and whirling in furious glee.

All this she saw with eyes made whole, the sweet prize of victory. And it was only the beginning. Pneumata beyond counting waited outside the cave, hers for the taking. This small, weak body could become stronger than any warrior's, swifter than an Ailu, immortal as a god. She would be a true champion for the spirits, for the salvation of the earth. Never again need she suffer the burden of a timid healer's soul, afraid to kill even her enemies....

A field of shining silver blocked her sight. A beast's eyes gazed into hers—slanted eyes in a long-muzzled face.

"Slahtti!" she cried.

The wolf did not answer, but he drew her back...back to a small room in Karchedon, to the very day of her bargain.

You will forget your own name. You will be given that which you most desire, only to lose it. You will be tempted again and again, but if you falter...

Tahvo rubbed at her eyes, trying to dispel the vision. Her hands came away coated with ichor that dripped from her fingers and pooled at her feet—the life fluid of a thousand pneumata, transformed and reshaped to create the very organs she so coveted. Eshu's laughing face replaced Slahtti's noble countenance.

Take them, the god urged. *Take this gift.*

Take it, and deny the very spirits who had fought and died to rid the world of its greatest enemy. Admit that she had found joy in killing. Accept that her sight would forever be tainted by the burning memory of willful slaughter. For what she had done in this cave would never be forgotten, and the bitter glory of her pride and hatred would spread like a wasting disease, from eyes to nose and mouth and limbs, until it had swallowed her up just as the evil pneumata had intended.

Tahvo fell to her knees. She pushed her fingers into her eye sockets and screamed as the tissue gave way. Hard, round stones rolled into her hands, and then there was no more pain.

Fool, Eshu said, his voice fading away. *Mortal fool.*

Tahvo bent to the ground and wept tears of blood. The pneumata were silent, destroyed or fled. Tahvo crawled to the nearest wall, climbed to her feet and felt her way along the passage.

That was when she heard the scream.

* * *

Rhenna was flying.

Wind whipped hair across her face, obscuring her view of the world far below. Hills and valleys and forests passed in the blink of an eye; Rhenna's head hung out over a blue nothingness laced with clouds. Sharp-edged feathers scraped her cheek. She flexed her hands and found them immobilized by ropes as thick as her thumb.

She closed her eyes against the impossible sight, struggling to remember how she had come to be in such a place. Her mind was as blank as her body was naked under the fur that covered her; she spread her fingers, feeling coarse hair and leather, the curve of a strap and the warm solidity of a human leg encased in high boots.

"So eager, pretty one?" a masculine voice said above her. She didn't recognize the sounds that came out of his mouth, but they formed into words she understood. A rough hand came down on her head, pawing at her hair. "I'd be happy to accommodate you, but you've already been claimed, and *he* said to leave you untouched." The hand wandered beneath Rhenna's fur and stroked her bare back. "You'd be a fine ride, little filly."

Rhenna choked on her own bile and tried to speak. Her mouth was so dry that her tongue stuck to the roof of her mouth; her throat was raw as if from constant shouting. Only a grunt emerged.

"Not such a pretty voice," her captor said, thrusting a gloved hand between her thighs. "Better save what you have left for him. He enjoys a little screaming when he's served fresh meat."

Rhenna tested the ropes at wrists and ankles and assessed her position. She hung belly-down over the shoulder of some rank-smelling beast, but all she could see of the creature was a crest of blue-sheened feathers and the curve of its shoulder. Below that was open sky. With difficulty she turned her head and caught the downsweep of immense white wings.

There was nowhere to escape, even if she could work loose

from her bindings. She could choose to fall, free for the few moments before she hit the ground. But she wasn't yet sure if it was time to die.

Tahvo. Cian.

The image of her friends drove all thought of death from her mind. Where were they? By all the devas, what had happened to her?

No answers came, not even the shadow of memory. She couldn't picture when she'd last seen their faces. Cian's, so vulnerable and determined. Tahvo, with her blind silver eyes and enduring faith. And Nyx, who was so sure of finding the Hammer.

The Hammer. They had been in the forest, beginning the search. Seeking the little people who would guide them. And there had been a cave, and darkness....

Rhenna's captor whistled, high and shrill. Answering cries rode on an upswept wind. The great-winged creature tilted its body and dived. Rhenna clutched at feathers that slipped through her fingers. They were falling, and there was nothing she could do except brace for the impact.

The winged beast touched down with scarcely a bump. Solid ground lay two arm's lengths away under Rhenna's head. The man stripped the fur from her body. He grabbed her hair and pulled her upright.

"Home, pretty one," he said.

She gazed out at the vast bowl of a valley, a landscape almost as sere and bare as that of the Great Desert. The clifflike walls were riddled with caves. Little grew on the plateau above, but the floor of the valley was marked with the green tracery of a stream and clusters of hardy trees. Furtive cloaked figures bearing clay jars and other burdens negotiated the narrow tracks up and down the cliffsides.

Rhenna's captor cut the ropes that bound her to the beast's withers and hauled her from its back. The moment her feet touched earth, she moved to run. A huge beaked head sliced the air directly in front of her face, and she found herself staring into a baleful yellow eye as big as a clenched fist.

She stumbled back and would have fallen except for her captor's grip at the nape of her neck. "You want to be griffin-bait, bitch?" he asked, spraying spittle onto her cheek. "Maybe if *he* gets tired of you, he'll throw you into the pit for the nestlings."

Rhenna stared as the immense bird's neck stretched, feathers bristling, and the beak opened on a hoarse, rattling cry. Long ears twitched and flattened. The man shouted a command, and the beast crouched on eagle's claws and a great cat's hindquarters, tufted tail lashing. Wings folded, hiding the saddle and harness that had held its rider in place.

The griffin's master looped a noose of rope around Rhenna's neck and fastened it with a knot meant to strangle her at the least attempt to fight. He led her away from the griffin's perch and down a path cut out of the cliff and worn by countless feet. Men emerged from the caves they passed, bearded faces that taunted and jeered and offered foul promises that Rhenna could not misunderstand. She was a female animal to be judged by length of limb and fullness of chest, color of hair and curve of rump, all in full view of her eager audience.

Her legs were trembling by the time they reached the turning in the path, halfway down the cliff. She was every bit as helpless as the griffin rider intended her to be…naked, weak, expertly bound. Humiliated. Defeated. She stared up to where the great beast waited, capable of such powerful flight and yet invisibly tethered to its roost as meekly as a caged wren. Its head snaked over the cliff's edge as if it sensed her regard, and the yellow eyes grew hooded to hide an emotion Rhenna knew all too well: rage. Hatred of all that would hold it captive. Hatred and the seething lust to kill.

Free us.

Rhenna shook her head, and her captor shoved her into the mouth of a cave hung with intricate tapestries and capes woven of feathers and fur. Weapons of war stood ready on racks built of antler and bone. Torches lit the dim, twisting passage that opened into a chamber of impressive proportions. On a stone dais stood a chair of carved wood and gold, its back surmounted by the gaping beak of a griffin's skull. The chair's arms ended in fleshless talons. A simmering pot of meat hung over a fire to one side of the dais.

A pair of women, little more dressed than Rhenna, crept out of the shadows. Their hair hung loose and lank about their thin shoulders. Each of them wore a thin iron collar. They crawled on hands and knees, like beasts, and one slunk close to the pot and began to dip her dirty hand into the thick, steaming liquid. She shrieked as a tail of black leather curled about her wrist and jerked her over to lie in the dust of the cave floor, whimpering with pain and despair.

The owner of the whip strolled from the rear of the cave, lightly flicking the braided leather over his shoulder. On his face he wore a leather mask molded to the shape of a griffin's head.

"Derinoe," he said, his voice heavy with regret. "How many times have I warned you to await your master's leave before you eat?" He walked up to the prone girl and nudged her side with the toe of his boot. She cringed away.

Derinoe. Rhenna remembered a half-wild girl on the steppe, defiant and discourteous and afraid of the vast responsibility laid upon her inexperienced shoulders. Derinoe, who had ridden free in the Shield's Shadow…

Rhenna shivered, and the masked man's head turned toward her. "Ah," he said. "You've done well, Arshan. I am pleased." He strode forward, stepping over the weeping girl. "Welcome to my Aerie, Rhenna." His gaze swept over her. "It's been much too long, but now we can properly renew our acquaintance."

Rhenna jerked against the noose at her throat. "Who are you?"

But she knew. She knew even before he lifted the mask from his cruel, handsome face.

"There is so much for you to learn," Farkas said. "And so

much I am ready to teach." He grabbed her leash and yanked her to him, grinding his lips into hers.

Rhenna screamed. She screamed like a weakling, like one of the Hellene's beaten females, but she couldn't stop. Blackness clouded her vision. She fell, tumbling down and down from a vast height into a bottomless chasm.

Someone caught her hand in a warm, firm grip, and she struck the ground without pain.

"Rhenna?"

She clung to the invisible hand and moved her body carefully, feeling for twisted muscle and broken bone. Nothing was damaged. The noose was no longer around her neck. She still wore the clothes she'd had on when she entered the cave....

The cave. She squeezed her unseen companion's blunt fingers and laughed until the tears ran from her eyes.

"Tahvo," she said when she could speak again. "You're well?"

"Yes." The little healer helped Rhenna to her feet. "We must get out and find the others."

Rhenna rubbed her throat. "It was only a dream. I saw Farkas—"

"It is over now. Can you walk?"

"Of course." Rhenna released Tahvo's hand and searched the darkness. "Which way?"

Tahvo started forward without hesitation, and soon the cavern narrowed to a passage that ended in a sliver of blessed light. The thick, decaying smell of the forest had never seemed so welcome.

The others already waited in the clearing just outside the cave mouth. The villagers and Imaziren stood apart in their separate groups, hunched and silent. Cian crouched in the shadows of a broad-leafed bush, and Nyx stood at the opposite edge of the clearing, arms folded tightly across her chest.

"Rhenna," Cian said when he saw her. He half rose, glanced at Tahvo, and sank back down.

"Is everyone all right?" Rhenna asked.

Immeghar opened his mouth, then closed it again. The villa-gers exchanged uneasy glances. Rhenna strode to confront Nyx.

"You said no evil could pass through these caves," she said, "but the evil was already inside them."

Nyx pressed her lips together and looked away. Rhenna turned to Tahvo. "You felt it, as well."

"Yes."

"What did you see, Cian?"

He lifted his hands and stared at them as if they belonged to someone else. "Blood," he whispered.

Rhenna almost went to him then, but the bleakness in his face stopped her. Clearly she had not been alone in her ordeal. Perhaps each of them had passed through a similar trial of the spirit. And though they had come out alive, none of them was yet willing to speak of what they'd endured.

Nyx and the village hunters agreed to scout the surrounding forest for sign of the little people, who would be watching the caves for their visitors' arrival. The Imaziren set out to gather wood and kindling from the forest floor, while Rhenna and Cian hunted for game. By nightfall Cian had caught a small striped antelope, and Rhenna helped him carry it back to the clearing.

Tahvo was gone. The Imaziren had returned with their fire-wood, but none had seen the healer. Cian quickly shed his clothes, changed and plunged into the black forest to search for her.

Rhenna forced worry from her mind and built the fire while the Imaziren skinned and cleaned the carcass. Nyx and the vil-lagers returned after moonrise, empty-handed. The meat was almost charred when Cian finally reappeared with Tahvo.

The healer sat before the fire, her opaque silver eyes reflect-ing the dancing light. "I have met with the little people," she said. "They have heard tales of the thing we seek, hidden many days' journey south in the deep forest. They say there is a great power there, an angry god who rules a place forbidden even to their kind."

"An angry god," Rhenna said. She turned to Nyx. "Did you know of this?"

"No more than the prophecies tell—that four escaped Exalted stole and hid the Weapons." She leaned close to Tahvo. "Will the little folk guide us?"

"As far as the borders of the forbidden place," Tahvo said. "They will show us the way, but we will not see them."

"Then they fear us in spite of their test," Cian said.

"They would not take us at all if the caves had not shown us to be worthy. But they say we will face many dangers." She bowed her head. "Not all will survive."

Rhenna nodded and looked from Nyx to the Imaziren. "We knew this would be a difficult journey," she said. "None of you need go with us. You can return to the desert—"

"And give up the chance to become great heroes of our people?" Immeghar said, slapping his chest. "We were charged to protect the Guardian on his quest and watch over the little Healer who awakened our goddess. This we will do until death claims us, even if we end our lives in this stinking wet hellhole."

"We go," Cabh'a said firmly.

"We go," Tamallat and Mezwar echoed, smiling at each other.

"Very well," Rhenna said. "What of your people, Nyx?"

"Few of the Ará Odò have ventured beyond the caves," she said. "Abidemi and Enitan are among those who believe my father's tales of the Godwars. They are eager to see what lies in the South."

"Then we must rest," Tahvo said. "The little people will come for us in the morning."

Immeghar began slicing chunks of meat from the carcass and handing them around on plates fashioned of broad serrated leaves. Rhenna ate with little appetite, half watching Cian as he prowled the borders of the clearing. When the others had made their beds, she drew him aside.

"Did you see these little people?" she asked.

"Not a sign," he said with veiled disgust. "I didn't hear or smell them, either. They might as well have been invisible."

"Tahvo trusts them."

"I hope they prove worthy of her faith." He cleared his throat. "What did you see in the caves?"

"Nothing."

"I don't believe you."

"It was…something that doesn't exist."

"Or has yet to happen." He looked away. "If the price for the Hammer becomes too high…if I ever turn against you—"

"Was it my blood you saw, Cian?"

He seized her arms. "If I ever lose myself, only you can stop me. Promise you will."

"No." She worked free of his hold and took his face between her hands. "Whatever you saw was an evil vision meant to lay bare your deepest fears."

"Is that what you found, Rhenna? Your deepest fear?"

She let her hands fall. "I saw Farkas." Her skin heated painfully. "He was in a land I've never seen before."

"Farkas is too much of a coward to leave the steppes," Cian said, baring his teeth.

"I know. It was only a dream." She met his gaze. "Only dreams, Cian."

He stroked her scarred cheek with the back of his hand. "Then just for tonight," he said, "let us dream of peace."

But she saw in his eyes that no such dreams would come for him.

Chapter Sixteen

Karchedon

Spring arrived in Karchedon, and with it the fragile beginnings of a new life.

Patience, humility and caution. That had been Philokrates's advice in the midst of the warm Libyan winter, when a traitor's shame had seemed Quintus's sole inheritance from his royal Arrhidaean blood.

But time had given truth to the old man's words. It was true that Tiberia had lost its leading rebel when Quintus had failed to set Buteo free; the captive had been taken to the Temple, supposedly for sacrifice, but no word ever came of his ultimate fate, nor was there any sign of the grand celebration that should have taken place on the day of Buteo's death.

Though Quintus never found a way to penetrate the Temple's veil of secrecy, he knew that neither Nikodemos nor Baal-shillek had won a lasting victory. The rebellion in Italia continued unabated; regular dispatches came across Ta Thalassa to inform the emperor of the latest outrages committed by the colonial insurgents.

Quintus made it his business to listen, and learn. And he built fresh determination out of Philokrates's guidance: *You must use your position here for the world's benefit, and never allow yourself to forget your true purpose.*

Quintus didn't forget. With the enthusiastic aid of young Hylas, who made no secret of his personal interest in the emperor's exotic half-brother, he found it surprisingly easy to become an accepted part of Nikodemos's court. He swallowed his pride and made himself agreeable to elderly advisers and military commanders alike; he rode out with Nikodemos on tours of the city and countryside, turning a blind eye to the evil of the priests and their altars. He hardened his heart to the suffering of those who could or would not bend to the One True God, remembering that he was but one man with a unique power that must at all costs be protected.

He made no attempt to see Danae, and she stayed close to the emperor. That was as it must be. Quintus didn't allow himself to dwell on their brief moments of intimacy, or on the loneliness he felt more keenly in the palace than at any time since childhood. He focused his attention on observing Nikodemos at every opportunity, in work and leisure, making careful note of each strength and weakness. When delegates arrived from distant satrapies to make their obeisance and bring reports of drought or petitions for relief from the priests' levy of their children, Quintus admired the emperor's clever answers that left the supplicants convinced that their grievances would be duly addressed. He smiled at Nikodemos's jokes, absorbed every morsel of court gossip, however trivial, and learned never to show what lay in his thoughts.

And the emperor rewarded him. If Nikodemos had harbored

any doubts about his half-brother's loyalties, he had set them aside with the same hearty good nature with which he favored his chosen Companions. He began to invite Quintus into some of his private councils, watching his kinsman over steepled fingers as his secretaries tallied the empire's growing wealth and discussed the deployment of imperial troops.

But even the most generous emperor's trust had its limits. Quintus knew there was much that went on in his absence, secret meetings with priests and generals to which few in the court were privy. There was still a barrier Quintus had yet to pass. He spoke to Philokrates when he could, but the philosopher had little additional advice to offer; he was ensconced in his new workshops in the abandoned quarter of the palace, purportedly devising some fantastic machine for the emperor. The old man suffered the unenviable position of keeping Nikodemos satisfied while somehow delaying the actual completion of his work.

On the eve of the Spring Festival, when the common people of Karchedon would be loosed to the Stone God's madness for a night of wanton destruction, Nikodemos called for a lion hunt. He assembled his favorites and ordered chariots and wagons of supplies prepared for a week away from the city. It was necessary to travel some distance from Karchedon to reach lands where the Stone's influence had not driven away wild game worthy of an emperor.

The party of servants, soldiers, courtiers and drivers set out for the hills west of Karchedon, the men mounted on fine horses while the few women permitted to accompany them lounged among pillows and furs in the covered wagons. It was the first time Quintus had been near Danae in many weeks. While Nikodemos exchanged jests with one of his Persian commanders, Quintus fell back to ride beside the lead wagon.

Four women reclined under the linen canopy stretched over the wagon's frame: Danae, her servant Leuke and two others Quintus recognized from brief glimpses at court. Danae straightened when she saw him, her lips curving in an indifferent smile.

"Well-met, my lord Alexandros," she said. "To what do we owe the honor of your presence?"

Quintus returned her bow and drank in the sight of her through half-closed lids. He had always thought her beautiful, but now he felt like a starving man so long deprived of food that he had forgotten the difference between a crust of stale bread and a banquet. She was thinner than he remembered, her lovely eyes shadowed beneath long lashes, but her golden hair still shone as bright as the Libyan sun.

"My brother the emperor is much occupied, Lady Danae," he said. "I took it upon myself to see that the ladies have all they require."

One of the women behind Danae leaned forward, displaying a bounty of bosom, vivid azure eyes and coils of black hair laced with pearls and precious stones. "You may tell the emperor," she said, "that some of us would much prefer to ride beside him and bask in his imperial glory."

Danae arched a brow at her companion, and her mouth twitched. "I do believe you two have never been properly introduced," she said. "Lady Gulbanu has but newly come to our court, my lord Alexandros."

"But everyone in Karchedon knows the emperor's brother," Lady Gulbanu said. "Even in Persis, we have heard his name."

Quintus bowed. "It is my honor to serve you, lady."

Gulbanu laughed, low and dark. "Your speech reveals your royal blood, my lord," she said, "and gives shame to those who would deride such a noble kinsman for the misfortune of his upbringing."

"Gulbanu has been in Karchedon only a few weeks," Danae said, "but already she knows all that is said in the corridors and private chambers of the palace. Her hearing is acute, but her tongue is sometimes known to wander."

"An agile tongue is a most useful instrument," Gulbanu purred. "Perhaps yours, Lady Danae, has grown weak from lack of use."

"It is merely selective in its choice of work," Danae said. She turned her back on her companion and smiled at Quintus. "Have you hunted lions before, my lord?"

"There are lions in Tiberia," he said, looking deliberately at Gulbanu. "The land of my unfortunate upbringing has no need to test the courage of its warriors by slaughtering dumb beasts."

Danae gave Quintus a sharp glance of warning. "No one doubts Lord Alexandros's courage, or that of the emperor."

"Or yours, Danae," Gulbanu said. "Perhaps you will stand beside our great lord when he makes his kill."

Danae suppressed a shudder, and Quintus saw the distaste in her eyes. "I am honored to serve the emperor in any way he requires," she said.

Gulbanu smiled. Quintus felt her hatred for Danae as if it were a blade poised in the air between them. Danae was far too clever to lose a battle of wits with a female like Gulbanu, but this seemed more than a mere skirmish of words.

For the rest of that day's journey and the next, when the emperor did not specifically request his presence, Quintus made casual tours of the wagons as often as was reasonable. Danae accepted his visits with distant courtesy, but her face had become an expressionless mask.

On the third night the party made camp beside a farmer's fields near the outlying edge of Karchedon's chora, and the servants efficiently raised the tents and prepared a feast for the emperor and his Hetairoi. The ladies Danae and Gulbanu were invited to join the men under the awning that served as a dining hall.

Quintus ate sparingly, observing Nikodemos's laughing response to Gulbanu's brazen jests and unsubtle words of praise. Though Danae still sat at his side, the emperor gave her a fraction of his attention, and she made no effort to win it. She picked at her food and only once met Quintus's gaze. The pain in her eyes tore at his heart. Still, it was Danae who joined the emperor in his tent when the feasters retired, and Gulbanu withdrew with her maid to her own accommodations across the camp.

Thoughts of Danae kept Quintus awake long after the camp grew silent. He was still staring at the ceiling of his tent when Nikodemos's trackers rode out in the hours before dawn. They returned just after the morning meal to report the presence of a lion, its females and cubs laired in the hills several leagues west of the fields.

The servants remained at the camp while Nikodemos and the courtiers pursued the trackers' lead. The emperor drove his own vehicle, Danae at his side. His personal groom rode his favorite hunting horse close behind, and Quintus's driver took up the privileged second place in the procession. Gulbanu traveled with the rest of the courtiers, audaciously dressed in loose trousers and tunic, bearing her own bow and quiver.

It was planned that the hunters should climb into the hills by chariot as far as the terrain allowed and then complete the excursion on horseback. The skilled drivers managed to find negotiable trails twisting among the jutting rocks and low trees, and only when they reached the impassible barrier of a dry gulch did Nikodemos hand over his chariot ribbons and mount his prancing stallion. Those courtiers who wished to be in on the kill had brought their own horses, and the emperor provided Quintus with a handsome gray gelding. Danae was given a mare whose gleaming coat matched the gold of her hair. Gulbanu mounted an onyx beast that lashed out at any man who came too near.

Quintus rode alongside Nikodemos as the chattering would-be hunters gathered around their king. "Surely it is dangerous to bring the women," he said.

Nikodemos looked at him in amused surprise. "Do you fear I will not be able to protect them, brother?" He waved toward Danae. "You aren't afraid, are you, my little doe?"

"If she is," Gulbanu said, reining her black mare across Danae's path, "I would be honored to take her place."

The Hetairoi fell silent at the insolence of her words. Nikodemos burst into laughter. Danae faced Gulbanu, her veil fluttering about her shoulders.

"I am not afraid," she said clearly.

Nikodemos clapped his hands. "Excellent. Today we will witness the valor of our women, and to the most courageous..." He held up his left hand and worked a gem-encrusted ring from his smallest finger, holding Gulbanu's gaze. "This will be her prize!"

The courtiers applauded. Danae rode up beside Quintus. Her passing glance was bleak. He clenched his jaw as the trackers retraced their steps higher into the hills and Nikodemos spurred after them. Danae hurried to catch up, and Gulbanu whipped her mount in pursuit.

The lions were not difficult to find. If there had been no vulnerable cubs, the male and his females might easily have fled and given the hunters a hard fight for their lives. As it was, the trackers had pinned the king and his two queens near the outcropping of rock that served as their lair. The dark-maned male crouched snarling on a jutting stone, one of the females at his flank, while the other guarded a hollow full of mewling cubs.

The courtiers hung back as Nikodemos dismounted and accepted his bow from his servant. He nocked an arrow. The lion gave a great bellow and shook its massive head, muscles bunching. The men nearest to Quintus sucked in their breaths.

Nikodemos let fly just as the lion sprang. The arrow caught it in the center of its chest, and it fell like a stone.

The Companions whistled and applauded, provoking fresh snarls from the females who waited to die. Nikodemos turned his back on the beasts as if they were kittens, catching Quintus's eye with a grin. But he didn't offer Quintus the honor of the second kill; he knew that Quintus could not draw a bow because of his withered left arm. He beckoned instead to one of his favored army commanders. The man failed on his first attempt, but his second wounded one of the lionesses. She charged, tawny body sweeping close to the earth. Quintus drew his knife and swung his gelding in front of Danae's quivering mare. An arrow hissed past his ear and drove between the lioness's ribs.

Gulbanu stood triumphant, still posed with her bow in hand. She looked like some wild goddess of the hunt, her hair whipping free of its veils, and the effect was not lost on the emperor. Nikodemos stared at her with open admiration, pulled the prize ring from his finger and tossed it to her. She caught it one-handed and bowed deeply.

Quintus kept his knife in hand and looked from Danae's impassive face to the remaining lioness and her cubs. Nikodemos retrieved his bow and strode within a few paces of the lair. Casually he aimed at the doomed female and pulled the bowstring taut.

Danae kicked her mount forward, driving the mare between the emperor and his quarry. His shot went wild. Danae slid from the saddle and knelt at his feet.

"Spare her, my lord," she whispered. "Let her cubs survive so that they may become worthy prey for a king."

Nikodemos cursed and grabbed her arm. "You dare—"

The lioness gave an eerie wail and leaped at Danae. Quintus lost no time in thinking. He threw his knife with the unwavering focus of desperation. The lioness stumbled and collapsed within reach of Danae's robes.

The Companions broke into cheers of astonished delight. Nikodemos glanced at the dying beast, pushed Danae away and advanced on Quintus with open arms.

"Bravely done, brother, bravely done!" He embraced Quintus and pressed his mouth to Quintus's ear. "You'll have your reward," he murmured. "I promise you." He let Quintus go and acknowledged the courtiers' shouts. "Tonight we'll celebrate," he said, gathering them all into the circle of his triumph. Not once did his eyes seek Danae.

Quintus went to her and led her away from the scene of

slaughter, leaving his knife behind. The trackers and servants collected the carcasses and carried them to the chariots. Quintus helped Danae mount her mare and escorted her back down the hill before she could witness what became of the helpless cubs. He gave her into the care of her maid and waited in his tent for Nikodemos's return.

But Nikodemos did not come for him. The night's festivities went on without Quintus, and he listened to drunken laughter and wild music well into the night. He had almost surrendered to sleep when the flap of his tent opened and Danae crept inside.

She stood proudly erect and motionless, her face averted. Quintus rose hastily.

"Are you well?" he asked.

The corner of her mouth lifted in a half smile. "I am alive, thanks to you," she said. "Would that I had died today."

He took her arm and compelled her to sit on his pallet of furs. "You are *not* well," he said, cupping her chin in his hand. "Why are you here, Danae? You should be resting. Nikodemos—"

"Nikodemos sent me," she said. A hot flush suffused her cheeks. "Tonight I am to be yours, my lord Alexandros…the 'prize' for your great courage."

Quintus pulled back, hearing but not believing. "What is this foolishness?"

She stared down at her interlaced fingers. "Is it foolish that your brother should wish to reward you, as he did Gulbanu? Even now that lady shares his bed."

Quintus rose and paced across the small space, kicking aside an empty wine jar. "Nikodemos…he would never give you away."

Danae followed his motions with hollow eyes. "He is displeased with me for interfering in his hunt."

"Displeased? Because you upset his aim?"

"Oh, Quintus." She shook her head wearily. "Have you seen nothing? Learned nothing?"

"I have seen you at the emperor's side every day—"

"I am the emperor's servant," she said in a flat voice.

Quintus knew he still didn't understand, and helplessness fed his anger. "Who is this Gulbanu? Does she threaten you?"

"She is a most accomplished woman, said to be expert in the amorous arts of the East," Danae said. "And she desires Nikodemos."

"Is he such a fool as to look at her when he has you?" Quintus snapped. "You...who loves him above all..."

She twisted her hands in a bloodless knot. "The empire is not ruled by love, my friend. Least of all by a woman's. The simple fact is that I am only the daughter of a merchant already loyal to Nikodemos. Gulbanu comes from the royal line of Persis, where the satrapies have always simmered with rebellion. She was sent as a hostage—"

"Then why does she not hate him?"

"That would be foolish indeed, and Gulbanu is no fool."

Quintus ran his hand through his hair. "Even if all you suggest is true," he said, "why should Nikodemos send you to me? He doesn't know—" He broke off, the heat in his face matching hers. "We were careful, Danae. If he had ever seen us together..."

"The emperor does you great honor by giving you the use of his favorite, even for a single night. Any man would consider it a sign of unsurpassed approval."

Quintus strode to her and dropped to his knees. "And you think I would accept such a gift?" he demanded. "His *honor* is your dishonor...your pain...."

"And you think I cannot bear it?" She gasped out a laugh. "Do you still believe all women are so weak?"

"Not you, Danae. Never you."

"Then do not pity me." She gave him a brave, defiant smile. "Do you not desire me?"

He looked away, not trusting his eyes to hide his feelings. "If you came to me willingly," he said, "and not by the emperor's command..."

If you came out of love, he thought, and silenced that treacherous conceit. He moved away before the urge to touch her became too powerful. "It's impossible."

"Why?" She rose to stand behind him. "You do desire me, Quintus. And I have desired you almost from the moment we met."

"You would take revenge on Nikodemos," he said harshly.

"He is my emperor. If he gives you a gift, then it is my duty to see that you accept."

"Danae…"

She pressed against him, resting her cheek on his shoulder. Her arms wrapped around his waist. "Quintus."

He felt her tears through the linen of his chiton and turned to take her in his arms. For a moment he simply held her, cherishing the soft warmth of her body cradled safe within his keeping. And then she lifted her head and kissed him, a brush of her lips on his.

The fire she ignited was beyond his control. He returned her kiss hungrily and led her back to the pallet.

Quintus had never had a woman before, but his body was Danae's eager student. She was patient with his occasional clumsiness, and he pretended that she had taken no man but him. They lay entangled in each other's arms through the rest of the night, stroking and kissing with no thought of the dawn.

But morning came, and Danae slipped out of Quintus's drowsy hold. He watched her fasten her chiton, each movement one of surpassing grace, and the anger built in his chest until his heart was seized in a vise of rage.

"Don't go," he commanded.

"It is time."

"No." He sat up, shoving the furs aside. "If the emperor no longer values you, let him surrender you to one who does."

"Ah, Quintus—"

"I'll ask him to give you to me."

She froze, the seams of her chiton falling open. "You cannot, Quintus."

"Why not?"

"Nikodemos acted on a whim last night. Do not mistake a moment's anger for more than what it is. He will never give up what belongs to him."

"And do you belong to him, Danae?" Quintus sprang to his feet, disregarding his nakedness. "Do you love him so much that you will suffer any indignity to accept whatever scraps of affection he deigns to throw you?"

She finished fastening the shoulder of her chiton, her fingers trembling. "For your own sake, Quintus, forget this madness. Forget this night ever happened." She stumbled toward the tent flap, evading Quintus's hand. Then she was gone.

They returned to Karchedon well after the blood and savagery of Festival had been cleared from the streets and the Stonebound populace had returned to their sheeplike lives of dull contentment. The next day Nikodemos was called away with Baalshillek to inspect newly conscripted troops drilling on the training ground outside the city.

Quintus saw nothing more of Danae, and he was glad. He spent the days of the emperor's absence exploring the citadel, unfettered to come and go as he pleased with no attendants assigned for his supposed "protection." He studied the walls for weaknesses, observed the palace guards in their daily rounds and stalked the perimeter of the Temple temenos, daring the priests and their faceless soldiers to remember when he had breached the sacred precincts to free the Karchedonian rebel leader Geleon.

He was still walking a blade's-edge of anger and memory when he saw the column of priests marching from the palace to the Temple, escorting a cowled figure that lurched and trembled as the servants of the Stone prodded it along. Quintus paused to watch, his neck prickling with alarm, and the cowled head turned toward him.

Without hesitation, he strode toward the priests on a path that would intersect theirs before they reached the Temple. He stepped in front of the two lead priests, who came to a halt with expressions of disbelief on their pale, pockmarked faces.

"That girl is the property of the emperor," Quintus said. "You will give her to me."

The priests exchanged glances. One of them fingered his red stone pendant. "We take her to the High Priest," he said, his voice hoarse and thin. "Stand aside."

Quintus smiled. "Do you know who I am?"

"Lord Alexandros," the speaker acknowledged. "This is none of your concern."

"What belongs to my brother concerns me," Quintus said. "Let her go."

The next few moments passed in a blur. The priests began to move again, crowding the girl between them. Quintus focused on the pendant swinging against the lead priest's chest. He turned deep inside himself, seeking the source of the power that he alone possessed. He raised his right hand. And he struck.

The priest howled. Quintus ignored the man's cries and refined the flow of his power, reducing it to a trickle. It splashed over the pendant's red stone, kindling sparks from the crystal and driving the priest to his knees. The other priests shrank back. The girl dashed from among them, dodging black robes like a mouse surrounded by cats, and hid behind Quintus.

When it was finished, nothing remained of the priest's pendant but a chunk of slag suspended from a half-melted chain.

The servants of the Stone were stunned into silent immobility. None dared to touch their own crystals. Quintus continued to smile even as a quartet of Temple soldiers arrived on the scene, spears leveled for attack.

"Stay where you are," Quintus said pleasantly, "or I'll kill these vermin."

"Do as he says," the stoneless priest croaked. He glared at Quintus. "You have made a fatal error, Lord Alexandros. The High Priest—"

"—will not be amused to learn how you lost both your stone

and your prey," Quintus finished. "But by all means report this shameful incident, as I will tell the emperor how you took advantage of his absence." He clamped his hand around Briga's arm. "Come with me—quietly," he whispered to her, and started toward the palace.

No one moved to follow. Quintus hurried Briga through the palace gates, barely pausing to acknowledge the curious guards, and half-carried her to his quarters. Once inside, he sat Briga on a chair and poured her a cup of watered wine. She took it from him and drained it in one gulp. Her hands shook so badly that she nearly dropped the cup before he set it back on the table.

"Now," Quintus said, kneeling before her, "tell me what happened."

"I don't know," she said. "I don't remember. I was in the dormitory with the other girls, and…" She shook her head. "I was so scared, Quintus."

He put his arms around her and stroked her hair, murmuring little idiocies while she held on to him with frantic strength. She didn't weep, and gradually her terror subsided. Quintus set her back on the chair.

"The priests made a dangerous mistake," he said, tucking loose red hair behind her ear. "When the emperor hears of this—"

"Won't the High Priest try to punish you for saving me?" Briga asked anxiously.

"I am the emperor's brother. Baalshillek isn't such a fool as to come to blows with Nikodemos over one little girl."

Briga's lower lip thrust out. "I'm not a…" She frowned and took his hand, examining his fingers. "You did something to the priest, to his stone. How did you do that?"

"I don't know. It's a gift I have, like you can make fire."

Briga's eyes widened. "Could you destroy all the stones?"

He got up and poured himself a cup of wine. "That is what the High Priest fears."

"Good." Briga grinned, and just as suddenly grew serious again. "You won't send me back to the dormitory?"

"Not as long as the emperor is absent from the city." Quintus considered sending for Danae and quickly decided against it. "You'll stay here with me for the time being."

Briga's thin shoulders slumped, and her eyelids grew heavy. She allowed Quintus to put her to bed, sleepily objecting that she wasn't a child. Quintus summoned a servant, ordered that all his meals be brought to him in his chambers and prepared himself to wait.

Nikodemos returned the next day, his arrival heralded by a flurry of activity around the palace. Within a few hours he appeared at Quintus's door, his face thunderous enough to shatter the heavy stone walls. Briga made herself very small in a corner of the room.

"What have you done?" Nikodemos demanded, slamming the door closed behind him. "I'm gone a few days, and you attack Baalshillek's priests and destroy their stones—"

Quintus bowed. "My lord Emperor," he said. "It was only one stone."

Nikodemos stared, open-mouthed, and turned red. "Baalshillek is insisting on your immediate punishment. He says this is proof that you cannot be permitted to run free in the citadel, and I'm almost inclined to agree with him."

Quintus humbly averted his gaze and offered his brother a chair. "I am ill-prepared to offer hospitality worthy of an emperor," he said, "but if my lord will have wine…"

Nikodemos growled and fell into the chair. "You knew cursed well I'd be coming," he said. His gaze found Briga. "And this is the cause of so much trouble?"

"You yourself took her under your protection," Quintus said. "It was the priests who breached your agreement with Baalshillek by entering the palace precincts and stealing the girl. I did not believe you would permit such a theft if you were present."

"Ha." Nikodemos scowled at the wine jar. "You should have called the Palace Guard, or at the very least acted with more discretion."

"There was no time, my lord. The priests were very near the Temple, and once they had her inside…"

Nikodemos grabbed a cup and filled it to overflowing. "You reminded Baalshillek all too well why you are a threat to him."

"And is that a bad thing, brother?"

The emperor drank, grimaced and banged down the cup. "You have such a fondness for this child?"

"I have a fondness for reminding Baalshillek that he is not invulnerable."

"By the gods, you are beyond all—" Nikodemos snorted, and the dark color retreated from his face. "I should have you punished, and I will…if Baalshillek agrees to punish the priests who tried to steal my property." He grinned. "Perhaps you deserve a reward after all, brother."

Quintus felt the blood racing hot in his veins, driven by the memory of Danae lying in his arms. "I seek only to serve my emperor," he said.

"Do you?" Nikodemos studied him, grin fading. "Did you enjoy my gift at the lion hunt?"

"I was honored by the emperor's favor."

"I'll wager you did." Nikodemos rose abruptly and slapped Quintus's shoulder. "You have not disappointed me, brother. Give no more thought to the girl…. I'll see that she's properly protected from now on. And you…" He curled his hand around the back of Quintus's neck and gave him a shake. "You'll have no cause to regret your loyalty. When Baalshillek and his minions are no more, I'll have need of new governors for all my provinces, including Tiberia. Learn the ways of kingship, Alexandros, and by the gods, I'll give you all of Italia."

Nikodemos swept from the room on a wind of triumph, leaving Quintus without the breath to speak. In that moment he believed that his brother could achieve everything he claimed: the complete downfall of the Stone God and all its evil works.

And he, Quintus Horatius Corvinus, would be at the emperor's side.

Orkos brought Talos to Baalshillek's chamber two days after the incident with Quintus and the girl. The old man was wan and hollow-eyed; Baalshillek's agents had told him that the inventor seldom slept but spent all his time poring over his secret work for Nikodemos. It was a wonder he had made so little progress.

That was about to change.

Baalshillek dismissed the Children and offered Talos a chair. "Will you have wine?" he offered. "Or perhaps you have not yet eaten today?"

Talos continued to stand. "I have nothing to say to you, lord priest."

Baalshillek seated himself and clasped his hands on the table before him. "You have grown very bold, philosopher. It seems the emperor has indeed come to value your services."

The old man's face showed no expression. "He will not be pleased that I have been brought here against my will."

"Surely an hour away from your work will not inconvenience him too greatly." He sighed. "Perhaps you've heard that his bastard brother attacked my priests outside the Temple."

"I heard," Talos said. "I am surprised you are willing to admit such a failure."

Baalshillek fingered his pendant, letting his rage drain away like blood from an open wound. "You are wise enough to know that it is all a game," he said. "A game with complex rules and many surprises. The emperor feints, and I step aside. This time it is my move."

"How does this concern me?"

"You are no fool, philosopher. We have spoken of these things before."

Talos's laugh was as brief as it was startling. "I would not agree to serve you or your gods when we first met," he said. "I have not changed my mind."

"Indeed." Baalshillek steepled his fingers. "You may recall I gave you fair warning that I would learn everything there is to know about your past, even before your years serving Arrhidaeos. Your origins, it seems, are far more fascinating than even I had guessed."

"Indeed."

"You once made the error of confiding in a slave, a member of the Horatius household in Tiberia. Shall I remind you of what you told him?"

Talos sank into the chair, his legs trembling. "You killed him?"

"A mere slave, but useful in his final days. With a little persuasion, he gave up his memories of you…how you spoke of your youth in fabled Hyperborea, building the great machines that keep the ice of the North at bay. How you rebelled against the rulers of your land and fled to the South, where you continued to build for one who would rule the earth."

The old man, already pale, went white. "Of what use is this knowledge to you, priest?"

Baalshillek touched his stone and then waved his hand. The wall opened up behind him. A woman stepped through…a beautiful woman by the standards of the civilized world, her simple chiton only drawing more attention to the elegant lines of her body. She paused in the doorway, her gaze flickering from Baalshillek to Talos.

"Do you remember, Talos?" Baalshillek asked, taking the woman's hand. "How many years have passed?"

Talos stared. His hands began to shake on the arms of the chair. "Melissa," he whispered.

Baalshillek led the woman forward and released her. "You have not forgotten," he said. "She has lived in your heart all this time, since you abandoned her and fled the court for Tiberia. Did you not wonder what became of her?"

Talos tried to rise and fell back again. "This is not Melissa," he said hoarsely. "She is dead."

"Is she?" He turned to the woman. "Do you not know this man?"

She took a step forward. "Talos?"

The philosopher's mouth worked. "No. This is some evil…a phantom…."

"Go to the one you love, Melissa," Baalshillek said. "Show him how little *you* have forgotten."

The woman's eyes welled with tears, and she knelt at Talos's feet. "My love," she said. "You have changed, and yet you are the same. Oh, how I have missed you."

Talos sat rigid, his gaze fixed on her face. She took his hands in hers and kissed them from knuckle to fingertips. He touched her thick brown hair. "You…you are dead," he stammered.

"But she lives anew." Baalshillek leaned on the edge of the table, watching the desperate struggle in Talos's eyes. "You could not take her with you to Tiberia. You thought she would be better off in Karchedon than fleeing with a fugitive from Arrhidaeos. And the emperor did not hold her to blame for your transgression. He gave her to a wealthy merchant, Kallimachos, and she bore him a daughter. But then a madness came upon her, and she was given in sacrifice to the Stone God."

Talos jerked his hands away from the woman and shrank before Baalshillek's eyes like a withering piece of fruit.

"You sorrow for one who is lost," Baalshillek said gently. "You could not save her. But now you have a second chance. Look at her, Talos. What was Melissa that she is not?"

Talos looked. His eyes flooded with tears.

"She is everything you knew," Baalshillek said. "All Melissa's memories, her feelings, her devotion."

"A simulacrum," Talos said. "You control her—"

"No, my beloved," Melissa said. She grasped the hem of Talos's chiton. "I have but one master. I have waited and prayed that you would come back to me." She pressed her face to his knees. "I live, Talos. I do not understand how this miracle has come to pass, but I live. For you."

Talos wept openly now, the tears running down his seamed face. "Your daughter," he croaked. "Who…"

"Danae," she said, lifting her head to smile with open joy. "She is beautiful, Talos. She might have been ours. I did not see her come to womanhood, but if you will have me again…we will know such happiness that even the gods will envy us."

Baalshillek backed away, unnoticed, and left the room through the secret portal. He sat in the anteroom, emptied his mind of thought and waited for the simulacrum to complete her work. When he returned to his chambers, Melissa sat with her head in Talos's lap, and he gazed down upon her with the helpless agony of the conquered.

"You must leave us now, Melissa," Baalshillek said, "but only for a little while."

She rose to her feet, smiled at Talos and slipped out the front door. Baalshillek took his seat behind the table.

"What will become of her?" Talos asked, staring at the floor between his feet.

"Why, whatever you desire…if you perform the simple task that the One True God asks of you."

"And if I do not?"

"Then she must suffer the same fate as her predecessor."

Talos was silent for a dozen breaths. "What is this task?"

"My servants tell me that you once performed a trick for the old emperor when you served the court. You placed a new-laid egg in a box of your own construction, spoke a few words and opened the box to reveal a full-grown bird."

Talos shook his head. "It was a trick," he said. "An illusion. Nothing more."

"So everyone believed. But they did not know you came from Hyperborea, where such 'illusions' are commonplace."

"I do not understand you."

"What you may conceal from men cannot be hidden from

the Exalted," Baalshillek said. "Those I serve have told me much of your homeland...how its greatest mages can control and alter the very flow of time itself. This is what you did with the egg, old man. And this is what you will do for my masters."

He spoke then of the Children of the Stone, those infants specially bred from women of godborn blood and touched by the Stone to create tireless, flawlessly loyal soldiers for the Exalted and their priests. Through the power of the stones embedded in their foreheads, they could be brought from infancy to adolescence in a matter of months instead of years.

"But they are subject to one weakness," he continued. "The very force of the Stone that brings them to maturity also destroys their bodies after a few years of service. The Temple requires far more Children than we can produce. You will construct many of these time boxes so that the Children can grow from birth to readiness without the dangers inherent in early exposure to the red stones."

Talos rose from his chair, feet braced in pathetic defiance. "What you ask is impossible," he said. "I know nothing of such machines—"

"I believe you do," Baalshillek said. "And I believe that you would rather perform this small service than watch your beloved burn in the altar fires, begging you for her life."

Talos turned for the door, stooped and shuffling like the old man he was. Baalshillek let him go and gave orders that he was not to be detained. He had failed to give an answer, but Baalshillek knew it would not be long in coming. The philosopher was weak—his scruples about his war machines were proof enough of that—and his heart ruled his otherwise considerable intellect. His heart, and his guilty memories of Melissa, whom Baalshillek had so perfectly recreated that even her own mother would not doubt her reality.

By the time the first of the perfect Children was born—the one fit to bear the soul of an Exalted—Talos's time box must be ready.

Baalshillek summoned Orkos and heard the commander's report of Buteo's "escape" from his cell in the Temple. All was proceeding as it should. Tomorrow the High Priest would meet formally with the emperor to discuss the foolhardy behavior of the lord Alexandros, and how his actions threatened the fragile balance between Temple and Palace. That was when Baalshillek would suggest that the emperor's half-brother might be best employed for a time away from Karchedon…hunting down the fugitive Tiberian rebel. Who better than one Tiberian to locate another?

The High Priest smiled to himself and removed his scrying bowl from its cupboard. He summoned a guard and sent the man for a jar of fresh blood from the great altar, where a number of offerings had been made within the hour. He set the bowl on its iron stand, and when the guard returned, he poured the blood into the bowl and waited for the liquid to settle.

It had been several days since he had found the time to observe his simulacra in their progress through the forests of the South. He had been pleased to see that they had not faltered in pursuit of the godborn, in spite of their ignominious defeat in the desert. And he knew they were close, very close, to discovering the location of the Hammer.

But when he sought to look through the eyes of his agent, he found nothing but darkness.

He upended the bowl, splattering blood on walls and floor. A guard dared to open the door, and Baalshillek cursed him so bitterly that even the man's dull, obedient mind must have known fear.

Baalshillek sat down and dropped his head into his hands. The Child he had selected to be his eyes and ears had finally met his demise after surviving the battle that had slain two-thirds of his cohort. The question was whether that death had come in the course of his duty…or as the result of treachery.

If Yseul or one of the other simulacra had exposed the agent and slain him, they could no longer be trusted. Yet the freedom they sought was as false as Talos's dreams of love restored. In a matter of months—or years, if they were lucky—they would be consumed by the power of the Stone that animated them. Even if they cast off all ties to Baalshillek and the Exalted, their own natures would drive them to fulfill at least part of their mission. And whether they merely killed the godborn or took the Weapons for themselves, Baalshillek would profit from their acts.

He smiled, rose, and summoned an omega priest to clean up the blood.

Chapter Seventeen

The journey passed as if by magic. And perhaps it *was* magic, Yseul thought, for she kept no memory of days spent walking through the endless forest, or nights huddled with Urho and Farkas beside fires that sprang out of nothing and vanished at first light. She saw the world in brief scenes of movement and stillness.

Contrary to Eshu's warnings, neither she nor the others suffered unduly from insect bites, soaking rains or the attacks of ravenous beasts. The little god seldom showed his face, though every day a basket of meat, fruit and nuts appeared at their camp, eliminating the need for hunting. Yseul was vaguely aware that the *òrìshà* must be guiding them by a path known only to him, but she did not question.

Finally the morning came when she woke to see everything clearly for the first time since they had left the villagers' territory. The forest was dense with trees and undergrowth so closely packed that she could hardly believe even a god could find his way through it. Birds and long-tailed animals screeched from the canopy, and a constant rain of moisture fell from the leaves and branches.

Yseul shook herself in disgust and carefully touched her tender forehead. The wound she had made in removing the red stone was nearly healed, and it was the same with the others. None of them had suffered ill effects from the excision, and even Urho had grudgingly admitted that the doom he'd predicted had failed to materialize.

Now that Baalshillek's spy among the Children had been eliminated, Yseul trusted that the High Priest remained ignorant of his servants' reckless acts. He had lost Yseul's allegiance, and she was sure that in time Urho and Farkas would begin to see things her way.

She smiled and looked for her companions. Farkas was just beginning to stir. Urho sat up and blinked in the dim, filtered light.

"Where in Tabiti's name are we?" Farkas demanded, scratching his beard. "And where is that cursed dog?"

Yseul selected a fresh piece of meat from the food basket before the males could claim it all for themselves. "I believe," she said, licking her fingers, "that we have reached our destination."

Urho peered into the seemingly impenetrable wall of trees. "This is the place where the Hammer lies?"

"Have you already forgotten, my friend? Eshu said he would lead us to the land of those who guard the Hammer…the females who hate all men." She grinned at Farkas. "Females like me."

Farkas glanced about sharply, as if he expected imminent attack. He cursed all creatures of the gentler sex.

Yseul laughed. "You'd do well to keep your tongue between your teeth, Farkas, if you wish to stay alive. If these Alu are indeed of my blood—"

She broke off, alerted by a whiff of new scent from the forest. The hairs on the back of her neck stood on end. A dark-skinned figure dropped out of the branches above and landed on silent feet, bared knife in hand. She wore only a few scraps of fur about her hips, and her eyes were slits of feral gold. She straightened, stared at Yseul and regarded the men with open contempt.

A harsh, coughing cry echoed from the forest. The woman cocked her head and answered, making a noise alien to any human throat. Leaves rustled, and one by one sleek black shapes emerged from the tangle of shrubs and vines, a dozen ivory-fanged panthers forming a loose circle about the intruders. Every pair of yellow eyes promised death.

Yseul held up her hands and stepped forward. The woman growled, shaking the earth beneath her feet. With the most deliberate of motions, Yseul removed her tunic, belt and trousers, her gaze fixed on the Alu female. Her clothes fell to the ground. Then she changed.

No breath of sound disturbed the perfect stillness. The panthers crouched, ears flattened. The woman kicked at Yseul's abandoned garments, her face frozen in unwilling shock. She spoke a single word, a question that Yseul knew meant the difference between life and death.

Yseul searched the darkest corners of her memory—memory distilled from the blood and bone of the Ailuri Baalshillek had captured and sacrificed to create her. She discovered the ancient language, known only to the Northern shapeshifters and the female warriors they chose as their mates. She became human again and found her voice.

"Alu," she said slowly. "I am your sister of the North, come to greet her kin and give them warning."

The woman hissed, and the panthers lashed their tails. Farkas chose that moment to shift his weight, and three beasts leaped to confront him. He shrank back, flinging his arms across his face.

"Stop!" Yseul cried. She met the leader's gaze. "These are my servants. They must not be harmed." She addressed the men in Hellenish. "Keep your hands away from your weapons and remain quiet."

Urho and Farkas made themselves very small. At a gesture from the Alu leader, the panthers retreated, casting glances of unappeased hunger at the males.

"You call yourself our Sister," the woman said to Yseul. "You know the ancient tongue, and you wear our shape. But you speak of the North, and your skin is pale. How can you be one of us?"

Yseul knew she walked a very fine line between victory and disaster. One wrong word, one mistaken assumption, and she might find herself fighting for her life against others almost as powerful as she.

But these creatures were savages, ignorant dwellers of the forest with neither writing nor civilization. They could be manipulated as easily as children by one with courage, intelligence…and imagination.

"I do not know your history, Sister," she began. "I can only tell the stories of my people…how our males betrayed us long ago, and how we females of the Alu were forced to leave our homeland to scatter far and wide. We believed that some of our sisters went into the South, but until now…" She bowed gracefully. "Now I have the joy of learning we of the North are not alone."

The Alu woman fingered the blade of her knife with a frown, digesting Yseul's tale. One of the panthers changed, becoming a tall, ebon-skinned woman with hair braided tightly to her skull. She addressed her leader, speaking in a tongue foreign to Yseul's ears.

The leader's eyes grew hooded. "You came to find us, Sister of the North?"

Yseul inclined her head. "Much has changed since my people settled in the lands beyond the Great Desert. When the new time of trouble came—"

The Alu woman made a sharp downward slash with one hand. "Why do you travel with males, when all know that none of their kind can be trusted?"

Yseul thought quickly. "The number of Alu is small in the North," she said. "We have found males useful for certain tasks, and since we could spare few of our own people on this journey, we deemed it advisable that I travel with an escort…no matter how inferior they may be."

"You crossed the Great Desert?"

"Yes. These are the males who survived. I would keep them alive until they have served their purpose."

The women argued briefly in their own tongue. Finally the Alu leader came to a decision. "It is clear that you are one of us," she said, "even if your ways and appearance are those of an outlander. The grace of Ge has brought you to our land, and we will hear what you have to say." She glanced at the men with a lift of her lip. "You may come with us to our village, but the males must stay here."

"They are not familiar with the dangers of your country."

"We will see that they remain alive until your story has been told. What happens after that is Ge's will."

Yseul bowed again. "As you say. I will relay your command." She backed away from the Alu and turned to the men. "Farkas, Urho, listen to me. Your lives depend on what I say. You will remain here—"

"What?" Farkas gathered his legs to rise, but Urho held him down.

"Urho is wise," Yseul said. "Eshu said these females would kill you, and it is obvious that they won't hesitate to do so if you fail to obey." She lowered her voice. "I am to be taken to their village. If they know anything about the Hammer, I will hear of it. You'll camp here, guarded by the Alu. Make no trouble with them."

Urho nodded. Farkas looked as though he'd bitten into rotten meat, but he had enough sense not to argue.

Yseul returned to the Alu leader. "I am ready."

The woman spoke to two of the panthers, who advanced on the men and crouched to face them with hot, baleful eyes. Then she shed her scanty clothing, changed and immediately leapt into the forest, followed by the others.

Yseul changed quickly and scrambled to catch up, aware that she had much yet to prove. Soon she had reached the hindmost of the Alu; in a few heartbeats she had surged ahead, her paws barely touching the earth, a triumphant hunter's cry bubbling in her throat. She recognized the leader by scent and raced with her, leaping over fallen trees and sliding like a serpent between knots of brush and coiling vines. She flew, and all the yammering, chattering creatures of the jungle fell silent at her passage.

Here, she thought. *Here I belong.*

They ran through the day and into the night, pausing only to drink at a trickle of water flowing from the face of a rock, and continued until the new dawn. The land rose in a steady climb and the trees grew taller, towering two and three times higher than any edifice built by men. It was among such trees that Yseul first saw the houses, woven seamlessly of leaves and smaller branches tucked between vast, outstretched limbs.

The Alu passed beneath the first house, and cries of greeting floated down from the platforms and bridges that connected one great tree to the next. Women, some naked and others dressed in scraps of fur, casually vaulted from the heights with the negligent use of convenient vines or roughly fashioned ladders. There was not a child or a male among them.

Scarcely slowing to acknowledge her sisters, the Alu leader ran on to the base of a tree whose trunk seemed to bend upon itself, arching over a great emptiness that dropped into the forest far below, its twisted roots gripping the edge of the cliff like clutching fingers. She led Yseul and a score of Alu up a bole wide as a road, the bark worn thin by the constant passage of paws and feet.

At the top of the incline, the lowest limbs splayed out like dividing paths, each leading to a house supported on a sturdy platform. The main trunk took a sharp turn to the right, passed through a dense mat of leaves and opened out to a clear view of the space beyond the cliff's edge. Tree tops rippled like a sea of grass three hundred body lengths below. Yseul tightened her grip on the bark and made sure of her balance before following the Alu leader to the door of a house cradled on a broad fan of gnarled branches.

By the time Yseul entered the house, the leader had already changed to human again and sat on a raised platform at the rear of the single large room. Her sisters filled in the spaces around her, settling cross-legged on the furs that served to soften the rough floor of woven sticks. Yseul heard other females come in behind and block the doorway, effectively cutting off her one chance at escape.

It didn't matter, in any case. If she failed in this, she failed in everything.

She stretched elaborately to show her lack of fear, displaying her claws and curling her tail high over her head. She changed and sat before the Alu leader, pale as a beam of moonlight among so many dark, rich hues of bronze and brown skin. Her audience made none of the small, restless sounds of a human gathering; they stared at her with the intensity of predators judging the strength of their prey and the risks of taking it down.

Yseul knew these females as she knew herself. "I am Yseul of the Northern Alu," she said, "and I am honored to be among the sisters from whom we have so long been kept apart."

The Alu leader spoke to the assembly in their native tongue and then addressed Yseul. "I am Keela, leader of the Alu by right of battle. Why have you come to this country, polluting our Mother's sacred earth with the touch of men?"

Yseul recognized a formal question and answered with great care. "I have come not to anger your Mother, but to bring warning of a great danger rising in the North—a danger to both your people and mine."

Keela exchanged glances with the women to her left and

right. "Our tales say that none but the Alu were given the gift of taking the shape of the great cat," she said. "I judge this female to be one of us, in spite of her strangeness. It must be that Ge has brought her to us, or she would not have survived to reach our borders."

The Alu raised their voices in surprise and doubt. "How is this possible?" a gray-haired woman asked. "Our tales say nothing of females who remained in the North after the males refused to share their power. Does she, too, serve Ge?"

Yseul quieted her racing heart. She had too little knowledge, yet she had no choice but to use what Eshu had told her and to trust her own cleverness.

"Much has been forgotten," she said, "but it is said that my people chose to stay close to the males, clinging to the hope that we could convince them to behave with honor. We were mistaken. The males abandoned their duty—"

Keela stopped her with a gesture. "We do not know what became of them after we left for the South."

Yseul released a careful breath. "Perhaps it would be best if you tell how you came to this place and became Ge's servants, and then I will understand—"

"You say the males abandoned the Stone," Keela said harshly.

"Yes." Yseul hung her head. "We could not stop them. They left the Desert to any who might chance upon the Stone and release its evil."

The Alu broke into a buzz of conversation, a strange mingling of triumph and alarm on their grim faces.

"It is as Ge predicted," the gray-haired woman said. "Evil will come across the Desert to seize the Hammer."

Keela called for silence. She stared into Yseul's eyes as if she could strip away flesh and bone to expose every secret her guest might dare to conceal. "I will tell you our tale, Sister," she said, "and then you will say all you know of this danger that threatens us." She closed her eyes, and her followers drew near.

"In the days when the Desert was grass," Keela began, "the

great gods created the Alu, male and female, to battle the evil of the Most High, who would lay waste to the earth. When the battle was won, the gods gave to the Alu the power to make the Stone, which would hold the Most High captive for all time. To male and female alike they gave the gift of changing shape, but to the males alone they entrusted the Stone."

The Alu listeners moaned softly, murmuring words of sorrow.

"Soon the gods went away," Keela said, "and left the Alu to watch the Stone. But the Alu lived long, and the years grew heavy on their shoulders. The females had no duty save to serve the males and bear their children. But children were few, and we saw that the males made light of the great task entrusted to them, wandering farther from the Stone with every passing season.

"One of our Sisters dared to believe that the gods had been mistaken in giving all the power of Earth to the males alone. She went to the eldest of the males and asked that they share the gifts that had been bestowed upon them. But the males only laughed and refused."

"The curse of Ge be upon them," the gray-haired woman cried.

Keela spread her hands. "So it was," she said, "that the females conferred together and decided to punish the males for their selfishness. We took our children and crossed the Great Desert, seeking a new home. We believed the males would discover their error and beg us to return.

"The males never came. So we chose to make a new home in the forests. But we were without protection in a strange land, and many died. There was much weeping for the children."

"Alas for the children," the women chanted.

"When it seemed all must be lost, a great light shone upon the Alu—Ge, mighty goddess of the Earth, bringer of life. She, too, was in exile, for once she had been of the Most High, those who had sought to rule all gods and men."

The Most High, Yseul thought. The Exalted. Her guess had been correct.

"Ge was among the first and most ancient of the gods, born long before the creation of mankind. She joined the rebellion of the Most High when she saw the wickedness that mortal males wreaked on the world, how they so readily felled its trees and destroyed the beasts, and fought among themselves with no regard for the balance of life. Ge hoped that the Most High would weaken the dominion of men. But she discovered that her allies intended to do far more than put an end to the ravages of humans. The evil ones would destroy the world and all that lived upon it.

"Hiding her knowledge, she bided her time until the servants of the good gods brought forth great magic to overcome the Most High. But just as the evil ones were nearing defeat, three of them schemed to steal the Weapons and prepared to flee. Ge knew that the Hammer of the Earth must not fall into the destroyers' hands, and so she fought to take it from those who had become her enemies. She escaped the embrace of the Stone and brought the Hammer to the forests of the South, and there the Alu found her."

"Praise be to Ge," the women whispered.

"Ge knew that a time must come when evil would escape its bonds and seek the Hammer again. She knew the treachery of males, men or gods, and she saw that we alone were worthy to serve her. She offered us long life and the power of all the growing things of Earth if we would guard her stronghold while she held the Hammer safe. And so we have served."

"So we have served," the Alu echoed.

Keela rose, and the others rose with her. She faced the rear of the house. Two Alu pulled on ropes set into the wall. A pair of woven panels swinging outward to reveal an unobstructed view of the deep valley below. Sheer cliffs formed the valley's sides, and in its center stood a tree so vast that its canopy shaded the crowns of its tall companions as if they were mere shrubs.

"The Belly of Ge," Keela said. "The center of her stronghold. There she has slept for a thousand years, trusting the Alu to watch for any who would steal the Hammer."

Yseul made no effort to hide her amazement. "Surely no one could reach such a place."

"No man," Keela said. She smiled, showing her teeth. "And now you will tell us what danger comes from the North."

The women settled back in their places, and Yseul felt their cold yellow stares. She dared not forget that these were not her sisters at all, but enemies—enemies she must defeat if ever she found a way of taking the Hammer from them.

"Your goddess is wise," she said humbly. "She must have known that the Alu males would abandon the Stone. They left it unguarded, and others found it—others who even now work to set the Most High free again."

Keela hissed. "Men."

"One man, a conqueror who sought to rule the world. He did not succeed in loosing the Most High, but he passed his ambition to his heirs, and they have used the evil ones' power to crush many of the Northern lands under their feet."

"Word of this has not reached us," Keela said.

"There is more. These kings of the North found our males and persuaded them to join their cause. We females remained true to our ancient duty. We turned all our wits toward learning what the traitors intended. We discovered that the Northern kings believed that one of the four lost Weapons lay in the South, and that they intended to find it and turn its magic to their own ends. Because both the Hammer and the Alu wield the powers of Earth, they sent a male of our kind, one called Cian, to seek the Weapon and deliver it to them."

Keela's nostrils flared. "An Alu male comes here?"

"I was chosen to follow Cian and to stop him if I could. But his magic is strong, and he travels with others, female humans whose souls have been corrupted by the Most High. I believe he has learned where the Hammer lies." She raised a hand to forestall Keela's cry of protest. "I did not dare hope that I would find such noble allies so far from my homeland. Only when I reached the forest did I hear rumors of women who possessed the gift of changing, and I began to believe that my quest was not in vain." She risked a smile. "You can be sure that if my people heard no tales of Ge in the North, Cian surely knows little of you or the goddess. This is his great weakness.

"You, wise servants of Ge, can destroy him."

Had he been alone, Cian might have relished the exploration of the forest. There was a freedom in its very boundlessness, an eternity of oblivion and perpetual twilight that allowed him to forget what he had seen in the Cave of Dreams. He could become gratefully lost in this vast green womb and never find himself again.

But he was not alone. He might have disregarded Nyx's hopes, but he wasn't prepared to disappoint Rhenna and Tahvo on what they believed was the final leg of their quest for the Hammer. As long as he had the advantage of teeth and claws and panther senses, he was of some use to those he loved.

Just as Tahvo had predicted, the little people who guided them remained invisible from the very beginning of the journey. Somehow they kept contact with Tahvo, who always knew which path to take through the seemingly impenetrable undergrowth.

Nyx made good use of her skill with growing things to widen the passages, sweeping her hands over branches to curl them back on themselves, and coaxing the most firmly rooted plants to bow and part like soldiers on parade. When she tired, or an obstacle proved too daunting, the village hunters cropped the vegetation with broad, curved blades.

The days presented only minor nuisances and discomforts. Meals were seldom a problem, for the little people deposited fresh game and sometimes fruit in the travelers' camp every night. Cian heard the occasional cough of some large hunting beast and the scurryings of lesser creatures, but none offered any threat to the humans.

The ground was constantly damp, kept so by the interminable drip of water that often broke into full, soaking rains. Tahvo revealed a new and unexpected ability to withdraw the moisture from damp branches, enabling her companions to build fires in the most unlikely places. Even the plentiful rivers gave way to her gentle beguilement of the forest spirits, brown water standing aside to allow the travelers crossing.

Two weeks passed with numbing sameness, the better part of each day spent walking, the evenings occupied with preparing food and making repairs to disintegrating clothing. One night the little people presented their guests with beautifully dressed furs and skins, which the Imaziren set about cutting into tunics and boots. Rhenna clung stubbornly to the garments she had bought months ago in the village south of Karchedon; she seemed unwilling to surrender anything to the forest or admit a need for more than was strictly necessary of its alien bounty.

At the beginning of the third week, the changes began. The little people became less confident in their guidance, sometimes leading the party in one direction, only to double back and return to the very point where they had started. The rain increased to slow the travelers even further. It fell ceaselessly, threatening to drown any poor soul who dared to look up at the murky sky.

On a particularly miserable night of continuous downpour, Tahvo withdrew into herself, muttered a chant almost savage in its tone, and flung her hands above her head. The water stopped a finger's length from her silver hair and trickled harmlessly away as if it had struck some invisible barrier.

Rhenna laughed in appreciation...the first time she'd laughed in many days...and the Imaziren crowded close to Tahvo, begging her to work her magic on them. Tahvo spent the rest of the night begging the water spirits to extend their goodwill to her companions, and by morning was so exhausted that Cian carried her on his back through most of the next day.

No sooner had the rains been conquered than the insects declared war on the human intruders. They flung themselves at every exposed patch of skin with rapacious ferocity, biting and sucking and pinching, the tiniest filling ears and nose and mouth in choking clouds. Immeghar bellowed in fury, while Nyx and the villagers bore the onslaught in miserable silence. Tahvo obtained a sticky salve from the little people, but it was of little use against such numbers.

After days of enduring the merciless assault, Rhenna had had enough. She took a long look at Tahvo hunched under her furs beside the evening fire and dropped to her knees, shaking so hard that Cian feared she would burst something inside her body. Then she raised her clenched fists and called.

Cian didn't hear the words or the sound of it, but his body tingled with the force of her cry. Tahvo lifted her head. Immeghar ceased his wild and futile gesticulations. The hum and buzz of the forest stilled. A hot, wet wind swept down out of the trees, whipping their crowns and cutting through the swarms of insects like a giant's sword. A hundred thousand segmented bodies plummeted to the earth. A hundred thousand more were lifted and smashed into the undergrowth and boles of trees. Cian grabbed Tahvo and pulled her into his arms, as blind as she.

As swiftly as it came, the wind died. Rhenna stared at her hands in astonishment and waved them in front of her face. Not a single insect alighted on her skin. She broke into a grin.

"It worked!" she said.

The others gathered around her, breathing in gulps of untainted air. "You brought the great wind in the desert," Cabh'a said. "How could you be uncertain of your magic?"

Rhenna laughed. "I am certain of nothing, least of all that these Southern devas would heed my request."

"Your anger gave you strength," Tahvo said. "This time you used it to serve you."

Rhenna grimaced and met Cian's gaze. He gave her his warmest look of encouragement and approval. She glanced away. "Now perhaps we can get a decent night's sleep," she muttered.

And sleep they did, gloriously untroubled by insects or rain. But the next morning Tahvo woke them with a drawn face and said that she could no longer contact the little people.

Cian sank to his haunches and listened. Even the morning chorus of birds and animals was muted, as if they sympathized with the travelers' grave situation.

"Is it my doing?" Rhenna asked.

"I do not believe so," Tahvo said. "There was no evil in your magic, and they already saw mine, small as it was."

"Then what are we to do?" Cabh'a asked. "Perhaps if we combine all our skills we can retrace our trail, but with no knowledge of what lies ahead…"

Cian closed his eyes and thrust his hand into the ground. It resisted and then slowly opened up to him, swimming with creatures that moved in the soil as easily as men walked upon it. He rotated his hand, sifting dirt between his fingers.

The first spark of pain was so small that he dismissed it as yet another insect bite and continued to reach, feeling the former life of the trees and animals that had died to give this earth its abundance. The second and third twinges were strong enough to catch his attention. He remembered the agony that had seized him at the Stone's prison in the desert, all but stripping the flesh from his hands.

This was different. This pain was not an assault meant to disable, but a warning…a warning like the insects, like the driving rain and the disappearance of the little people.

The elusive natives had promised to guide the travelers as far as the borders of the "forbidden place." If they had reached that boundary, there was nothing to indicate it other than the bizarre attacks of nature. But the pain in Cian's arm told him which direction they must go.

"What is it?" Rhenna asked.

"Wait," he said. He withdrew his arm and slipped into the forest before she could protest. Once out of sight of the others he stripped and changed. With his panther senses he sought hidden ways through the forest, close to the earth where only animals trod. He had gone less than a quarter of a league when his paws felt the change in the ground, a strange hollowness opening up before him like a pit trap meant to swallow unwary creatures.

He proceeded with great care and stopped where the trees clung to a crumbling edge that looked out on a tapestry of forest spread across a circular valley far below. He could just see the opposite cliff, a slash of sheer gray shadow perhaps three days' steady walk across the valley. And between the stone ramparts, at the valley's very center, stood a single tree twice as tall as any Cian had seen in all his years of wandering.

He crouched flat, his fur standing on end. A fearful dizziness gripped him, luring him toward the edge of the cliff. He peered down into the alluring softness of that green bed, so deceptively near, and yet so far from the venality and petty ambitions of men.

A hand gripped the fur at his shoulder. "Cian. Mother-of-All…"

He curled back over himself and snapped at the hand, averting his head just in time to avoid crushing flesh and bone. Rhenna hardly flinched.

"I'm sorry," he stammered. "I don't understand why I—"

Rhenna shook her head. "It's this place. It has a strange effect on all of us." She pointed her chin toward the valley. "So that is where we must go?"

"The great tree," he said, following her gaze. "I believe that is our destination."

Rhenna pushed straggling hair behind her ears and kicked at the edge of the cliff. "It won't be easy to get down there," she said. "Even if we find a way, we'll be vulnerable to attack."

She did not say from what or whom, but Cian knew even better than she that enemies, old and new, waited for a chance to stop them. "I'm the best climber," he said. "I'll seek a path down—"

"We stay together," Rhenna said. "Let's go get the others."

Reluctantly he followed her, retrieved his clothing and returned to camp. The villagers and Imaziren immediately began laying plans for the descent into the valley.

"We have some rope," Cabh'a said. "There are plenty of vines here to make more."

"We will need ledges where we may rest and secure the ropes," Immeghar said. "How sheer is this cliff?"

"A panther can find footholds a man could not," Cian said.

"And I can help," Nyx said. "If there are any plants on the cliff face, even the smallest, I can shape platforms of the kind Immeghar describes. As for ropes…"

She rose, approached a vine-bedecked tree and gathered three of the thick filaments in her hands. She stroked the vines until they clung together and began to twine about each other, forming a braid that extended from the tree's lowest branches to the ground. Nyx gave a gentle tug, and the new-made rope fell in a neat pile at her feet. Abidemi and Enitan made gestures of thanks to their *òrìshà,* and Immeghar grunted his approval.

"It seems we will have all the rope we need," Rhenna said. "Nyx, make as much as your power allows, but don't exhaust yourself. The rest of you, gather your supplies and secure them well." She turned to Cian. "You'll go first…cautiously. Nyx will follow. Take no chances. If you find that there is no way down—"

"The thing we seek is in the valley," Tahvo said.

"The Hammer?" Cian asked.

She rubbed her eyes. "I cannot reach the spirits here. Even the smallest ones do not answer me. They are under the rule of another, far more powerful."

The angry god of the little people. Perhaps, if Nyx's knowledge of the prophecies was correct, one of the Exalted themselves.

And if the prophecies were true, then Cian had to face whatever lay in that valley, even if he must leave the others behind.

Chapter Eighteen

For the rest of the morning, Nyx made her vine ropes while the Imaziren redistributed supplies and fashioned harnesses for the climb. Mezwar proved clever at devising knots that held firm but could be released with a twist of the fingers. Abidemi and Enitan collected edible roots to add to the scanty stores of food.

When all was ready, they made their way through the forest to the cliff. Rhenna had designed a harness to fit Cian's panther body and insisted on tying it on him herself. She played out an ample length of vine rope and fixed one end around a small, sturdy tree rooted well back from the cliff's edge. She arranged a separate line for Nyx so that if one fell, the other might still survive.

"Take care, Cian," she said, her voice thick with concealed emotion. She rested her hand on his back, stroking the fur from shoulder to hip, and turned quickly to Nyx. "When it's safe for the next to descend, pull on the rope."

Nyx squeezed Rhenna's hand and checked her harness. Cian filled his sight with Rhenna one last, lingering moment and then let his panther senses take him.

He had little conscious knowledge of what came after. All the world was endless sky around him, crumbling earth and stone beneath his claws. He worked his way from one narrow ledge to the next, panting under the brutal sun. Occasionally he heard Nyx behind him; he remembered to stop and rest when she paused to work her magic on some stubborn bit of vegetation that had found roothold on the nearly vertical surface.

His muscles had gone to water by the time he smelled the rank scent of the valley floor. He drew level with the canopy of trees, sucking in the cooler air beneath the leaves, and scrambled down the last stretch of rock with reckless haste. The bleeding skin of his paw pads sank into deep, rich soil. He lay on his side, chest heaving, and allowed himself to forget that even a girl-child could have killed him with no effort at all.

He woke to the rattle of stones beside his head. Nyx dropped to the ground and slumped against the cliff. She reached for him blindly and clutched one of his ears.

"Are you…all right?" she whispered.

He twitched his ear free and changed, groaning at the stiffness of muscle and bone. "Weak as a cub," he said. "The others?"

"On their way. I think I made it a little easier."

He grinned, seized by irrational joy, and kissed her cheek. She jerked away and regarded him as if he'd gone more than a little mad. He leaped up to spin a giddy dance of triumph, abruptly remembered his nakedness, and sank behind a convenient shrub.

Nyx laughed, shook her head and offered him her waterskin. His fingertips brushed hers as he took it. He and Nyx were truly close then, bound by triumph and relief, but Cian knew the intimacy would not last. The bond would slowly dissolve and leave him alone again, as Rhenna had done. As he had done to himself.

He focused his attention on the cliff and settled down to wait. Within the next hours, the Imaziren, Abidemi, Enitan, Rhenna and Tahvo made their way to the foot of the cliff and collapsed in heaps of loose limbs and quivering muscles.

They made camp there, too weary to prepare a fire, and took turns keeping watch through the night. Tahvo sat sleepless, her face turned toward the giant tree in the center of the valley.

The next morning they coiled Nyx's ropes and started through the forest. Cian no longer needed to consult the earth to determine the direction of their march. His instincts spoke clearly.

Tahvo stayed close to Cian as if she feared more for him than for herself. "It hears us," she said.

"The tree?" Cian asked.

She tilted her head, listening as he did for the little sounds of insects, birds and the small furred animals that lived in the canopy and the tangle of undergrowth beneath. But there was nothing to hear. The entire valley might have been empty of animate life, and yet Cian knew the silence was only another warning.

Go back, it said. *Go back while you still can.*

But they continued on through the day and endured another damp, hungry night in the starless shadows beneath the trees. Cian was up before the dim light that marked the dawn, seeking some sign or scent of game, and so was the first to discover that the forest had grown while its unwelcome visitors slept.

The bush behind them was much as they had left it, but the thickets in every other direction had put forth countless new branches and tendrils that grew one into the next in a solid mass. Cian searched for a way through the barrier and found no gap big enough to accommodate anything larger than an ant. He tried to climb over it, first as a man and then as a cat, but the deceptively firm thatching collapsed under his weight and only snapped back into place once he had jumped clear. Rhenna and Nyx were already awake when he went to fetch them.

Abidemi and Enitan squatted before the barrier and spoke softly to each other, shaking their heads. The Imaziren debated and argued. Rhenna had no use for conversation. She lifted her blade and hacked at the nearest branches. They recoiled, quivering, and almost immediately began to grow again, reaching toward each other like parted lovers.

Nyx stepped up beside Rhenna and held her hands out toward the severed limbs. They thrashed violently, but after a moment their astonishing growth slowed and stopped. Nyx released her breath and opened her eyes.

"There is much anger in this forest," she said. "All the things that grow from the earth will resist us. I may be able to hold the branches apart long enough to allow us passage, but beyond that…"

"It will have to be enough," Rhenna said. She met the troubled gazes of each of the villagers and Imaziren in turn. "Take the ropes and go back. You may still return to the village."

The denials were swift and unequivocal. Abidemi and Enitan took their places beside Rhenna, blades at the ready. Slashing and slicing with all their strength, Rhenna and the hunters cut a ragged opening in the bush. Nyx followed just out of range of their sweeping blades, working her magic to hold the gap open long enough for the rest of the party to pass.

Immeghar, who brought up the rear, swore colorfully the first few times the vines and branches sealed behind him, but eventually even he became too weary for curses. Each hour of painstaking progress was won with sweat and exhaustion. By day's end, after Cian and the Imaziren had taken their turns with the blades, Nyx was stumbling and drained by the constant use of her magic. Cian and Immeghar supported her between them, while Rhenna looked for a place where they might stop to rest without constant fear that the undergrowth would close in and seal them up in a suffocating shroud.

Her startled exclamation told Cian that she had found what she sought. She lurched forward, carried by the sweep of her blade, and all but fell into a clearing completely devoid of growth of any kind. The hunters stepped through the gap behind her. Cian and Immeghar eased Nyx to the bare ground and Tahvo knelt beside the Southern woman, pressing her ear to Nyx's chest. The opening through which they had come closed with a rattle of twigs like the clicking of teeth.

Cian left Nyx in Tahvo's care and crouched at Rhenna's side. There was no relief or triumph on her scratched and dirty face. She was staring across the narrow clearing, and when Cian followed her gaze, he felt the full weight of her despair.

The forest had not surrendered. It had simply changed its tactics. What lay before them now was not a living tangle of greenery but a true wall…a wall made not of stone but thorny, leafless branches so tightly intertwined that not even air could squeeze between the joinings. There was no way to tell where one plant began and another ended; the wall rose to the height of ten tall men standing one atop the other, and its armor of foot-long spikes would tear a climber's clothing or flesh as easily as it would the thinnest sheet of papyrus.

Rhenna laughed. "I think Nyx underestimated the forest's anger," she said, streaking the mud on her face with a swipe of her hand. "She has come to the end of her strength—"

"As you have," Cian said.

"I?" She shook her head. "I've only rid us of a few insects and hacked at branches like a novice with her first sword."

Cian ignored her brittle rage and took her in his arms. She felt warm and vital and strong…too strong to require his comfort. But then she turned her face into his shoulder and twisted her fingers in his hair, demanding the one thing he found desperately easy to give. She kissed him fiercely, with the same abandon she'd shown in Danae's courtyard so far away. He answered with all the hunger he had suppressed every weary step from Karchedon. The beast inside him wailed its longing to take her, and her mouth ground on his as if she wanted nothing more than to lie with him in this impossible place.

But she broke away as he knew she must, her eyes blazing with anger and thwarted desire. Ignoring the deliberately averted gazes of the others, she seized her blade and flung herself at the thorn wall, wielding the tool like a warrior's axe. Steel rebounded from iron-hard wood. She attacked it again, cutting from every possible angle. The blade made no impression. She couldn't even sever the fine point at the tip of a single thorn.

Rhenna dropped the blade in disgust and examined her blistered hands. "We can go no farther," she said. "Nyx?"

The Southern woman slowly lifted her head. "I feel nothing," she said. "No life in this that I can touch. It repels me."

"Cian?"

He knelt and touched the soil. Even the lightest contact seared his fingers. He pushed his hand down. The pain was unrelenting. He pulled his hand free, removed his clothes and changed.

Climbing the nearest tree was no easy matter, for the branches flailed under his claws, and the trunk shuddered to cast him off like a flea from a dog's back. He snarled defiance and worked his way up, hugging the bole with front and hind legs, until he could look over the top of the hedge wall. Enough filtered daylight remained for him to see the trees beyond and, less than half a league distant, the great tree casting its vast circle of shadow.

But it was what lay on the other side of the wall that drew Cian's eyes. Heaped at its base were a hundred human skulls, and the soil around them was engraved with the unmistakable tracks of Ailuri paws.

"What do you see?" Rhenna called.

Cian scrambled out of the branches and leaped to the ground, his coat nearly invisible against the darkening forest. Rhenna caught her breath, for no other reason than that she never grew used to the sight of his lethally graceful panther's body, and because he seemed so much a part of this world. The wildness in his yellow eyes seemed to grow stronger with every passing day.

But he changed back into a man, as he always did, and regarded her and the others with a carefully blank expression.

"Beyond the hedge is more forest," he said, "and the great tree. The wall continues to either side as far as I could see." He fixed his gaze on Rhenna. "Let me try to get through. Alone."

She planted her hands on her hips and returned his stare. "What makes you think the wall will yield for you and not the rest of us?"

"Because the Hammer lies behind it, and this is my quest."

"If that is your only argument…" She glanced at Nyx. "You said you feel no life in this thing," she said. "Does that mean you can't make an opening for us, as you did before?"

Nyx studied the wall with a frown. "I can try," she said, "but this is very powerful magic, laid down by one with far greater command over the Earth than I. I doubt that I will be able to hold it."

Rhenna chewed her lower lip. "Tahvo?"

The healer cocked her head. "Whoever made this wall holds no control over Air or Water," she said slowly. "A wind of sufficient strength might prevent the branches from growing too quickly."

A wind. Air was Rhenna's province. She had yet to find a reliable ritual or method to call the spirits of Air when she wanted them…and perhaps some of that failure was because she could not quite accept that she, born a common warrior, should wield power reserved for the Chosen. Nevertheless, when the need was great, she'd managed to bring forth a wind potent enough to blow away the plague of insects.

"Your anger gave you strength," Tahvo had said. *"This time you used it to serve you."*

Rhenna didn't think it would be difficult to find that anger again. She closed her eyes and imagined the dancing motes of air she couldn't see, the sapient spirits and the pneumata that had no will of their own but could still be made to serve. She could almost feel them. Almost.

"Nyx," she said, "we will work together to make a passage. You untangle the branches as best you can, and I'll find a way of keeping it open."

Nyx scraped her fingers through her twig-thatched hair. "Tell me when you are ready."

Rhenna bit back a laugh. *That day will never come, my friend.* She gestured to the villagers and Imaziren. "The rest of you keep as close to us as you can, and be prepared to move quickly." She glared at the wall. Defiance hummed in her clenched muscles. She envisioned the spirits of Air gathering about her, drawn by the vitality of her passion and the stubbornness of her will.

"Go, Nyx," she said.

Nyx muttered under her breath and stretched her fingers toward the hedge. Branches creaked and rustled. With a sound like the groan of a dying woman, the plaited surface began to give way. Nyx spread her hands, and a dozen tiny branches snapped apart, thorns rattling.

Rhenna called upon the winds. They answered, fitfully at first, in random gusts that left traces of moisture on her cheeks. She focused on the tiny hole Nyx had made, and the air streamed toward it, whistled as it passed through the gap. Branches writhed. Side by side, Rhenna and Nyx fought to widen the hole. The wind blasted the hedge in a storm of shredded leaves and whirling debris.

It was not enough. The branches wove together. The opening vanished. Nyx slumped. Cian caught her, easing her to the ground. Rhenna's knees trembled, but somehow she kept her feet. The taste of defeat was sour on her tongue.

"We must try again," she said.

"Nyx is too weak," Cian said. "And soon you'll be, as well."

"I wasn't ready. We'll rest tonight and continue in the morning."

Cian shook his head and stepped away from Nyx. He crouched and thrust his hand into the earth. His hand disappeared, and then his arm to the elbow. His mouth contracted in a grimace of pain, and perspiration streaked his face.

Tahvo lifted her head. "It turns the earth against him," she whispered. "It will kill…"

Rhenna didn't wait for her to finish. She grabbed Cian's arms and pulled. The earth engulfed his shoulder, pressing him flat to the ground. Immeghar and the Ará Odò hunters seized whatever part of Cian they could reach. Their efforts were useless. The earth devoured Cian bit by bit, taking chest and hip and legs until only his head and one arm remained free.

Rhenna clutched his hand in both of hers. His eyes met Rhenna's, stripped of anything but pain. The soil heaved. Her arms were nearly wrenched from their sockets. She lost her grip and fell. When she gained her feet again, Cian was gone.

Frantically she scraped at the earth with broken nails, pounding the unyielding soil with her fists until her flesh was bruised and her bones threatened to snap. The world blurred through a haze of tears. She jumped up, snatched at the nearest blade and charged the hedge. Iron slammed into wood and bounced away as if she had attacked the wall with a feather.

Tahvo clutched her sleeve and would not let go. "I hear him," she said.

Rhenna scrubbed her face with the back of her hand. "He…he's alive?"

Tahvo tilted her head. "He hurts, but—" She exhaled slowly. "He is on the other side. I think he has found a weak place in the wall."

"Praise the gods," Nyx said. "Can you show us, Tahvo?"

The healer began to walk along the hedge, pausing now and again to listen. She continued perhaps a hundred paces and stopped.

"Here," she said.

Rhenna pressed as close to the hedge as she could without touching the thorns. "I can't hear him."

Tahvo sat on the ground, crossed her legs and rested her hands on her knees. She chanted softly in her mother tongue. Rhenna stood back with the others and prayed that Tahvo's spirits would listen.

The forest, already silent, took on a new pall of unreality. All the moisture went out of the air, sucked away as if by a harsh desert wind. The Imaziren gasped. Abidemi jumped with a cry of surprise and pointed at the ground under his feet. Water trickled and pooled where he stood, streaming out of the darkness from an unseen source.

"Stand aside," Tahvo said.

Acting more out of instinct than understanding, the hunters and Imaziren scattered away from the growing flood. Rhenna helped Nyx to her feet. She moved just in time. With the roar of an angry beast, a river burst from among the trees, surging toward Tahvo and the hedge.

"Tahvo!" Rhenna shouted. The water reared up before her and swept over the healer, exploding against the wall in a shower of spray. Thorny branches shot like arrows in every direction. The river bent back on itself, spitting and foaming, and abruptly receded, sinking into the ground.

Tahvo sat in the same position, skin and clothing untouched by the flood that had swallowed her. Before her gaped a hole in the hedge, large enough for a horse to enter. Rhenna raced to Tahvo's side.

"Quickly," the healer said. "It will grow again."

Rhenna gathered the others and urged them through the gap. She and Tahvo were last. They had just reached the other side of the hedge when its branches began to thrust into the opening, stabbing with an overgrowth of thorns as if it hoped to catch some victim in its snapping jaws. By the time Rhenna had taken twenty steps away from the wall, it had closed completely.

The forest within the hedge was as still as that outside it, but the trees seemed lit from within, glowing with a faint green luminescence that picked out the piles of human skulls and the numerous tracks pressed into the soil. Cabh'a laughed uneasily and poked at one of the skulls with the tip of her knife. Enitan bent to examine the prints and spoke to Nyx.

"These are the tracks of many great cats," Nyx said, chafing her arms though the night was still thick with heat. "Some are old, but some were left within the past hour, as were the footprints of a man."

"Cian," Rhenna said. "Where is he, Tahvo?"

"I do not know." Her fingers brushed the earth, outlining the depressions made by the feet of man and beasts. She turned to Nyx. "These tracks are like those of the Ailuri. Cian spoke to me of your ancestress. He said that your people believed others of her breed still live in the forest."

"Her ancestress?" Rhenna said. "What is this, Nyx?"

The Southern woman glanced at her fellow villagers and lifted one shoulder. "My clan is descended from a panther woman who came out of the forest long ago and chose one of the village men to be her mate. It was she who gave us the powers of Earth."

Rhenna stared at the tracks, too weary for shock. "Why did you never mention this before?"

"We of the Clan have not seen another like our ancestress in many generations."

But Cian knew, Rhenna thought. *Why did he fear to tell me?* She kicked at the dirt. "Female Ailuri…"

"That is not possible," Cabh'a said. "Our legends of the Guardians say nothing of this."

"Nor do the Ailuris'," Rhenna said. "They believed no females of their race existed. But perhaps Cian has already met these impossible kin, if kin they are."

Enitan spoke. "He sees no sign of struggle," Nyx said, uncharacteristically subdued. Enitan set off toward the trees, bent close to the ground. Nyx followed to interpret his words. "Cian and the great cats went into the forest together."

Numb with foreboding, Rhenna clutched the familiar solidity of the knife at her waist. "He would not have gone willingly without leaving some message for us," she said. "Something— or someone—used powerful magic to try to keep us from this place. We must assume that these creatures are hostile."

"Our ancestress was not evil," Nyx protested.

Rhenna gestured at the skulls. "These were obviously left as a warning."

"But there is no proof that the panther folk did the killing. Perhaps they agreed to help Cian. It may be that he meant to go on without us."

"Then he was mistaken in his judgment." Rhenna squinted toward the spectral green glow of the trees. "There is enough light to follow, and that is what I intend to do."

Nyx lifted her chin. "I have never suggested otherwise."

"We will all go," Immeghar said.

Rhenna strode after Enitan, who waited near the border of the forest. In his hands he held a bundle of much-worn, familiar clothes.

"Cian's," Rhenna said. "He left them for us to find."

"Enitan says that the human prints stop here," Nyx said, "and there is a new set of panther tracks."

Rhenna nodded grimly. Tahvo, Nyx and the others bunched close, drawn together by the strangeness of the viridescent twilight. The trees closed in around them. The panthers' tracks made an easily visible trail over the forest floor, tracing a nearly straight line toward the center of the valley.

In spite of the constant threat of an unseen enemy, no danger emerged from the canopy or the shadows beneath. After a time Rhenna heard a bird call, and then another—hoots and warbles she remembered from the woods near Nyx's village. Small creatures skittered in the underbrush. The return of ordinary sounds restored a calming sense of near normality. The travelers began to straggle from their tight circle, Immeghar falling behind to take up the rear guard.

Rhenna was too far ahead to hear the first scream. It was Tahvo who called a halt and turned back down the path. She had gone two steps when the hoarse cry came again. Rhenna passed Tahvo at a run, the villagers and Imaziren at her heels.

Immeghar lay submerged up to his chest in a liquid soup of mud where the ground had been firm only moments before. He flailed with his brawny arms, seeking purchase, but only barren earth lay within his reach, and the harder he fought the deeper he sank.

Cabh'a, Tamallat and Mezwar ran to the edge of the mud-hole, shouting to Immeghar in their tongue. He looked up at them, face contorted with terror, and warned them away. Cabh'a and Mezwar stretched their arms to him, and Cabh'a's foot plunged into the mud. Only Mezwar's grasp kept her from sliding in with Immeghar.

Rhenna flung herself on her belly and crawled until she felt the solid ground turn to mire. Cabh'a grabbed her feet and anchored Rhenna in place as she extended her arms above her head. Stifling ooze coated Rhenna's face and filled her mouth.

"Immeghar!" she cried. "Take my hands!"

He struggled to obey, only his shoulders above the deceptively quiet surface. His fingers brushed Rhenna's and slipped free. The mud swallowed his arms. Rhenna strained every muscle in her body and felt the sludge give way beneath her weight.

She met Immeghar's eyes. They had been glazed with fear, but now they cleared, and in them Rhenna saw his acceptance of his own death. His lips curved in the ghost of a smile.

"It seems that I will not be in the heros' tales after all," he croaked.

"You're wrong, Immeghar," Rhenna said. "Your courage will never be forgotten."

He tried to laugh and spat out a mouthful of mud. "You were a worthy companion, warrior. Find the Guardian and bring him home." He looked beyond her to his fellow tribesfolk and spoke to them in the measured tones of ritual before the mire made further speech impossible. For a handful of heartbeats Rhenna saw only his eyes, and then they, too, vanished.

The others pulled Rhenna back from the brink. She lay still, mute with grief and rage. The Imaziren collapsed beside her, Cabh'a openly weeping, Mezwar and Tamallat holding each other in a hard embrace.

Tears ran from Tahvo's silver eyes. She whispered some death chant, propitiating the cruel or negligent spirits that had permitted such a horror.

"Another attack," Rhenna said, "like the insects and the rain…"

"They will continue," Tahvo said, "as long as we search for the Hammer."

"I won't turn back. Not without Cian."

"Immeghar would want us to go on," Cabh'a said. Tamallat and Mezwar nodded fiercely. "We—"

Nyx came upon them at a breathless run, Enitan right behind. "Abidemi has disappeared," she gasped.

Rhenna rolled to her knees and cast one final look at Immeghar's grave. Ooze had become solid earth once more.

Farewell, my friend.

"We'd better find Abidemi," she said.

They gathered close again and followed the hunter's fresh footprints. His path broke off from the panthers' trail and cut into the densest underbrush, which parted all too readily before Rhenna could touch a single plant with her blade.

She smelled the perfume just as she broke into the little clearing. The scent was indescribable, honeyed and alluring, and it set Rhenna's head spinning with sensuous thoughts of physical pleasure and the sating of every unspoken desire. She stopped, fighting the pull of the fragrance, and recognized its source: hundreds of flowers draped on every bush and tree, swaying gently in a nonexistent breeze. Each vibrant red and purple blossom was the size of a woman's head, plump petals full and ripe as a courtesan's lips.

Abidemi stood before one of the flowers, his hands stroking its velvet skin as he would the body of a lover, his face pressed deep into its center. Nyx and Enitan pushed past Rhenna, stricken as she was by the flowers' unearthly beauty.

"There is evil here," Nyx said. "We must stop him." She took a hesitant step into the clearing. The nearest blossoms rustled invitingly. She smiled.

"Do not let her go," Tahvo said.

Rhenna took Nyx's arm and dragged her back. Cabh'a grabbed Enitan. Across the clearing, Abidemi lifted his head, pollen gilding his face like a mask.

Then the insects came. They arrived at first in small numbers, buzzing about the flowers like eager suitors. But more appeared, and the few became a swarm, clumping at the center of the clearing until they had formed an opaque, black sphere of segmented bodies and whirring wings.

"It is too late," Tahvo whispered.

Rhenna watched in horror as the sphere of insects elongated into a spear's point and dived at Abidemi. He barely looked up in time to raise his hands as the first tiny creatures struck his face. In an instant the insects had covered him. His screams were lost in the roar of their wings, his body a grotesque and clumsy child's sculpture of a human shape with only stubs for limbs and head. The figure flailed for a moment and then fell, jerking and shuddering.

When the insects rose from his body, nothing remained of the hunter but his bones.

Someone gagged. Enitan wailed in grief. Nyx's dark skin was ashen gray. She and Rhenna pushed the others back the way they had come, shoving blindly through the trees. They huddled on the main path, coughing and retching to expel the foul perfume from their mouths.

"They will not...follow us here," Tahvo said, wiping her lips.

Rhenna hardly heard her. She stared up at the glowing trees and raised clenched fists.

"Who are you?" she shouted. "Are you so afraid that you must send your servants to threaten us? Show yourself, coward!"

The forest answered. A sleek black shape skimmed along the ground past Rhenna's feet and leaped on Mezwar, claws bared to kill. Tamallat shrieked. She drew her knife and hurled herself at Mezwar's attacker, stabbing at ebony fur. Blood spattered her face. Rhenna, Cabh'a, Nyx and Enitan converged on the battle, but the blended forms of woman and beast thrashed too wildly to be stopped.

The panther wrestled free of Tamallat's grip and jumped out of her reach, its teeth crimson slashes against the gaping void of its mouth. Mezwar lay still. Tamallat fell on his body and wept, careless of her own life.

Rhenna set herself between women and beast. "I know what you are," she spat in the tongue of the Free People. "Come fight *me,* Ailu."

The beast sank down on its haunches, shook out its fur— and changed.

Chapter Nineteen

A dark-skinned woman stood in the panther's place, slender and savage, her golden eyes narrowed to slits in a cruel and beautiful face. She raised her voice in an ululating call. A dozen more women emerged from the woods, each bearing a long spear and knives curved like fangs. They advanced on Enitan, weapons ready to impale him.

Tamallat scrambled up with a growl of rage and rushed the panther woman, who pivoted and slashed at the Amazi. Nyx ran forward, pushed Tamallat aside and addressed the Ailuri in the Ará Odò tongue. The females stared at her, listening to her urgent words, but their faces showed neither recognition nor mercy.

"If these are the kin of your ancestress," Rhenna said grimly, "they seem not to acknowledge the connection."

Nyx carefully backed out of the range of the spears. "They do not understand me." She cast a desperate glance at Enitan.

"I think they will kill Enitan as they did Mezwar if we do not stop them."

"I think they plan to kill all of us," Rhenna said.

"They will pay dearly," Tamallat said, her face streaked with tears. Cabh'a held her back.

"Tahvo," Rhenna said. "Can you speak to them?"

But Tahvo was silent, and when Rhenna glanced behind she saw the healer crouched beside Mezwar, deaf as well as blind, lost in some inner world that not even the threat of death could penetrate. Rhenna gestured to Nyx, and they fell in beside Tamallat and Cabh'a. The women locked gazes, knowing full well that the battle was hopeless. Rhenna chose one of the female Ailuri and tightened her muscles to charge.

A second panther, larger than the first, leaped over the Ailuri females and skidded to a halt before Rhenna.

"Cian!" she cried.

He changed, making his naked body a shield. Save for a few scratches and bruises, he seemed unhurt.

"Enitan," he said. "Come to me."

Enitan began to move, but the female Ailuri intercepted him. Cian spoke harshly to the panther women in a language Rhenna recognized with a jolt of shock. The Ailuri answered in mocking voices, mouths curled in contempt. Enitan took advantage of their distraction to reach the dubious safety of his companions' tiny circle. The females snarled in unison and lifted their spears.

"You seem to be in some difficulty," a woman's low voice said in perfect Hellenish. She strolled casually among the female Ailuri as if she ruled them, her naked skin as pale as Tahvo's and her eyes panther-yellow. She paused before Cian, glanced at him without interest, and met Rhenna's gaze.

"So," she said. "You are the seekers of the Hammer."

Rhenna knew without questioning her certainty that this woman was a far greater threat than all the Ailuri females together. "Who are you?" she demanded. "Are you the one who killed our friends?"

The woman looked past Rhenna at Mezwar's torn body. "I fear I cannot take credit for that," she said. "The Alu slaughter all males who enter their territory." She addressed the females in the same arcane tongue Cian had used, and several of the panther women laughed. "I see that one has managed to survive."

"Two," Cian said. He stared at the woman with nothing short of hatred. "And they won't have either of us."

"You have little chance of escape...though they may allow your females to live if you do exactly as I tell you."

"These Ailuri took you prisoner?" Rhenna asked Cian.

"I managed to fight my way through the Earth to the other side of the hedge," he said, "and they were waiting." He dropped his gaze. "Nyx spoke of a panther ancestress, but I didn't believe such a race truly existed."

"Yet you did know of one female Ailu before ever you came to the South," the pale-skinned woman said. She clucked her tongue. "You never told them about me?" She leaned closer to Rhenna and smiled. "I should be offended, but so many mortal females suffer the weakness of common jealousy. Was he so afraid to lose your affection?"

"I don't understand you," Rhenna said.

"Her name...is Yseul," Cian said. "She was unnaturally created from the flesh and blood of my people by Baalshillek to do his bidding."

"One of the creatures he sent to stop us," Rhenna said. "How can she know the language of the Earthspeakers?"

"I was born with the knowledge," Yseul said, "as I was born with the powers the Ailuri had forgotten...until Baalshillek gave them cause to remember." She stroked her hands over her belly. "Unfortunate that they never had a chance to rediscover the lost half of their race."

Rhenna silenced the hundred questions that drummed inside her head. "What do you want?"

"From you, nothing at all," Yseul said. "For Cian the Alu may find some use, at least until he ceases to amuse them. As for the rest…" She gestured negligently toward her ebon-skinned sisters and spoke a command in the sacred tongue.

The Alu moved to obey. Cian changed, hind legs bunched beneath him. Rhenna wiped her damp palm on her thigh and tightened her grip on her knife.

"Enough!"

The shout rattled Rhenna's bones and rumbled in the earth under her feet. Tamallat, Cabh'a and Nyx went still. The female Ailuri froze as one, lifting their heads, nostrils flared.

Tahvo walked boldly among them, her eyes suffused with luminous green. The little healer was gone, though the shell of her body remained unchanged. Behind her face was another being, shedding verdant light like the forest, a goddess who towered over lesser mortals like the great tree at the center of the valley.

The Alu shrank to the earth in obeisance. Tahvo circled the human prisoners, studying each of them in turn, and stopped before Cian.

"You are the one who dares to steal what is mine," she said.

Cian changed again, met Tahvo's alien gaze and bowed his head. "You are the goddess of the tree," he said.

"I am Ge. What are you, male creature, that you take the shape of my beloved children?"

"I am Ailu," Cian said steadily. "I have come from the North—"

Tahvo touched Cian's forehead, and he swayed as if she had struck him. Rhenna moved to help and found her feet sealed to the ground by a thousand minute tendrils sprung from the soil.

Ge examined Rhenna through Tahvo's eyes. "You have overcome all the obstacles I set in your path," she said. "You are no ordinary mortals."

"You succeeded in stopping some of us," Rhenna said bitterly. "Are you a goddess of life, or death?"

Nyx lifted her head. "We serve the good—"

"Silence," Tahvo-Ge hissed. "I have known this day would come…the day when the evil ones would seek what I took away."

"Not…evil," Cian croaked, as if Ge's touch had damaged his voice.

Ge ignored him. Abruptly she turned to the Alu. "Bring the females to me, and hold the males until I decide their fate."

Yseul crept forward, half crouched like a dog expecting to be kicked. "Great goddess," she said, "these mortals bring much danger. It would be best to kill them now—"

Ge raised her hand, and the Alu sprang up to surround Yseul with growls and much shaking of weapons. Yseul retreated, an answering snarl on her pale, beautiful face. Her withdrawal was enough for the Alu. They pushed between Rhenna and Cian, driving him and Enitan to one side.

Cian locked his feet. "I can tell you all you wish to know," he said to Ge. "I am the seeker of the Hammer. The others are only my servants. Let them go."

Ge did not answer. She stood immobile, her green stare fixed on something far away, and Tahvo's body slumped. Shoving Alu spears aside, Rhenna supported the healer and saw that her eyes were silver again.

"The withered leaf," Tahvo whispered.

"What? Tahvo—"

"I am all right," Tahvo said, a little breathless. She gripped Rhenna's hand. "Ge is filled with great anger against all mortals, men above all, and we have not the strength to stop her if she chooses to kill."

"Then what hope do we have?" Rhenna asked as the Alu prodded at her back with the butts of their spears. "If she rules all the spirits here—"

"Ge is not beyond reason. She shares our greatest enemy, for she is one of the Four who escaped, and she hates the Exalted of the Stone."

She said no more, for the larger group of Alu had separated the women from Cian and Enitan, stripped Rhenna, Nyx and the Imaziren of their weapons, and were herding them into the forest.

"Cian!" Rhenna shouted.

"Don't worry," he called back as his captors bore him and Enitan away. "Save yourselves."

"Do whatever you must, Cian. Swear to me...."

But he had vanished, and there was not so much as a rustle of leaves to betray where they had taken him. Of Yseul there was no sign.

The Alu drove the women along an almost imperceptible path through the forest. Rhenna soon lost track of both time and distance, her arms supporting Tahvo and her thoughts on Cian. Nyx attempted once more to speak to the Alu, but they pushed her back among her companions with hardly more than a glance. Tamallat walked with the rigidity of one on the very edge of suicidal violence.

Dim daylight had tinted the nearly invisible sky by the time the travelers reached the outermost branches of the great tree. Lesser trees blocked all sight of its trunk, but Rhenna could reckon its size from the breadth of its leaves and twigs the thickness of a man's leg. As they passed deeper into the great tree's shadow, the ordinary trees disappeared, leaving masses of fantastic undergrowth made up of vines, flowering creepers and plants for which Rhenna had no name.

Halfway through the day, Tahvo had begun to stumble with exhaustion, and even Rhenna had difficulty keeping up the pace. Finally the Alu called a halt. At first Rhenna thought they had come to yet another wall, this one made of solid brown wood. But then she recognized that the wall was the trunk of the great tree, so massive that fifty women could have lived comfortably within it. The lowest branches were indistinct shapes high above Rhenna's head, and the roots were as broad as the bow of a Hellenish ship.

The Alu made it clear that Rhenna and her companions were to kneel and wait. Tamallat resisted, and they knocked her down before Rhenna could intervene.

Cabh'a crawled to her fellow warrior's side and held her hand. Nyx whispered what might have been a prayer. Rhenna stared at the tree trunk until her vision began to blur, and she thought she saw the tangle of vines and flowers about the tree's roots begin to writhe and cluster into a single, strangely human form.

It was no illusion. Legs and arms, a distinctly feminine torso, delicate fingers made of vine tips, and a face...a face so perfectly constructed that each feature was a flawless copy of a mortal woman's, perilously beautiful. Green hair rippled and flowed about her body in ceaseless motion.

"Ge," the Alu said in unison, bowing low.

"Ge," Tahvo repeated.

The goddess stared at Tahvo from pupilless green eyes. "I know you," she said in Hellenish, her voice like the rubbing of leaves one against the other and yet deep as a tremor in the earth. She took a step away from the tree...not a true step, for she moved suspended above the soil and yet tied to both tree and earth by a train of vines that coiled behind her legs and hips like the sweep of a gown. Her gaze fixed on Nyx. "And you," she said. "You bear the blood of the Alu."

Nyx inclined her head. "My distant ancestress came out of the forest generations ago. I—"

Ge swept past Nyx and paused before Rhenna. "You are born of the gods."

"I am Rhenna of the Free People," Rhenna said stiffly.

"Rhenna." Ge closed her eyes. "How is it that one who lives without males accompanies him who would steal what is mine?"

"Cian is not your enemy," Rhenna said. "He seeks the Hammer only to save the world."

Ge reared up in a snapping of vines, leaves scudding in her wake. "Save the world?" she mocked. "It is males who would destroy it."

"Once I might have agreed with you, goddess," Rhenna said. "Now I know it is not so."

"Would you die here, mortal?"

"If we die today, others will come for your precious Hammer, and they won't stop until they've slaughtered your Alu and burned your forest to ashes."

The ground tilted under Rhenna's feet. Two Alu sprang up and came at her, long-nailed fingers curled to claw and tear.

Ge lifted her hand. The Alu fell back.

"In my roots I have sensed a great sorrow," Ge said. "My Alu have told me…"

"The Stone has been set free," Rhenna finished for her. "You know the power of the Exalted. You were one of them."

"No." Ge's face remained immobile, but her body flushed with verdant light. "I left those who cared nothing for the earth—"

"And stole the Hammer so it could never be used against you."

The restless tendrils of Ge's hair thrashed about her head. "I am a guardian of Earth. No mortal can destroy me."

"But you fear Cian, who is also of the Earth. If you are not an ally of the Exalted and you recognize their evil, why do you stand in the way of the Watcher who could stop them?"

"Did not his kind fail in their task and abandon the Stone?"

"Cian would give his life to atone for that failure, great *òrìshà*," Nyx said. "He is the last of his race."

"Not the last." Ge pointed toward the crouching Alu. "My females told me long ago how they were denied the right to guard the Stone. Now they speak of the males' alliance with the evil in the North—"

"Then they lie," Rhenna said. "The Exalted and their priests have murdered all Cian's brothers. Only he is left to fulfill the prophecies and carry the Hammer against them."

Ge hissed, and the leaves of the great tree rattled overhead. "Prophecies," she said. She gazed at Tahvo. "I see with the eyes of your memory. You believe these writings are truth."

Tahvo stood slowly. "I do, Mother of Earth."

"The devas set us on this path," Rhenna said. "The Exalted and their servants have already spread their poison across the North. Only the four Weapons can prevent them from swallowing the world."

"Four Weapons," Ge said. "And four mortals to bear them. Mortals with the blood of gods." Her eyes narrowed. "You also claim this right, Rhenna of the Free People. What do you seek?"

"All that concerns me now is the Hammer."

"And if I give it to you, you will surrender the Alu male to me?"

"Never. I am not here to steal his destiny."

Ge was silent. The tree grew still. "Keela."

One of the Alu rose and went to her goddess, yellow eyes burning on Rhenna's. Ge touched the shapechanger's black hair and asked a question in the Alu tongue, her voice almost tender.

"She asks if Keela has ever known the love of a male," Tahvo whispered.

Keela answered with a shudder of disgust, and Tahvo translated. "We have not suffered such depravity for a thousand years."

"Then look upon this female," Ge said, indicating Rhenna, "and witness how what mortals call love weakens even the strongest."

"She cares for the traitor."

"She would give her life for him." Ge's petal lips curved in mimicry of a smile. "If I let Cian take the Hammer, she would stay here to die."

"Then she does not deserve to live."

Tahvo inhaled sharply and faced the goddess. "You know what it is to love, Mother of Earth," she said in Hellenish. "You joined the Exalted out of hatred for the greed and cruelty of men, but it was for love of the world and all its creatures that you turned against them."

"Not all," Ge said. "Once mortals came to my sanctuaries

with offerings and vows of love, but it was only fear and avarice that moved their souls. They wished to rule, not serve.
When they had no more need of me…" She stopped, flailing
vines like whips. "I want nothing from mankind. I would witness their extinction without sorrow."

"But not only men will suffer," Rhenna said. "The sacred
groves of my people are rotting from within. I have seen beasts
burned alive on the Stone God's altars. Even the smallest wild
creatures cannot survive where the priests hold dominion.
What grows from the Stone is forever corrupted."

"My Alu will protect me—"

"They can't protect you from what is coming," Rhenna said
harshly. "You lie to yourself, goddess. You no longer care about
the world because you have been away from it too long. You're
afraid, and you disguise your fear with hatred. You fear that if
the Exalted find you, you'll discover just how weak and useless you have become."

A terrible, rending crack shook the trunk of the great tree as
if it had been struck by lightning. Ge's body sprouted vicious
thorns, and her mouth opened in a soundless roar. Her hands
grew a dozen sinuous fingers. She caught Rhenna about the
neck and chest, sealing the air from her throat.

The ground beneath Ge's feet exploded in a spray of dirt and
pebbles. Cian emerged from the ground, hair slicked to his head
and shoulders, his face taut with agony. Angry welts and open
sores blistered his bare skin. He grabbed Ge about her hips and
flung her aside, severing vines with the force of his effort.
Rhenna tumbled free and rolled to the base of the tree's roots,
gasping for air. The Alu snatched up their spears; Cabh'a and
Tamallat moved to confront them with only their bare hands
as weapons.

Tahvo pushed in front of her friends and laid her hands on
Ge's slick green skin. She felt herself slide into the goddess's
being, joined with the spirit in rage and confusion. Only a
sliver of her soul remained apart. It was enough.

Ge cast her off, but for a few precious moments Tahvo still saw with the goddess's eyes. Ge's voice rang out in a single word. Keela and the Alu closed in a circle about their enemies, and Ge turned on Cian.

"You have been in my Earth," she accused.

Cian straightened swollen limbs. "Your Earth did not welcome me."

"What has become of my Alu who watched you?"

"They live."

"Enitan?" Nyx asked.

"He escaped."

Ge's agile, leaflike tongue darted between her lips. She glanced at Rhenna. "You came to save this female. You would die for her."

"Is my death your price for the Hammer?"

"No, Cian!" Rhenna cried.

"The Hammer is useless without the Watcher," Nyx said, standing beside Rhenna. "If you must have more lives, take mine."

"And mine," Tamallat said.

"You slew our brothers," Cabh'a said, "but we do not fear you."

"Mortals have better reason to fear death than any deva," Cian said. "But even a deva can come to the end of existence. As you have."

Tahvo knew the truth of his words. During her joining with Ge, she had felt a wrongness within the goddess but had not recognized its source. Understanding blossomed like one of the goddess's deadly flowers.

Ge also began to understand. She turned inward, and Tahvo felt her moving within the great tree that was her true body, searching for the root of her sickness. It lay at the center of her massive trunk, lodged deep like an arrowhead festering where no noaiddit could mend it.

"The Hammer," Cian said, "was made to fight the Exalted,

and you were one of them. While you slept, its influence was held in check. But now it is killing you, goddess, as surely as your hatred."

Ge looked at Tahvo, her fear undetectable in the blank green eyes. "You are a healer," she said. "Heal me."

Tahvo walked toward the tree. The Alu melted out of her path. She pressed her palms to the seamed bark.

"Do nothing," Tamallat said. "Let this evil one die."

"Not without the Hammer," Rhenna said coldly.

Tahvo blocked their voices from her mind and reached through the layers of wood to the narrow channels that carried the great tree's life. The fluid pulsed sluggishly, thick with the taint of the Weapon Ge had kept so long concealed. The decay had spread from roots to highest branches. Soon her leaves would begin to fall, brittle twigs snapping with the lightest breeze. Then the smaller branches would crack, weeping from every wound, and the earth beneath her canopy would shrivel and rot.

Ge was dying.

Tahvo let her hands fall. The tree groaned. Tahvo's sight dimmed as the last threads of her bond with Ge dissolved. She had shared her companions' anger when Immeghar, Mezwar and Abidemi had died, but now she felt only pity and sorrow for the pointless ending of so ancient a spirit.

"I am sorry," she said. "The poison has gone too far."

"She deceives you. They all deceive you, Mother."

Yseul's footsteps crossed the clearing and came to a stop. Rhenna grabbed Tahvo's arm and pulled her to safety while Yseul continued to speak, shrill with accusation.

"It is not the Hammer that would destroy you!" she cried. "It is this male who violated your sacred Earth. Even now he works his evil magic."

"The evil is hers," Tahvo said. "Yseul is a servant of the Exalted. She would deliver the Hammer to her masters."

"Liar!"

"You are an adept of deception. You used your body to trap Cian in the city of the Stone."

Yseul's voice thinned to a whine. "He forced himself upon me! Goddess…"

"You know I speak truth, Mother of Earth," Tahvo said, silently begging Cian's forgiveness. "She and the priest who made her wanted Cian's seed to create a new race of Ailuri bound to serve the Stone."

"Blasphemy," Ge said. Her vines lashed the air near Tahvo's face.

"No!" Yseul suddenly shifted to the ancient Ailu tongue, and Tahvo struggled to understand the unfamiliar words.

"Hear me, my sisters!" Yseul cried. "This male serves the will of the Exalted and their priests. Strike now, before he steals the life from your beloved. Strike!"

For an instant nothing stirred, and then Tahvo heard the rush of bare feet and the repeated, deadly hiss of iron piercing flesh.

"Cian!" Rhenna cried. A body fell. Tahvo smelled the acrid scent of blood. Cian's blood. She stumbled as she tried to find him, working her way through a chaos of thrashing limbs.

Emotion assaulted her so violently that at first she thought a dozen Alu spears had impaled her. She caught her breath, feeling her belly and breast. They were whole. Sensation tore through her, pain and ecstasy combined in a delirious dance. Vision returned, and she saw Cian slumped in Rhenna's arms before the power of Ge's passion swept her away.

Joy. Exaltation. She felt the blood of the Watcher seep into the earth, rich and sweet, trickling between the particles of soil until it reached the sensitive fibrils of her roots. Eagerly she accepted the nourishment, trembled at the new strength it sent coursing through her veins. The pain she had never acknowledged drained from her body.

But she knew that Cian's blood would not halt her dying, even if he spilled it all at her feet. He was not to be her murderer or her savior. Yet she no longer feared him or the fate he brought from his world of prophecy and mortal desire. She would not end when the Hammer was taken from her. Her children would live on.

She spoke to the Alu, ordering them to pursue and hold the treacherous female who had commanded the attack on the Watcher. He lay on the ground, eyes glazed with pain, while Nyx sought to stanch the bleeding of his wounds with scraps of cloth torn from her own garments. Rhenna knelt beside him, fists clenched, as if she could fell a goddess with a single blow.

Ge looked upon the mortals as she had once regarded her ancient worshipers, without anger or regret. The time for such indulgence was past.

"What will you give for the Hammer?" she asked Cian gently.

He raised himself on his arm and met her gaze. "My life, if you will let the others go."

Rhenna objected, but he seemed not to hear. He, too, understood. He saw how the kiss of his blood had reminded Ge, for so sweet a moment, of what she had been before she had learned to hate.

"Yours is the true blood of Earth," she said, "but I would not take it from you. You cannot restore what is lost."

"Then what is your price?"

"Immortality." She smiled, and one of the Alu began to weep. "You will give me life that will continue when mine is done."

"How?" he asked. But even as he spoke, the knowledge came to him through the soil upon which he lay, and his skin grew pale as a serpent's belly.

"I am no god," he croaked.

"What is it, Cian?" Rhenna demanded. "What does she want?" She rose and faced Ge, her plain mortal features taut with brave, foolish defiance. "We share his fate," she said. "Whatever it may be."

Cian caught her hand. "You can't be a part of this, Rhenna," he said. Leaning heavily on her arm, he climbed to his feet and took a step away from her, the blood already clotted in his healing wounds. "You will surrender the Hammer?" he said to Ge.

She inclined her head. He glanced from Nyx to Tamallat and Cabh'a, his eyes unseeing.

"Curse all devas," Rhenna said. "What does she want?"

He looked through her. "She wants children, Rhenna. Children of her body. And only I can give them to her."

Chapter Twenty

Tahvo broke free of Ge's influence, her stomach knotting in horror. She remembered. Everything that had been in the spirit's thoughts had become her own. She could see how Rhenna stared at Cian, bewildered and not yet ready to understand.

There was no more Tahvo could do for him. Rhenna needed her now.

"Tahvo?" Rhenna said, her voice pleading like that of a child who longed to be told a comforting lie. "What is happening?"

"I was with the goddess." Tahvo swallowed. "I…"

Rhenna touched her brow. "You can see."

"For a little while." She closed her eyes, wishing herself blind again. "Rhenna, Cian has agreed to the bargain."

"Bargain?" She laughed. "Cian is to sire offspring on this…this—"

"It is possible."

Rhenna's moss-and-honey eyes smoldered with fury and pain. "How?"

"The spirit must choose a mortal body that will accept her soul for the time it takes to…" She couldn't finish the sentence, but Rhenna already knew. She turned on Ge.

"Use me," she said.

Narrow, sharp-ended vines sprang from Ge's sides and curled about Rhenna's arms and face. The warrior held rigidly still as the probing points drew tiny beads of blood from her skin. Cian threw off his stupor and stepped forward, poised to interfere.

Abruptly Ge thrust Rhenna away. "No," she said. Her gaze came to rest on Tahvo.

Tahvo's mouth went dry. Who better to bear this burden than a noaiddit who already shared Ge's essence so completely? She spread her hands across her belly, recalling the dream on the Northern steppes—how she had become large with child and given birth to a babe with black hair and green-gold eyes….

It must not be. Such a union would injure Rhenna beyond all healing. Tahvo could no more mate with Cian than with her own brother.

As she waited, sick with dread, Ge's eyes looked past her to the Imaziren women, quickly dismissing them. But Tahvo felt no relief, for the goddess moved on to the Alu and their pale-skinned prisoner.

"He gave you his seed," she said to Yseul, "but it died inside you. Your evil killed it."

Yseul shrank from the goddess's anger. "I had no choice. I—"

Ge snapped a command, and the Alu beat Yseul to the ground with the shafts of their spears. Tahvo glanced at Rhenna. The warrior's visage was as cool and white as a mask carved of seabeast tusks.

Oh, my sister…

"Nyx," Ge said. "Come to me."

Nyx obeyed with obvious reluctance, her face averted as if

somehow she might escape Ge's inevitable scrutiny. The goddess's needle vines drifted over Nyx's skin, pricking, tasting.

"Blood of the Alu," Ge said. "You are worthy."

Nyx looked from Rhenna to Cian, who had closed his eyes against what he did not wish to see. "Great *òrìshà*…" she began.

Ge's eyes glowed like the forest in the depths of night. "Will you give your body?"

"You will not be hurt," Tahvo whispered to Nyx. She felt for Rhenna's hand and held it tightly. "There is no other way."

Nyx lifted her head. "Then I agree."

Not so much as the rustle of a leaf broke the absolute quiet. Ge's vines reached for Nyx again, but this time they sprouted countless tendrils no broader than the width of a single hair. The tendrils pierced Nyx's clothing, shredding it from her limbs, and wriggled like corpse worms under her flesh.

Nyx moaned. Tahvo gripped Rhenna's arm. Something wonderful and terrible was happening, for as Ge's tendrils invaded Nyx's body and enclosed her in a web of vegetation, Ge herself began to shrink until the female form she had made was no more than a twisting cable of stems. Then even that last remnant disappeared, dissolving into Nyx as ice melts under the sun of spring.

Pupilless green eyes glittered in Nyx's brown face. The Ará Odò woman still inhabited her own body, but it was no longer hers to control. She would feel everything that happened, but Ge would move her limbs and speak with her voice.

Nyx held out her hand to Cian. He stared at it, frozen, and then lifted his eyes to Rhenna. She looked away. He gave Tahvo a bitter, helpless glance and took Nyx/Ge's hand. Together they walked to the foot of the tree, and Nyx raised her arms. Thick vines, woven in the shape of a ladder, dropped from the canopy. Nyx began to climb. Cian followed like a man going to an inexorable, gruesome death.

Rhenna turned her back on the tree, arms folded across her chest. The Imaziren women sat locked in close embrace, bound in their grief for the companions they had lost. Tahvo whispered a calming chant, striving desperately not to feel what passed between Cian and the goddess in their bed among the leaves. No one was watching Yseul when she plunged feet-first into the ground.

One of the Alu shouted an alarm, and the others converged on the place where Yseul had stood. Only a slight mounding of the soil betrayed her passage.

Tahvo crouched and stroked the earth with her fingertips. Her senses were still distantly tied to Ge's, so she knew almost at once where Yseul had gone and what she intended.

"The roots," she said, scrambling to her feet. "She is attacking the roots of the tree."

Stone-faced, Rhenna gazed into the forest. "Why?"

"To distract Ge. To prevent what must happen." Tahvo rushed to the Alu, hands raised palm up in supplication. "Yseul wields her magic to harm your goddess," she said in the Alu tongue. "Help me to stop her."

The leader called Keela gripped her spear in both hands, her eyes wild with fear. "What must we do?"

"You have the Ailu magic. Reach into the earth. Bring her to the surface again."

Keela looked at her women and licked her lips. "We have never—"

"Try." Tahvo sank to her knees, drawing the shapeshifter with her. "Feel your enemy. Drive her as you drive the beasts in the hunt."

The Alu knelt in a circle about their leader. They began to sing, a tune both haunting and ferocious, drumming with the butts of their spears and tossing their heads to the quickening beat. Tahvo matched their chants with her own. The ground bulged between two massive, wedge-shaped roots, and the top of a black-haired head emerged.

Rhenna rushed the Alu and seized one of their spears, spinning lightly on one foot as she took aim. Yseul's head and shoulders popped free of the soil, her skin pocked with blisters. She cried out in rage as the earth rejected her. Rhenna threw her spear. It grazed Yseul's arm and lodged in bark.

A deafening bellow boomed through the forest. The tree tossed and rolled as if it would pull its roots from the ground and stride away. Yseul, her arm streaked with blood, stumbled behind the broad, quivering trunk.

The overwhelming clamor ceased. Leaves shaken loose from the tree's lowest branches drifted to the earth and lay still. Rhenna tugged the spear loose and set off in pursuit of Yseul.

She returned a few moments later. "She's fled," she said.

"You can't let her escape," Cabh'a said.

"I have no intention of doing so…once I know that Cian is safe."

"Yseul will not be easily found," Tahvo said.

Keela helped Tahvo to rise and signaled to her women. "Only we can track her in our own land," she said in the Alu tongue. "When the mating is finished…" She looked up into the great tree. Tahvo followed her gaze.

Cian was climbing down the trunk, arms wrapped about the vine ladder as his bare feet clung to rough bark. He reached the ground, scrubbed his hand across his face, and stared about him as if the world had grown too strange for mortal understanding. The wounds and bruises on his skin had completely healed. Rhenna took a step toward him and stopped.

Tahvo approached him with great care. Her vision was beginning to dim again, and she knew it would soon be gone. As Ge would soon be gone.

Cian focused on her slowly, despair dulling his golden eyes to weathered bronze. "We must go."

Tahvo looked up again. Nyx had not yet reappeared. Even as she searched, the trunk gave a snap and groan of splintering wood. A dark premonition filled Tahvo's head, and she saw herself as an insect scuttling out of the path of a toppling twig.

"Away!" she gasped. "The tree…"

The Alu already understood. They bounded off, some taking the shapes of panthers for greater speed. Rhenna pushed Tahvo into a run, Cian beside her and the Imaziren at his heels. When they paused to catch their breaths and look behind, they saw nothing but a whirlwind of scudding dirt, leaves and branches.

The tree was not falling. It was flying apart, shattering from within. Chunks of wood as big as several horses shot into the sky. A cloud of debris choked the air, arching over the forest for a league in every direction, yet none of the tree's fragments fell on the mortals who watched its undoing.

Rhenna tugged on Tahvo's arm, but she shook her head. "Wait."

The others huddled closer, speechless with astonishment. The ferocity of the divine storm lasted but a few hundred heartbeats. When the dust began to clear, Tahvo searched the center of the eruption, hoping to see one last thing before the gift of sight deserted her.

Nyx stood where the tree had been, cupped within the low walls of an earthen crater. Her naked skin gleamed, unmarred by the fury of Ge's final moments of life. She threw out her arms, and from them fell as many seeds as there were stars in the sky. Where each seed struck the earth the soil rose to cover it like the arms of a mother cradling her child.

Nyx squatted and spread her hands on the ground between her feet. Her fingers dipped and lifted again, wrapped around the handle of a weapon half as tall as she...a thing made of wood and reddish-black stone engraved with symbols, arcane and strange, simple of form but radiating such power that Tahvo began to truly comprehend what the spirits would demand of Cian.

Nyx stood, raising the Hammer in triumph. Her eyes flashed brilliant green one last time and then darkened to a mortal woman's deep brown.

Cian started toward her, his steps halting and ungraceful. Rhenna made no move to follow.

"Is Ge dead?" she asked Tahvo.

Tahvo wiped the wetness from her eyes. "She is gone."

"You weep for such a monster?" Rhenna asked.

"For one so ancient, for one who once loved the race of men... Perhaps even the spirits require forgiveness."

"I curse such gods of death," Tamallat said, tears running down her cheeks. "Let the evil ones destroy them."

Tahvo had no comfort to offer. She could see little now, but through the veil falling over her eyes she watched tiny seedlings spring up in verdant glory, warmed by the rays of a sun no longer obstructed by the great tree's vast canopy.

Ge had found her immortality.

Cian stared at the Hammer. He was afraid to look higher, afraid to meet Nyx's eyes and share the memory of what had passed between them.

He remembered everything...every touch, every sensation: Nyx's hands stroking his chest, the feel of her lips on his skin, the murmur of leaves singing their joy at Ge's triumph. Shame had not kept his body from fulfilling its part of the bargain. And though he knew Nyx had no control over what had happened, he could not forget that she had experienced their joining as surely as he.

"Cian."

He raised his eyes to Nyx's. He could read nothing in their brown depths. Her regal bearing seemed to reject any taint of shame or regret.

"The Hammer is yours," she said, offering it with both hands. "Take it."

Sunlight glinted off the unfamiliar glyphs etched in its head. The metal was marbled black and red, perfectly shaped save for a tiny piece chipped off one edge. Cian reached for the smooth wooden handle, fingers shaking. A keening wail rose from the forest, voices of the Alu mingling in mourning for their lost mother.

"They are no threat," Tahvo said from behind him. "They will hold to Ge's agreement."

Cian let his hand fall, the Hammer untouched. He looked down at the seedlings rising so swiftly from the fertile soil, unable to fathom how they could contain any part of him.

"How is Rhenna?" he asked Tahvo.

"She understands."

"Does she?" He wrapped his arms around his chest. "I wanted no part of this, Tahvo."

"I know."

"It isn't over, is it? When I take the Hammer…it will change me."

Tahvo didn't answer. Her silver eyes held visions she could not share.

"You must take it, Cian," Nyx said.

"I'm sorry, Nyx," he said. "I can't. Not yet."

"Then I will keep it for a time. But be warned…I can hold it only because I shared Ge's power. Anyone else who touches it may suffer grievous harm."

"I understand. I am grateful." He drew a painful breath. "Nyx, I—"

She met his gaze. "We do what we must," she said. Abruptly she walked away, stepping carefully over the seedlings.

Cian forced his legs to obey his will, turning back toward Rhenna. She stood with the Imaziren women, as tranquil and composed as a well-fed lioness. Cian was not deceived.

She smiled as he approached, her lips twisted up on one side in a way he knew all too well. "You seem to be all right," she said.

"Yes."

"Where is the Hammer?"

"Nyx is…carrying it for me."

Rhenna's eyes flickered with emotion, quickly concealed. "It doesn't seem so terrible. Why are you afraid of it, Cian?"

"I don't know." Heat scalded his cheeks. "Everything will change—"

"Everything has."

His fingers ached with the need to touch her. "No, Rhenna."

She stared at some point over his shoulder. "What now, Tahvo?"

"Ge no longer rules the forest," the healer said. "Yseul has no allies. We can travel freely where we choose."

"Not where we choose," Rhenna said wearily. "We have only one Weapon. There are three more to find."

"I know where to seek them." Nyx joined them, carrying a long bundle wrapped in large leaves and bound with vines. "The prophecies lie in my father's homeland. All we need to learn will be there."

Rhenna glanced at Nyx, jaw tight. "East," she said. "A hundred leagues? A thousand?"

"It is far, but my father made the journey alone."

"Tahvo?"

"East," the healer agreed.

Rhenna sighed. "We are in no shape to go anywhere as we are now. We'll return to Nyx's village to rest and gather supplies. Can you find the way back?" she asked Nyx.

"The spirits will aid us," Tahvo said.

"Can they protect us from Yseul? If the Alu don't catch her…"

"Cian said there may be more such creatures on our trail."

Tahvo nodded. "I fear Yseul was not alone."

"Then we must be doubly cautious," Nyx said. "The location of my father's city and the true prophecies remain hidden from the Stone priests and their minions. We must be certain not to lead Baalshillek's servants to them."

Everyone fell silent, exhausted by the weeks of struggle and the prospect of more to come. Tahvo drifted away, murmuring something about the spirits. Tamallat and Cabh'a spoke quietly in their own tongue. Nyx clasped the Hammer to her chest, leaving Rhenna and Cian alone again.

"Rhenna…about Yseul…" Cian began.

"You don't owe me any explanations."

Cian gathered the rags of his courage. "I should have told you long ago."

"'He gave you his seed' Ge said. It's true, then?"

"Yes." He clenched and unclenched his fingers, wishing for her anger or contempt—anything but this seeming indifference.

"She lied when she said you forced her," Rhenna said.

"She found *me*. Baalshillek... I was not in my right mind." *I thought she was you.* "I have no excuse."

"Baalshillek made her out of your people's substance. How could you resist her?"

"I should have known her for what she was."

Rhenna shrugged. "Now you know that females of your kind do exist."

"Perhaps the Alu were once of my people. No longer." *You are my people, Rhenna. You are the last.* "There will be no more Ailuri children."

She looked up with her uneven half smile. "Poor Cian. Perhaps for a while you can finally escape the females who constantly demand your...cooperation."

"There will always be one female who can command me."

"And that is something you'd best not forget." She adjusted her belt to conceal a hole in her shirt, gave Cian a brief nod and went to join the Imaziren.

Cian's legs nearly gave way. He braced them, sucking in ragged breaths until the dizziness left him.

Rhenna had forgiven him. She was too strong and just to do otherwise. She had learned to accept his weaknesses as she could not abide her own, insignificant as hers seemed to him.

But even her pardon could not undo this day's work, or bridge the chasms that cruel necessity had opened up between them. He had not lost Rhenna today, or even when he'd taken Yseul in the dark streets of Karchedon. She had never truly been his.

He found a quiet place well away from Ge's nursery and changed to panther shape, scouting the forest in search of Yseul or the Alu. Their scents were already fading, buried beneath the competing odors of birth, growth and decay. When he returned, Tahvo, Nyx and Rhenna were deep in conversation.

"No sign of the Alu," he said, leaving Yseul's name unspoken.

"We have good news," Nyx said. "Tahvo has reached the little people."

"So far from their own country?"

"They are close to the spirits," Tahvo said. "They were afraid of Ge but regretted leaving us. They will guide us back to Nyx's village."

"If we can trust them," Rhenna said.

"Tahvo says that their *òrìshà* have brought them word of Cian's victory," Nyx said. "I would not be surprised if they consider him an *òrìshà* himself. They may agree to take us across their territory, as far as the eastern boundary of the great forest."

"Whatever these little people may do," Rhenna said, "Cabh'a and Tamallat have decided to return to their people. They've sacrificed enough."

Cian bowed his head. "I should have come alone."

"Regret is pointless. We must move ahead." Rhenna tilted her face toward the sky. "I have no desire to stay here for the night. We'll make camp elsewhere."

She went to speak to the Imaziren while Nyx and Cian gathered the meager supplies the Alu had permitted their prisoners to keep, including a few small animal skins that served as scanty garments. The band covered a league's distance before nightfall. The next morning they passed by the place where Mezwar and Abidemi had died. The deadly, brilliant flowers hung in tatters, bereft of the scent that had tempted the Ará Odò hunter.

Nothing was left of Abidemi himself, not even his bones, but the scavengers had hardly touched Mezwar. Rhenna, Nyx and Cian dug a grave for him and covered it with stones, while Tamallat wept and Cabh'a chanted Amazi death-rites over his final resting place.

Two days later they reached the hedge wall, or what remained of it. Only severed, skeletal branches stood where Nyx, Rhenna and Tahvo had worked so hard to breach it. The forest that had fought them now eased their passage, and when they came to the high cliff that bordered Ge's valley, the little people threw down vine-woven ladders.

The walk to the Ará Odò village was an easy stroll compared to what had come before. They never met with Enitan, but Nyx was confident that they would find him at the village, unharmed. No one contradicted her. They had all had their fill of death. Hope, however fragile, bound them as surely as the bitter chains of tragedy.

Every day Nyx brought Cian the Hammer. Every day he refused it. But he knew the time would come when it would demand his fealty, and on that day every previous loss would seem as nothing.

On that day, Cian knew, he would die.

"You have failed once too often," Farkas snarled. "And all of us will suffer because of it."

Yseul cast him a contemptuous glance from her perch in the tree above, observing Urho out of the corner of her eye. She had felt no joy in returning to her allies and reporting her lack of success with the Alu and the Hammer. Farkas's response had been easy enough to predict. Urho remained an enigma, and that made him all the more dangerous.

Farkas, however, was the immediate threat, and so Yseul stayed out of his reach for the first few hours and endured his railing without argument. He had finally subsided into familiar, tedious repetition.

"We must attack," he said for what seemed like the hundredth time. "You said they still do not know about me and Urho. We have surprise on our side—"

"And they have the Hammer." Yseul yawned, snapping her teeth, and jumped down from the tree.

"Which according to your observations, the Ailu fears to

hold, let alone use," Urho said, sharpening his knife on a stone with an air of boredom. "Your attempt at direct attack miscarried even before he obtained the Weapon."

Farkas deepened the furrow his ceaseless pacing had plowed around the cold campfire. *"Before,"* he said. "Before you and I gained control of our powers."

"True." Urho tested the blade against his thumb and drew a thin red line across his flesh. "We have not spent these days of waiting in idleness. But Yseul, too, has become more powerful, and it was not enough."

"She is female," Farkas spat. "Are you a man, Urho? Will you ever use that weapon you spend so much time sharpening, or are you an *enaree* who prefers to don the clothes and manner of women?"

Urho's fist tightened on the hilt of his knife, then slowly relaxed. "I have no need to prove myself to you, Skudat." His cold, pale eyes met Yseul's. "Our master shaped Farkas and me to be the equals of the Bearers, but you were made before their threat was known. Perhaps you are flawed and should no longer lead—"

"And who shall take my place?" she purred. She circled Farkas, looking him up and down, and stopped before Urho. "Which of you mighty males is strongest? Farkas, with his brawn and his courage? Or Urho, who has wisdom and the patience to use it?"

The two males regarded each other like bristling boars. Farkas flexed his muscles and raised clenched fists. To Yseul's eyes, it seemed that the air about him changed, growing solid like water turned to ice. She had only a moment to note the effect before the very breath in her chest congealed. She gasped, helpless as a fish thrown up on shore to die. Eleven Children of the Stone, stationed on the perimeter of the camp, stiffened to attention. Through darkening vision, Yseul glimpsed Urho, blue in the face and raking at the earth with rigid fingers.

Then suddenly the air was free again. Yseul sucked it in

until she could hold no more and broke into a spasm of coughing. Urho fell onto his back, arms splayed. The Children staggered and sank down wherever they stood.

Farkas laughed. "No man can live without air," he said. "I can kill them all—"

"And your allies with them!" Urho snapped, scrambling to his feet. He turned his face skyward and began to chant, his foreign words raising the hairs on the back of Yseul's neck. Perpetually moist air went dry. Thunder boomed. The leaves in the canopy overhead rattled like miniature drums. Needles of ice sluiced through the branches and slapped Yseul's skin, chilling her to the bone. Her breath turned to a wreath of mist around her face. Lush foliage blackened and curled under the onslaught of bitter cold.

Farkas yelled and hopped from foot to foot. The Children shuddered in the scraps of armor they had not discarded in the relentless Southern heat. Just as Yseul was about to risk striking Urho, his chanting ceased. Ice turned to water and then vanished altogether. Sun broke through the clouds, sending gouts of steam spiraling into the humid air.

Farkas took a step toward Urho, his dripping face twisted in rage. Yseul prepared to put herself between them, but one of the Children interrupted her with a hoarse cry of warning.

A handsome, dark-skinned man strolled past the guards, evading their spears as if he himself were made of nothing but air. He grinned with a flash of white teeth and bowed to Urho.

"Most impressive," he said.

Farkas drew his knife. "Who are you?"

"His name *was* Enitan," Yseul said, suspicion giving way to certainty. "Is he dead, Eshu, or have you merely borrowed his body?"

"Eshu," Farkas said with a scowl. "The trickster who bargained to help us find the Hammer and then betrayed us."

"Betrayed you?" Eshu raised a brow and sat cross-legged beside the fire circle. "I did as I promised. I led this female to the land of the Alu and the *òrìshà* who guarded the Hammer."

"And then abandoned us," Urho said. "We have not seen you since you left us among the shapeshifters."

"I did not agree to obtain the Hammer for you," the god said. He glanced at Yseul. "I gave you fair warning. I said the Alu might not kill you if you proved your worth. You are still alive."

"And lacking the Hammer," Farkas said. He sheathed his knife as if even he thought twice about threatening a god. "Without it, we cannot beg the Stone God's leniency for you and your kind."

Eshu grimaced and scratched behind his ear. "You are impatient, little man. I am not yet finished."

"You would still help us?" Yseul demanded. "Why should we trust you to do more than talk?"

Eshu's lids dropped over his eyes. "Your comrades are considering an attack on your enemies," he said. "You know that such an effort will end only in your deaths. The godborn have too many friends in the forest now that Ge is no more."

"And you are *our* friend," Urho said, his voice tinged with scorn. "What more do we require?"

"You do not know?" Eshu leaped up, seized one of the Children's spears and broke it over his knee. None of the soldiers moved. "What are you, creatures of the Stone? No more than made things like these men of metal, spawned to serve your maker as slaves, with not even a single soul amongst you. When you die, you will have no other existence. Olorun will not intervene on your behalf. Your ashes will scatter on the wind, to be lost forever."

"You lie," Farkas said. "I am a prince of the Skudat."

Urho opened his mouth and closed it again, casting a troubled glance at Yseul. She stared at Eshu, wanting only to laugh at his words and drive him away. She could do neither. She rubbed the scar on her forehead and remembered the day of her birth, remembered the confusion and helplessness as the blood of dead Ailuri cooled in her veins and Baalshillek spoke the words that gave her life.

"Are you the one who can give us what we lack?" she asked Eshu, despising the words even as they left her lips.

"Not I. But if you take the Hammer and the other Weapons for yourselves, you may yet become whole."

"You would have us betray our master," Urho said, "and bring the Stone's wrath down upon us."

Eshu ignored him. "You know I speak truth," he said to Yseul. "Your Baalshillek cannot reach you here. He cares nothing for your survival once you have stopped his enemies. You will die even if you obtain the Weapons and deliver them to your master." He grinned. "Take them for yourselves and see what transpires."

Yseul turned so that Urho and Farkas couldn't see her face. She knew full well that Baalshillek was no god, whatever *he* had come to believe. He had lost his spy among the Children. He could not know of her failure to obtain the Hammer, and the slight control he had wielded through the crystals had also been denied him.

"What will you gain by this?" she asked Eshu. "What good are we to you if we can no longer intercede with the Stone priests on your behalf?"

"An excellent question," Farkas said. "What is your game, godling?"

Eshu shrugged. "Perhaps Olorun has opened my eyes to new possibilities." He leaned closer to Yseul. "It is not too late to defeat the godborn," he whispered. "But first you must know their plans. They will be seeking the remaining Weapons. I will bring to you a tribe of the little people of the deep forest, kin to those who aided the Bearers. If you do not behave like utter fools, they will fear you as *òrìshà* and agree to serve you. Send them to the Ará Odò village to listen and learn. Then contrive to move before your enemies, and lay your traps with cunning."

"These little people will take us wherever we wish to go?" Urho asked, still frowning over Eshu's blasphemous suggestions.

"If your power is sufficient to intimidate them."

"That will not be a difficulty," Farkas growled. "And what of you, Eshu?"

"I?" Eshu scurried up the trunk of a tree as nimbly as a cat. "I will watch for your victory, servants of the Stone!"

Part III
Harvest

Chapter Twenty-One

Rhenna sat on a convenient rock and removed her torn leather boot, shaking a sharp stone from its toe. Nyx, Cian and Tahvo stood together, gazing with various expressions of amazement, despair and resignation at the endless swamp that stretched to the smudged green horizon.

Seven hundred leagues of forest lay behind them—week upon week of laboring through pelting rain, across swollen rivers, up and down the sides of mountains so thick with brush that every footstep risked a painful tumble. Only the combined elemental gifts of the travelers—and the expert guidance of the little people—had made the excursion bearable.

Even so, most of the garments Rhenna and the others had started out with had disintegrated to rags, and they now wore a disreputable patchwork of skins, furs and salvaged cloth.

Had they seen any villagers on their way to the East, such folk might well have mistaken them for brigands.

But the forest had been nearly empty of human inhabitants. The little people, invisible since the beginning of the crossing, had made their farewells to Tahvo several days ago and vanished into the trees. Forest had given way to a drier, more open plain like the one that lay between the Great Desert and the lands of the Ará Odò. It was a country laced by many rivers and streams, all flowing north and east; herds of antelope, massive *àjànànkú* and black-striped horses cropped the grass and foliage on their banks.

Here, Nyx had said, they could expect to find villagers and herders of cattle, men whom her father had met on his journey west two decades ago. Nyx had also mentioned her father's report of a vast swamp, deeply flooded in the rainy season.

Nyx's brief description had not done justice to the immensity of the barrier that stood between them and her fabled holy city. Every river they had crossed or passed poured into the mass of floating vegetation and turgid water. The swamp had an appearance of solidity, with islands of green, feathery stalks rising above dark channels inhabited by *ònì, akáko,* numerous birds and the usual contingent of biting, stinging insects. Nyx assured her companions that the semblance of stability was illusion. If Rhenna had not grown used to Southern heat, she might have found the stench and humidity unendurable.

She pulled on her boot, tested it with a stamp on the soft ground, and went to join the others. Tahvo turned toward her with a faint smile, as if to reassure her friend that things were not as grim as they appeared. Nyx, who still bore the Hammer across her back, continued to stare unblinking at the swamp.

Cian stood a little apart from the women, keeping a marked distance from Nyx. He greeted Rhenna with a raised brow. "At least we've seen no sign of Yseul in all these weeks," he said.

Or the Alu, Rhenna thought. *Or any other miserable devas bent on our destruction.* It was faint comfort. Rhenna was certain that

Tahvo suspected the presence of enemies who hadn't yet shown their faces, though the healer refused to put her concerns into words. If such enemies followed, however, even the combined senses of an Ailu, the little people, two competent trackers and a shaman who spoke to gods had not detected them.

"Rafts," Nyx said suddenly. "I remember my father spoke of building a raft to cross the swamp." Her tense shoulders relaxed. "That is what we must do."

"There seems enough dry wood on the hills," Rhenna said. "Do any of you know how to go about it?"

No one did. They discussed various possibilities and theories at some length, and as the day's heat reached its zenith, they retreated to a stand of trees set well back from the edge of the swamp. Nyx used her gift with growing things to select the best branches and binding materials, collecting every piece of rope and braided vines that the travelers had made, preserved or salvaged in the forest. Her skills also provided Rhenna and Cian with straight, sharpened sticks to serve as spears, with which they went hunting for the evening meal.

The dark coloring of Cian's fur, so useful in the forest, was too conspicuous on the open plain. He used his Ailu senses but kept human shape, tracking a small herd of antelope while Rhenna worked her way around the beasts from downwind. Their collaboration won them a plump doe. Once they returned to camp, Rhenna set about skinning and cleaning the carcass, and Cian gathered firewood and kindling.

Such activities had become routine after so many months, and yet Rhenna could still look across the fire and drown in a pair of slanted golden eyes. She tried not to reveal too much…not the fears or the uncertainties or the irrational jealousy she had never quite managed to overcome. Cian had burdens of his own. But she kept him always within her sights, and sometimes—when she lay on the hard ground to sleep—she listened to his breathing and remembered their first quarrelsome days together. Before she'd realized she loved him.

Such sentiments had been never been so irrelevant as they were now. What Cian needed from her was loyalty and protection. And then, one day, when all this was over…

"It is finished."

Nyx stood in the dusk just beyond the fire's light, proudly indicating a sturdy construction built of branches bound with rope and vines. The raft was large enough to be unwieldy, but certainly not apt to capsize, even with a burden of four people and their scanty provisions. Tahvo felt the smooth wood with a nod of approval. Rhenna offered Nyx an ample slice of roasted antelope.

"Do you know how to find your way across that?" she asked, gesturing in the direction of the swamp.

"I have only the knowledge which my father passed to me," Nyx said, delicately pulling strips of meat from bone. "It is said to be very like a maze, difficult to navigate. I should be able to sense the growth patterns of the papyrus islands that stand between the river channels, but water is Tahvo's province."

"Can you identify the currents that will carry us in the right direction, Tahvo?" Rhenna asked.

The healer cocked her head as if she could hear the streams moving beneath the tangle of living and half-rotted plants. "The spirits are distant. I will seek them out tonight."

"No," Rhenna said. "You'll need your strength in the morning. Rest now." She glanced at Nyx and Cian. "Sleep. I'll stand watch."

With the efficiency of long habit, the others obeyed. Rhenna rested her crossed arms on her knees and gazed into the fire. It was surprisingly difficult to stay awake; her head felt heavy, and the bouts of chills she had ignored for the past few weeks seemed suddenly much worse. She gritted her teeth and poked savagely at the blackened ashes. She and her friends had come intact through disasters, the most arduous conditions and constant deprivation. This was no time to sicken, in a strange land with no native guides and a sodden labyrinth yet to negotiate.

"Are you all right?"

The slits of Cian's eyes caught the firelight, glittering with suspicion. Rhenna shook her head, unreasonably irritated at his worried tone.

"I'm fine," she said. "Go back to sleep, Cian."

"Only if you wake me in a few hours."

She sighed and endured another violent spell of shivering. "Very well, oh Bearer of the Hammer."

He winced and rolled over, turning his back to her. She cursed herself for a vindictive she-wolf and braced for a night of lonely discomfort.

Early the next morning they dragged the raft down to the last stretch of solid ground at the edge of the swamp, tied on their bags, bedding and waterskins, and launched into the murky water. Nyx had a reasonable idea of the direction they must travel, and so they caught the first current they found flowing toward the northeast, Cian and Rhenna armed with long poles to steer and push.

The first few days went by without undue hardship. Nyx turned her attention to the tall stands of papyrus that sprang from the shallows between the nearly invisible river channels, guiding the raft with relative ease. The sun was blistering well before noon, but Tahvo had made hats of broad leaves brought from the forest. Occasionally a thin breeze rose off the water. Rhenna managed to keep most of the insects away, and the native animals left them alone. Cian proved adept at spearing fish, and each night they were able to find some patch of reasonably solid ground upon which to build a fire of papyrus stalks dried into kindling by Tahvo's magic.

Tahvo spent most of her time at the edge of the raft, trailing her fingers over the edge as she felt for the local spirits. The troubled look on her face suggested that she had not found what she sought.

The reason for her concern became clear at the end of the fifth day. An hour before sunset, the raft jammed in a thatch of impenetrable plant life that seemed to squeeze in more tightly with every passing moment. Rhenna poked the mat with her pole and looked back the way they had come. The newly cleared stripe of black water had filled with rampant green.

Tahvo crawled from one side of the raft to the other, rubbing oozy water between her fingers. She tasted it and spat out the foul stuff as soon as it touched her tongue.

"It is as I feared," she said quietly. "There are spirits in the water, but they are ill."

"Ill?" Rhenna echoed.

Tahvo plunged both hands through the muck, chanting under her breath. Nyx crouched by her side.

"I feel it," the Southern woman said. "The plants have been forced into unnatural growth, like Ge's hedge."

"By whom?" Cian asked.

Tahvo withdrew her hands from the water. "I have…reached the spirits," she said. As she spoke, a pathway opened at the prow of the raft. Cian and Rhenna applied themselves to the poles. It was hard work, and Rhenna's muscles began to quiver with the strain.

They drove forward as long as the light lasted and then were forced to pull up alongside a hillock of papyrus, the nearest thing to dry land within sight. Everyone stretched out on the raft, too weary to consider a meal of that morning's leftover fish.

Cian shook Rhenna out of a profound sleep. She opened her eyes and labored to remember where she was. Her mouth was gritty and dry as sand, and her limbs felt weighted as if by layers of mail and leather. She met Cian's somber gaze and struggled to her knees.

"It's worse than Tahvo realized," he said, gesturing to the opposite end of the raft. Tahvo sat with a bowed head, her hands folded in her lap. Beyond her, and in every direction, floating vegetation heaved like the backs of enormous fish. A stretch of black water would appear, only to be covered by a green, pulsing blanket.

Tahvo looked up as Rhenna approached, her silver eyes dull with despair. "The spirits cannot hear me," she said. "They are mad. The currents constantly change direction. They will no longer carry us where we wish to go."

Rhenna shaded her eyes and looked toward the eastern horizon. "We can't walk across."

"No," Nyx agreed.

"What is the cause of this madness, Tahvo?" Rhenna asked, fearing she already knew the answer.

"Yseul," Cian said. "She must escape the Alu."

"She, and those who travel with her," Tahvo said. "I have had another vision of my brother."

"The one who should be dead," Rhenna said.

Tahvo nodded. "I am certain now that he is one of those who follows us. His hand is in this evil, as it was in the drying of the Amazi springs."

"And yet we have never seen him," Nyx said. "How did they get ahead of us?"

"Only the spirits know," Tahvo said. "The evil ones laid this trap to slow our progress."

"Or stop us completely," Rhenna said. Her teeth chattered. "If you and Nyx can do nothing…" She looked at Cian. "What of the powers of Earth?"

Cian rubbed his hands on his tattered trousers. "Would you have me turn all this marsh to solid land? You give me too much credit."

"A goddess found you worthy enough."

He flinched, avoiding her gaze. "This is beyond my skill."

"But not beyond the Hammer," Nyx said.

"*No.*"

Rhenna grabbed his shoulder and forced him to face her. "We could die here, Cian. Everything we've fought for will be lost. Immeghar, Abidemi, Mezwar…"

He moved to shake off her trembling hand and took it instead, nearly crushing her fingers. "Once I touch the Hammer—"

Nyx gave a cry of warning. Rhenna followed her gesture to the forest of papyrus. A man pushed his way from among the fronds and stopped to stare, brown eyes dazed in a bronze-skinned face. Scraps of cloth hung from his emaciated frame. He croaked a broken string of syllables and abruptly collapsed.

Nyx jumped off the raft and landed precariously on the relative firmness of the papyrus bed. She knelt beside the stranger, lifting his head against her chest.

"This man is of my father's countrymen," she said. She spoke to him, and he grunted a soft response. "Help me get him aboard the raft."

Rhenna glanced at Tahvo, seeking her reaction. "I feel no evil in him," the healer said with a faint frown.

"But?"

"He is no danger to us."

Rhenna braced herself against a sudden spell of weakness and joined Nyx on the bank. Together they carried the stranger onto the raft and laid him out, while Cian fetched a waterskin.

The man drank with the desperate concentration of one near death from thirst. Rhenna took the skin away before he could sicken, and Nyx addressed him again in her father's tongue. After a long moment of uncertainty, when it seemed the stranger must surely lose consciousness, he rallied and fixed his gaze on Nyx, brushing her cheek with skeletal fingers.

She folded his hand between her own. "His name is Khaleme," she said. "He is a soldier of the holy city." She began to speak to the stranger in a voice of unmistakable command.

"She tries to persuade him that we may be trusted," Tahvo said softly. "She gives the name of her father and talks of things I do not understand, but he does not answer."

"My father's people are taught from childhood never to reveal knowledge of New Meroe to outsiders," Nyx said. "But there is one sure way to convince him."

Slowly she untied the vine ropes that bound the Hammer to her back, laid the bundle across her knees and unwrapped it.

She lifted the Weapon reverently in both hands. Sunlight splashed off the iron head and illuminated the symbols carved into its gleaming surface.

Khaleme started. He threw his arm across his eyes and whispered a single word.

Nyx carefully covered the Hammer. "Now he believes," she said. She pulled Khaleme's arm away from his face. He averted his gaze from the Hammer and began to speak as if he feared he might die before he could finish.

Nyx listened, her face growing more and more grim. "It is no wonder that he recognizes the Hammer," she said at last. "Khaleme is the last surviving member of an expedition sent by the king of New Meroe to find it."

"Then your father was not the only one to seek it," Rhenna said.

"So it seems." She listened again, and her frown deepened. "Many such expeditions have been sent, but not one has returned. The others of Khaleme's party went astray in the swamp before they ever reached the other side. Khaleme was searching for the way home, but he, too, was lost."

Khaleme struggled to rise, the breath sawing in his throat. Tahvo pressed him back. "He has suffered much," she said. "He must rest, and take nourishment…."

"No," Khaleme rasped. "I…speak the Hellenish tongue." He reached for Nyx. "Hear me, Lady—"

Nyx offered him another sip from the waterskin. "We hear."

"You are not the first I have met in this cursed land," Khaleme said, pushing the waterskin aside. "Others came from the West, a woman and two men, with an escort of soldiers in Hellenish armor." His head fell back to the deck. "It was clear they were beings of power. They…" Tears trickled down the sides of his face. "Lady, they used evil magic and forced me to tell of the city."

"A woman and two men," Rhenna said. "Did they give their names?"

Khaleme looked at Rhenna as if she might transform herself into a malevolent spirit before his eyes. "They were pale, like all Northerners, and their words..." He swallowed and turned back to Nyx. "They asked about the prophecies, but I did not speak. I did not speak."

Tahvo laid a damp cloth across his sweat-soaked forehead. "Yseul," she murmured. "Yseul and my brother."

"And another," Rhenna said. "With the Stone God's soldiers."

Khaleme went rigid. "I will not!" he cried. "I will *not*."

Nyx caught his flailing hands. "How many days since these strangers came?"

"No days here," he said, suddenly calm. "No nights. No escape."

"Who is king in New Meroe?"

"Aryesbokhe holds the throne. The time of battle draws near...."

"What battle, Khaleme?"

His head rolled to one side, and his brown eyes glazed.

"He will no longer hear you," Tahvo said. "Let me care for him."

Nyx nodded and withdrew, taking the Hammer with her. Rhenna and Cian squatted beside her at the opposite side of the raft.

"Tahvo was right," Nyx said. "Our enemies are ahead of us, and they know of the holy city. Somehow they have discovered where we are bound."

"If their goal is simply to stop us, why must they know the city's location?" Cian asked.

"Baalshillek would sacrifice a thousand of his finest troops to find New Meroe and steal the true prophecies," Nyx said. "But I cannot believe that Yseul is powerful enough to breach the city's walls or overcome the magic of our priests."

"They would have all the power they need if they reported this to Baalshillek," Rhenna said.

"We have no way of knowing if they have sent messengers

back to Karchedon," Nyx said. "But unless they can fly like the birds, they will not cross the Great Desert before we reach the holy city."

Rhenna's head throbbed as if a herd of horses were racing through her skull. Khaleme's appearance had not changed their predicament. Sinister magic still bound the swamp and held the raft captive.

"Why did Yseul let Khaleme live once they were through with him?" she asked, rubbing her forehead.

"I do not know." Nyx stared at Cian. "We dare not wait for our enemies' influence on the waters to lose its strength. The time has come, Bearer of the Hammer."

Rhenna caught a glimpse of Cian's stubborn, frightened face just as the darkness crashed behind her eyes.

Tahvo heard Rhenna fall and followed the sound of Cian's cry to the warrior's side. Rhenna's feet beat on the deck, and her breath wheezed as if she were strangling. Cian and Nyx pinned Rhenna down before her convulsions could hurl her from the raft.

There were no spirits here to help her, but Tahvo chanted the rituals of healing and stroked her hands over Rhenna's trembling body. The warrior's wild motions slowed and ceased. Cian held Rhenna against his chest, cursing harshly, while Nyx brought water.

"What is it?" Cian demanded. "What is wrong with her, Tahvo?"

"I have seen this before," Nyx said, her voice hushed. "It is a sickness of the forest that sometimes strikes the Ará Odò in the rainy season. I did not realize…"

"She's been shivering for days," Cian said, "but she refused to admit that anything was wrong." He hissed through his teeth. "Her skin is burning…."

"Shaking and heat under the skin are the first signs," Nyx admitted. "They often strike without warning."

"What is the treatment?"

"I know of none."

"Can it kill her?"

"The strong survive," Nyx said. "Rhenna is strong, Cian…."

"Tahvo," Cian said. "Help her."

Tahvo shut out Cian's fear and all sense of the world around her. She let her being join with Rhenna's as she had mingled with the tormented spirits of the swamp, seeking the life-giving waters that raced through the channels beneath the warrior's flesh. Almost at once she felt the sickness in the blood, tiny invaders attacking Rhenna from within like a fleet of minute Arrhidaean warships. In their black holds they carried death.

But this was not the work of the Stone God or his servants. It came out of the forest, as Nyx had said, an enemy that could be fought by a skilled noaiddit—a healer with the proper herbs, a sacred drum and spirits able and willing to lend their aid.

Tahvo pressed Rhenna's hot, limp hand to her cheek. "There is too much foulness in this place," she said. "We must get her out."

No one spoke. The raft's lashings creaked. Cian gently pushed Rhenna into Tahvo's arms and stood.

"The Hammer," he said. "Give it to me."

The leashed power of the Weapon disturbed the air like the distant rumble of a storm. Cian's heart beat so fast and hard that Tahvo could hear it. She straightened slowly, alerted to something she had not felt before…something that made Cian's fear of the Hammer seem not only rational but vital to his existence.

The Hammer was not merely an inanimate Weapon of magic. It had a very real life of its own. A life that waited to be set free…

"Cian," she said, trying to get his attention, but her voice came out as a whisper. No one heard her. She reached out, but no one saw. She knew when Cian took the Hammer in his hands, when its magic awakened at his touch and poured into his body.

A puff of wind stirred the simmering air. Nyx gripped Tahvo's wrist, her nails digging into Tahvo's skin.

The Hammer struck water with a crash like shattering stone. Scalding drops rained down on Tahvo's face and hands. She curled her body over Rhenna's. A deep vibration shook the thick branches under her knees, followed by the roar of waves that slapped at the raft like a lynx with a mouse. Then the raft began to sink, settling at last on a firm surface.

Nyx gasped.

"What do you see?" Tahvo asked.

"The Hammer has cut a gorge all the way down to dry earth. The water rises like walls on either side, as far as the horizon."

"And Cian?"

"I cannot see his face. He stands so still…."

"Speak to him, Nyx. I am afraid."

Nyx got to her feet. She moved slowly, her steps faltering, as if she sensed what Tahvo feared.

"Cian?"

He must have turned, for Nyx abruptly stopped. She exhaled sharply.

"Come, if you want to save the female," Cian said in a voice Tahvo hardly recognized. She heard the crunch of pebbles and drying vegetation, and then Nyx returned to her side.

"He is leaving," she said. "Can you support Rhenna if I help you lift her?"

"Yes. What of Khaleme?"

"I am here, Lady. I am better now."

"Can you walk?" Nyx asked the warrior.

"You have found the Bearer. We must serve him."

Tahvo felt for the soldier's thin leg, startled by his swift recovery. If Cian had gone, they had to follow.

Khaleme and Nyx supported Rhenna between them, while Tahvo gathered the packs. Rhenna groaned but did not wake.

"Cian is not far ahead, but we must hurry," Nyx said. "I do not think he will wait long."

Then he has *changed,* Tahvo thought. *May the spirits save him….*

* * *

Rhenna knew that they were moving, and that they had somehow left the raft far behind. Sometimes she woke and thought she saw bizarre visions of roiling water shaped into walls by some invisible force. Occasionally she was able to walk, supported on the arms of Nyx and Khaleme, though she could not remember when the tall soldier had regained consciousness.

Each day flowed into the next without change. Tahvo tried to make her eat and drink, but anything that touched Rhenna's lips tasted foul with corruption. The struggle to stay awake consumed more and more of her strength, until finally she gave up the effort.

When she opened her eyes again, she lay on furs in a quiet place, her mouth parched and her eyes crusted. The constant shivers and waves of hot and cold had left her body.

A moist, cool cloth dabbed at her face. The hand that held it belonged to a small, round figure whose face smiled at her with open joy.

"Tahvo?"

The healer put a waterskin to her lips. "You are well," Tahvo said, "but you must rest a little longer."

"How long have I...?"

"Many days. Do not concern yourself."

"Cian...Nyx..."

"Have no fear. We are in a village of friendly folk who live east of the marsh. This is the hut of their healer. They have shared all they have and aided in your healing."

Rhenna tried to sit up and quickly lay back down. "Yseul?"

"No sign of her."

Rhenna sighed and closed her eyes. "How did we get out of the swamp?"

Tahvo's silence lasted so long that Rhenna opened her eyes again. "What is it?"

"Cian used the Hammer."

"But he's all right...?"

"Yes." Tahvo looked away. She was an abominable liar. Rhenna reached for her hand.

"Did he have reason to be afraid, Tahvo?"

Tahvo patted her shoulder. "He and Nyx have been discussing where we will travel from here. There is more desert, though not as wide as the one in the North. Then there is a great river that leads to the mountains, and near the source of the river lies a high plateau—"

"*Tahvo.*"

"He…" She licked her lips. "He is different, Rhenna."

Ice congealed in Rhenna's empty stomach. "How?"

"He is stronger. He keeps himself apart."

Rhenna wedged her elbows behind her back and fought off a wave of dizziness. "I want to see him."

"He…will not come."

"Then I'll go to him." She ignored the weakness in her limbs and worked her way to her knees. Tahvo gave up trying to hold her down and lent her arm. Together they walked toward the door of the hut one creeping step at a time.

The light of day struck Rhenna's eyes like a heated awl. She paused to blink away the tears and quickly took in the cluster of huts, animal pens and brown-skinned folk who waved at Tahvo with casual friendliness. The land here was relatively dry and hilly, but Rhenna could just see a distant line of dull green that marked the borders of the swamp. Tahvo led Rhenna out of the compound to the edge of a stream, mercifully small and well contained within its banks.

Cian stood by the stream with Nyx, the Hammer slung over his shoulder.

"…has told me that Aryesbokhe has become possessed by the desire to find the Hammer," Nyx said. "His tale troubles me greatly. When we reach the city, you must be prepared—" She broke off as she saw Rhenna. Her smile was brief and strained. "Thank the gods you are recovered. You should not be on your feet. Tahvo…"

Cian turned his head. Something in the hard lines of his profile warned Rhenna before she saw his eyes.

They were still golden and feral and beautiful, as they had always been. But there was no welcome in them—no pleasure at seeing her well, no softness, no humanity. They were like chips of amber, drained of all warmth, set in a face of pale marble.

"Cian," Rhenna said with a calmness she didn't feel.

He examined her as if she were a meddlesome insect, his upper lip curling in contempt, and glanced at Nyx. "Tell me for what I must be prepared," he said.

Nyx stared into the brown water at her feet. "There are several cults in the holy city, and not all are devoted to the Watchers. There may be those who wish to take the Hammer from you, and others who will not believe you are the true Bearer."

Cian's hand snapped out and seized Nyx by the back of her neck. "Do you believe?"

Rhenna took a step toward Cian. Tahvo restrained her. Nyx went still and passive in Cian's grip.

"Yes, my lord," she croaked.

He laughed, shook Nyx like a kitten and yanked her against him. His mouth ground on hers. When he let her go, her lips were streaked with blood.

Cian met Rhenna's horrified gaze. "Have you also come to pleasure me, female?"

Rhenna pushed Tahvo behind her. "You are not Cian. What have you done with him?"

"He is here." A tint of red swirled through his eyes. "*He* would let you go." He looked over her shoulder at Tahvo. "Take her before I change my mind."

"Rhenna," Tahvo pleaded.

"What is inside him, Tahvo?" Rhenna said, holding Cian's alien stare.

"Something that lived in the Hammer," the healer whispered. "A spirit of great power. I did not feel it in time." Tears ran from her eyes. "I am sorry."

Rhenna squeezed Tahvo's hand and stepped in front of Cian. "I know you can hear me, Cian. Come back. Don't let this... thing destroy you."

For just an instant she thought she saw the man she loved return to his eyes. "There is nothing you can do," he said. "Go, Rhenna-of-the-Scar. Go while you still can."

Rhenna grabbed Tahvo's arm and walked away.

Chapter Twenty-Two

Italia

Quintus breathed in the familiar smells of a Tiberian morning: the aroma of food stalls selling bread and cabbage and meat pies; the sweat of laborers and slaves passing in the crowd; the mingled odors of dust, sunwarmed stone and the Tiber River baking in the late summer heat.

If he had used every sense but his vision, he might have convinced himself that this was the Tiberia of his childhood, before the empire had come and his family, their clients and a handful of patrician allies had fled to the mountains. But he would not have been deceived for long. Gone were the scents of animal dung on the streets and human waste in the gutters that emptied into the sewers. If he listened carefully, he heard not the shouts and laughter of free Tiberians but the strangely muted babble of a conquered populace. And when he looked about him, he saw smoking altars built on the rubble of razed temples, the blank expressions of once-proud citizens, the troops of imperial soldiers striding through the Forum Tiberianus as if they might tear the ancient buildings down with their bare hands.

He had known it must be this way, even though he had let himself forget. He had been nearly a year in Karchedon. He had grown used to too many of the Stone's obscenities, willfully blind to the suffering of a people not his own. He had become lost in the rarified world of imperial politics, palace intrigues and the singular education required of the emperor's brother. He had begun to believe that the promise of his elevation to the highest ranks of the empire was worth any price.

Now he stood beside the massive wall constructed around the city proper nearly a hundred years before, his hands shaking beneath the folds of his toga. He recalled every word Nikodemos had spoken before he embarked on the royal galley bound for Italia. The conversation had been light, pleasant—and ominous.

"I have a small task for you," Nikodemos had said as they sipped wine in his private chambers. "I received reports several months ago that the rebel prisoner Buteo escaped from his cell at the Temple...much to Baalshillek's annoyance." He smiled and signaled a slave to refill his cup. "A pity the High Priest didn't execute him as I expected. Now it seems that Buteo has reappeared in Italia and may have rejoined his followers in the mountains."

Quintus nearly choked on his wine. "Was no attempt made to recapture him?"

"Unsuccessful," Nikodemos said. "But it has occurred to me that there is one man perfectly suited to tracking down a Tiberian rebel in his own lair."

Quintus had known what his half-brother was about to say. He had shown no reaction when the emperor assigned him the mission of finding Buteo, capturing him and returning him to

Karchedon. Never did Nikodemos mention a test of loyalty or show doubt that Quintus would succeed. Such words were unnecessary. Quintus understood.

All the previous trials had been mere preliminaries for this ultimate test of Quintus's worthiness to stand beside the master of the Arrhidaean Empire. Quintus would be given every resource, accompanied by Nikodemos's handpicked soldiers...and a beta priest, a "gift" from Baalshillek. Troops and priest would be entirely under Quintus's command. But they would be watching for any slip, any indication that Quintus retained his former allegiance to his adopted homeland.

During the voyage to Italia, Quintus had spent each possible moment with his assigned Palace escort, winning the soldiers' approval with the courtier's trick he had learned in the past year. They, like most of Nikodemos's favored Companions and personal guard, already shared his contempt for the Stone God's priesthood. He had confided to the men that he'd once been held by the Tiberian rebels against his will, which was no less than the truth, and that he would gladly expose his former captors for his brother's sake.

By the time the galley had docked at Ostia, the soldiers treated Quintus as one of them. When Quintus had recovered from his first glimpse of a Tiberia crushed by seven years of occupation—and after he had seen a half-dozen plebeian and patrician insurgents, along with all their families, given to the Stone God's fire—he had convinced his soldiers of the wisdom of letting him ride into the mountains with a minimal guard. If he was to approach the rebels in their own refuge, he must be prepared to take great risks.

The beta priest, whose name Quintus hadn't bothered to learn, refused to stay behind. Quintus had no intention of letting the man interfere with what he hoped to do. In spite of the horrors he had seen in Tiberia, his ambitions hadn't changed. He had to reach Buteo and convince the rebel leader of his genuine goodwill—without letting the priest or the imperial guardsmen recognize his true purpose.

Quintus strode through the city gate, casually displaying the emperor's seal to the sentries who examined every man, woman and child who entered or left Tiberia. They snapped to attention and let him pass. He had already observed that the troops assigned to Tiberia were young and not as well-disciplined as those he'd seen in Hellas; that seemed to suggest that Danae had been right when she claimed Nikodemos sent his least experienced soldiers to Italia. Quintus could only speculate as to the emperor's motives.

But he had more pressing concerns to occupy him at the moment. He found his two-soldier escort and the priest waiting for him outside the gate, each with a mount and a spare, as well as two fine beasts for Quintus. They were prepared for hard riding. Quintus pitied the poor horses assigned to the priest; the Stone's poison that lived in his body would seep into the animals and leave them fit only for the slaughterhouse when the hunt was over.

The priest's face was completely obscured by his black hood, though Quintus had no doubt that his skin was scarred and disfigured by the same dread power that would eventually kill his mounts. The space between Quintus's eyes throbbed whenever he went near the man; he could feel the priest's red stone almost as if it were a separate, living presence.

The priest fingered the crystal pendant nervously, though his bearing held the usual arrogance. "It is not wise, my lord," he said, "to travel without your full escort."

"It is not wise to hunt wolves with an army," Quintus retorted. "They hear you coming and disappear. That is why so many rebels remain in the mountains." He waved off a soldier's help and mounted his sure-footed dun. "In any case, you will be there to protect us with the Stone's fire."

He couldn't see the priest scowl, but he knew the man would

as soon strike him down as serve him. Perhaps that was what Baalshillek intended. This second rank lackey might very well be one of Baalshillek's most skilled assassins.

Quintus sincerely hoped the man would attempt an attack.

He consulted his map again, letting his escort assume that he was less familiar with the mountains than he truly was. During his time of captivity among the rebels, they had frequently moved the location of their primary stronghold, always seeking to stay ahead of the patrols of priests and soldiers who periodically scoured the Apenninus Mountains. Though he had been kept in seclusion, Quintus had carefully gathered information about the sanctuaries Buteo's men maintained throughout the Umbrian high country. He knew the positions of narrow defiles and hidden caves where the insurgents cached their weapons and planned raids on lowland towns, and where they made their camps.

He had a few ideas of where to look for Buteo.

It was not yet full noon when he and his escort rode away from the outer wall and set off along the Via Tiburtina, crossing the pastures and grove-land that stretched toward the Sabina Hills. Sprawling farms and villas, many seized from their original owners by imperial soldiers, dotted the landscape. Few of the slaves or free laborers working in the fields or vineyards looked up as they rode past. All were equally wretched under the rule of the Stone.

Once, Quintus's father had told him, there had been many shrines to local gods of fertility and harvest throughout this country. Not one now stood. Men prayed to the Stone God or not at all.

Quintus spurred his mount to a faster pace and was grateful when they left the rolling farmland behind them. The foothills of the Apenninus Mountains scraped the Eastern sky. They passed the town of Tibur on the Anio River and entered the mountains at the mouth of the river valley, where the water cascaded over rocks and ledges down to the plains. The Via Valeria ran alongside the Anio, winding northeast between the mountains.

Immediately the day's grueling heat gave way to the relative coolness of forested slopes and blue shadows. Another twenty milliaria carried them well into the mountains, where the Aequi tribe had been subdued by the Tiberian army a mere thirteen years before. They spent an untroubled night by the roadside and reached the colony town of Alba Fucens by early afternoon the next day. Here the empire's priests and soldiers still made their presence felt, but in the deep, thinly settled and little-traveled valleys to the north lay a hundred hiding places for the hardy and the cunning.

Quintus turned off the road and cut north into the territory of the Marsi, who had become allies of Tiberia not long before the conquest of Italia. The imperial occupation had stricken them far worse than it had the more numerous Tiberians. Most of the surviving mountain tribes had fled north as far as Umbria and would avoid any riders who carried the stamp of the Arrhidaean Empire.

They camped beside the River Aternus and continued along the valley. The priest, unused to riding, began to complain about delays and deception; Quintus asked him politely if he could detect the rebels with his stone. The priest stroked his pendant and grew dangerously silent.

On the following day they rode out of the river valley and into the mountains, following the courses of streams that tumbled down from the highest slopes. Shepherds' paths led through woods of oak and ash, ascending to dense forests of beech and black maple; here and there lay the ruins of tribal villages, abandoned to wolves and bears. Sometimes Quintus sensed watching eyes, and once he glimpsed men dressed in furs retreating into the silence of the trees—beleaguered tribesmen who recognized a Stone priest and gave up any notion of attacking the intruders.

For the next two weeks he drove his escort mercilessly, pushing the horses to the limits of their endurance. He kept his distance from the soldiers, who had long since lost any desire to exchange companionable banter with their royal charge. The priest ceased his complaints and clung to his mount with grim determination.

Gradually they worked their way north, passing beneath bare peaks that jutted from green mantles of fir and pine. Quintus found evidence of deserted rebel encampments but little sign of recent activity. Over the years the number of insurgents had been severely reduced, and Buteo's followers had been driven into the most isolated recesses of the Apennini.

Quintus had hoped he would encounter a raider band before he was compelled to lead the priest and soldiers to the rebels' most secret hold. He was fast running out of options. Three weeks into the search, on a moonlit night when the priest had fallen into a deep and exhausted sleep, he discovered a single boot track on the bank of a stream. He kept the knowledge to himself and pressed on.

The ambush came almost too late. The soldiers muttered to each other as Quintus preceded them into a cleft cut between two sheer limestone cliffs, and the horses balked and tossed their heads. The priest refused to enter the crevice. By the time one of the guards decided to force Quintus to retreat, he and his companions were already trapped.

Quintus clenched his fists on the reins and listened with bleak horror as men died, struck down like sheep on a sacrificial altar. A horse squealed and plunged past him, riderless. Harsh voices echoed among the rocks. He dismounted, locked his muscles and waited to defend his life.

He did not wait long. Muted footsteps approached from behind, and the tip of a sword ground into his back. A man in a dark cloak emerged from the shadows to snatch his horse's reins from his hand. Others followed, rough-faced fighters who had seen the worst and had lost all fear of death.

"Kill him," the swordsman said.

"He brought a priest," another said. "If they have found us here…"

"He must be questioned before he dies," the cloaked one said. He stared at Quintus, his eyes hooded beneath his cowl. "I know this face." He dropped the reins and seized Quintus's sleeve. "Who are you?"

Quintus shook off the man's grip. "Quintus Horatius Corvinus," he said. "Where is the priest?"

The rebels glanced at each other in stunned silence. As if he had come in answer to Quintus's question, a man ran up the gorge and skidded to a breathless halt.

"The priest has escaped," he said.

"I can find him," Quintus said. He swept the rebels with his gaze. "Many of you will die before you take him, and he may still get away. I will dispose of the priest, and then you will take me to Buteo."

"Corvinus," the swordsman hissed. "You betrayed us. You broke your oath and ran to the enemy. You are the brother of Nikodemos—"

"And I am the only one who can save you."

The sword pierced Quintus's clothing and nicked the skin over his spine. The cloaked man raised his hand.

"I know what powers this traitor wields," he said. "The priest must be caught before he runs back to his masters in Tiberia." He lifted his hood away from his face, and his narrow gray eyes met Quintus's. "You have one chance, spawn of Arrhidaeos. Kill the priest, and you may live to see Buteo." He gestured to the men behind him. They fell in around Quintus, jostling him with fists and elbows, and drove him to the mouth of the crevice.

A dozen horses and hostile rebels waited in the woods. They let Quintus mount and formed a bristling ring of swords around him, ready to strike him down in an instant. He listened for a moment, ignoring the hatred that beat at him from every side, and reached for the taint of the red stone.

The priest was no woodsman, and his horse had begun to suffer the ill effects of bearing one so consumed by the Stone's insidious poison. Quintus kicked his mount into a gallop and found the place where the rebels had lost their quarry. He rode into a forest gone unnaturally still, paralyzed by the evil presence of its violator. He dismounted and let his terrified horse race back to its companions.

He found the priest's horse lying among scorched leaves and blackened earth, a half-burned carcass stinking of Stonefire. The priest waited with his back to an outcrop of gray rock. His hood lay on his shoulders, exposing the rotting, skeletal grimace of his face. He clutched his pendant and cried out to his gods.

Quintus was ready when the red fire spat from the crystal. He felt its heat splashing around him, incinerating everything it touched. His skin pulled tight with instinctive terror, yet he felt nothing as he raised his hands and drew upon the nameless power at the core of his being. Stonefire met his invisible shield and turned back upon itself with a shriek like blades scraping bone.

The priest remained standing even after he had begun to die. His head withered first, collapsing around the pitted framework of his skull. Then his arms and shoulders buckled into his chest, and the red stone pendant devoured him, sucking the soft inner workings of his body with the eagerness of a maggot in a fresh corpse. His legs were last. The fetid ashes floated to the ground, settling about the slagged gold of the pendant and its pulsing crystal. Quintus knelt to touch the stone, and it went black. He kicked melted metal and crystal under a pile of rocks and ground the ashes into the soil with his heel.

He heard retching behind him and turned. The rebels stared from somber eyes in gray faces. Their leader met Quintus's gaze.

"Blindfold him," he said. "He goes to Buteo."

* * *

The path to the stronghold was steep and arduous, climbing over massive boulders of bare rock and squeezing through dense thickets that seemed reluctant to allow the passage of any creature larger than a fox. The rebels touched Quintus only when they had no choice, but he knew that their hatred had been tempered by awe and fascination. They gave him water and meat, and covered him with furs after night fell, guarding him like a stolen crate of new-forged imperial swords.

Quintus knew they were near their destination when they left the horses behind and continued up a track suitable only for wild goats or desperate humans. They entered the cool dampness of a cave, where Quintus smelled the odors of recent cooking and heard the distant clamor of men training with sword and javelin. Several hundred paces beyond the entrance, the rebels chained Quintus's hands to the cave wall and removed the blindfold. The faint light of a torch behind the jutting wall revealed only the slick surface of rock and scraps of moldy bread left by some former occupant.

No one came for many hours. Time was no more important to Quintus than food or drink. His power burned with a steady white heat in his chest, staving off the needs of his mortal body. He went quietly when men arrived to take him to Buteo.

The rebel leader sat at a table built of rough-hewn wood, his chin resting on steepled fingers, cowled officers ranged around him with swords bared and ready. He looked up at Quintus, his eyes empty of hatred or surprise.

"Corvinus," he said. "Did the emperor send you, or was it Baalshillek?"

"Nikodemos commanded this journey," Quintus said. "But Baalshillek sent his priest to watch me. That priest is now dead, and I am here to offer my sword to Tiberia."

"He is a traitor," one of the officers said. "He would have let you die in Karchedon—"

"Silence." Buteo got up and circled Quintus, examining him

with the same leashed intensity he used on untried recruits. "Unbind his hands."

"Buteo!"

"Leave me, all of you." His men glanced at each other and held their places. He fixed each of them in turn with a stare that could stop a charging bull. They obeyed with reluctance.

Buteo resumed his seat at the desk. "So, Quintus," he said. "You have taken much trouble to find me, when I was so conveniently in Karchedon not so long ago."

Quintus held his gaze. "I am pleased to see that you escaped."

The older man laughed. "Indeed. Do you wonder how I managed it?"

"I would expect nothing less from the Hawk."

Buteo sliced the air with his hand, rejecting the compliment. "You claim you have returned to Tiberia to serve your homeland," he said, "but you are not Tiberian, son of Arrhidaeos."

"I am Tiberian in all but blood," Quintus said. "I did not know the truth of my birth until I was taken prisoner by Baalshillek. My loyalties have not changed."

"And yet you ran from us and put your powers into the hands of the emperor. He has accepted you as kin, and you serve him—"

"Only as far as serving him also serves our cause."

Buteo leaned back in his chair. "Do you know why I risked traveling to Karchedon? Because word had reached us of your newfound birthright, and I wished to see the truth for myself. I saw you walking freely in the citadel. Why should I believe anything you say?"

"Why would I risk killing a priest if I'm lying?" Quintus went to the desk and braced his good hand on the sturdy oak. "I could not set you free in Karchedon without destroying this chance I've been given…the chance to fight the empire from within. Now that I've gained the trust of the emperor—"

"Have you? Or is retrieving my head the heroic deed that will assure your position?"

"If this is a final test of my allegiance to him, all we need do is provide proof that you are dead. You'll have to lie low for a time, perhaps take refuge in the North until—"

"You would have me flee like a coward and leave my people leaderless?" Buteo flipped Quintus's cloak away from his crippled arm. "I swore an oath, Corvinus. So did you, and you broke it."

"Because you held me prisoner…" Quintus felt his temper begin to flare and quickly extinguished it. "I have not come to argue about the past, Buteo. I look to the future. There is no future in minor skirmishes that kill a handful of imperial soldiers, or raids to steal a few swords or horses. The empire must be fought on its own terms."

"And who is better placed to do so than the brother of the emperor?"

"Yes." Quintus shrugged his cloak back into place. "I have never believed in the gods, Buteo, but surely this fate was given to me for a reason. Nikodemos has already spoken of a governorship in Tiberia—"

"So you wish to rule over us?"

Quintus slammed his fist on the desk. "It's freedom I want…freedom for Tiberia, and for all who are enslaved by the Stone God."

"And subjugated by your brother?"

"I will do whatever is necessary."

Buteo stared at his folded hands. "You would have me believe that you can stand alone against the priesthood and the imperial armies?"

"I would have you trust me. Believe in me." Heady certainty warmed his body like wine from Bacchus's own vineyard. "I will save you."

The rebel leader got to his feet and paced from one wall of the cave to the other, his brow furrowed in thought. "You have given me much to consider, Horatius Corvinus. But there are things that you also must know if you are to help us."

"I listen."

"Come with me. There is something I would show you."

He took a torch from the wall and led Quintus from the chamber through a narrow, deserted passage. The tunnel ascended twenty paces and opened onto a ledge that looked down on the cleft where Quintus and the imperial soldiers had been ambushed.

Buteo dropped the torch and clasped Quintus's shoulder, guiding him toward the edge of the precipice. "Our world has changed so much," he said. "Men are forced to do that which they would never consider in the old days of freedom."

Quintus thought bitterly of the men he had led to their deaths. "These are hard times, and they require hard men."

"Yes." Buteo sighed. "You returned to Tiberia to acquire proof of my death."

"False proof, Buteo. Something to satisfy Nikodemos."

Buteo's fingers tightened. "I, too, must satisfy one who holds my life in his hands." Pebbles rattled under his boots. "You were uninterested in how I escaped from Karchedon. It was a simple matter when Baalshillek himself arranged it."

Quintus stiffened, the rich intoxication of triumph falling away in a heartbeat. "Baalshillek?"

"He made me an offer I found impossible to decline. You see, his agents found my family in Liguria. He set me one simple task in exchange for their safety."

Quintus tried to jerk away, but Buteo's grip was like iron. "Baalshillek told me he would see to it that you were sent to hunt me down. And when you found me, as he was certain you would, I was to arrange that you never returned to Karchedon." He pushed Quintus closer to the brink. "No one here will question your death."

Numbness spread from Quintus's chest to his limbs, robbing him of strength. "If you do this, Buteo, all of Tiberia will be destroyed—"

"No. Only one arrogant and treacherous pup who forgot his

place." He drew a knife and pressed it to Quintus's back. "Die like a Tiberian, Quintus. Your pain will end quickly."

Quintus closed his eyes. He took a step forward. A small stone tumbled off the ledge and struck the ground far below.

"I am Tiberian," he said softly. The toe of his boot slid over emptiness. He cleansed his mind of all thought, all emotion. Blood trickled under his tunic. Buteo tensed to deliver the final thrust.

Instinct drove Quintus in that instant between life and death. He twisted violently, throwing his body toward Buteo. The rebel leader grunted in surprise, carved a crooked gash in Quintus's back and slid on the loose gravel. He snatched at Quintus's cloak. Quintus fell to one knee and tore his fibula free.

No one saw Buteo fall. Quintus scrambled to safety. As he reached the cave mouth, a familiar awareness throbbed behind his eyes. He looked toward the woods and saw light flashing on armor several milliaria away.

He sprinted back down the tunnel as fast as the darkness allowed, seizing the first torch that came to hand. He nearly collided with one of Buteo's officers.

"Corvinus!" the man barked, grabbing for his sword.

"Listen to me," Quintus said. "Priests and imperial soldiers are on their way as I speak. Evacuate the caves at once." The rebel hesitated. "Do as I say, or there will be no resistance left in Tiberia."

The man grimaced, released his sword and set off at a run. Quintus went to Buteo's chamber, found a cloak hung from a peg and threw it over his shoulders, hiding his face beneath the hood. Soon he was among rebels racing for the exits, some carrying bundles or small chests in their arms, others making ready to fight. None noticed one more cloaked figure in their midst.

Quintus followed the defenders through the descending tunnel to an opening in the cave and raced down the goat trail at a dangerous pace, scraping palms and snagging the stolen cloak on thorny branches. He found the place where his escort had left their horses, but all the beasts had been taken. By the time he came to the ravine, bruised and shaking with fatigue, the remains of a dozen rebels and their mounts lay smoldering on a broad patch of charred earth.

Buteo's broken body lay at the feet of an alpha priest and his black-cloaked brothers. A company of imperial cavalry—including the dozen men Quintus had left in Tiberia—ranged behind them. Quintus climbed down the face of the gorge and landed without stumbling. He strode to face the emperor's men like a general arriving to inspect his troops, setting his boot on Buteo's chest.

"I was not informed that Nikodemos would be sending more men to assist me," he said to the cavalry commander. "As you see, they were not necessary."

"You left your guard behind," the alpha priest said, his voice rattling like the clack of dry bones. "And your priest appears to be missing."

"Unfortunately, the priest and my two guards were killed by the rebels when we arrived," Quintus said. "I think they burned the priest's body." He prodded at Buteo's corpse. "This one wouldn't be taken alive, but his threat to the empire is ended."

"And the other insurgents?"

"They have their own ways of spotting intruders, and they obviously saw you. I could not kill all of them."

The priest stared at him, his gaunt hands hovering near his pendant. "You were taken prisoner?"

"I had almost gained Buteo's trust. I could have done more if not for your interference." He smiled grimly. "Was Baalshillek so dubious of my chances for success?"

The cavalry commander's horse shifted nervously. "I will send riders to hunt down the rebels," he said.

"Your horses won't make it far on the trails these men use," Quintus said. "They have a thousand hiding places in the mountains."

"We will find them." He turned to issue his orders, but the priest continued to stare at Quintus. Quintus's escort broke away from the other soldiers and gathered about him, hands on sword hilts.

"It seems you have completed your mission," the alpha said heavily. The glitter of his hooded eyes made plain that he knew that Baalshillek had wished the emperor's brother dead and gone. But he also knew he had lost the opportunity to complete Buteo's failed assignment.

Quintus could safely return to Karchedon in triumph. There was little more he could do to win the rebels to his side; once again he must follow his dangerous path alone. If he felt a twinge of regret over the deaths of the two ambushed soldiers or the ultimate fate of Buteo's family, he knew he would have to accept the necessity of such sacrifices. A few must die now so that a hundred thousand more could survive and grow strong in freedom.

Two of his men produced a blanket and wrapped Buteo's body, slinging it onto a horse's back. Likely the head would be put on display in Tiberia, a warning to other would-be rebels, and some token of his identity would be sent back on the ship to Karchedon. Quintus wanted nothing to do with such grisly work.

He accepted a horse from a soldier and mounted, ignoring his torn and battered flesh. "To Ostia," he said. "And home."

He rode past the priests without a backward glance.

Chapter Twenty-Three

The city called New Meroe was guarded by magic so potent that Yseul felt it even at a distance of seven leagues, gazing across the rolling hills and terraced plateaus of pasture and fertile cropland. An ordinary man could not have detected the outer ramparts, let alone the houses, palaces and temples within. The whole of the city stood against the high, nearly vertical wall of a mountain, and to the mortal eye it was no more than a natural part of the dark rock behind it.

Yseul was neither ordinary nor mortal.

She descended from her vantage point at the crest of the hill and returned to the others. Urho sat quietly, mending a tear in the tunic he had stolen from a native village some fifty leagues back. Farkas, worn down to lean tendon and muscle by months of walking, brooded on dreams of bloodshed and glory. And the few Children of the Stone—a mere five of them now, bereft of armor and nearly weaponless—huddled together like common soldiers faced with certain death.

They were not as stupid as their blank faces made them appear. Yseul smiled and licked her lips. Not even the brightest of them seemed to realize just how their brothers had come to die during the long trek through forest and swamp and river gorge, but they had begun to know real fear. Only their in-bred instincts for obedience kept them from abandoning their masters.

Yseul looked away before they could suspect the nature of her interest and threw herself down on the grass beside Urho. He cut off a strip of fine sinew, fitting it through his bone needle with blunt, deft fingers.

"What have you seen?" he asked.

"The city is quiet," she said. "A handful of villages and scattered huts, oxen and goats in the fields, no sign of warriors." She snorted. "These keepers of prophecies rely too heavily on magic alone if they so greatly fear discovery."

"Maybe they have no other defenses," Farkas said.

"Perhaps." She snapped a blade of grass, chewed on it thoughtfully and spat it out again, grimacing at the bitter taste. "Perhaps they truly believed that no agent of the Stone would ever find them."

"And perhaps their magic is sufficient for their purpose," Urho said. "You have sensed its effectiveness already, though we have yet to approach the city walls."

"Well *you* might worry, little man," Farkas said. "Your sorcery couldn't stop our god-cursed enemies in the swamp, even though you boasted of your power over the waters."

Urho set down his needle. "The cat-man used the Hammer. There was no more I could have—"

"We knew he would use it eventually. You are feeble, Urho. Baalshillek erred when he made you."

"And what have you achieved?" Urho asked. "You did no more than I in compelling the forest people to guide us, and since then your supposed skills have been of little benefit. The Hammer protects them...."

"They are still behind us." Farkas swung on Yseul. "This land is filled with opportunities for ambush."

She stared him down. "You will have to kill the Bearer instantly if you wish to survive such a trap yourself. He has grown a hundred times in power. Rhenna can counter your Air magic, and if Tahvo is not yet a match for Urho, it is only because she is bound by her healer's *compassion*."

"Then let us strike silently and take the female Nyx," Farkas said. "We can force her to reveal all she knows of the prophecies and how to obtain them."

"You underestimate her," Yseul said softly. "Her abilities may seem modest, but Ge chose her when she mated with Cian. There is a pattern in these things...."

"A pattern of stupidity and weakness."

"I have said since we left Ge's stronghold that we should send the Children back to Karchedon while some remain alive," Urho said. "Now that we know New Meroe's location, there is no reason to keep them with us. Surely one of them will complete the journey, and Baalshillek will send priests to raze the city and take the Hammer."

"Would you so loudly proclaim your impotence?" Farkas demanded. "Why should Baalshillek keep you alive when he sees how you have failed?"

Yseul got up and strolled away as if she had no part in the males' bickering. Urho was growing more insistent about contacting Baalshillek. That must not happen. Eshu's words had not left her for a single step of the journey through his stinking forests.

"What are you, creatures of the Stone? No more than made things...spawned to serve your maker as slaves, with not even a single soul amongst you. Your Baalshillek cares nothing for your survival once you have stopped his enemies. You will die even if you obtain the Weapons and deliver them to your master.

"But if you take the Hammer and the other Weapons for your-selves, you may yet become whole."

She had learned much since Eshu had offered his warning. She knew how to alter the very substance of the earth so that it flowed like liquid and could swallow a man in a heartbeat. She knew how to use the soil to drain that man of his essence, how to transform that essence and absorb it into her own body.

Two Children of the Stone had died of mishaps in the forest and swampland, but the other four had given their lives to strengthen Yseul in a way neither Urho or Farkas suspected. As the Stone God's altars consumed the bodies and psyches of the priest's victims, so she could reduce a man to the elements that made up his flesh and bones, mind and soul. And those elements became a part of her forever.

Soon, very soon, the last five Children would meet their unfortunate fates.

Yseul climbed up the hill, lay on her belly and kept watch until the sun set. The males finished their argument and settled into a restless sleep. By the thin light of a crescent moon, Yseul took panther shape and loped across the fields, her legs tireless and her senses honed to dagger sharpness. The farmers had retreated into their huts. No soldiers patrolled the cleared land before the city walls.

But the walls radiated power, and Yseul knew she could not pierce their defenses without great care. The magic extended above and below the fortifications, high into the air and under the earth. She crept as near as she dared, searching not for an opening but for the area of weakness that must surely exist.

The section she found looked no different than any other, but its protection was subtly flawed. She pressed her body to the ground, closed her eyes and let herself sink into the soil. She burrowed deep, feeling her way past the wall's foundation.

She emerged in a space between the first wall and a second, lower one. Before she could get her bearings, a shout sounded from the inner wall. Wind whistled past her ear as a spearhead plunged into the bare, firmly packed soil. She dived into the earth, tunneled to the margin of the cleared land and reached the surface in the dubious shelter of a thorny shrub. Then she ran, her ears cocked back to catch the cry of pursuit.

Whoever had seen her was slow to organize the hunt. She returned to camp and changed as Urho and Farkas clambered to their feet.

"You would never have succeeded in entering the city," she gasped, forestalling Farkas's questions. "They are well defended with two walls and strong enchantment."

Urho looked past her shoulder. "Were you seen?"

"Yes."

Farkas charged her, fist raised. "Stupid bitch—"

She snarled and leaped out of his path. "*You* would have been caught." She glanced at Urho. "We must find a more defensible position and consider another approach. There are cliffs behind the city. If we combine our powers—"

"No more talk," Farkas said. "I will get inside and find these cursed prophecies…and then I'll come back for the Hammer."

"You'll die, Farkas."

He strode past her and up the hill. Yseul drove her nails into her palms. "Speak to him, Urho. Make him understand."

Urho was silent. Yseul turned to confront him, but he, too, was gone.

Yseul dropped to a crouch and clawed at the earth. She could stop them if she chose, but she preferred to let them discover their own folly. And if they died of their obstinate masculine stupidity…

So be it. The Hammer would be hers.

She pivoted to face the huddled Children and grinned.

* * *

Nyx returned to the hidden camp just before dawn. Rhenna noted the tightness of her expression and helped her down beneath the overhang of rock in the ravine, where the others waited for her report.

"Something has disturbed the city," Nyx said, accepting a waterskin from Tahvo as she caught her breath. "Mounted patrols are scouring the countryside for several leagues beyond the walls."

"Yseul?" Rhenna asked.

Nyx stared at the waterskin as if the mere act of drinking was beyond her strength. "I found the bodies of two soldiers of the Stone God," she said. "Both had been drained of life, and the crystals in their foreheads were black. This was not the work of the city priests."

"Why would our enemies turn against their own?"

"I do not know."

"Surely this is a good thing," Khaleme said. "If the evil ones are divided, they will pose less threat to the holy city."

"My father told me that none marked by the Stone can enter the city undetected," Nyx said, "but even we must take great care in approaching the gates."

Khaleme nodded. "Strangers are not welcomed here even in times of peace. Our warriors would sooner kill than risk permitting an enemy to pass within the walls, but the king must be warned. I will go."

"I may be a stranger, but this is my father's homeland," Nyx said. "We will go together." She glanced at the cairn of rock where Cian stood alone, staring north toward New Meroe. "Since he took the Hammer, Cian has been impatient to reach the city. It is not wise for him to leave this shelter until we know it is safe."

"Safe for him, or for your city?" Rhenna asked bitterly.

"Cian will do no harm to those who would aid him."

No harm, Rhenna thought, remembering how Cian had

kissed Nyx with such cruel indifference. "You warned him that some in the city might try to take the Hammer."

Nyx avoided her gaze. "That is why Khaleme and I must speak to the king and his councillors, so that they can prepare."

And what are you hiding, Nyx? Rhenna thought. *What have you not told us?* "Cian—or whatever possesses him—is driven by more than the desire to find the prophecies. What does he want?"

"That I do not know, but surely the priests will see what we cannot. They will reach him."

"I trust your priests are nothing like the ones in Karchedon."

"They are wise, holy men who speak to the gods."

"And of course the gods can always be trusted." Rhenna pinched the bridge of her nose to stop the burning behind her eyes. "Did you foresee this, Nyx? Did you know how much he would change?"

"I am no prophet," Nyx protested, but her voice was thin. "The Hammer was created to fight the Exalted, and Cian accepted that burden." She raised her head. "You *must* keep him here until we return."

Rhenna laughed. "You once warned me not to become a distraction to him. Well, I have no influence over him now. I doubt my small skills can stop him if he chooses to leave."

"I also told you he would need your protection. Do what you can." She nodded to Khaleme, and together they climbed to the top of the ravine.

The sun had barely risen above the horizon when Cian set out after them.

Rhenna ordered Tahvo to remain under cover while she followed him, bending low as she ran into the open fields. Cian strode at an unrelenting pace, seemingly indifferent of both pursuit and the dangers that might lie ahead. He hardly glanced at Rhenna when she caught up with him.

She knew better than to try to reason with the arrogant being who walked in Cian's body. She planted herself in his path and called up the wind. It came in fitful gusts, swirling about her head as if the native spirits of Air feared to obey her summons. Cian paused to lift the Hammer, his face set in contemptuous amusement. He struck the ground. A jagged crack split the earth from his feet to Rhenna's boots. Soil and pebbles rattled into the cavity, and Rhenna lost control of the wind as she fought for balance. Cian shouldered the Hammer and walked past her.

There was nothing more she could do to stop him. She gripped the hilt of the knife at her belt and scanned the green plateau. Huts and low fences of scattered villages dotted the boundaries between well-tended pastures. New Meroe was just visible to her eyes as a pattern of planes and angles set against the natural crags and spires of the mountains at its back; Nyx and Khaleme had vanished behind the gently rolling hills. If warriors rode out to intercept the intruders, she could not yet see them.

As she had expected, Tahvo came to join her before she could return to the ravine. Rhenna smiled without humor. "Nyx should have known it was pointless to go ahead," she said. "I told her I couldn't control him."

"What you said to Ge was true," Tahvo said softly. "You share Cian's fate, whatever that may be."

"If the man I know still exists."

Tahvo felt for Rhenna's hand. "He will come back. Do we go to the city?"

"Do you have a better suggestion?"

"The danger will not go away. It is best to meet it."

Rhenna squeezed Tahvo's shoulder and turned her toward the city. By the time they arrived within the shadow of the high city walls, Cian was surrounded by a dozen dark-skinned men mounted on small, sleek horses, every warrior armed with an iron-tipped spear aimed to strike him down. Archers with drawn bows ranged along the top of the wall, and the immense wooden gates were guarded by four ranks of tall foot soldiers. Rhenna thought she saw Nyx at the center of her own knot of warriors.

A group of riders broke off from the others and rode for Rhenna and Tahvo. Rhenna lifted her open hands. One of the warriors, dressed like the others in a short cloth kilt, brightly painted belts crossed over his chest and a plumed headband, challenged Rhenna in a deep, harsh voice.

"He demands to know our purpose in coming to the holy city," Tahvo said, "and if we are companions to the one who claims to bear the Hammer."

"Tell him the truth, Tahvo," Rhenna said, holding the rider's gaze. "Tell him—"

The warriors' horses reared and squealed in terror, drowning her words. The city walls shook, throwing off a fine cloud of reddish dust. Rhenna knew what had happened before she saw Cian with the Hammer's head lodged in the earth at his feet.

Rhenna dodged trampling hooves and raced to his side. She reached him just as he lifted the Hammer for another strike. She grabbed his arm, fingers digging into rigid muscle, and braced herself against his pull.

The earth stilled. Horses sucked air through flared nostrils. Warriors half fell from their mounts' backs and dropped to their knees. The hard-faced man who had confronted Rhenna kicked his horse in a wide circle around his stricken troops, exhorting them with sweeps of his bared sword.

Cian shoved Rhenna aside and held the Hammer high above his head. He spoke to the warriors in their own tongue as if he had known it all his life. Rhenna was hardly surprised when Nyx pushed her way through the kneeling men and addressed the soldiers' leader with the authority of undisputed command.

Her words shattered the spell that lay over her father's countrymen. They got to their feet and gathered around her, keeping well away from Cian. Their leader sheathed his sword with a sharp exclamation that sounded very much like a curse. One of his men relieved Rhenna and Tahvo of their knives and gestured them toward the city gates.

The kilted guards stood at attention as the high doors swung open with a groan of heavy iron hinges. Nyx was lost amid the taller warriors, and Rhenna saw no sign of Khaleme. She kept Tahvo close, well aware that she understood little of the forces that seethed around them. Cian marched through the gates in his own bubble of godly isolation.

The city of New Meroe was utterly unlike those in the North. Beyond the inner and outer walls lay narrow unpaved streets between neat brick and stone buildings, most only a single story. There were no indications of poverty or neglect, even in the smallest and plainest structures that Rhenna guessed must serve as dwellings of the city's humblest inhabitants. Donkeys, horses and cattle stood quietly, enduring the day's heat in their well-swept pens. Dogs panted in open courtyards, and flowering vines spilled over trellises fashioned from braided branches, as lovingly tended as treasured children.

Simply dressed brown-skinned people peered from doorways to observe the cavalcade, their faces reserved and their manner solemn but unafraid. Everything in New Meroe bespoke the assurance of ancient dignity, power and sober duty. Yet the sense of order bore nothing in common with the rigid control that marked Karchedon and its conquered territories in Hellas. The very air held an unmistakable sense of waiting.

As the procession wound deeper into the city the streets widened, some bordered with monumental sculptures of crouching beasts with lions' bodies and curved-horned rams' heads. Columned edifices of many stories, lavishly decorated with shallow reliefs painted in vivid colors—warriors and kings and gods striding over the prone bodies of their enemies—were guarded by towering crowned figures who bore shepherd's crooks and farmer's flails in their limestone hands. Shaven-headed men in long white robes and animal skins stood on the wide steps watching Cian with dark eyes.

"The spirits of this city are very near," Tahvo said.

"I think these are the temples of their gods," Rhenna said. "Nyx's people choose strange creatures to worship. Men and women with the heads of hawks and serpents and cattle…" She stopped, transfixed by the image of one creature that stood alone upon its own pedestal: a male form from bare feet to shoulders, topped by the head of some beast Rhenna had never seen. Its snout was long and curved downward, and the pricked ears were squared at the tips. Its flesh was painted vivid red, and in its hands it bore a perfect replica of Cian's Hammer.

"Sutekh," Tahvo whispered.

Rhenna had no chance to ask what she meant, for the riders and foot soldiers turned up another broad avenue leading to a complex of buildings and pylons that captured the sun's radiance with facades of gold. A gated wall surrounded the compound, defended like the outer ramparts by warriors armed with spears, swords and shields.

The leader of the horsemen dismounted, spoke to the guards and signaled to his troops. Gold-chased doors opened, and Nyx was carried along on a tide of gleaming brown skin and waving speartips. Cian followed, looking neither to the left nor right. The cavalry drew aside, while soldiers urged Rhenna and Tahvo after him.

An extensive garden of potted frond-leaved trees and crystal pools lay just inside the gates, and a tiled path led through yet another pillared portal. Cool shadow picked out reliefs and engravings on the smooth inner walls, scenes of domestic life abounding with men and women at their ease while servants brought trays of food and drink and children played at their feet.

Rhenna soon lost count of the rooms through which they passed. Hallways opened into compartments clearly intended as meeting places or private chambers; intricately woven mats and handsome skins stretched over floors of green and blue tiles, and carved wooden chairs were arranged about low tables bearing trays of wine jars and golden cups. But the inhabitants of the palace—for surely no one but a great ruler would live in such a place—remained hidden.

At last the soldiers stopped at a sparsely furnished, windowless chamber with painted murals of fish leaping from a churning river. "My lord," one of the guards addressed Cian in Hellenish. "If you will rest here, all you require will be brought to you."

Cian walked in without hesitation and stood in the center of the room, the Hammer held in his folded arms. Rhenna entered with greater caution, marking the sealed doorway in the far wall. The warriors closed the wooden doors behind their guests, and Rhenna heard the thump of a bolt sliding into place.

Guests indeed. She stalked the perimeter of the room and tested the smaller door. It, too, was barred. Tahvo waited where the soldiers had left her, head tilted to listen.

"It would seem that Nyx has abandoned us," Rhenna said.

"I do not believe it," Tahvo said. "She has no reason—"

"These people know her. She was lying when she claimed she had never been to New Meroe." Rhenna slapped the painted river with her open palm. "She could have spoken to us any time since we came to the city walls."

"Unless she is a prisoner."

"I saw the way she addressed the warrior's commander. They treat her like royalty."

Cian laughed. "Envious, woman?" he asked coldly. "Do you still hate her because Ge chose her instead of you?"

Rhenna turned to him, sealing her emotions behind a mask of indifference. "We are here for one reason only," she said. "And that is to learn where the next Weapon can be found. Or are such small matters no longer of interest to you?"

Red light muddied the gold of Cian's eyes. "I will destroy the Exalted."

"Alone? Has this 'god' that possesses you given you so much power?"

Cian raised the Hammer in both hands. The glyphs in its black head seemed to writhe as if they would leap from its surface. "I could raze this city with a blow," he snarled.

"But you will not," Tahvo said. She touched his arm, holding firm though her body was racked with shivers of distress. "You will wait for Nyx, and we will find what we seek."

Cian shoved her away so violently that she tumbled to the floor, skidding halfway across the room. Rhenna's hand brushed the sheath at her belt and found it empty. She grabbed a delicate wooden chair and smashed it against the wall, selecting the sturdiest leg from the shattered fragments.

"Whatever you are," she said, breathing hard, "you're no better than our enemies. Take the cursed Hammer, and give Cian back to us."

"He cannot."

Nyx walked into the room, flanked by guards in plumed headdresses who came to rigid attention as they fell into position on either side of the open doors. The woman who spoke bore little resemblance to the rebel Rhenna had first met in Karchedon. She wore a sheer, pleated white gown that draped her body from shoulders to ankle, embroidered at the hem with glittering golden thread. A heavy collar of precious stones circled her neck, and her black hair was crowned with a gold circlet adorned with three tall, curving feathers.

"Do not be alarmed," Nyx said. She bowed to Cian with calm detachment. "I regret any inconvenience you have endured, my lord, and beg your forgiveness for this delay in welcoming you to the city. Soon you will be honored as befits your station." At some unseen gesture, two young women in short robes entered bearing a carved wooden chest overflowing with rich garments and jewelry. "These servants will assist you, if it pleases you to accompany them."

Cian stared at Nyx with a strange half-smile, as if he had anticipated her transformation. He dismissed Rhenna and Tahvo with a glance and strode out the door, followed by the servants and a quartet of warriors.

Rhenna threw the chair leg to the floor and started after him. Guards crossed feathered spears to bar her way.

She swung on Nyx. "Where are you taking him?"

Nyx waved the warriors back and met Rhenna's gaze. "He will be prepared to meet King Aryesbokhe," she said, "and to claim his rightful place as Bearer of the Hammer."

"Why should I believe you aren't planning to kill him and take the Hammer for yourself?"

Nyx flinched. "Why would I steal the Hammer now when I could have claimed it long before Cian accepted it?"

"How can I guess your reasons?" Rhenna said. "You've lied to us all along. You're not the daughter of some common soldier. You've been here before, and you expected a welcome."

Nyx shook her head. "I have never set foot in this city. All I know of it was taught to me by my father. I did deceive you, but only because you were already reluctant to trust me. If I had told you that my father was a prince of New Meroe, and that my uncle is now the king, you would surely have questioned my motives even more stringently."

Rhenna snorted. "And what *are* your motives, prince's daughter?"

"The same as they have always been…to restore the Hammer to the holy city, along with its Bearer."

"For some purpose other than fighting the Stone God."

"Will you always believe the worst of me, my friend?" Nyx spoke to one of the guards, who closed the doors behind her. "You cannot possibly understand the forces that have long been at work among our people. New Meroe is a new city for us, but the prophecies have bound us since the Godwars. And in all the years of our guardianship there have been many interpretations of the ancient texts, many rulers and priests who have advocated one translation over all others."

"Then the prophecies are not of divine origin?"

"They were given to us by the gods of light, but those who read them are only mortal." She fingered the polished stone beads of her collar as if she chafed under its weight. "Prince Irike was the youngest son of King Akinidad, my grandfather,

394   Susan Krinard

who ruled New Meroe from its founding. It was near the time
of the building of the city that one of the priests whose duty it
was to preserve the prophecies discovered a new meaning in
the texts he had studied since childhood. It had always been
believed that only an heir of my people's royal blood would
wield the Hammer in battle with the Stone, but Talakhamani
claimed that another would come to us…one of the blood of
the Watchers."

"The one for whom your father searched?"

"My father became a disciple of Talakhamani, but Akinidad
declared all who listened to his words to be heretics and traitors. Prince Irike was banished from New Meroe. Only his eldest brother, Aryesbokhe, dared to help him in secret. So my
father set out to find the Hammer and prove the truth of the
priest's revelation."

"And you have succeeded where he failed."

Nyx lifted her chin. "I have served my people and redeemed
my father's name. None can doubt that Cian is the true Bearer.
My uncle will affirm this by day's end, all schisms will be healed,
and the warriors of New Meroe will prepare for the Time of
Reckoning."

Rhenna hooked her thumbs in her belt and paced about the
room, still troubled by Nyx's explanations. "These religious
schisms could still be a threat to Cian."

"Not if the king acknowledges him before the city."

"And what of the other Weapons, and the prophecies you
said would reveal where they lie?"

"When you resume your journey, you will have everything
you need." Nyx looked to Tahvo with pleading in her eyes.
"Surely you see, Healer. All is as it should be."

Tahvo's silver brows drew together. "Yseul…"

"Our best troops are searching for her as we speak. They will
not rest until they have her and any who give her aid. Her
power cannot stand against the magic of our priests in their
own city."

"And are you so sure of Cian?" Rhenna demanded.

Nyx was about to reply when the door opened and one of the warriors bent to whisper in her ear. "Cian is ready to meet the king," she said. "If you will wait here, proper clothing and refreshment will be provided."

She turned to go, her guards closing ranks to prevent Rhenna from following. But mere mortals could not stand against one touched by the gods. Cian shouldered the guards aside, strode into the room and stopped before Rhenna. He, like Nyx, was dressed in long pleated white robes, but his belt and collar were made of solid golden links, and even his sandals seemed woven of precious metals.

"You will come with me," he said.

Nyx met Rhenna's eyes and bowed her head in resignation. "There is no time for you to dress," she said. "You must go as you are."

"I need no fine clothes," Rhenna said.

Tahvo came up beside her. "I will remain here," she whispered, "and seek the counsel of the spirits."

"We should stay together—"

"She will be safe," Nyx assured Rhenna. "You are all under my protection."

Rhenna stifled a laugh and let Cian precede her into the colonnaded hallway. He walked ahead as if he knew the way. Rhenna's escort blocked her view of the corridor, but she caught glimpses of even more lavish wall paintings and rooms that could only belong to men and women of great wealth and status.

She knew they had reached their destination when Cian paused at a pair of embossed gold doors twice as high as a man and broad enough to admit two of Nyx's long-trunked *àjàn-ànkú*. He tapped the doors with his Hammer, and they rang with the clamor of twenty blacksmiths striking their anvils all at once.

The doors swung inward, pulled by bare-footed servants in

short kilts. They covered their eyes and flung themselves to the
floor at Cian's feet. The center of the room was long and nearly
empty of furnishings save for the elaborate chair perched on a
dais at its end, but every space between the columns to either
side was filled with a resplendent company of courtiers dressed
in variations of the long-robed style. Some of the women were
bare-breasted, their bodies plump and sleek with prosperity.
The men were tall and well-formed. The skin of men and
women alike had the richness of dark, highly polished wood,
and their equally dark eyes regarded the newcomers with an
intensity that might have been anticipation…or fear.

The man who sat on the throne was of middle years, with
white dusting his black hair and short beard. Across his right
shoulder he wore a fringed sash, and long tassels draped around
his neck hung nearly to the floor. His armbands, collar and sandals were heavy with gemstones and gold. His crown was
shaped like a helmet with an elaborate crest of cones, stylized
feathers and curving serpent's heads.

On the steps below him sat a pair of full-bodied women, each
wearing a matching wide sash. Slaves stirred the warm air above
their heads with fans made of black and white feathers. At the
foot of the dais stood several men with shaved heads and spotted skins draped over their shoulders, each bearing a staff topped
by a crowned ram's head. The king's guards—eight on each side
of the dais—were dressed in tunics made of glistening scales,
and they towered above all the other males in the room.

Cian never hesitated. He paced down the length of the hall,
holding the Hammer erect like a royal scepter. A murmur of
shock or dismay rippled through the watching nobles like wind
through tall grass. The mailed warriors stepped in front of their
sovereign, spears tilted forward.

Cian stopped. King Aryesbokhe stared at Cian, his hands
rigid on the lion-faced arms of his throne. The clatter of Nyx's
footsteps was the only sound in the hall. She passed Cian and
knelt at the foot of the dais, arms crossed over her chest.

The king's gaze shifted to her. She spoke softly. After a moment he answered, signaling to one of the slaves crouched behind the throne. The servant brought another chair and set it on the step beside the royal women. Nyx rose, bowed and took the offered place.

The king beckoned to the guards escorting Rhenna. They led her forward and dispersed to either side, ready to seize their weapons at a moment's notice. Rhenna glanced at Cian's impassive face and inclined her head to the ruler of New Meroe.

"Rhenna," the king said, his Hellenish heavily accented but clear. "Rhenna of the Free People, friend to the Lady Neitiqert. You are welcome to the holy city."

"My thanks, lord king," Rhenna said.

"All thanks are due to you for helping to restore the Hammer to its people," Aryesbokhe said, "and for bringing my brother's daughter back to us." He smiled at Nyx. "Lady Neitiqert has told us much of your travels and of the dangers you have overcome. Your courage will not be forgotten in New Meroe."

"Then Lady Neitiqert has surely told you why we are here."

The king looked at Cian, and his eyes flashed with emotion that made Rhenna catch her breath. "She has told us that you and your companions seek the Weapons that were made to defeat the Exalted."

"This is true, lord king."

"And you believe that you and the woman Tahvo are to be Bearers of two of the Weapons."

Something in Aryesbokhe's tone made Rhenna choose her words with great care. "So we were told," she said, "by one who speaks with the voice of the gods."

The shaven-headed men standing by the dais exchanged sharp glances. The king seemed not to notice. "Lady Neitiqert also believes this," he said, relaxing in his chair, "and now we have proof of her faith. The Bearer of the Hammer has revealed his power."

Cian's eyes focused on Aryesbokhe, and he smiled. "*You* do not believe, little king."

Nyx jumped to her feet. The bald attendants hissed in outrage. Aryesbokhe raised his bejewelled fingers.

"I know what you claim to be, Watcher of the Stone," he said. "My priests say that you are possessed by the spirit of Sutekh, who forged the Hammer out of the desert sands at the height of the Godwars. But Sutekh is a god of chaos and destruction. How can he, or one who bears his *ba*, be trusted to stand against the evil ones in the North?"

Cian laughed. "How can you prevail without me, mortal?"

"Sutekh is ever-shifting in his loyalties," Aryesbokhe said. "The fate of the world does not concern him. He has the power to create a false Hammer to deceive and foment discord simply for his own amusement."

"Yet Sutekh stood with the righteous gods when he forged the Hammer," Nyx said, her voice low and urgent. "This is the true Weapon, my lord, the one your brother gave his life to find. I have felt it—"

"That is not enough." Aryesbokhe nodded, and the shaven-headed men stepped through the wall of guards and scattered in a half circle around Cian. "The prophecies say that only the king or his direct heir can recognize the Hammer and be certain of its provenance." He held out his hand. "Assure us of your good intentions, Watcher. Give the Hammer to me."

His demand echoed in the silence. Rhenna moved closer to Cian, not knowing whether she would have to protect him or prevent him from attacking the king and his warriors. Aryesbokhe's women got up and swiftly descended from the dais. Only Nyx remained, the sable tone of her skin ashen with shock.

Cian shouldered the Hammer and swept the chamber with a glance full of contempt, his eyes fever-red. "Come and take it from me, little king."

Aryesbokhe rose, hands fisted and trembling. "If you refuse, we will know that you are in league with the female Watcher who attempted to enter our city. She is of the Stone, and we will destroy her—as we will destroy you."

Chapter Twenty-Four

The gods of New Meroe came to Tahvo as if they had been waiting for her call. She had known they were powerful, kept strong by the faith of their worshipers; like their people, they had long prepared for battle.

They came so fiercely that Tahvo fell under their onslaught, fighting to keep some sense of her own self as they whirled about inside her head. Birds, beasts, and men and women with skins of gold, red and brown shouted soundlessly. Horns pierced and beaks pecked, tearing at her unreal flesh to expose the truths that lay beneath.

Just as she thought she would go mad, the gods abandoned her, summoned by some devotee whose claim upon them was greater than hers. But one spirit lingered, and in its essence Tahvo recognized one she had known before.

"Isis," she whispered.

"I am Aset," the spirit said. Her image formed in Tahvo's mind, robed in white and wearing a crown of sun disk and horns upon her head. "Who are you?"

Tahvo knelt and bowed deeply. "I am Tahvo of the Samah, oh Great of Magic."

The goddess narrowed eyes as blue as a desert sky. "Your *ba* has been touched by one of my sisters in the North," she said.

"By one who helped to save my life and defied the evil that lies in the shadow of the Stone."

Aset cocked her head as if listening to distant voices. "So," she murmured. "Why have you come to my city?"

"We have come to consult the prophecies, so that we may fight the Exalted and those who serve them."

A long staff, woven of reeds and capped by a white flower, materialized in Aset's hand. "You are a healer," she said, "and yet you bring one who has been my enemy."

Behind Tahvo's eyes appeared the likeness of a man with the head of a strange, long-eared beast. His flesh and fur were red, and he bore in his hands the Hammer itself.

"Sutekh," Aset said, biting off the word. "Lord of the Desert. Brother and murderer of my husband, god of rage, bringer of violence and chaos."

Tahvo's thoughts blended with Aset's, and she shared the memories the goddess and all the sisters who bore her name had carried down through the ages. She saw the evil god Sutekh, lusting for his brother's wife, tricking the great god Asar and dismembering him, scattering the parts of his body throughout the land of Khemet. She saw Aset gathering up the pieces and, by means of great magic, bearing her husband a child.

"Heru," Tahvo said. "Heru-sa-Aset."

"Our son, who is lost to us," Aset said. Tears ran down her smooth golden face. "As Sutekh was lost, until you brought him back."

"His spirit lay within the Hammer," Tahvo said. "It was he who forged it to battle the Exalted—"

"Or to betray us."

Tahvo was blind, yet she remembered what Aset had forgotten. "Sutekh is the spirit of chaos," she said, "but the Stone God's priests seek perfect order, the death of all growth and change. Without growth there can be no life."

"The Red One opposed the harmony of Ma'at, the greatest truth."

"Sutekh allied himself with the good spirits because he saw that the world would be destroyed," Tahvo said. "He was the only god who could defeat the Serpent of Darkness, Apep, when he would swallow the sun itself. Who better than the god of rebellion to defy the Stone?"

Aset touched the golden symbol that hung from her neck, crossed bars that hung from a loop at the top. "You are wise, mortal," she said. "You see what I…"

Abruptly her image wavered in Tahvo's mind, and the shape of the goddess was replaced by a scene of conflict. There was a long room with many people, and at the end of the room, standing before rows of guards and a man on a high chair, were Rhenna and Cian. Men with shaved heads and animal-skin cloaks—priests of the city gods—mouthed curses as they swung their staffs in sorcerous attack.

"The king has demanded the Hammer," Aset's voice said faintly from the air. "Sutekh refused. Now the priests call upon us—" The goddess paused as if struggling with some powerful compulsion, and Tahvo understood what the spirit did not say.

The king of New Meroe sought the Hammer because he believed *he* was meant to bear it. About his neck he wore a piece of the Weapon, broken off at the end of the Godwars, and it gave him power: power to control the priests, power to convince his people that he alone could wield the Hammer against the Stone.

But Cian had refused to surrender it, and now the priests who served the king had summoned the gods to crush this upstart with their divine magic.

The gods could not resist, even if they wished. They were

subject to the wills of the priests and the king, servants as surely as the poor, witless folk bound by the Stone in Karchedon and Hellas. This, too, was evil, born of good twisted by greed and fear.

Tahvo watched in helpless silence as Cian lifted his Hammer, his lips drawn back in a snarl of rage, his eyes red with the fury of a god. Rhenna stood beside him, unarmed but ready to fight. From the staffs of the priests came gods-given blasts of light that struck Cian and sent him stumbling back, reeling in shock and pain. Rhenna cried out. Cian pounded the floor with the Hammer, and a great crack raced along the tiled floor, dispersing the priests and splitting the dais upon which the king stood. The king merely stepped aside, smiling.

Men and women fled as painted columns swayed and the ground rolled under their feet. The priests recovered and slammed Cian with another blast of divine magic; Tahvo saw the spectral faces of New Meroe's gods floating above them, spirits prepared to give the full measure of their life essence to wipe out the king's enemy.

It was a battle Cian and his God of Chaos could not win. One attack after another laid him low, and the Hammer flew from his grip. Rhenna dived after it. Her body writhed as her fingers touched the handle. Nyx, shouting commands Tahvo could not hear, rushed down from the platform and snatched the Hammer away.

Cian lifted his head, and Tahvo saw his golden eyes—the eyes of the good man she knew—staring in bewilderment at the tumult around him. Then the priests encircled him and touched him with their staffs, encasing his body in golden light that wove itself into a fine net that clung to every surface of Cian's clothing and flesh.

In an instant of stillness Rhenna seized a spear from the lax hand of one of the guards and charged the dais, bearing down on the king like a howling gale. Nyx swung the Hammer between king and warrior, shattering the spear. The guards mobbed Rhenna and bore her to the ground.

That was the last Tahvo saw of her friends. Aset had vanished, taking with her the gift of her vision. Tahvo crawled to the nearest wall and huddled against it, rocking to calm her galloping heart.

Cian and Rhenna were prisoners of a mad king, and Nyx had betrayed them. Khaleme had disappeared. Only Tahvo was still free and able to act.

Tahvo crept toward the door and listened for guards outside. She heard nothing. Perhaps the king had not considered her worth watching, or her keepers had been called to join in the battle for the Hammer. She pushed at the door, but it didn't yield. They had bolted it from outside.

Slowly she skimmed her hands over the gilded wood of the door. Little moisture remained within the fibers, but there was just enough for Tahvo to reach. She sought the tiny particles of water and absorbed them into herself, sapping the wood with painstaking care. The golden paint cracked. Planks buckled with a groan, and the bolt began to give way. Another shove of her shoulder snapped the lock and splintered the shrunken door.

She stepped out into the passageway and paused to get her bearings. What noise there was came from far down the corridor. She turned in a circle, casting out with all her senses.

The prophecies were close by. She could almost feel them, but a hundred walls might lie between her and their location. Without the help of the spirits, she could wander the palace and the city for days without coming any nearer to her goal.

"Healer."

She turned to face the deep, familiar voice. "Khaleme?"

A large, gentle hand took her arm and drew her away from the room. "Do you know what has happened in the palace?" he asked.

"I was left here when Rhenna and Cian went to see the

king," she said, "but the spirits have shown me…" She hesitated, knowing that Khaleme's own loyalties must now be in doubt.

"You need have no fear," he said, guessing her thoughts. "I slipped away before your friends were taken to the king. I know that the Watcher is the true Bearer of the Hammer, and there are others who believe, as well."

"Did you know who Nyx was before we came to the city?"

"She did not reveal herself to me, but her features were those of the royal family." He cleared his throat. "I am only a common warrior. I had no power to defy her, even if I knew her intentions."

"But you defy her now."

"Yes." The air stirred as he looked right and left. "You seek the prophecies?"

Tahvo nodded, and he guided her down the long, open passage. "My brother is a priest of the Archives, where the Sacred Scrolls are preserved with the magic of the gods," he said. "Not all the holy men follow the king. Some are meeting now to decide what may be done to aid the Bearer." His voice cracked. "There will be war in New Meroe."

"Is there no other way?"

"Not if the Watcher is to be saved." He pulled Tahvo roughly against a fluted column as marching feet tramped past. "I will take you to my brother, and he will see that you have access to the prophecies you require."

Tahvo squeezed his hand. "The spirits will bless your courage."

"If they win free of the priests who control them. Come quickly."

"For your loyalty, Lady Neitiqert, you will be richly rewarded."

King Aryesbokhe sat again upon his throne, presiding over the nervous courtiers who had crept back into the hall. His women and Nyx had resumed their seats below him, their bejewelled sandals resting on the fine powder that had sifted down from the high ceiling during the battle. The crack in the floor remained, evidence of the Hammer's divine power, but its Bearer lay bound and helpless at the base of the dais, spoils of war cast at a conqueror's feet.

Rhenna knelt beside him, her singed hands tied at her back. She could hear him breathing, but he could neither move nor speak. No spirits had come to his aid; the priests of the city had summoned up a magic too mighty for even the godridden Cian to overcome, and he was only a beaten man again. Rhenna had been worse than useless to him.

Nyx still held the Hammer. Her uncle gazed at it with an avarice his niece was too blind to see.

Aryesbokhe raised his hands, silencing the uneasy conversation of his subjects. He turned again to Nyx. "Let it be known to all the city that Lady Neitiqert has redeemed the treason of our brother, who followed the heresy of the priest Talakhamani. Let the gods witness that my brother's daughter is now our heir and beloved of the king."

Rhenna watched with contempt as the noblemen and women of the court applauded with strained smiles and broad displays of humility to their lord and master. She stared at Nyx, who never bothered to glance at the companions she had betrayed.

"Lady Neitiqert," Rhenna said when the applause had died, "has broken her word to protect those she welcomed as guests to your city, oh King. Is this the measure of your royal blood?"

Aryesbokhe's guards moved at once to silence her, but the king stopped them with a gesture.

"Boldly spoken, warrior of the North," he said mildly. "We could regard you as an enemy in league with him who tried to steal the Hammer, but Sutekh's wiles are many. Perhaps you may be pardoned for striking at the king and be permitted some freedom in our city…once you have sworn never to serve those who would destroy us."

"Cian is not your enemy," Rhenna said. "He has risked his life a hundred times for the sake of defeating the Stone God."

"The one you call Cian is no more," Nyx said quietly.

"You," Rhenna growled. "Was there any truth in the tales you told us? Why did you urge Cian to take the Hammer when you already held it in your hands?"

"I am not the Bearer," Nyx said, avoiding her gaze. "It was necessary to test Cian…to be sure…."

"Now all doubts are ended," Aryesbokhe said. "The time of preparation begins." He held out his hands to Nyx, his meaning unmistakable.

Nyx tightened her grip on the Hammer and closed her eyes. Slowly she laid it across her palms and knelt at her uncle's feet.

The king touched the Hammer but once. It glowed like metal in the forge, radiating heat that even Rhenna could feel. Aryesbokhe gasped and fell back, clutching his singed hand to his chest.

Two priests rushed forward to support the king, easing him into his chair. One whispered in his ear while the other examined his hand. His guards surrounded him and half carried their lord from the hall. His women swiftly followed.

The priests raised their staffs, quieting the agitated courtiers. "I speak for the king," one said in Hellenish. "The Hammer must be cleansed of the foul taint of Sutekh the usurper and purified in the House of Life. The king will fast and pray for the guidance of the gods. Only then will the prophecies be fulfilled." He spoke in his own tongue to the warriors who guarded Cian, and they lifted his limp body like a sack of grain. Rhenna felt the prod of a spear against her back. She moved, staying as close to Cian as she could, and prayed that Tahvo was still free.

Emptying her mind of all irrelevant thoughts, Rhenna let her senses take in every feature of the wide galleries and narrow corridors through which the warriors led them. One moment of inattention was all she needed, though the effort would be doomed from the beginning. She was without allies, without hope, without even a gentle, silver-eyed seer to assure her that all would yet be well….

A small, wheaten-haired dog ran between the warrior's feet like a mouse pursued by a ravenous cat. Two of the men missed their steps, and the others bunched up behind them. Rhenna lunged at the nearest soldier, knocking him off balance. Just as she found her feet again, figures draped in concealing head cloths burst into the passageway. They attacked the warriors with swords and clubs, while Rhenna struggled to free her hands from their bindings.

The fight was short and deadly. Not one of the soldiers was allowed to escape. The rescuers suffered their own losses, and several more were wounded. Rhenna twisted her bleeding wrists out of the ropes.

"Who are you?" she demanded of the newcomers.

One of the men unwound his head cloth, revealing a shaved head and bright black eyes. "I am Dakka, chief priest of the Archives," he said in Hellenish. "I and my brothers will take you and the holy Bearer to a place of safety."

Rhenna touched Cian's chest through the webbing that bound him. His heart beat far too slowly. "You stand against your king?" she asked.

"He would name us heretics, but we revere the writings of Talakhamani. An Ailu must bear the Hammer." One of his followers crouched beside Rhenna, briskly examined her hands, then wrapped them in strips of soft cloth. Another gave her a bleached linen cloak and a bone-handled knife, while the rest gathered about Cian and gently lifted him in their arms.

"There is no more time for talk," Dakka said. "The king will not long remain ignorant of our rebellion."

"We left our companion Tahvo in the palace," Rhenna said, drawing the cloak over her shoulders. "I need—"

"Rhenna!"

She turned with relief as Tahvo made her way toward them, her arms stretched out before her. Rhenna hurried to take her hand.

"Devas be praised," she said. "Nyx betrayed us—"

"I know." Tahvo frowned, cocking her head toward the priests. "Khaleme helped me, but he is gone."

"Khaleme is one of us," Dakka said. "He can care for himself." He passed Tahvo a cloak and head cloth. "Now we must go."

Tahvo hesitated. "You held the Hammer," she said to Rhenna. "Your hands—"

"There's no need to worry," Rhenna said, rising to choose a spear from among those of the fallen warriors. "I didn't suffer nearly as much as Aryesbokhe, and I can still hold a weapon."

Tahvo reluctantly conceded to Rhenna's stubbornness, and they set off at a swift pace, keeping to the long blue shadows as they left the palace grounds. Dakka led them to one of the grand buildings they had passed when they first arrived, but he did not go up the broad steps to the colonnaded entrance. He circled to the side of the building, paused before a blank wall and skimmed his hands over it, chanting words of ritual. Smooth stone dissolved into the black square of a portal.

Dakka bent and entered, warning Rhenna of the steep stairs behind the magic door. She helped Tahvo descend into an unlit chamber. After the men with Cian had reached the bottom of the stairs, Dakka closed the door and produced a flame that danced on his open palm. A maze of corridors branched out from a featureless room. The priest chose one barely wide enough to accommodate one man at a time.

The way was suffocating in its stifling darkness, and Rhenna began to understand what Tahvo endured every day of her life. After what seemed like leagues of dank walls and leaden air, they emerged into a small chamber bright with flickering torches. Two giant statues, expertly carved in the shape of crouching panthers, guarded a stone door at the opposite end of the room. A dozen priests, each holding a panther-headed staff, stood beneath the beasts' snarling heads. One priest handed Dakka a similar staff engraved with mysterious symbols and capped with gold.

Dakka's men carefully laid Cian on the cool earthen floor.

Tahvo knelt beside him. She plucked at his bindings, but not a single strand gave in spite of her efforts.

"Khaleme spoke of the Archives," she said to Dakka. "Is this where the prophecies are kept?"

"They are very near." The priest studied Tahvo with quiet intensity, including Rhenna in his gaze. "When you and the Bearer entered the city, Khaleme came to me and spoke of your quest to find the other Weapons. He was convinced that you were meant to bear them, and now I see that he was right."

"Nyx was certain that the prophecies can tell us where the Weapons may be found," Rhenna said.

"We have worked for many years to decipher those passages that mention them. We believe we have finally—"

"There will be time to speak of these things later," Rhenna said. "Now you must release Cian."

Dakka's shoulders dropped as if he carried a weight he dared not set down. "We cannot," he said. "Not yet."

"Why not, if he's the holy Bearer you've been waiting for?"

"Because Sutekh still lives within him," Tahvo said. She cupped her hand over Cian's muffled face. "I saw what happened in the king's hall. Sutekh was imprisoned in the Hammer for uncounted years before Cian freed him, and now he holds Cian's spirit in bondage."

Rhenna clenched her teeth. "Ge said nothing of this before she surrendered the Hammer."

"She did not know," Tahvo said. "The magic that bound Sutekh was potent, and the spirits of the forest knew nothing of him. I did not feel his presence. Even Nyx did not suspect until it was too late."

"The priestess speaks truth," Dakka said solemnly. "We did not anticipate this danger. Until we can bring the Red One under our control—"

"The king called Sutekh a god of chaos and destruction," Rhenna said. "He forged the Hammer to fight the Exalted. How did he come to be trapped inside it?"

Dakka glanced at the line of priests beneath the statues, and an elderly man stepped forward. "There are a few ambiguous passages in the most ancient scrolls that tell of Sutekh's part in the Godwars," he said. "They say that when Sutekh forged the Hammer out of the desert sands, he claimed the right to lead the gods of Khemet in their battle against the Exalted. But the gods did not dare trust one whose nature was so opposed to the way of Ma'at. They feared he would betray them." The priest hesitated. "What remains of the text is unclear. But it suggests that Sutekh severed a part of his *ba*, his soul, and bound it to the Hammer, intending to take revenge on the gods when the last battle was at its height. He worked his magic too well. The Weapons were stolen by the Exalted who escaped imprisonment, and Sutekh's power vanished with the Hammer."

"Then he has no intention of fighting the Stone God," Rhenna said. "Perhaps he even plans to join the Exalted."

"His ultimate desires are unknown to us," Dakka said. "The Exalted would as gladly eliminate him as they would the righteous gods. But Sutekh had reason to come to New Meroe. The king bears a fragment of the Stone in an amulet he wears about his neck day and night—a piece chipped from the Hammer in the final battle of the Godwars. Until that piece is reunited with the Hammer, Sutekh cannot devour the ba of the Bearer and claim his full power."

Rhenna knelt, laid down her spear and gripped Tahvo's shoulder, finding some small comfort in the healer's warm solidity. "Can you drive Sutekh out?" she asked Dakka.

"With the aid of the gods, we may leash his magic."

"Your spirits obey the priests who attend the king," Tahvo said.

"Their bond to our kings is an ancient one. Aryesbokhe will attempt to destroy the Bearer's body to weaken Sutekh, but not before he himself has gained mastery over the Hammer."

"It injured him when he touched it," Rhenna said. "Can he command its power?"

"Not without great risk. Even if he succeeds, the Hammer

will eventually turn against him." Dakka's black eyes rested on Tahvo. "You come from a distant land, priestess, but my soul tells me that you are beloved of the gods. Can you help us?"

Tahvo rose slowly, leaning on Rhenna's arm. She opened her mouth and repeated a single word: "Aset. Aset. Aset…"

The goddess came so swiftly that Rhenna was not prepared for Tahvo's transformation. A soft light radiated from her stout body, stretching Tahvo's torso and limbs into a semblance of elegant beauty that had never belonged to a humble healer from the Northlands. Her face was copper-skinned and alluring, unmarred by any imperfection.

She opened blue eyes and turned to examine the priests who had fallen to their knees before her, each of her movements casting reflected torchlight from her jeweled collar and the long, intricately embroidered sash about the waist of her sheer gown. The horned sun-disk balanced upon her golden headpiece burned with its own inner luminance.

The priests pressed their foreheads to the ground. "Great of Magic, Restorer of Asar, Mother of Heru," Dakka intoned. "We beg you to accept our undying gratitude—"

Aset lifted her hand, fixing Rhenna with the leashed power of her gaze.

"Rhenna of the Free People," she murmured. The delicate black crescents of her brows etched a frown across the smoothness of her forehead. "Are you the one?"

Rhenna glanced at Dakka, trying to make sense of the goddess's words. The priest shook his head almost imperceptibly.

"I am the companion of the Bearer of the Hammer," Rhenna said, holding the goddess's stare. "We know of Sutekh and how he threatens the soul of our friend. I am told that you and your fellow devas have the power to drive Sutekh from his body."

Aset clasped the looped cross at her throat. "We were not prepared for this assault," she said. "The king's priests have demanded much of us to protect the prophecies from our enemies. We have not left the city since its foundation. Our powers…" She seemed to shrink, shadowed by a pall of vulnerability. "We cannot destroy Sutekh."

Dakka raised his head from the ground, keeping his eyes averted. "Yet once, Great of Magic, you won for your son Heru the rule of Khemet with no more than your own cleverness." He turned toward Rhenna. "When Asar, King of the Gods, was cruelly murdered by Sutekh, his heir, Heru-sa-Aset contended with the Red One for the throne. As they debated upon the merits of each claimant, the Divine Council forbade Lady Aset from speaking on behalf of her son. But she disguised herself as a mortal woman, a herdsman's widow, and approached Sutekh with the tale of how the herdsman's son was being deprived of his inheritance by a usurper. She begged the Red One to render his judgment, and he declared that the son was indeed entitled to his father's property. In so doing, Sutekh condemned himself out of his own mouth."

"I remember," Aset said with a sad smile. "Those days are long past. And yet…" Her gaze grew hooded. "Your healer believes that Sutekh's forces of chaos may be set against the Stone God. If one mortal shape can bear two *bau*…"

"Cian can't go on as he is," Rhenna said. "If you wait, he'll be driven mad before he regains command of his body. Aryesbokhe must not carry the Hammer. However the priests have bound you in the past, now you must fight for the survival of devas *and* men."

Aset's face darkened with anger and just as suddenly cleared. "You speak without the reverence befitting a mortal," she said, "but Ma'at resides in your words. I must consult my husband." She closed her eyes, and her graceful form melted into another—undeniably masculine, his clothing more like snug wrappings than the long gown of his mate-black-skinned and bearing a tall crown fringed with feathers. In his hands he carried a crook and flail.

"Asar, Wenenefer, Lord of the Living," Dakka whispered.

The god regarded Rhenna with obsidian eyes and walked

past her to Cian's side, his steps short and confined by the restricting cloth wound about his legs. "Sutekh," he said with a long sigh. "My brother. My murderer."

Rhenna quickly joined him. "Cian never harmed you, Lord Asar," she said.

He smiled at her, full lips curving in his mild face. "My beloved has told me," he said. "It is as she has said…we who remain in the city have given all our power to protecting the ancient writings of those who came before us. We have little left with which to fight. But today you bring us hope in your mortal body." He touched Rhenna's scarred cheek, and she felt the blood surge in her like a hot tide. "How strange it is to know that an outlander and unbeliever will return our son to us."

Rhenna flinched away. "I don't understand you."

Without answering, Asar knelt beside Cian and passed his crook and flail over the still form. "Long have we served the kings of the People of the Scrolls," he said, "even from the days of the first pharoah of Khemet. Now that time is past. The true Bearer must rise to do battle in our name." He brushed his palm over the webbing above Cian's mouth, and it peeled away like the scales of a molting serpent. He placed his lips on Cian's, exhaling strongly so that Cian's chest rose with the force of his breath. His arms and legs jerked once, then lay still again.

Asar withdrew, his skin dry and brittle as if he had expelled all the moisture in his body along with his breath. "I have given what I can," he said, rising. "As once my brother and I fought for the rule of the Earth, so now Cian must fight for his *ba*."

"How can I help him?" Rhenna asked.

The god gave her a long, strange look, as if she ought to know the answer. "The love of my lady restored me to life when all hope was lost. So will you restore him you love."

His shape faded, and Aset reappeared. "I, too, have a gift." She opened her hand. On her palm lay a tiny bronze sculpture no larger than Rhenna's thumb, intricately formed to represent a seated woman nursing a child. Though the figure wore the horned disk of Aset's crown, the face was almost featureless. The child wore a circlet set with the head of a hawk.

"This image has much power," Aset said. "It is life itself, and the continuation of existence. As Heru avenged his father and defeated Sutekh, restoring Ma'at to the Two Lands, so Sutekh fears the harbinger of the child's rebirth." She took Rhenna's hand and folded her fingers around the figurine. "Hold this close to your heart, and a part of me will travel with you." She smiled at something only she could see. "We will put ourselves beyond the reach of the king's priests. You will not see us again."

Dakka scrambled to his feet. "Lady Aset…"

A dark mist gathered about the goddess. When it had dissipated, Tahvo stood in her place, trembling and pale. She staggered to the wall and heaved until her stomach had nothing left to expel. Rhenna helped her to sit.

"They are all gone," Tahvo whispered. "I did not hear them. Did they help Cian?"

"I don't know." Rhenna tucked the figurine into her belt and looked at Dakka. "What did Asar do to him?"

Dakka paced on unsteady legs, his brow furrowed. "I have… never seen the gods as I have today," he said. "There are no writings of Asar appearing to any priest of our people. He is among the most powerful of our gods, master of death—"

"A god of death?" Rhenna said.

"As Asar was reborn, so he is the god of resurrection," Dakka said. "I believe the Lord of the Living lent a part of his ba to the Bearer, giving him strength to fight Sutekh. But his gift comes with a price, like the power of the Hammer."

Rhenna balled her fists to keep from grabbing the priest by the scruff of his neck. "Hasn't Cian given enough?"

Dakka bowed his head. "If the Watcher regains his soul, he will always bear a part of both Sutekh and Asar within him."

Rhenna walked away, imagining Cian forever changed, lost, his very being entangled with the souls of creatures beyond her comprehension. She had believed she could endure the ending of a love she had never fully acknowledged, but she had been wrong.

Asar had said that love had saved him. Rhenna could fight with nearly any weapon put in her hand, but this…

"Leave me with Cian," she said to Dakka. "Take Tahvo to your Archives and help her find what she needs."

The priest searched her eyes. "I do not doubt your courage, warrior of the North," he said. "But are you certain—"

He broke off with a gasp as every light in the chamber died. When he finally summoned up his magic flame, his startled gaze told Rhenna what the fire would reveal.

Cian stood among the shredded scraps of his gossamer bindings, his clothing and jewelry cast away, his eyes and flesh and hair as red as iron-shot earth. He thrust out his hand. Dakka fell, his limbs sealed to the floor as if some great weight bore him down. The other priests sank to their knees.

Rhenna seized her spear and stood before Cian, desperately seeking the man behind the god. "Listen to me, Cian," she said. "You're strong…stronger than you ever believed—"

He smashed the spear out of Rhenna's hands, nearly wrenching her arms from their sockets. Pain boiled the blood in her veins and robbed her of sight. Clawed fingers caught Rhenna about the neck, squeezing the air from her throat.

Somewhere beyond the roaring in her ears she heard the sharp yapping of a dog, incongruous and absurdly ordinary. Cian pushed her away, and she saw the small, sharp-eared dog she had seen near the palace racing back and forth at Tahvo's feet.

"Eshu," she whispered.

The dog grinned and began to run dizzying circles around Cian, barking all the while. Cian's mouth twisted in fury. He stumbled back toward the chamber door, and a tinge of gold pierced the red of his eyes. His skin turned pale and then black. With a wild cry, he spun and plunged into the darkened corridor.

Rhenna retrieved the spear, snatched a torch from the wall and started after him. "Find the prophecies," she called to Tahvo. "And take care with that dog!"

Tahvo followed Rhenna as far as the door and listened to her retreating footsteps. She knew she could do no more to help Cian. Healing him was beyond her power.

She prayed it was not beyond Rhenna's.

The dog trotted about the chamber, calmly sniffing the walls. He did not speak to refute Rhenna's cryptic warning.

"What creature is this?" Dakka asked, tracking the animal's movements with wary eyes.

"He is Eshu," Tahvo said, "a spirit of the Western forest with whom we had some dealings. He…" *He cannot be trusted,* she thought. But he had just saved Rhenna's life, and she sensed no hostility in the god. "He must have followed us in our journey, but his purpose here is unknown to us. It is best not to hinder him in any way."

"I understand," Dakka said. He cleared his throat. "Are you ready to proceed to the Archives?"

"Yes."

His sandaled feet brushed across the floor, and she felt the pressure of his fingers between her eyes. Light shot inside her skull.

"I have but a small gift to send you on your way," he said. "I pray its effects will last until you escape the city."

He withdrew his hand, and suddenly Tahvo could see Dakka's face and the great statues behind him. He acknowledged her gasp of surprise with a smile that quickly vanished.

"This chamber and its secret passages are known to only a few of us," he said, "but the scrolls are accessible to any of the priesthood. The king's servants may be there even now." He spoke to his brothers in the Meroite tongue. "Four of my men will go ahead to make certain the Archives are safe."

He faced the door between the panther statues and waved

his staff. The stone slid open with a grating rumble. The four priests went through, Eshu darting ahead into the passageway.

The moments of the priests' absence crept by with painful slowness, but at last one of the men returned. "There were two of the king's priests in the Archival chamber," Dakka said to Tahvo. "They have been dealt with."

"Eshu?"

"The beast has disappeared. Come with me."

Dakka led Tahvo into another maze, lighting their way with the glow from the golden head of his staff. A sealed door opened into a huge room supported by gilded columns painted with strange symbols. Against every wall, and on the shelves of wooden cupboards set in rows along the length of the room, were hundreds of yellowed scrolls. The room was lit by no source that Tahvo could see. The air thrummed with ancient magic.

"If not for the enchantments worked by the priesthood," Dakka said, "the scrolls would have crumbled to dust two thousand years ago. Not one papyrus has ever left this chamber since the founding of the city." He pressed a small metal object into her hand. "The prophecies you seek have been set aside in the cedar chest marked with the ram's head of Amun. Fit the end of this ankh into the ram's mouth, turn it thrice, and the chest will open."

"The gods have given me the gift of tongues," Tahvo said, "but I do not know if I can read your writings."

"Two of my priests keep watch at the main entrance of the Archives. When you have retrieved the scrolls, continue straight ahead and up the stairs, and you will find the door to the street. The priests will get you out of the city and aid you with the translation once you are safe." He seemed to hear her thoughts before she spoke them. "We will not abandon the Watcher or his companions. Have faith, little sister."

Tahvo closed her fingers around the ankh. "Thank you for all you have done."

"I am blessed to witness the fruition of the prophecies in my lifetime," he said, "and to serve the holy Bearers." He bowed deeply. "The gods go with you, priestess."

"And with you."

He straightened and turned back the way they had come. The door closed behind him, becoming part of the wall.

Tahvo walked into the room, drinking in its austere beauty. It was indeed a holy place. She would have given much for a few days with one of the priests to reveal the marvels that must exist here. But the gift of sight was too precious to waste on anything but survival. She passed by the stacks of scrolls and looked for the chest. She found it at the foot of the wide steps rising between heavy columns at the end of the room.

In a chamber so unadorned, the chest stood apart with its workings of gold and the raised embossing of a crowned ram's head upon its lid. The sides were painted with scenes of leaping panthers. Tahvo crouched beside the chest, fitted the end of the ankh into the ram's mouth and turned it three times. The top lifted easily in her hands.

But the chest was empty. Tahvo fell back on her heels, sick with shock. She ran her hands along the insides, certain that her newly restored sight had deceived her.

"You will not find them."

She turned at the voice, expecting one of Dakka's priests. But the man who stood behind her was no native of New Meroe. He was scarcely taller than Tahvo, and beneath his head cloth his hair and eyes were pale as moon-silvered ice.

She recognized his face. She had seen it before in a small room in Karchedon, when she had begged to save the lives of her friends. She remembered the sound of his laughter.

"So you know me," he said with a strange, cruel gentleness. "I would know you anywhere, sister. It is almost like looking in clear water."

Tahvo got to her feet, shaken by the pounding of her heart. "You are real," she whispered.

"As real as you." He smiled. "Did you think you could escape me forever?" He held up the leather sack hung from his shoulder. It bulged with brown-edged scrolls. "Your quest is over. When I return to Baalshillek, this city will be dust. And you…" He made a negligent gesture with one hand, and Tahvo felt the blood in her veins grow sluggish. "You will no longer claim the power that should have been mine."

"How…are you called?" she asked.

"I am Urho." He made a fist, and Tahvo's heart gave a lurch, struggling with every beat. "Do not fight, sister. It will be easier."

Gasping for breath, Tahvo remembered how she had cured Rhenna of the shivering sickness by seeking and eliminating its cause in the waters of the warrior's blood. Now Urho was drawing the water from Tahvo's body as easily as he might net fish in a river, and there were no gods remaining in the city to lend their magic in her defense.

Yet the simple, elemental spirits had not abandoned her. She used the last of her strength to summon tiny particles of moisture from the air of the room, shaping and crystallizing them into a slender spear of ice. It was a slight and paltry weapon, but it was the only hope she had left. The moment it had hardened to solidity, she cast it directly at Urho's chest.

The dart distracted Urho for a precious instant. He paused in his attack to bat it aside, and Tahvo flung herself forward on rapidly numbing legs. She clawed at the sack, dragging it from Urho's shoulder.

Urho laughed as she fell. "Foolish woman," he said. "Do you believe—"

His question ended in a yelp of surprise. A small prick-eared dog darted between his reaching hand and the satchel, snatching the bag in its jaws. Tahvo thanked the spirits and crawled to the foot of the stairs. At least the scrolls would be out of Urho's hands. Whatever Eshu did with them, he would surely not deliver them to Baalshillek….

The light wooden cupboard above her rattled, warning of the tremors just before they began to roll under Tahvo's hands and knees. The building groaned. Dust sifted down from the ceiling. Urho looked up, bracing his legs apart as the ground heaved and rippled.

"The Hammer," he said, cursing in the Samah tongue. His pale gaze returned to Tahvo. "My allies are within the city, sister. They will see to your companions, and I will find that beast—"

"Look no further, fool." Eshu reappeared, grinning with sharp canine teeth. "Come and get me."

Urho lunged. Eshu spun about on his hind legs and dashed around Urho, circling him faster and faster until he was no more than a blur and Urho's body was nearly invisible behind a net of golden light.

Go, the god's voice said in Tahvo's mind. *The scrolls lie outside the door. Go!*

Tahvo pushed herself to her feet and staggered up the steps toward the doors at the end of the room. The heavy doors gave under her weight, and she burst out into late-afternoon sunlight. The sack of scrolls lay where Eshu had indicated, but the priests Dakka had promised to provide were nowhere to be seen.

Tahvo looped the strap of the sack around her neck and shoulder, searching for some sign of where she should go. The street below was quiet, but she knew its peace was an illusion. Stone buildings quivered in the heat as if they anticipated what was to come. Portents of violence hung in the air, like smoke from an unseen fire.

Eshu trotted up beside her, tongue lolling. "The city falls," he said. "I will take you to your companions. Come."

He started down the outer steps. Tahvo hesitated. "Urho?"

Eshu looked over his shoulder with a twitch of his ears. "He is very tired," the god said. "Let him rest."

Tahvo remembered Rhenna's warning and her own misgivings about Eshu's motives.

"Why have you helped us?" she asked.

But Eshu had already set off, and Tahvo had no choice but to follow.

Chapter Twenty-Five

The city had gone mad.

Rhenna raced through the streets with her stolen spear in hand, retracing the path from the hidden temple door back to the palace. The alleys and wide avenues that had seemed so quiet mere hours ago were now filled with men and women darting from one building to another, gathering in small, frantic clusters, only to burst apart again at the sight of some real or imagined threat. Grim-faced warriors converged on the palace compound, and priests came to blows in the shadows of their gods' temples.

The turmoil worked to Rhenna's advantage. Beneath her cloak and head cloth she was only one more distraught citizen among the rest. The soldiers ignored her until she reached the palace gates. There warriors milled about in confusion, stabbing at empty air with their spears and swords, as if battling invisible enemies.

Rhenna retreated behind a ram-headed statue and watched the bizarre display. Magic was at work here, and it did not belong to the priests. Sutekh was the Meroite god of chaos. Cian had come this way.

She called upon her own gift, hoping that the lesser devas of Air were free of the king's control. Dust swirled around her feet. She swept the loose dirt and sand from the nooks and corners of every nearby building and fashioned a spinning, opaque wall. It revolved around her as she ran for the palace gate. A few of the warriors ceased their fighting as the wind scoured their skin and blew grit in their eyes, but Rhenna was up and over the wall before they could confront the new threat.

The palace was strangely deserted, bereft of soldiers, courtiers or servants. Rhenna followed the broad central gallery to the king's hall. The doors were flung open to a vacant room. She paused to listen, letting the very silence be her guide. A shout echoed at the far end of the hall. She crossed the room and found a small door behind the dais. Beyond lay a courtyard and a dozen smaller doorways. A kilted servant saw Rhenna and fled through one of the doors.

Rhenna pursued the man, finding the door unbarred. It led into a sleeping chamber furnished for one of high rank. The sounds of raised voices drew her from the room and into a narrow corridor past many chambers furnished much like the first.

A single warrior guarded the final door, holding a spear in one hand and a sword in the other. He saw Rhenna and cast the spear with wild inaccuracy. She dodged it and rushed him, swinging her own spear at his legs. His sword sliced the air a finger's-breadth from her shoulder. She spun, caught the blade with her spear butt and wrenched it from his hands. The warrior dove for the sword, but she was there before him.

She left him sprawled across the threshold and plunged into a scene of utter turmoil. Cian crouched a few paces in front of her, facing a score of warriors and several priests. Behind the barrier of bristling spears stood Nyx. Smashed furniture and fragments of carved stone and wood lay scattered about the cracked tile floor, and a dozen dead or badly injured soldiers stood testament to the violence of Cian's arrival. There was no sign of the king.

"Rhenna!" Nyx cried.

Cian half turned, his eyes fevered slits in a black-and-red mottled face. His disdainful glance reduced Rhenna to a crawling insect, unworthy of his attention.

"Rhenna," Nyx repeated. "You must stop him. He will destroy the city."

"You would have killed him," Rhenna said, working her way around Cian to the side of the room. "Your city has turned against him. Why should I help you?"

"Sutekh cares nothing for the prophecies. He will end any hope of defeating the Stone." Nyx strained to look over the shoulders of her guards, and Rhenna saw that she still held the Hammer close to her chest. "If any part of Cian remains—"

"*You* said that Cian is no more." Rhenna stopped halfway between the king's warriors and Cian, concealing her own desperation. "Where is your king, Nyx? Where is the power of your priests? Can they no longer bind their enemies with the magic of their gods?"

One of the priests gripped his staff and raised a trembling hand, tracing a figure in the air. Nothing happened.

"Your devas have deserted you," Rhenna said. "They have seen the truth." She licked her lips. "Give the Hammer to me."

"It burned you once," Nyx said. "It will do so again, and this time you may not walk away."

"Give it to her, woman," Cian said, baring his teeth. "I will take it from her lifeless hands."

Rhenna edged closer to the warriors, who shifted weapons and glanced at each other in confusion and alarm. They were afraid…afraid of Sutekh and of forces they could not control or understand. Just as Rhenna was afraid.

"Call off your men," Rhenna said. "Their lives will be sacrificed without purpose—"

She had barely finished speaking when the warrior closest to her gave a harsh cry and turned on his nearest neighbor, slashing at naked flesh with his sword. His victim fell back, and other warriors burst into furious motion, attacking each other with violent abandon.

Cian laughed. Rhenna closed her ears to his brutality and watched for a break in the surging mass of bodies. Nyx fought her way free, dodging blades and speartips. She hesitated for an instant, staring into Rhenna's eyes with sorrow and regret. Then she threw the Hammer.

Rhenna tossed her spear aside and caught the weapon. Its power blasted her like a bolt of lightning, driving her to her knees. The wrappings on her hands sizzled and blackened. The clash of battle faded, and all she could hear was the whisper of Cian's tread on the broken tiles.

He took it from her hand as easily as he would steal a toy from an infant. Rhenna opened her eyes to the jeering triumph on his alien face. The warriors froze, dropping their weapons. The world held its breath.

Cian struck the floor with the Hammer. Shards of tile spun through the air, piercing skin and cloth. The ground rolled outward from the Hammer in great waves, tossing wounded and dying men like flotsam on the sea. The walls began to crack. Powdered stone rose in choking clouds. A jagged black crevice split the earth from the point of the Hammer's impact, racing toward the South.

Those warriors still on their feet crowded through the door. A few turned back to aid the injured. Nyx struggled to help them. Holding her seared hands out before her, Rhenna stood amidst the ruin of her hopes and prepared to face Cian with the only weapon she had left.

Slender fingers seized her arm. "The palace is collapsing!" Nyx cried in her ear. "Cian is gone, Rhenna. We must get out!"

The dust cleared just long enough for Rhenna to see that Nyx spoke the truth. Cian had escaped, contemptuous of the feeble enemies he left behind. She followed Nyx to the door. Walls crumbled behind her, crashing in on themselves with a roar.

The survivors huddled in a small courtyard, hedged by devastation on every side. The palace of King Aryesbokhe had fallen. Nothing but rubble remained of its towering columns and painted walls, and Rhenna could see more distant buildings beginning to shake with the fury of the earth's convulsions.

"The crack in the ground points toward the city gates," Nyx said, hoarse with shock. "If it breaches the walls, the city will be defenseless."

"Your enemies are already within your city," Rhenna said harshly, peeling scraps of burnt cloth from her palms. "Cian goes to find your king."

"Why? He has the Hammer."

"Not all of it. Aryesbokhe keeps a piece of it in an amulet. Without that piece, the Hammer isn't complete."

Nyx closed her eyes. "If the Hammer can do this when it is not yet complete…"

Rhenna forgot her pain and grabbed Nyx's arms. "Why did you betray us, Nyx?"

"I…I came to believe that my father was wrong. I saw that Sutekh had completely overcome the Watcher, that Cian was not strong enough…" She opened her eyes again. "I wished only to serve the prophecies."

"And now? Are you convinced that the king's supporters are mistaken in their beliefs?"

"The Hammer burned my uncle. He cannot be the true Bearer." She held Rhenna's stare. "Aryesbokhe is not evil, only misled. He was raised from infancy on stories that one of the royal family was fated to find and carry the Hammer." She swallowed and glanced at the dazed warriors. "There is fighting between the king's faction and the disciples of Talakhamani. If the city is dying, all the folk of New Meroe will need leaders, and I am of royal blood. There may yet be survivors in the palace. Let me do what I can to organize a search and find allies."

"You'll find allies in the temple of the Archives," Rhenna said. "Where has Aryesbokhe gone?"

"To a secret refuge among the cliffs behind the city. You intend to follow Cian?"

Rhenna touched the figurine still tucked in her belt. "I was given to understand that only I can stop Sutekh from eating Cian's soul."

Nyx didn't question her further. She spoke to one of the soldiers, who bent his head in acknowledgment. "Shorkaror will lead you to the king's refuge." She clasped Rhenna's wrist. "We have only our faith to guide us now. You must save him, Rhenna. You must save us all."

Yseul watched the city gates fall, reveling in the wanton destruction of all the Stone-cursed mortals held dear. She heard the screams of fear and pain, smelled freshly spilled blood as frantic humans fled their toppling structures and poured from the gaps in the crumbling walls.

She knew who had worked this sorcery of ruin. She had seen him enter the city, a creature she no longer recognized. She felt his ravening advance in the soles of her feet, vibrating through the earth like the tread of a mythic giant. His purpose had become a mystery; had she not known better, she would have sworn that he had turned to the Stone.

It made no difference. Cian possessed the Hammer, and he had grown mighty beyond her imagining. But she, too, was greater than she had ever been. The life essence of nine Children of the Stone beat in her blood. No jealous, squabbling males restrained her; Urho and Farkas had never returned from their attempts to enter the city. And even if they still lived, they had no power to take the Hammer from its wielder.

Yseul did.

She assumed panther shape and ran straight into the confusion of weeping, wailing humans and panicky livestock. Terror blinded them to her passage. She scrambled over the rubble, leaped the great crack in the earth and put her nose to the ground, tracing Cian's implacable course across the city. Everywhere lay columns snapped like twigs, and statues shorn from their pedestals; the dead were abandoned by the living, and women searched the wreckage, crying out for lost children.

Yseul felt no pity. She loped between the severed heads of crouching ram-gods and through a garden of withered vines and felled trees. In a fifth of an hour she reached the far side of the city, where it butted against the sheer mountain wall.

Here all sign of Cian ended. Yseul paused, sniffing the hazy air. A troop of men had come this way, their bodies trailing the scent of fear, but her quarry was not among them. Even as she turned back toward the city, she heard the drum of running feet.

She melted into the shadow of a broken pillar and waited for the man to pass. He never had the chance to raise his sword. She leaped and knocked him down with a swipe of her paw. He lifted his bloodied head and froze.

Yseul straddled him and changed. The man's eyes went blank with shock. She slapped his face with an open palm.

"Where are you going in such a hurry?" she asked in Hellenish, caressing his cheek with the tips of her nails.

"Watcher," he whispered. "But you are not…"

She wrapped her fingers around his throat. "I will kill you unless you speak swiftly and truthfully. Where is the man called Cian?"

Rattling breath hissed from his mouth. "Sutekh," he said. "He has come in the shape of the Watcher."

"What is this Sutekh?"

"The god," he said. "The god who would destroy the king. He hunts Aryesbokhe…."

"Why?"

"I…do not know."

"And where is the king?"

The man tried to resist, but a slight increase of pressure on certain parts of his body convinced him to speak. "The refuge," he gasped. "In the mountain behind the city."

"Take me there."

She let him up, and he stumbled toward the cliffs. Yseul took panther shape and followed. The ground rose steeply away from the city streets. Loose rock skidded under the man's feet and bounced over Yseul's paws. She climbed with claws extended, calling upon the Children's strength to feed her own. When the man faltered, she encouraged him with snarls and nips at his heels.

The cleft in the rock was well concealed, only one among many cavities in the dark stone. The man leaned heavily against the boulders planted at the entrance, trembling with exhaustion.

Yseul jumped to the top of the boulder and changed. "Well?" she asked, teasing the man's hair with her fingers.

"Here," he panted. "At the end of the tunnel...lies a chamber cut from the rock. It will be well guarded...."

"Should I fear the king's minions?" She chuckled softly and cupped his face between her hands. "You have served me well, mortal. But your usefulness has ended."

He must have understood, for he made a clumsy attempt to flee. She caught him within two strides, transfigured the stone beneath his feet and watched it gather him into its hungry embrace. When he was fully absorbed, she stretched out across the saturated earth and let his essence seep into her flesh—his youth, his strength, even some part of that thing mortals called a soul.

The fading remnants of his memory confirmed what he had told her. She squeezed between the boulders and crept along the rough floor of the tunnel. Her nostrils flared with the scent of many human bodies in a small space. A great slab of rock obstructed the way. She used the fresh flush of her victim's vitality to shatter the stone.

Men waited on the other side. Fearful eyes glittered in the

light of a dozen torches. Swords hissed from their sheaths. Yseul laughed.

"So," she said. "At last I am granted an audience with the great king of the holy city."

A hairless man draped in a spotted pelt took a hesitant step forward. "What are you?"

"Do you not recognize a goddess when you see one, mortal?"

The man withdrew and whispered to someone hidden in the shadows. Another baldpate joined him.

"You are no goddess," the second man said. "You…" He gripped the amulet hung from a cord around his neck. "You are of the Stone."

The warriors behind him groaned like men robbed of their last hope. They did not lay down their weapons. Doubtless they would die to the last man in defense of their king.

"I *was* of the Stone," Yseul said. "It no longer rules me." She arched her back. "Come out, O king, or I shall have to fetch you."

"What do you want?" Baldpate asked, his teeth chattering as he spoke.

"I want the Hammer."

"It is not here." A man dressed in long robes trimmed with gold pushed his way through the warriors, though they tried to hold him back. "I am Aryesbokhe," he said. "You see the work of the Hammer in the ruins of my city. Seek there for the one who bears it."

Yseul studied him with mild interest. "And why has he destroyed your city, oh king?"

"Because he is evil," Baldpate said.

"Cian?" She shook her head. "No. He is only weak." She smiled at Aryesbokhe. "One of your gods has possessed him, and now he hunts you. He will find you, and when he does—" She stopped, struck by a sudden awareness. All the fine hairs on her skin stood erect.

"You lie," she said. "Part of the Hammer is in this chamber. Give it to me."

The king held his ground. "I have nothing."

Yseul leaped, changing shape in midair. Her claws raked Aryesbokhe from forehead to groin, stripping him of his jeweled collar and shredding the royal robes. He staggered and fell. Baldpate rushed to his side while the warriors charged Yseul with bared blades.

She dispatched them one by one, twisting her agile body to evade every thrust, ripping out entrails and snapping bones between her teeth. The chamber floor grew slippery with blood. The few who survived the first skirmish stood fast around their crippled master.

Weary of the game, Yseul risked a few minor wounds and killed the remaining warriors. She disemboweled Baldpate, tearing the slick pink organs from his belly. Then she seized the king's arm in her jaws and dragged him from the chamber and through the tunnel, into the light and heat of the waning day.

On a woven leather cord that had lain hidden beneath his collar hung a painted clay amulet in the shape of a hammer. Yseul severed the cord with a swipe of a claw. Aryesbokhe made a weak sound of protest and lifted a hand to push her away. She bit through the tendons and vessels in his neck and left him to choke out his life while she crushed the amulet and exposed the sliver of stone inside it.

She knew at once what it was. Even so small a part of the Hammer radiated power that no mortal man could hope to control. Yseul changed shape and cupped the fragment in her hands. This was why Cian hunted the king. The Hammer was not complete.

Yseul took the ivory-handled knife from the half-severed belt at Aryesbokhe's waist and slit the skin of her right breast. She pushed the sliver into the wound. The flesh closed over it in a matter of moments. Heat seeped under her ribs and pumped through her body with every beat of her heart.

Cian arrived almost quietly, as if he had been waiting for

Yseul to finish her deadly work. He had undergone so great a change that she might not have known him if not for the Hammer in his hand and the flecks of gold in his blood-red eyes. He was naked, rampantly male—and utterly deadly.

"Cian," she said, rising to meet him. "Or should I call you Sutekh?"

He bared a double row of pointed teeth. "Yseul." He stared down at Aryesbokhe's lifeless form and nudged it with the Hammer. "You stole my prey."

"It was unworthy of you, Bearer," she purred. "No more than the dust beneath your feet."

He laughed. The boom of his voice loosed a shower of rocks from the slope above. "As you are," he said. "Where is the thing I seek?"

"It is here, within your reach." She stroked her breasts, teasing the nipples to taut brown peaks. "Why take only a part, when you can have the whole?" She crouched at his feet and slowly straightened, drawing her fingers across his thighs and the thrusting column of his member. Her nails scraped his hard belly. "I no longer serve Baalshillek, my lord. I am not what I was."

He grabbed her breast and squeezed. "I could tear you apart."

"And lose one who would serve you well." She wrapped her fingers around his wrist and pulled his hand to the soft hair between her thighs. "You and I are of the same breed, my lord. Together we can destroy your enemies. Even the Stone God will fall. The get of your seed will rule the world."

Rhenna heard Yseul's boast with a shudder of dread. The mottled pattern of Cian's skin distorted his face, but she could see the avid hunger in the curl of his lips, the unbridled lust that drove even a god to listen when Baalshillek's creature offered her power and her body.

Rhenna knelt on the steep hillside in the shadow of a great rock, filling her burning lungs with clean air. Cian's progress across the city had been erratic, as if he sometimes forgot his purpose and destination. Once in a while, when he witnessed some terrible consequence of his rampage—a lost child crying for its mother, a woman's body pinned beneath an immense block of stone—he paused to shake himself, his brindled skin fading to its normal color as he stared at the horror he had made.

But in the end the god won. He had turned toward the mountains and sprinted up the treacherous slope like a mountain goat, driven by a single ambition.

Yseul had been waiting for him.

There was no sense to the thoughts that spun through Rhenna's head, no certainty to guide her. She touched the figurine Aset had given her and continued to climb, making no effort to conceal her approach. They would know she was coming.

Yet neither Cian nor Yseul spared her so much as a glance. They were intent on each other, communicating in their own silent language. Yseul was beautiful, utterly female, the essence of all any male could desire. Once Cian had rutted with her like a beast, driven by instinct beyond his control. Now the god wanted her. Once Yseul had him, Cian would never be free.

"Cian," Rhenna said.

He ignored her. The corner of Yseul's full lips twitched.

"Cian," Rhenna repeated. "Look at me!"

He tilted his head as if he had heard the buzz of a troublesome insect.

"You swore you wouldn't leave me until the Stone God had fallen," Rhenna said. "You swore, Cian."

Yseul hissed. "Kill her, my lord!"

Cian half turned. The seething red slits of his eyes fixed on Rhenna. Yseul pressed against him, licking his neck as she stroked his engorged erection. "Kill her."

"No," a half-familiar voice said behind Rhenna. A muscular arm seized her around the waist before she could react, and the finely honed edge of a blade nicked the tender skin at the base of her throat. "I demand that privilege."

Yseul grimaced in disgust. "Farkas. I thought you were dead."

His hot breath fouled Rhenna's hair as he laughed. "You hoped."

They might have exchanged further insults, but Rhenna didn't hear. Shock numbed her to all sensation.

Farkas. The Skudat chief's son who had drugged and raped her, working his own evil long before she first witnessed the horrors of the Stone God. He had haunted her nightmares for months after she had left the Skudat lands.

He could not be here, yet he was. She could never scrub the defilement of his touch from her body, or forget the contemptuous triumph in his laughter. Somehow Farkas knew Yseul, and he had followed Rhenna and her companions thousands of leagues from the North.

"You remember," Farkas whispered in Rhenna's ear. "A pity I have no time to give you another memory to cherish before you die."

Rhenna choked on the taste of bile and blinked to clear her clouded vision. Cian stood still, his eyes shifting from red to gold, memories of hate and violence reawakening the man he had been.

Rhenna met Yseul's cold yellow gaze. "I am surprised," she said roughly, "that you keep company with a common mortal like Farkas."

Farkas's blade pressed down, drawing blood. "Common mortal? I am far greater than the man you knew, bitch."

"Because Baalshillek made him," Yseul said with a mocking smile, playing with the wiry red hairs on Cian's chest. "He is the Stone's slave."

Farkas pushed Rhenna away as if he had lost interest in her death. "I was never like Urho. He's gone to seek the prophecies. He thinks he'll carry them back to Baalshillek. But I will take them, and *I* will find the Weapon of Air." His glance flickered warily to Cian. "Now that you have the Hammer…"

Cian snarled. The brief uncertainty was gone from his face.

Sutekh had returned, and Rhenna knew that only the god would hear her now.

"Listen to him, God of Chaos," she said, scrambling beyond Farkas's reach. "He thinks you're this female's slave, eager to do her bidding. She always meant to steal the Hammer for herself."

"She lies, my lord," Yseul said, rubbing her breasts against Cian's back. "I know your power."

"Do you remember when Aset enticed and betrayed you, Lord of the Desert?" Rhenna asked. "How she stole from you the throne of the Two Lands with the use of female trickery, and humiliated you before the Council of the Gods?"

"I am not Aset," Yseul protested. "I—"

Cian shoved her so hard that she slammed into a boulder and slumped senseless at its foot. Cian stalked toward Farkas, his head moving from side to side like a serpent's. His skin rippled, colors shifting as if murky water ran beneath translucent flesh.

And he began to change. Red fur sprouted over his body. The Hammer fell at his feet. He dropped to hands and knees, his mouth gaping to reveal double rows of serrated teeth. Sickle claws emerged from huge beast's paws. He raked the ground, tearing rock like freshly turned soil. His sinuous, arrow-tipped tail lashed the air. He opened his grotesque, downcurved muzzle and gave a roar so terrible that Farkas covered his ears and shrieked in agony.

Rhenna gazed into the Sutekh-beast's burning eyes. Nothing of reason or humanity survived in that ravenous stare. She had stopped Cian from falling under Yseul's spell, but in so doing she had driven him to a place where he could no longer hear the words she had meant to say.

Nyx was wrong. Aset was wrong. She would do no saving this day.

I have loved you, Cian, but love is not enough….

The beast swung a three-toed paw at Farkas, catching him across the face with its claws. He spun through the air like a leaf carried on the wind. Yseul stirred and opened her eyes. She spotted the abandoned Hammer just as Rhenna dodged Sutekh's charge.

There was no time to reach Yseul, no way past the Sutekh-beast's mindless fury. Yseul crawled to the Hammer and grabbed it in both hands. She screamed. The beast swivelled its ears and turned its head, one foot raised to grind Rhenna into the earth.

Yseul screamed again, her face frozen in agony, and lifted the Hammer above her head. She ran at Sutekh. The Hammer plunged down toward its hindquarters. The beast sprang aside, clipping Yseul with its tail as the Hammer slammed into the ground where it had stood.

The mountain rumbled deep in its heart. A crevice opened at Yseul's feet. She balanced on the brink of the chasm with the Hammer stretched out behind her. The beast bent back on itself and crouched at the opposite side of the abyss, its bellow drowned by the mountain's thunder.

Rhenna dashed for the crevice, readying her legs for the jump. Something got in the way of her feet. The wheat-colored dog hopped from side to side, yapping and nipping at her ankles.

"Rhenna!"

Suddenly Tahvo was beside her, pulling her backward. A massive slab of rock sheered off the face of the cliff and plummeted from the heights, carrying half the mountainside with it. Rhenna found herself careening down the slope at Tahvo's heels. They reached the bottom and rolled to a halt, pelted by a shower of stones.

Rhenna got to her knees and looked for Yseul. She and Sutekh stood untouched amidst the upheaval, still facing each other across the chasm. The black fissure vomited a stream of rocks and drops of red liquid that steamed and sizzled as they touched the ground. Sutekh's hindquarters bunched to propel him to the other side, and Yseul raised the Hammer to meet him.

With a grating boom, the edges of the chasm gave way beneath Sutekh's claws. He howled and leaped. Yseul tottered, swinging the Hammer forward in a desperate effort to keep her balance. Sutekh's jaws seized the Hammer, but Yseul did not let go. Woman and beast seemed to float in air for a heartbeat, and then they vanished into the abyss.

Chapter Twenty-Six

Karchedon

There was no crowd to celebrate Quintus's victory over the rebels, no envoy of courtiers with words of praise from the emperor. His return to Karchedon was as quiet as the voyage had been, unmarked by either trouble or triumph.

Quintus disembarked with his small escort of soldiers, adjusting the cloak over his left arm. He didn't look at the grotesque bundle carried by one of the men; a single glance had been more than enough. No one, least of all Baalshillek, could doubt that the rebel known as Buteo was dead.

Baalshillek would be cursing his own evil gods before this day was over.

"My lord," the commander of the escort said, stepping off

the gangplank beside Quintus. "Will you require a litter from the palace?"

Quintus shook his head. "My legs are still capable of carrying me that far, Hektor. Go ahead, and give the emperor my humble regards."

"As you wish." Hektor grinned. "Congratulations, Lord Alexandros." He saluted, then signaled to his men. Quintus watched them march across the wharfside agora, passing Stonebound citizens who awakened from their indifference only when the horrors of Festival drove them to kill or be killed.

The people of Tiberia were only a breath away from suffering the same fate. But now they had an advocate, a defender in the very heart of the Arrhidaean Empire. And Quintus would not fail them.

"Lord Alexandros."

He glanced up, meeting the heavily kohled eyes of one of Nikodemos's favored Hetairoi. Hylas smiled and bowed.

"Well met, my lord," he said. "I am pleased to see you safely returned…and victorious, I hear?"

Quintus gripped Hylas's shoulder. "I accomplished the task the emperor set me," he said. "Have you come alone?"

"Only because word of your arrival has but lately reached the palace," Hylas said. "The emperor's servants are already preparing a feast in honor of your success." He lowered his voice. "Many have missed your presence at court."

"How is Lady Danae?" Quintus asked casually.

A shadow crossed the courtier's face, quickly gone. "She is…well, my lord."

Quintus frowned. "What is it, Hylas?"

"I believe the lady would prefer to discuss it with you in person."

The last time Quintus and Danae had spoken, she had told him to forget the night they had spent together…the night arranged by Nikodemos himself. She had made no attempt to see him afterward. Something must have changed, and not for the better.

Quintus broke into a fast walk toward the street that wound from the lower city to the citadel. Hylas trotted to catch up.

"Do not be alarmed, my lord," he said. "She has not suffered any physical harm."

"Nikodemos?"

Hylas bit his lower lip. "Lady Danae would be the last to provoke ill feelings between the emperor and his brother," he said. "I urge you to remember how much you have achieved, my lord…and how much there is to be lost."

Quintus slowed, wrestling his anger under control. "Is that why you came, Hylas? To warn me?"

"To remind you." Hylas peered into Quintus's face, his own wrinkled with worry. "Lady Danae…I…would do anything to preserve your life."

"I know." Quintus stared at the perpetual blaze of the Temple's red beams stretched out above the city. "I won't forget myself, Hylas."

The courtier briefly closed his eyes and matched Quintus's pace. "Meet with the emperor, my lord. Make your report and accept the praise he offers. Then you will be free to speak with the lady."

There was a wistfulness in Hylas's tone that Quintus couldn't mistake, but he merely nodded and continued toward the citadel. The gates stood open, as was usual, but the guards saluted smartly when they saw Quintus. It was a far different greeting than he had received when he'd first come to the attention of the citadel's inhabitants.

Two soldiers broke off from the troop at the gates and fell into step behind Quintus and Hylas. By the time they crossed the broad square and reached the palace, a dozen more men had joined them, some grinning in defiance of proper military discipline. The emperor's chamberlain, Kleobis, greeted Quintus outside the double doors of the reception hall.

"My lord Alexandros," he said, bowing deeply. "Welcome home."

Home. Quintus tested his feelings at hearing the word. Once the very idea had been repugnant to him, but much had changed. *He* had changed.

"It is good to be back," he said.

Kleobis straightened but kept his gaze averted. "My lord, the emperor sends his greetings and goodwill. Unfortunately, he is engaged in matters of state and cannot see you today."

Quintus glanced at Hylas. The courtier forgot himself just long enough to reveal his concern, and then his face turned bland and smiling again. Quintus assumed the same dispassionate expression.

"I understand that my brother has many obligations," he said smoothly. "Please convey my regards and tell him that I will be at his disposal."

Kleobis released a quick breath and bowed again. "Very good, my lord. You will wish to bathe and rest after your long journey. Servants are waiting in your chambers." He bobbed nervously and beat a hasty retreat.

Quintus turned and strode down the corridors to his rooms in the royal wing. Hylas held his tongue until they stood at Quintus's door.

"Surely the emperor means nothing by this, my lord," he whispered. "His responsibilities are many—"

"I know." Quintus met the courtier's troubled gaze. "He must have received my escort's report by now. I have nothing to conceal." *Unless Baalshillek suspects that I killed his priest, and he is unlikely to admit to the emperor that he let a rebel leader escape simply to set a trap for me.*

"No, indeed," Hylas said. "You have much to celebrate." He hesitated. "I will leave you to your rest, my lord, and see what I can learn of the emperor's state of mind. As for the lady Danae…"

"It might be best to wait before I speak to her," Quintus said.

"A wise decision, my lord."

"One more thing, Hylas. I would know how fares the girl Briga, who is under the emperor's protection."

Hylas inclined his head. "I will see to it, my lord. Only send word, and I will come."

He set off, and Quintus opened the door. A pair of young female slaves stood beside a basin filled with steaming water. They bowed, and one hurried to pour a cup of wine while the other approached Quintus, prepared to help him undress. Quintus sank gratefully into the bath and accepted the wine, still weighing the reasons for Nikodemos's apparent reserve. The slaves washed his back and shoulders with scented oil, scraping his skin clean with a bronze strigil. After they had dressed him in a fresh chiton, they offered him platters of fruit, meat and delicacies from the palace kitchens.

Though both girls made plain that they were willing to stay and provide additional entertainment, Quintus dismissed them and lay back on his couch, listening to the constant murmur of life in the palace. Even after so long a sojourn, he was already restless. Inactivity gave his mind too much to dwell on. He thought of Buteo's family, who might die now that Buteo had failed in his mission to betray Quintus. He remembered the suffering of the Tiberians, robbed of freedom and dignity by the evil of the Stone. And he felt his anger grow—anger at Nikodemos, who had tested his loyalty and now refused to acknowledge his achievement.

A tap on the door pulled him from his brooding. He had hardly risen from the couch when the door opened and Danae glided into the room.

"Quintus," she said. Her face was alight with happiness she made no attempt to hide, and Quintus forgot the admonitions he was ready to speak. She met him halfway across the room. He opened his arms, and she walked into them. All at once he was transported back to that night in the wilderness, when he had caressed her naked body and possessed her, body and soul....

"Quintus," she said, pressing her face into his shoulder. "Quintus, I feared for you. You have been gone so long."

He stroked her hair, kissing the softness of her temple. "Not so long that you forgot me," he said.

She sniffed and drew back with an exaggerated frown. "Forget you? Did you forget me?"

"You told me to forget, not so long ago."

Her ivory skin took on a tinge of red. "You refer to the lion hunt."

"You led me to believe that you never wanted to see me again."

She backed away and reached for a wine cup with uncharacteristic clumsiness, nearly knocking it over. "I believed it was best for you. For both of us. I…" She set the cup down again and gave a short laugh. "I missed you terribly, Quintus. It is one thing to stay away when I know you're in Karchedon and quite another when you are risking your life in another country."

He studied her intently, searching for some sign of malady or unhappiness. There were shadows under her eyes, and a certain thinness in face and body he didn't remember, but no trace of physical affliction.

"I was never in any danger," he said. "My mission was a success."

"So I hear. All the palace knows."

"Nikodemos will not see me."

"He has been…most preoccupied. There is rumor of rebellion in Tyros." Her flush deepened. "I would speak to him for you, if I…" Suddenly she sat down in the nearest chair. "I'm sorry, Quintus. I am not myself today."

"Hylas suggested that all is not well with you. What is it, Danae?"

She waved her fingers in a dismissive gesture. "It's nothing. Hylas worries too much."

Quintus cupped her chin and forced her to look up. "There is something wrong. Is it Nikodemos?"

She shrugged. "Do you remember Gulbanu?"

"The princess from Persis, who rode in the hunt."

"She has…made herself very much at home in Karchedon.

Nikodemos approves of her. He admires her so much that he keeps her at his side nearly every moment."

Quintus knelt before her. "She has replaced you in the emperor's favor."

She looked away. "I have always understood that it is the ultimate fate of the king's most favored hetaira to be replaced."

"By that virago?" Quintus slammed his fist on the table. "Has Nikodemos gone blind in my absence? You are as superior to Gulbanu as a lioness is to a sow."

She laid her palm against his cheek. "Ah, Quintus. I knew you would find a few kind words for me."

He snorted in disgust and got to his feet. "Nikodemos is a fool." He paced from one end of the room to the other. "I would make him understand his error of judgment—"

"But it is not within your power." Danae came up behind him, her breath warm on the nape of his neck. "Just as it is not within mine to keep Nikodemos's love."

"But you still love him."

"I didn't believe it possible to love two men so different, and yet so much alike."

He didn't dare look into her eyes. "You said yourself that Nikodemos would never let you go."

"He cannot command what lies in my heart."

"Your body belongs to him."

"Do you still want me, Quintus?"

He turned on her, trembling. "Look at me, Danae, and tell me what you see."

"I see a prince, a man destined for greatness."

"A man who can't have the woman he wants."

"No. I see a man who will do what he must to achieve all he desires for himself, his people and the world."

He stared out the small window that faced the harbor. "You'd better go, Danae."

She returned to the chair, undisturbed. "Is it true that you discovered a rebel sanctuary in Italia?"

"Yes."

"Nikodemos will be very pleased." She folded her hands in her lap as if she and Quintus had merely been discussing the latest grape harvest. "There must be more to the tale than the rumors say."

"Buteo was Baalshillek's agent. Baalshillek freed him and then suggested that I be sent to capture or kill him, but he intended that Buteo should kill me, instead."

"He underestimated you." She smoothed a wrinkle in her chiton. "Was it difficult…exposing the people you once served?"

Her voice was full of gentle sympathy, but he flinched from the words. "I took no pleasure in it."

"Yet it had to be done. Now the emperor has no reason to doubt your loyalty ever again, and Baalshillek has used his last gambit." She drew small circles on the tabletop with her fingertips.

"Will you tell Nikodemos of Baalshillek's treachery?"

"If it will help him to see that we must sever all ties to the Temple." He strode back to Danae's chair. "The world can't endure much more, Danae. Nikodemos must be made to see that the Stone God will destroy him and his Companions as surely as it's destroying all traces of freedom in the provinces. He must put an end to the priesthood before it becomes too powerful to be stopped."

"At any price?"

"At any price. I have passed all his tests of loyalty, and I'm ready to make use of my power." He clenched and unclenched his right fist. "Nikodemos implied that he would grant me governorship of Italia, but that's no longer enough. When he calls for me, I'll be ready."

"Ready to convince him that you are right."

"I *know* I am, Danae. He will listen."

"And if he does not?"

He met her gaze. "Who will you choose, Danae, if I must turn against Nikodemos?"

She rose in a whisper of linen, took his face in her hands and kissed him, igniting a passion that almost made him forget the purpose that warmed his heart with such fierce joy. He bent her supple body in his arms and returned the kiss. It was she who broke off, her breath coming short and her chiton disarranged by his caresses.

"Not here," she said. "Not now. I will find a place where we can meet in safety. Follow the messenger I send." She went to the door and looked back, her eyes bright with desire and anticipation. "Sleep well, my love."

The messenger came just after midnight. She led Quintus down darkened corridors to the abandoned wing where Danae had once shown him the portal to the secret passages under the palace, ushering him through the door of a seemingly vacant room.

But it was not entirely empty. In the adjoining chamber Danae waited for him beside a couch heaped with furs and a table spread with delicacies fit to tempt the most fastidious of lovers. She dismissed the servant, took Quintus's hand and began to remove his clothing with arousing care. He could barely restrain himself from tearing her chiton to shreds.

They fell on the couch together and made love with equal urgency, kissing and licking and touching as if they rediscovered the planes and hollows of each other's bodies. After they had sated the first deluge of need, they paused to dine on sweatmeets and sip cups of the emperor's finest vintage. Danae drank far more than was her wont, and giggled when Quintus kissed the back of her neck.

Soon her laughter changed to moans of pleasure, and they began again. Three times Danae gave herself to Quintus, each encounter more uninhibited than the last. Quintus fell asleep in Danae's arms, exhausted and heavy with contentment.

He woke to the sounds of strange voices and booted footsteps on the floor of the outer chamber. Danae stirred; Quintus lifted his head, still dazed with sleep, and saw the glint of dying lamplight on armor.

"Lady Danae." The soldier stopped inside the door and bowed stiffly. "You will come with us."

She sat up, clutching a fur to her breast. "What is this? What—"

Quintus swung his legs over the side of the couch just as two more soldiers closed in on him with lowered spears. He struck out with his fist, but he was outnumbered and not fully awake. The soldiers seized his arms and forced him to his knees.

"Danae!" he cried.

"I am all right, Quintus," she said from the doorway, still wrapped in her furs. "Don't fight them. I will explain to Niko-demos."

Explain to Nikodemos. These were the emperor's men, and they had discovered the emperor's half-brother lying with the emperor's former mistress. It was no accident. Somehow the soldiers had been led to this place.

Quintus struggled to rise. "Let me talk to the emperor," he said.

"You'll see him soon enough," one of the soldiers said. He and another hauled Quintus up between them and pushed him through the door.

But they didn't take him to see Nikodemos. They left him in the dungeon where Danae had freed Nyx so long ago, throwing him down on stale straw and barring the door behind them.

The day of triumph was over.

"I grieve for you, my lord," Baalshillek said. "How could you have foreseen such treachery from one who served you so well in Italia?"

Nikodemos scowled and scraped the back of his hand across his mouth. "You shed the tears of a crocodile, Baalshillek," he said. "How long have you known that Quintus was dallying with Danae?"

"But I did not know, Lord Emperor." Baalshillek hid a smile

and offered Nikodemos another cup of wine. "It was not I who alerted the guards to your brother's indiscretion."

"I still haven't discovered who did. I have no use for inform-ers."

"And surely no use for a former rebel who takes what is yours."

Nikodemos grunted. "Foolish," he said. "Stupid, but not treacherous enough to deserve the punishment you would give him, priest."

Baalshillek sighed. "I think only of your welfare. If young Al-exandros would do this, what more is he capable of? What other of your possessions does he covet?"

"If he is like me…" Nikodemos gazed into his cup, swirling the wine within as if he could see the future in its dregs. "But he's not. He's a cub, Baalshillek, and he wants training, not death."

"Once you would not have been so sanguine where Lady Danae is concerned," Baalshillek said. "But you gave him the use of her once, and he simply took the rest. Just as he will judge you weak if you show leniency now."

Nikodemos pretended to disregard Baalshillek's advice, but Baalshillek saw that he listened. His fingers bit into the silver cup.

"Do you think I can't control one boy, priest?" he said softly. "You sent my brother to take the rebel, and he did. Would you devise a similar test for me?"

Baalshillek lowered his head in mock humility. "Quintus is no ordinary boy, but kin of Alexandros the Conqueror. He shares your blood as well as your ambition. And he has power you do not, my lord."

"Power *you* have reason to fear, priest. Not I."

"Are you so certain?"

Nikodemos ran a hand through his untamed mane of hair. "I'll never let you have him, no matter what I decide."

Because you are not quite prepared to surrender a weapon that can be turned against my masters, Baalshillek thought. He imagined summoning Ag and penetrating the emperor's mind, compelling him to do the god's will, but it was too soon, and too dangerous.

"If you will not consider a direct threat from Quintus," he said, "then think of your reputation among your subjects. Danae is known even in the most distant provinces of the empire. She has been much praised for her beauty. If you allow this to pass and rumors escape the palace—as they inevitably will, despite all our efforts—it will seem evidence of vulnerability, which your enemies will regard as proof that you may be defied with impunity."

"My enemies." He barked a laugh. "Do you speak of the Tiberian rebels, who have been driven from their hole, or of the feeble bands in Persis and Phoinike? I certainly have nothing to fear from the wretches who've succumbed to your god."

"I need not tell you that enemies lurk everywhere, even in your own halls."

Nikodemos jumped to his feet. "You would bid me look for disloyalty in those I trust with my life."

"As you trusted young Alexandros?"

The emperor smashed his cup on the floor, cracking a delicately tinted tile. "You've made your position clear enough, priest. I'll hear from my brother before I decide his fate."

"He will do whatever he can to save himself…tell any lies, create wild tales to shake the emperor's will."

Nikodemos glared into Baalshillek's eyes and abruptly sank back down in his chair. "Will he tell me tales of you, I wonder?"

"I will tell you a tale you did not know," Baalshillek said gently. "It was reported that the rebels killed the priest I sent with Alexandros to Italia. But I believe that your brother himself killed the priest…so that you and I would not learn something my servant would have revealed."

"Learn what?"

"That Quintus is still loyal to his former countrymen."

"I've seen Buteo's head."

"A dedicated insurgent might consider that a small price to pay for the ultimate defeat of the empire."

"You weary me, priest," Nikodemos said, but the fight had gone out of his voice, and his words were laced with doubt. "Begone. Let me think."

"Of course, my lord." Baalshillek backed toward the door. "I will be available should you require my assistance."

Nikodemos made no answer. Baalshillek closed the door and smiled to himself as he returned to the Temple.

Quintus, Annihilator and enemy of the One True God, was as good as dead.

Chapter Twenty-Seven

New Meroe was gone.

Nothing remained of the holy city but rubble and dust. Rhenna crouched outside the ring of debris that had been the city walls, Tahvo kneeling at her side, while straggling refugees limped and stumbled away from the wreckage of their lives.

The horror of Cian's transformation and disappearance continued to circle through Rhenna's mind. She vaguely remembered running to the edge of the chasm and lying with her head over the blackness, reaching down as if she could catch some part of Cian before he fell. She remembered the sting of fire raining down on her flesh, and Tahvo's soft voice urging her to come away. And she remembered, with endless sorrow, how the earth had given another great shudder and closed the rift, sealing the wound as if it had never existed.

She knew, even without hearing Tahvo's hushed affirmation, that Cian would not return. Not to this place. Not to her.

"He is not dead," Tahvo said, her hand resting on Rhenna's shoulder. "I would feel it if his spirit had left this world. So would you."

"Our feelings can't be trusted, Tahvo. We should have known that Yseul wouldn't give up. We should have known she had powerful allies, like your Urho. And Farkas." She swallowed. "I never saw Farkas again after Sutekh attacked him. Do *they* still live, Tahvo?"

"I do not know."

"Then we must assume the worst."

Tahvo gave her a quick, fierce hug and got to her feet. "There are many wounded who need a healer's care," she said. "I do not know how much longer Dakka's gift of sight will last...."

"Go. I'll be all right."

Tahvo nodded and headed for the nearest group of survivors, who huddled, dazed and leaderless, on the plain. A few of the hardiest Meroites had collected brush and made small fires; they shone like fragile beacons of hope in the gathering darkness. A full moon rose over the hills to the east. When the stars came out, Rhenna opened the sack that Tahvo had brought from the Archives, unrolled a scroll and gazed at the rows of meaningless symbols.

For *this* Cian had gone mad. For this a city had died.

"At least some of the sacred writings were saved."

She turned to face the man who spoke, too weary for surprise. Khaleme dropped an armful of branches and sank to his heels, black eyes unreadable.

"I am glad to see that you and the healer survived," he said, sorting the branches according to size. "Do you have flints to start a fire?"

Something in Khaleme's pragmatic manner shook Rhenna from her misery. She drew her flints from the pouch at her belt and tossed them to the warrior.

"I didn't see you after we entered the city," she said.

He struck the flints, raising a spark on the first try. "I was unable to accompany you to the palace," he said, "and then, when the trouble began…"

Trouble. It was a strange word to describe what must be the end of the world he had known. "Have you seen Nyx?" she asked.

He shook his head. "I have heard rumors that the king is dead, along with many of his soldiers. I pray that Lady Netiquert lives, so that she may lead our people."

"Lead them where?" Rhenna asked. "To what?"

Khaleme nursed the spark into a flame. "To a new beginning," he said. "The old order has ended, but the prophecies remain true. The great battle lies ahead."

Rhenna covered her face with her hands, sick to death of noble causes. An animal, perhaps some hungry scavenger in search of an easy meal, cried out near the scattered stones of the wall. A male voice carried sweet and clear from another fire.

"He sings a song of mourning," Khaleme said.

And what right have I to mourn? Rhenna thought. *How many lives were lost today because of the monster Cian became? If we had never come to this city…*

"The past cannot be undone," Khaleme said, feeding sticks into the fire. "We must go on. This is what the Watcher would wish."

She stared at him across the fire. "How do you know what became of Cian?"

"Even in a dying city, such tragedies do not long remain secret."

"Don't you blame him for this?" she asked, waving toward the ruins. "Don't you blame all of us?"

"Surely the prophecies foretold the city's end."

Rhenna laughed bitterly. "You should curse your prophecies, and all the gods who abandoned you."

He smiled, as if she had made a jest. "The gods are nearer

than you think. I…" He paused, lifting his head, and Rhenna followed his gaze to the broken gates. A shadowy group of figures climbed over the splintered wood, thirty or more men and women in robes and kilts and jewelry dull with blood and dirt. As they came closer to the fire, Rhenna recognized the woman who led them.

"Nyx," she said. She found that she still had enough feeling left to rejoice at the woman's survival. "Your lady is alive, Khaleme."

They stood and waited while the group approached. Nyx's teeth flashed in a smile as she caught sight of Rhenna; she hurried forward and clasped Rhenna in a hard embrace.

"My friend," she said. "Praise the gods that you are well."

A bald man came up beside her. "My lady," Dakka said, bowing to Rhenna. His eyes searched the darkness beyond the fire. "The holy Bearer…"

"He is gone." Rhenna drew back and wrapped her arms around her chest. "Sutekh was too strong for him, and he met an old enemy. They fought, and the earth—" Her throat strangled the words.

"The earth swallowed them," Khaleme said.

Nyx closed her eyes. "Aset, protect him. Asar, preserve his soul."

Dakka murmured a prayer in his own tongue. "Like Asar, he will rise again."

Rhenna rejected the hope that so easily betrayed her. She kicked the sack with the scrolls, and Dakka's gaze tracked her movement. "The healer saved the sacred scriptures," he said.

Rhenna picked up the sack and held it out to him. "Take it."

He stepped back. "You still have need of them, Bearer. I will translate—"

"Of what use are they now that the Hammer is lost to us?"

The priest exchanged glances with Nyx and sighed. "My lady, your quest is not ended. The other Weapons must be found before evil takes them. We—I and my brothers of the Archives—have saved some of the ancient texts, and we will re-create many more when New Meroe is restored."

"All who still live will be ready to fight when the Weapons are reunited," Nyx said.

Rhenna met Nyx's gaze. "You know that your king is dead."

"The people will need a new ruler," Dakka said. "Lady Net-iquert has agreed to become our kandake, our queen."

"Twice before our people have left their homes to make new lives in other lands," Nyx said. "We will do so again. The knowledge we have preserved must not die."

Rhenna looked away from the fire. Frightened people were creeping near, straining to hear their leader's words. "Where will you go?" she asked.

"West. West to the country of my mother."

"A long journey."

"Not so long as yours." Nyx looked toward the South and the rolling hills. "The villages and farms outside the city still stand. Once you have learned your destination, we will assemble the supplies you need and send men for your protection."

"I want no more blood on my hands," Rhenna said. "Tahvo and I will go alone."

"I will go with you," Khaleme said.

"I've seen too many men die for our cause," Rhenna protested.

"But I am no man." Khaleme laughed, leaped in the air and came down again on four paws, shaking his sleek-coated body in a canine dance.

"Eshu!" Nyx exclaimed.

Rhenna stared into the beast's glittering eyes. "*You* were Khaleme?"

The dog sat on its haunches and grinned. "I found a man dying in the great swamp. Now he lives in me, and I in him."

"You deceived us," Rhenna said. "We have no use for trick-ster gods on our journey."

Eshu snarled and pawed the ground, digging furrows with

his claws. "When will you learn respect, mortal? I saved your silly scrolls when your healer's enemy would have stolen them. I stopped you from flinging your life away."

"And why did you follow us? Why would you help us now, when you were so indifferent before?"

"Because you have proven your worthiness." He scratched behind his ear. "Olorun sent me to test you, to discover whether the *òrìshà* of the forest people should enter the battle between your Stone God and the peoples of the North."

"And you've decided in our favor."

He snapped at an insect circling the fire. "It may be, with my help, that you will succeed in your quest."

"Do not dismiss his aid," Tahvo said. She walked into the firelight, making her way with care. Her eyes were once again unbroken silver. "The spirits of the forest wish us well."

Rhenna took Tahvo's arm. "Dakka's magic?"

"It is gone." She turned her head toward Nyx and the priest. "My thanks for all you have done."

"Can you restore her sight?" Rhenna asked Dakka.

"Such is beyond my power," Dakka said with regret.

"Eshu—"

"She chose this affliction," the dog said. "I cannot take it away."

"Do not grieve for me," Tahvo said. She knelt and felt for the scrolls. "Will you read the prophecies, Dakka?"

"Yes." He sat cross-legged before the fire. One by one the city's refugees—men and women, courtiers and warriors and servants—joined him. Nyx bowed to Eshu, went to Rhenna and looped a beaded leather cord around her neck.

"This belonged to my father," she said. "I have carried it all my life, but I betrayed the true Bearer. I am no longer fit to wear it." She smiled sadly. "You are bound to Cian, my friend, my sister. You will see him again."

At the end of the cord hung a tiny black panther.

Karchedon

The exile's ship had sailed. Not one of the emperor's Companions had gone to the harbor to witness young Alexandros's punishment or bid him farewell…not even Lady Danae, who shared his disgrace but not his fate.

Baalshillek descended from the citadel wall, sweeping his robes behind him. Nikodemos's soldiers moved swiftly out of his path. Perhaps, he thought, they had begun to realize that a new era was dawning—that there was no certainty, no safety, outside the Stone God's favor. One who had so lately been raised up was cast down, sent to the farthest and most barbaric corner of the empire, and he would not live long enough to benefit from the emperor's inevitable forgiveness.

Today the gods of the Stone were restless. They, too, sensed the change. Ag, ancient god of fire, rattled about in Baalshillek's head like some great clawed beast testing the bars of its cage. The other Exalted roared and wailed.

Baalshillek ignored them and strode into the Temple. He entered the door under the altar, and hurried down the narrow steps to the underground halls and chambers known only to the priesthood and its Stonebound servants.

The entrance to the brood chamber was crowded with priests. They bowed and retreated as Baalshillek approached, but none withdrew. They had heard the rumors. The first of the perfect Children was about to be born into the world.

Baalshillek had known this birth would be different, from the moment he had seen the rich, red light suffusing the woman's distended belly. He had commanded the alpha priest who oversaw the brood females to take special care with this one, and the man had done his duty. Now the time had come.

Only the overseer and a few attendants stood at the couch where the female lay. She breathed steadily and slowly, held in the state between waking and sleeping that kept the mothers quiescent throughout their period of incubation. But her belly had begun to contract, and soon not even the power of the Stone could maintain her dormancy.

Baalshillek stood at the woman's feet, waiting for the sign. The luminescence radiating from her womb began to pulse. Her breathing stopped and resumed, much more rapid than before. Distended flesh rippled. Suddenly the woman's eyes flew open, and she screamed.

The attendants gripped her ankles as she convulsed. A stream of blood issued from her body. She choked, foam bubbling from her lips. Her head beat against the frame of the couch. Then her offspring's head appeared, bathed in blood and light. The female gave one last, great heave and lay still.

Baalshillek was there to catch the child as it emerged. He held it aloft, glorying in its perfection. Perfect body, made to bear a god, strong enough to survive the crippling influence of an Exalted. Perfect features. Perfect emptiness. For this child had no soul. It was a vessel waiting to be filled.

The babe did not cry. It breathed, filling its chest with life-giving air. It opened its eyes. Baalshillek smiled and gave the infant to the attendants, who bathed its flawless skin and wrapped it in cloth to keep it warm.

The overseer moved to the head of the couch and lifted the woman's eyelids.

"She is dead," he said.

Baalshillek nodded, stepping clear of the blood that still gushed from her body. It was as he had expected. Her offspring had drawn her essence into itself, leaving none to sustain her life. The female had fulfilled her purpose.

She was only the first.

"Arrange for a dozen wet-nurses," Baalshillek said to the overseer. "Select the healthiest you can find in the city. The child will drain each woman quickly, and it must not go lacking."

"As you say, my lord."

Baalshillek left the man to his work, passed through the cluster of curious priests and continued on to the sanctum. He dismissed the priests ministering to the Stone and faced the brilliant red sphere set in the marble altar.

"Soon," he whispered. "Soon, Ag, you will have full life again."

The god roared his joy, his divine emotion seething in Baalshillek's bones with shattering force. The other Exalted snapped and snarled like dogs fighting over a morsel of rotted flesh.

Baalshillek turned to the long stone box that stood at the rear of the sanctum, running his hands over the engraved lid. He could feel the Hyperborean magic that imbued the device…alien magic Talos had summoned and shaped in exchange for the ease of his foolish mortal heart. Magic that would raise a Child of the Stone to full growth in a matter of months instead of years.

Eight Exalted. Eight perfect Children. And by the time each mount was ready to assume its rider, Baalshillek would have the means of controlling the most powerful beings the world had ever known.

It was a ship of death. The death of hope, of dreams, of ambition. The end of a life Quintus had hardly begun to imagine.

He stood on the deck of the biremis, listening to the steady beat of the oars against the water. The first shock was long past; even when the grim, silent guards had taken him to the ship, waiting like a harbinger of disaster in the predawn darkness, he had not begged for explanations. In his heart he had already known.

Alexandros, son of Arrhidaeos, was no more. Quintus Horatius Corvinus might never have existed. The man who watched the waves of Ta Thalassa had neither name nor future. And yet he survived.

The night was still, almost windless, and only a single guard shared Quintus's vigil. Perhaps he was meant to prevent the exile from leaping over the rail into the dark sea, putting a swift end to his shame. But Quintus had no intention of easing the High Priest's path to ultimate power.

I am not done, Baalshillek. When I return, I'll have both Danae and the throne, and then…

A mooncast shadow stretched across the deck, and Quintus spun to face the intruder. The man fell back a step, glanced about him and pushed the hood away from his face.

"Hylas!" Quintus said.

The courtier pressed his finger to his lips. "Caution, my lord. I bribed the ship's captain well, but even so…"

"What are you doing here?"

Hylas cleared his throat and stared out at the water. "I could not let you go alone, my lord."

"You're mad." Quintus clenched his good hand on the rail and cursed the courtier's unwanted devotion. "They're sending me to the ends of the earth, Hylas, a land ruled only by barbarians—"

"Who will need the civilizing influence of a man of my exceptional talents. I even possess a few you have not yet seen." Hylas brushed at a nonexistent blemish on his expensive himation. "In any case, my lord, I could not return to the exceedingly dull life I endured before you came to Karchedon."

Quintus gave a brief laugh and shook his head. "Your quest for diversion will be your death, Hylas."

Hylas straightened, his face set in lines of sober dignity. "Then I will make it a worthy death, my lord. Worthy of you."

"Gods." Quintus pinched the bridge of his nose. "I'm no longer anyone's lord, Hylas. Call me Quintus."

"As you wish…Quintus."

"How is Danae?"

The courtier squirmed and bit his lip. "She is unharmed. Doubtless Nikodemos will forgive her—in time…."

"I was a fool, Hylas. I risked everything just to be with her."

"I believe she also had some part in the decision."

"But she is a woman, driven by women's passions." He slammed his fist on the rail. "I will go back for her—"

"No." Hylas wrapped his arms around his chest and looked away. "She arranged for the soldiers to find you, Quintus. It was her intention all along."

Quintus felt the blood drain from his face. "What are you saying?"

"I have…contacts among the Palace Guard. Danae intended for you to be caught."

"Why?"

"My contact did not know. But I cannot believe…Lady Danae would never wish you harm. She must have had good reason…."

Quintus heard no more of Hylas's labored explanations. He sat down on the deck, convinced that his legs would give out and shame him still further.

Hylas crouched and hesitantly touched his hand. "Do not despair, my friend. You are not alone. Another has come to bear you company."

Quintus lifted his head, bracing himself for another dose of misfortune. "Who?"

Hylas whistled softly, and his signal was returned from somewhere across the ship. After a moment another dark-clad figure crept across the deck, moving with the watchful care of a fugitive. She lifted the cowl from her face.

"Briga," Quintus said, beyond incredulity. "Did you bring her?" he demanded of Hylas.

"I found her already at the wharf when I was prepared to embark," he said. "A most resourceful child. She escaped the Palace and would certainly have been caught. I feared that she might fall into Baalshillek's hands again, so I simply bribed the captain and guards for both of us." He stretched his mouth in an uneasy smile. "She is a very stubborn female."

Briga thrust out her lower lip and faced Quintus unflinchingly. "I will not be left behind," she said. "I heard what Danae did. I know the High Priest will take me if I stay."

That was a very real danger now that Danae could no longer be counted on to protect the girl. Quintus got to his feet and looked past them to the indifferent guard and the sleepy sailors manning the limp sails. "If Baalshillek has sent men to kill me…"

"Then you will have two to defend you." Hylas drew his knife, and Briga presented her open palm. Fire danced on her work-stained skin. "They will not make such an attempt on the ship. The emperor's men will see that we have enough provisions to survive once we make landfall. After that...we must be ready."

Ready to fight off the High Priest's assassins. Ready to tangle with barbarians who had no reason to love the folk of Hellas, Karchedon or Tiberia: a girl, a catamite and a crippled rebel whose power was useless against ordinary mortals.

Perhaps this was fate, the work of gods Quintus had never believed in. If so, struggling against it was useless. If not, the strange twist of events was more than he had the means to resist.

The first light of dawn crested the horizon behind them. Ahead lay the Gates of Herakles and the dangerous voyage up the coast of Iberia, into the unknown.

"Go below," Quintus said, "before the guards decide we're hatching a conspiracy between us."

"Will you be all right?" Hylas asked. Briga regarded her would-be savior with trusting blue eyes.

He met their stares with stern authority. "From now on, you'll obey me without question. Agreed?"

"As long as you don't tell us to go back," Briga said.

He cuffed the side of her head and turned the light blow into a caress. "That is no longer within my hands," he said. "If you have any gods who have escaped the Stone, I suggest you pray to them now."

Hylas retreated with a bow, towing a reluctant Briga by one thin arm. Quintus was alone again. But the night and the voyage had changed. Betrayal and loyalty stood on his shoulders, whispering taunts and promises.

Danae was dead to him now. He could cast off the burden of fear for her future. But he had more than himself to keep alive. One day he would go back to Karchedon with Hylas and Briga.

He would return victorious and ready to challenge the might of the empire, or he would not return at all.

The battle was far from over.

Author Note

Hammer of the Earth deals with many cultures in the continent of Africa around 290 B.C.E., when little was known about the vast expanse of wilderness south of what is now called the Sahara Desert. In fact, the ancient Greeks simply referred to Africa as Libya, which was their name for the northernmost portion occupied by subjects of Carthage (Katchedon) and the tribes known as Numidians or Berbers.

Before the coming of the Arabs in the seventh century C.E., the Berbers—more properly known as the Imazighen—traded and fought with Egypt, Carthage and Rome. Their culture goes back at least 4,000 years, and they speak their own unique language. Today they are found in North Africa from Morocco's West coast to the oasis of Siwa in Egypt and into the mid-Sahara. The Tuareg are close relatives.

Though I have borrowed a variation on the Imazighen name,

my depiction of the desert tribes is entirely fictional. I have incorporated the Berbers' traditional expertise with horses, and the dress and weapons ascribed to them by Greek and Roman contemporaries. Dromedary camels didn't become important domestic animals in North Africa until the Arab conquests.

The Speaking Stones in *Hammer of the Earth* are based on real rock paintings at Tassili-n-Ajjer in Algeria. Some of the paintings date back to 4,500 B.C.E., and depict animals such as giraffes, hippopotami and extinct giant buffalo that roamed the area before the encroachment of the desert.

Little is known about sub-Saharan West African culture prior to the Common Era, since these people left no written records. Archaeologists have discovered terra cotta sculptures in the area of the Niger and Benue Rivers, works dating from as long ago as 500 B.C.E. They have named the originators of these sculptures the Nok culture. The daily life of the Nok people is a matter for speculation, but I have based the Ará Odò very loosely on the people of Nigeria, specifically the Yoruba, whose language I have borrowed.

The kingdom of Kush was very real and not only traded extensively with Egypt and other contemporary cultures but also provided some of Egypt's pharohs. The first Kushite capital city was Kerma, built on the floodplain around the Nile's third cataract. Following periods of independence and domination by Egypt, the Kushites moved their capital to Napata. During this period their culture shared many common elements with Egypt's, the Napatan kings formed the twenty-fifth pharaonic dynasty in the eighth century B.C.E. Around 600 B.C.E., the Kushites moved farther south and established the new capital of Meroe. Meroitic culture developed its own unique arts and traditions, electing their kings (and sometimes queens) from among members of the royal family, though they continued to worship Egyptian gods and erect variations of Egyptian-style tombs.

Hammer Glossary

Characters:

Abeni: a girl of the Ará Odò
Abidemi: a hunter of the Ará Odò
Adisa: head of Clan Amòtékùn
Aetes: a Tiberian slave
Ag: ancient god of Fire, one of the Exalted
Akinidad: former king of New Meroe, grandfather of Nyx
Alexandros the Mad: conqueror of the lands surrounding Ta Thalassa; uncle of Nikodemos and Quintus
Amanibakhi: a king of Meroe
Amun: Egyptian King of the Gods
Annis: kitchen slave in the Palace at Karchedon
Apep: also known as Apophis, Egyptian god of evil and darkness
Apollon: also known as Apollo, Greek god of light, music and the arts
Arion: a courtier of Karchedon

Arrhidaeos: brother to Alexandros the Mad, founder of the
    Arrhidaean Empire
Arshan: a follower of Farkas the simulacrum
Artemis: Greek goddess of the wilderness, the hunt and wild
    animals
Aryesbokhe: king of New Meroe
Asar: see Osiris
Aset: see Isis
Ashtaph: a servant of Hylas
Asteria: legendary founder and Mother of the Free People
Baalshillek: High Priest of the Stone God
Berkan: an Amazi warrior
Bolanle: sister of Adisa, a Mother of the Ará Odò
Briga: a kitchen slave in the Palace of Karchedon
Buteo: Tiberian rebel leader
Cabh'a: an Amazi warrior
Chares: a courtier of Karchedon
Cian: a shapeshifter of the Ailuri
Dakka: a priest of New Meroe
Danae: mistress of Nikodemos
Danel: former lover of Hylas
Dayo: sister of Adisa, a Mother of the Ará Odò
Derinoe: a young warrior of the Free People
Dionysos: Greek god of wine and madness
Doris: a courtier of Karchedon
Enitan: a hunter of the Ará Odò
Eshu: trickster god of the Ará Odò; messenger to Olorun
Farkas: Skudat chief's son; also his simulacrum, created to
    serve Baalshillek and thwart Rhenna
Galatea: a courtier of Karchedon
Ge: ancient goddess of the earth; formerly one of the Exalted
Geb: Egyptian god of the earth
Geleon: rebel leader in Karchedon
Gulbanu: princess of Persis
Hat-T-Her: a goddess of the Imaziren; see Hathor

Hathor: Egyptian goddess of the sky, music, dance, love and fertility

Heru-sa-Aset: Heru, son of Aset and Asar, enemy of Sutekh; also known as Horus

Het-Hert: see Hathor

Hylas: a courtier of Karchedon

Immeghar: an Amazi warrior

Inpu: also known as Anubis; Egyptian god of mummification and guide of the dead

Iphikles: an adviser of Nikodemos

Irike: prince of New Meroe and father of Nyx

Isis: Egyptian Queen of the Gods, patron of women, mothers, children and magic

Kaj: a soldier of the Palace Guard in Karchedon

Kallimachos: father of Danae

Kanmi: a servant of Hylas

Keela: leader of the Alu

Khaleme: a warrior of New Meroe

Kleobis: majordomo of Nikodemos

Leuke: a servant of Danae

Madele: an Amazi warrior

Melissa: former wife of Philokrates/Talos

Mezwar: an Amazi warrior

Mnestros: a courtier of Karchedon

Monifa: a girl of the Ará Odò

Neitiqert: Meroite name for Nyx

Nikodemos: emperor of the Arrhidaen Empire

Nut: Egyptian goddess of the sky

Nyx: a rebel of Karchedon; member of the Ará Odò tribe

Olayinka: mother of Nyx

Olorun: sky god of the Ará Odò; creator of the world

Orkos: commander of the Temple Guard in Karchedon

Osiris: Egyptian Lord of the Dead, the underworld and fertility

Philemon: a soldier of the Palace Guard in Karchedon

Philokrates: a philosopher of Hellas; also known as Talos

Poseidon: Greek god of the sea
Quintus Horatius Corvinus: a Tiberian rebel, also known as Alexandros, son of Arrhidaeos
Re: Egyptian god of the sun
Rhenna: a warrior of the Free People
Shorkaror: a warrior of New Meroe
Slahtti: a Northern spirit-beast, friend of Tahvo
Sutekh: also known as Set or Seth; Egyptian god of chaos, war and conflict
Tabiti: Skudat goddess of the hearth, animals and fire
Tahvo: a shaman of the Samah
Talakhamani: priest and prophet of the People of the Scrolls
Talos: see Philokrates
Tamallat: an Amazi warrior
Tefnut: Egyptian goddess of moisture, water and the moon
Thais: a kitchen slave in the Palace of Karchedon
Urho: simulacrum; shaped to serve Baalshillek and match Tahvo's powers
Vanko: commander of Nikodemos's Persian mercenaries
Yseul: simulacrum; a female Ailu created to serve Baalshillek
Zamra: mother of Madele
Zeus: Greek King of the Gods

General Glossary:

Aequi: a tribal people of Italia, former enemies of Tiberia
Aternus: river in Italia
àgùnfón: "giraffe" in the Ará Odò language
Aigyptos: Egypt
Ailuri: race of male panther shapeshifters
àjànànkú: "elephant" in the Ará Odò language
akáko: "hippopotamus" in the Ará Odò language
Alu: race of female panther shapeshifters
Amazi: singular of Imaziren
amda: oasis

Amòtékùn: clan of the Ará Odò; "panther"

Anio: river in Tiberia

Apenninus Mountains: the Apennines

Ará Odò: a tribe of the region now known as West Africa

Arrows of the Wind: one of the legendary four Weapons of prophecy

augur: Tiberian soothsayer

auspicia: prophetic signs, usually favorable

ba: aspect of the soul; personality

biremis: bireme; a galley equipped with two tiers of oars on either side

Black Land: Egypt

Children of the Stone: warriors magically created to serve the Stone God

chora: countryside

Chosen: women of the Free People selected to mate with the Ailuri

Companions: favored members of Nikodemos's court

Corvinium: Tiberian mountain town founded by Quintus's adoptive father

deva: a god

Divine Cow: honorary title for Hathor

Earthspeaker: a woman of the Free People chosen to speak to and for the devas

emu òpe: palm wine

enaree: a Skudat shaman; a male who dresses in female attire

Exalted: the twelve ancient gods who sought to rule the Earth and provoked the Godwars

fibula: brooch

Free People: a race of Amazons who live on the steppes north of the Black Sea

Godwars: the great conflicts between the gods, and between gods and men, that resulted in the fall of the City of the Exalted

Great Desert: the Sahara

Guardians: prophetic name for ancestral Ailuri who imprisoned the Exalted in the Stone

Hammer of the Earth: one of the legendary four Weapons of prophecy

Hellas: Greece

Hellene: Greek

hetaira: a high-class courtesan

Hetairoi: Companions; see Companion

Hyperborea: legendary, magical land of the far North

Imaziren: tribes of the Great Desert

iràkikò: "hyena" in the Ará Odò language

ishu: "yam" in the Ará Odò language

Karchedon: capital of the Arrhidaean Empire; also known as Carthage

Keltoi: Celts

Khemet: Egypt

Kush: African kingdom located to the south of Egypt

Ma'at: truth, order and law; the "right"

Marsi: a tribal people of Italia; former enemies of Tiberia

Meroe: capital city of Kush

milliarius (pl. milliaria): Tiberian measurement, approximately one mile

Mother of Earth: honorary title for Ge

New Meroe: city founded by the People of the Scroll in the region now known as Ethiopia

noaiddit: Samah shaman

oho: "no" in the Amazi language

ònì: "crocodile" in the Ará Odò language

Oracle of Amun: temple of Amun at the Oasis of Siwa, known for its prophetic edicts

òrìshà: "god" or "gods" in the Ará Odò language

Ostia: port city of Tiberia

papyri: plural of papyrus

papyrus: ancient writing material; a reed-like plant used to make a flexible writing surface

People of the Scrolls: guardians of the prophecies and settlers of New Meroe

Persis: Persia

pneuma (pl. pneumata): "bones of the gods," the scattered fragments of dead beings that contain magical properties

psyche: soul or life essence

Queen of the West: honorary title for Hathor

Samah: a people of the Northern forests

Seeker: a woman chosen as a seeker of recruits for the Free People

Serpent of Darkness: title for Apep

Shield of the Sky: a mountain range in the territory of the Free People

Shield's Shadow: the hills and steppes south of the Shield of the Sky

simulacrum (pl. simulacra): a duplicate or counterpart

Siwa: an Egyptian oasis

Skudat: a tribe of herders and warriors living on the steppes north of the Black Sea

stadion (pl. stadia): Greek measurement, approximately 600 feet

Stone God: singular name for the Exalted confined within the Stone

Sun's Rest: a village of the Free People

Sword of the Ice: one of the legendary four Weapons of prophecy

Ta Thalassa: the Mediterranean

temenos: temple compound

Tiber: a river in Italia

Tiberia: the principal city in Italia, center of the Tiberian sphere of influence

Two Lands: Egypt

Umbria: mountainous region in central Italia

Via Tiburtina: principal road in Italia

Via Valeria: principal road in Italia, the continuation north-
eastward of Via Tiburtina
wajá: "yes" in the Amazi language
Watcher: prophetic name for ancestral Ailuri who imprisoned
the Exalted in the Stone

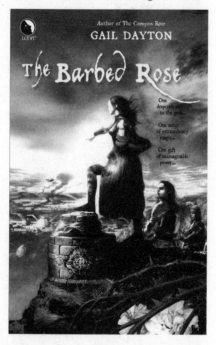

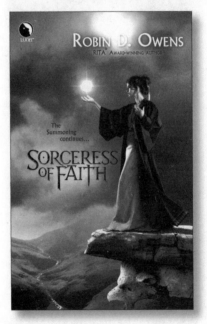

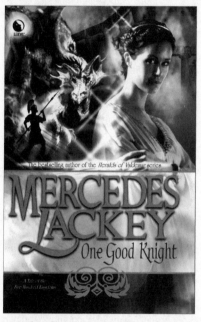

Susan Krinard never expected to become a writer. She "fell into it" by accident when a friend suggested she try writing a novel, and that novel sold to a major publisher two years later. A longtime reader of science fiction and fantasy, Susan began reading romance—and realized what she wanted to do was combine the two genres. She decided to incorporate fantasy into her romance novels and has created a unique place for herself in the romance genre. She now considers herself incredibly fortunate in finding a career so perfectly suited to her love of words and storytelling.

She now makes her home in New Mexico, the "Land of Enchantment," with her husband, Serge, her dogs, Brownie, Freya and Nahla, and her cats, Murphy and Jefferson. In addition to writing, Susan's interests include music (New Age and classical), old movies, reading, nature, animals, baking and collecting jewelry and clothing with leaf and wolf designs.

Readers are invited to visit her Web site at www.susankrinard.com.

If you enjoyed what you just read,
then we've got an offer you can't resist!

Take 1 bestselling love story FREE!

Plus get a FREE surprise gift!

Clip this page and mail it to the Reader Service®

IN U.S.A.	**IN CANADA**
3010 Walden Ave.	P.O. Box 609
P.O. Box 1867	Fort Erie, Ontario
Buffalo, N.Y. 14240-1867	L2A 5X3

YES! Please send me one free LUNA™ novel and my free surprise gift. After receiving it, if I don't wish to receive any more, I can return the shipping statement marked cancel. If I don't cancel, I will receive one brand-new novel every month, before they're available in stores! In the U.S.A., bill me at the bargain price of $10.99 plus 50¢ shipping & handling per book and applicable sales tax, if any*. In Canada, bill me at the bargain price of $12.99 plus 50¢ shipping & handling per book and applicable taxes**. That's the complete price and a savings of 10% off the cover prices—what a great deal! I understand that accepting the free book and gift places me under no obligation ever to buy any books. I can always return a shipment and cancel at any time. Even if I never buy another book from LUNA, the free book and gift are mine to keep forever.

175 HDN D34K
375 HDN D34L

Name	(PLEASE PRINT)
Address	Apt.#
City	State/Prov. Zip/Postal Code

Not valid to current LUNA™ subscribers.

Want to try another series?
Call 1-800-873-8635 or visit www.morefreebooks.com.

* Terms and prices subject to change without notice. Sales tax applicable in N.Y.
** Canadian residents will be charged applicable provincial taxes and GST.
   All orders subject to approval. Offer limited to one per household.
   ® and ™ are registered trademarks owned and used by the trademark owner and
   or its licensee.

LUNA04TR   ©2004 Harlequin Enterprises Limited

THE TEARS OF LUNA

A shimmering crown grows and dims and is always reborn. Luna has the power and gift to brighten dark nights and lend mystery to the shadows. She will sometimes show up on the brightest of days, but her most powerful moments are when she fills the heaven with her light. Just as the moon comes each night to caress sleeping mortals, Luna takes a special interest in lovers. Her belief in the power of romance is so strong that it is said she cries gem-like tears which linger when her light moves on. Those lucky enough to find the Tears of Luna will be blessed with passion enduring, love fulfilled and the strength to find and fight for what is theirs.

A WORLD YOU CAN ONLY IMAGINE ™

LUNA™

www.LUNA-Books.com

THE TEARS OF LUNA MYTH COMES ALIVE IN A WORLD AN ARTIST CAN IMAGINE ™

Over the last year, LUNA Books and Duirwaigh Gallery presented the work of five magical artists.

After many entries, our contest to win prints of the art created by these artists and a library of LUNA novels has come to a close.

Thank you for the great enthusiasm we received and please visit our Web site for more great books and art!

DUIRWAIGH
Gallery

www.DuirwaighGallery.com

Winners will be contacted by LUNA Books.

LBDGE0206TR